A Small
FORTUNE

A Small FORTUNE

ROSIE DASTGIR

First published in Great Britain in 2012 by

Quercus
55 Baker Street
7th Floor, South Block
London
W1U 8EW

A CIP catalogue record for this book is available
from the British Library

ISBN 978 0 85738 373 0 (HB)
ISBN 978 0 85738 374 7 (TPB)

10 9 8 7 6 5 4 3 2 1

Typeset by Ellipsis Digital Limited, Glasgow

Printed and bound in Great Britain by Clays Ltd, St Ives plc

For my father

One

The house where Harris lived was on a hill. After four years in the north of England, he had become adept at hill-starts, managing the steep gradients in that part of the world with a deft combination of clutch control and handbrake operation.

The neighbourhood was mainly Pakistani, yet this fact did not make Harris feel at home. Home was the Home Counties, where he had once lived with his wife and daughter; now that chunk of his life was over. His real name was Haaris, but upon arrival from Pakistan in the 1970s, he had found that people baulked at its pronunciation, recoiling from the long, flat vowel sound. So he had obligingly adopted the name Harris instead, after the celebrated tweed whose label was stitched inside a cap he had bought from the Scotch House on Piccadilly. It was stamped with the British royal crest, suggesting that Prince Philip owned one too, and Harris was convinced he had seen that very royal sporting something similar on a Christmas television programme.

He was a slight, elegant man of five foot five – or five foot six, depending on his mood when he was filling in official documents – and he was rather keen on smart clothes. Within weeks of his arrival, he had made himself familiar with all the best British labels, taking considerable pride in his newly suited look: Crockett & Jones shoes were purchased, along with Gieves & Hawkes shirts, and a suit and several ties from Austin Reed. The Aquascutum overcoat he wore during that first freezing winter still carried the white label proclaiming the brand on the left cuff. After his divorce, however, people noticed he'd lost his enthusiasm for style. He'd been forced to retrench and his beloved clothes were the first casualty. To get by, he depended on a stack of credit cards he carried everywhere in an old leather wallet, hoping and believing that one day, eventually, something would turn up. But nothing quite did. Not in this neck of the woods.

Harris had always felt a tincture of pride and guilt that he had vaulted to success from a Commonwealth country to southeast England, rather than having to hole up in the northern town ghettos like his less fortunate relatives. Now he was stuck in a part of a world he had once counted himself lucky to shun, a former mill town that had seen better days. Several of the terraced houses in his street were condemned, boarded up with punched-metal sheets blanking out the sunlight. Rickety loft extensions burst forth from cramped houses that struggled to contain their denizens from spilling on to the streets. The neighbourhood was a testament to unfulfilled DIY ambition. Cheap conservatories, rashly purchased, flapped unfinished in the wind. Dilapidated sheds, relics from an older generation of dahlia growers and diggers for victory, were filled with broken suitcases and unidentifiable chunks of self-assembly furniture.

His neighbours seemed quite unperturbed by their surroundings. Come rain or shine, the women threw on rubber flipflops, pulled flimsy emerald and fuchsia dupattas about them, and pegged out the washing in the forlorn hope that the English north wind might blow it dry before the next downpour. One or two elderly ladies tended brass cooking pots on open fires in their handkerchief-sized front yards. The braver ones ventured up the hill with old chapattis and burnt toast to feed the pigeons congregating by the swings and roundabout in the half-finished playground. At the end of the street lay an expanse of grassy wasteland bounded by a fence that trapped a billowing display of plastic bags. Here was a sodden black bench where Harris would sit on fine days, contemplating the view of the valley below, which was dominated by a disused textile mill. A number of his cousins and uncles and aunts had settled in the area during the 1950s and 1960s, and their continuing presence was the catalyst for his relocation to the rain-soaked northern town after the breakdown of his marriage.

The news that their wayward relative was returning to the fold had been greeted with unbridled enthusiasm by a coterie of male cousins. In the vanguard was Nawaz, a stocky, bearded fellow pushing forty, who waged a forceful campaign of persuasion that had resulted in Harris's purchase of a small terraced house, with a chocolate-brown hallway and no central heating. It had been going for a song and he could no longer afford to be choosy, as Nawaz was fond of reminding him. And so, with a modest down payment borrowed from the bank, he had managed to cobble together a mortgage to buy it — a temporary staging post, he'd thought, until something better turned up.

After he had moved in, Nawaz persuaded him to take over the lease of a Spar corner shop from a cousin who had got into difficulties with the rent. The shop would occupy his time as well as generate a modest income – at least that was the plan. Before long, Harris had bought himself a nearly new Citroën through *Exchange and Mart*; the French car was good for the steep roads, he'd declared when eyebrows were raised at his extravagance. And so it was that for a brief period, in the new place, with the new car, he had enjoyed an optimistic outlook. The upside of the situation was that he was surrounded by relatives: he was just a short drive from Nawaz and his family, who provided hot meals, friendly company and distraction from the pressing need to sort out his own life. The downside was that considerable work was required to make the house habitable and the shop profitable, and unfortunately Harris was neither a keen handyman nor a born grocer.

For the first six months in the new house, he'd struggled with the *Reader's Digest Complete DIY Manual* in an attempt to master the complexities of central heating installation. By the time his daughter, Alia, had come up from her mother's place to visit him that Christmas, gleaming white radiators hummed with heat in every room. She was eighteen years old, in her last year at school, and the prospect of A-level exams loomed that summer. While her father pottered about aimlessly downstairs, she had occupied a room in the attic, poring over her biology and chemistry notes at a wonky Formica desk. From time to time, her attention would drift to the changing landscape outside her window and the jagged hills that rose beyond the town. When the sun shone and split the clotted sky into inky streaks, the countryside reflected a glorious slaty greenness and she would head to Castle Hill for a run. Or, if it was raining, she'd escape to go shopping, moseying up and down Market Street, in and out of Peacocks or Topshop, wondering how long it would last, this precarious arrangement of her father's.

On Christmas Day, he'd roasted chicken in the English style for her, with frozen peas and boiled potatoes, and made a pot of hot, oily chickpea stew for himself. He'd decorated a small pine tree in a pot and ceremoniously handed out her presents from a festive Marks & Spencer bag – matching stripy leggings and jumper, plus a sleek red vinyl shoulder bag. As an after-thought, he'd given her a bar of white Toblerone, also from Marks & Spencer, having added it to his basket at the checkout as he stood waiting nervously to pay for clothes he was not entirely confident about. Sartorial style for him was one thing; a teenage girl was another matter.

The house had been warm and Harris cheery as the two of them ate meals together in the basement kitchen, though Alia had quickly begun to suspect it was all a front for her sake. Yet she'd been reluctant to upset the fragile edifice he'd created for himself, so she'd kept her fears under wraps as he laid bare his desperation. Life as a shopkeeper, he'd discovered, was no picnic. Rising at dawn, stacking shelves, sticking price labels on every-thing, had made him exhausted, despondent.

'Did I struggle to come top of my class for this? And let's not beat around the bush, Alia.'

'About what, Dad?'

'The profit margins in this game are laughable. I can barely make enough to survive, let alone live in any decent comfort.'

'Are things really that bad?'

'Worse than bad. But the biggest problem is this solitary life I've been forced to lead.'

'Can't you remarry?'

'Fat bloody chance.'

It was a conversation they'd had many times.

'I've had it with the constant trips to the cash and carry, day in, day out . . .'

'But you run a shop. It's what you're meant to do.'

'My car won't take it, the wear and tear and all. Alia, how can people guzzle so many Heinz Baked Beans and tins of Spam?'

She'd been unable to shed any light on the matter.

It made no sense to him whatsoever, English food. All those wretched tin cans, the leathery joints of meat, the vegetables pulverized in boiling water.

'But you love gravy,' she'd reminded him. 'When Mum did roasts.'

It was true. He had lapped up the salty brown elixir at the end of those meals like a famished animal.

The summer was over and Harris was in his bedroom unpacking a suitcase. He had just returned from a trip to Pakistan, having taken Alia with him for the first time. They'd been to the village, the place he'd escaped from to marry her mother when he'd come to England as a graduate student years earlier. They'd roamed around the country on trains and buses, eaten spicy snacks together, slept under the stars in the village, and visited his best friend, Omar, and his wife, Kamila, in the suburbs of Lahore. Now he was back in the north of England and she was far away in the south. It made him desolate, but it could not be helped.

He went downstairs to sort through the drift of post that had accumulated on the doormat during his absence and, as he knelt to gather it up, he noticed the fluted forms of his cousins Nawaz and Jamal appear through the ribbed glass of his front door. They were barely inside, the dust of their *salaams* hardly settled, before the nitty-gritty of retail business arose. Harris had left them in charge of the shop while he was away but now that he was back they were eager to air their grievances. It was barely eight-thirty in the morning. He envisaged a disgruntled cluster of customers gathering in front of the closed shop and gave a weary groan. Of course, neither Jamal nor Nawaz had actually been over there yet to pull back the metal shutters, undo the stacks of newspapers and throw open the doors to the locals agitating for their fags, their copies of the *Sun* and their cartons of milk.

'Did you leave a note on the shop door saying when you'd be back?' Harris asked.

Nawaz rubbed his nose and shrugged.

'I take that to be a "no", is it?'

Nawaz ignored this and made himself at home on the couch. 'How'd the tomboy daughter go down with the family back 'ome, then?'

'They loved her, of course. What do you expect?' Harris replied. 'They treated her like visiting royalty.'

'Did they indeed? I can imagine.'

Nawaz rolled his narrow eyes and cleared his throat. He didn't hide his disapproval of the Uncle's daughter and her wayward tendencies – the English boyfriends, the un-Islamic upbringing. It was a site of struggle between the cousins.

'Did you find an 'usband for her, then, Harris?'

'That wasn't the purpose of the trip.'

'All alone in that big bad city, though, in't she?'

'Oh, she's doing very well, back at medical school. It's a first-rate college, really is. One of the best.'

'She'll be supporting you before you know it.'

'I'm not counting my chickens—'

'That is, if she doesn't go off with an English boy first. You won't see her again if she does, mark my words.'

'Take my advice and worry about your own brood,' Harris snapped.

Nawaz had no fears on that front. His brood was safe within the confines of his family, but Harris's daughter was a different matter. He'd been a lab technician at the local comprehensive school and, with his degree in physics, he liked to believe he had all the answers. After snaring the bright young Safeena as his bride, he had quit his job and nagged her till she quit hers. He had swiftly taken over a takeaway restaurant, Royale Cuisine, installing Safeena behind the counter. It did not matter a bit that he knew nothing about cooking, for the dishes were limited to chicken tikka, kebabs, chips and pizza, photos of which were displayed on an illuminated menu. The point was, he had spotted an insatiable need in the community for tasty fast food and had filled it.

'What's been going on while I've been away?' Harris wanted to know.

'Cousin, we don't mean to come so early and that—' Jamal began.

'Only there's a problem,' Nawaz went on. 'Lemme tell him the score, orright?'

Before Harris could protest, his cousin scrolled down a list

8

of issues that had arisen during his absence. The biggest problem was cash flow.

'I'm diggin' deep in me own pocket, I am, and it can't go on.'

'I'll repay you,' Harris stammered. 'Have I ever not?'

Nawaz disregarded him. 'You need to fix that burglar alarm. Or is it just decoration?'

'It's a deterrent.'

'Jamal's refusing to work in the off-licence section, says it's *haram*.'

'We can sort this out, between us.'

'Trouble is, I'm like, neglecting me own baby, Harris,' Nawaz said, and for a moment Harris's heart softened, thinking he meant his infant daughter. But then he realized it was the take-away business Nawaz was moaning about.

'You could have gone over to keep an eye on it, why not?'

'Why not? See, you've no idea, 'ave you? I'll tell you why not. Shoplifting, cousin! Had to protect poor Jamal 'ere, didn't I?' Jamal was on the feeble side – short as well as skinny. 'They'd've slaughtered 'im, no question.'

'Well, what are you doing letting in these groups of school-children en masse? There's a sign on the door banning groups of more than two, unless you took it down.'

'We didn't. Cousin, you need a proper CCTV, like.'

'Those things make no difference. Like speed cameras, everyone ignores them.'

'They provide evidence,' Jamal piped up. Recently, he had been concerned for his own safety when confronted by a group of hyper teenagers who had refused to hand over pilfered stuff they'd scooped into their pockets. 'The girl said she'd do my face in,' he explained apologetically.

There was a long pause during which nobody spoke.

'Tell you what, I've an idea,' Nawaz said, as if it had just struck him. 'I'm looking for a bit of cash for the restaurant, to tart it up, like, and get a decent cook.'

'About bloody time,' Harris said. 'Before someone dies in there.'

'Right. So what do you say?'

'To what?'

'To stumping up a few grand.'

'Am I a cash machine all of a sudden?'

Nawaz ignored this. 'Why should I borrow from the bank and pay those crooks interest? *Riba* is *haram*, Harris, you're always saying so. Don't deny it.'

'Plenty of things you do are *haram*, Nawaz, so why the moral high ground all of a sudden, huh?' Harris said.

Nawaz made a grunt of protest and Jamal looked away. He was fed up with being owed weeks of wages for all the overtime he'd done to cover Harris's frequent absences: trips to London, the recent jaunt to Pakistan.

'Let me think about it, the cash injection,' Harris said, softening. 'But for now, you boys go and open the shop or we'll have a bloody riot over there. The locals need their cigs.'

Jamal bobbed his head in assent. Nawaz rose heavily, tucking in his shirt tails, which had ridden up to reveal a nap of coarse black fur spreading across his back. 'Best be gettin' along, then. C'mon, Jamal.'

'What about my situation, Cousin?' Jamal asked Harris meekly on his way out.

'I'll sort it out, don't worry. Your hard work will not be forgotten.' Though he feared that given the cash-flow problem,

Jamal might have to regard his labour as a sunk cost. '*Khuda hafiz*, brothers,' he said.

After they had left, Harris breathed a long sigh of relief and got on with opening the post. He stacked a bank statement and several credit card bills on one side of the dining-room table he had inherited from the previous owners of the house, then piled up the magazines on the other. The table's varnished veneer was cracked, he noticed, remembering that his only tablecloth was in the wash. It was overwhelming, the unending cycle of cleaning and clearing that was required simply to get by. In Pakistan there was always a retinue of people around to do such things: the sisters and wives in the village, the servants at Omar's house in Lahore. Tea and meals popped up from nowhere; chores were magically done. Here it was a different proposition. The laundry basket on the landing had toppled over, shedding its cargo of dirty washing down the stairs. The sink hosted a greasy sculpture of abandoned washing-up and globules of orange fat clung to the draining board. The khaki-grey remains of a chicken curry on the stove resembled the cratered surface of the moon. Peering with trepidation into the fridge, Harris saw that its sparse contents were welded to the sides like frosty relics of a prehistoric era.

I need to buy some food, he thought, panic rising. *Get organized. Go shopping. Cleaning can wait.*

Yet the prospect of combing the aisles and searching through the chilled-food sections for meat filled him with gloom. He always dreaded the slow hours, days and weeks that followed in the wake of a trip. He liked to go away as often as possible to avoid this dreary place. The painful realization dawned on him that he hated it; even after all his efforts – the layers of fresh paint, the installation of gas-fired central heating throughout – it would never quite be home.

What was the point in living here alone?

His spirits plummeted and not even the television, his usual solace, could lift his mood.

To distract himself, he tried tackling the remaining pile of post. The first envelope he slit open revealed a grainy photocopy of an ad for porn videos, available only by mail order. One tiny slip, a moment of carnal weakness, and now his good name was stuck indelibly on a shameful mailing list. He screwed the flier up into a ball and set light to it over the sink, watching its crimped edges glow and delicate black embers feather over the plates.

'Bugger that,' he muttered.

He turned his attention to the last unopened letter and noticed his solicitor's name and address embossed on the left-hand corner of the envelope. He felt a kick of adrenalin and his hands quivered as he opened it. The surface of the letter swam before his eyes, sentences fragmenting as he raced down the page. The sum he was owed from the ex-wife was far more than he was expecting.

It was £53,294.00.

Allah is great. Perhaps the anguish of divorce had been worth it after all.

Two

Harris spent a fitful night struggling over what to do with the money, as if it was imperative to decide immediately. There was the obvious option of simply leaving it in a savings account, accruing interest and providing him with a little cushion. But somehow he was loath to let the cash sit doing nothing. It was sinful, according to the Koran, to hoard money and assets that Allah had granted out of his grace while others around you were in need. He knew that for those who were niggardly about giving away their hoardings, a harsh fate awaited them on Judgement Day.

With this in mind, he toyed with how the money might best be disbursed. Paying off the mortgage was not in his sights; that would be sorted out upon his death. He aspired to do something greater, something transformational for others in need, relieving him of the burden of riches. A power generation plant in the village? A generous donation to the half-finished mosque that people were eagerly planning in his neighbourhood? The spiritual enrichment was appealing yet there were too many scoundrels caught up in that particular project, and he was wary of handing over anything to them. The money was like a net that trapped him; the more he struggled, the more entangled he became.

Then he thought of Khalid Ali, his cousin in the village. His house was makeshift, fashioned from an unhappy marriage of mud and cement, boasting just one room for the family. He lived there with his wife, Nasreen, and their three children, two girls and a boy, in an open-plan arrangement. There was no kitchen, so Nasreen cooked outside on an open fire. In winter, they slept huddled under a *resai*. In summer, they slept outside on rope cots, sharing the hot breeze from a battered fan. The bathroom was open to the elements, its door a sheet of cloth. Khalid Ali had recently lost his job as a labourer on the railways and been compelled to make a sideways move into horoscope-casting instead. But the work was scant, and when his clients didn't pay up, he was too soft-hearted to pursue them, preferring to provide the service, more often than not, free of charge.

Khalid Ali was ten years his junior, and Harris owed him his life – that is to say, his life in England. When Harris had left the village, and refused to marry Nasreen, Khalid Ali had stepped into the breach. Everyone was shocked that somebody better, somebody English, had cropped up and ousted Nasreen, who was considered quite a catch. Years later, Harris's divorce from the English lady caused consternation in that corner of the world, and also much heated discussion.

'It is all final?' Khalid had probed his cousin, when he'd visited with Alia in the summer. They had been sitting on crates in the courtyard, watching the children's baby rabbits frolic in the sunshine. The rabbits were kept as pets, but sold regularly when money was scarce.

'*Insha'allah*, yes.'

'So you are getting some money from the iron lady, then?' Khalid was incredulous. 'I thought that in England the law favours the wife and you are paying her for all the rest of your time on earth?'

'I'll get my remaining share of the assets. It's not a fortune, but still.'

Khalid was silent for a moment. 'That's good,' he said, clearly wishing he were a tenth as lucky.

'I'd like you to have something, Khalid. You deserve it.'

'Me?'

'Yes, you and your family.'

'Cousin, I couldn't possibly. You're too generous.'

'Maybe. But I owe it to Nasreen.'

'You owe her nothing.' Khalid's voice was hoarse.

'Please. For my sake. When you married Nasreen—'

'Don't say it. It was my duty and I accept it.' Khalid looked down at his lap and sighed. 'Thank you. You are a good man, Harris.'

'It's nothing. Just promise me you won't sell any more of these rabbits, OK? Leave them be for the children.'

Khalid wiped his nose and sniffed. 'You're a kind soul. I promise, or Allah strike me down.'

The precise details of the conversation – what was promised, what was declined – eluded Harris now as he twisted and turned in his bed, until sleep finally overtook him. He awoke before dawn with a jolt of clarity, swiftly did his ablutions and said his prayers in the chilly lounge by the flickering blue flame of the gas fire. It was obvious, crystal clear. His nearest and dearest must benefit from the money. He would not leave it sitting in the bank; not let those cousins up the hill get their hands on it. Yet who to choose? The list of deserving cases was long. He stared out of the window as the refuse trucks heaved along the street and watched the sun rising over the rooftops. His heart pounded; his feet felt slippery with sweat.

In the murky streaks of daybreak, he thought of Alia – his only child, his best hope, the light of his life. During term time, she seldom visited him up here in his house at the end of the north wind and after their summer trip together, he felt her absence more keenly than ever. He had an idea, a proposition, that would mean going to see her.

It was drizzling that morning when he drove south to London, armed with little more than an overnight bag, a light mackintosh and a tiffin carrier containing a puddle of leftover prawn curry and two slices of white bread.

The act of fleeing his house never failed to lift his spirits. The world unspooling outside the window as he sped down the M1 gave him a sense of purpose and progress. It was a four-hour drive to London and he usually brought his own food on motor trips. Not because he was fearful of encountering non-halal food – unlike the northern cousins who took a hard line on such things – but rather because he loathed spending money on the rubbery fry-ups they served in motorway service stations. The curry he had brought along sloshed messily on the seat beside him for ninety miles or so, at which point he grew peckish and tried spooning it into his mouth as he drove, but this proved too dangerous. The soupy concoction splashed his shirt, clean that day, and the car veered dangerously into the middle lane.

He pulled into a service station off the M1, so he could eat without crashing the Citroën, his pride and joy. When he was done, he rang Alia to alert her to his imminent arrival, sheepishly aware that she was not expecting to see him again until at least Christmas. He knew better than to show up on her doorstep without prior warning, even if it was just a courtesy call from a motorway service station to announce he was on his way. She didn't like surprise visits, he'd learned from bitter experience. But this was different. He called her mobile several times, leaving a slew of voicemails, fearful that she might be off somewhere. The notion that she might be with other people – boys or girls, people beyond his orbit – was a painful reminder that she lived a separate life that not only excluded him but was contrary to his way of doing things. It was the English way of putting freedom and pleasure before family and duty. Everybody did that here.

In his world it was different. People could drop in on each other any time of the day or night and expect boundless hospitality in the form of meals and lodging and sundry comforts, with no fixed dates for arrival or departure. Alia wasn't like that. She was a modern girl, born and bred in England, and he did not want to provoke or, worse, lose her. She shared little of her life with him now that she was a student, no longer living at home. She spoke of 'needing space' and, though he didn't dare ask her what that space was for, he harboured painful suspicions.

A few hours later, he pulled up outside the student house where she lived near the Whitechapel Road. It was a tall, narrow red-brick Victorian terrace, sandwiched between an atrophied hospital building and the Commercial Road. She occupied the first floor, with a stream of changing housemates. The ground floor was rented by a halal meat dealer who came and went at random times of the day to empty and refill a huge freezer that squatted in the window with carcasses of meat. Harris peered through the grubby net curtain but the space was dark. Surely he could stay a night or two in her place. He remembered that she'd said her housemate had moved out and she'd not mentioned a replacement. A lanky young man with unruly hair and a five o'clock shadow came to the front door.

'Oh, hello,' Harris said, taken aback. 'Are you the new housemate?'

'Kind of, sometimes,' came the reply.

'I see. Is Alia there – is she in?'

'Sorry, she's just gone to get her hair cut.'

'I see,' Harris said, alarmed by the degree of inside knowledge about Alia's movements that he seemed to have at his disposal. 'Will she be long?'

The young man didn't know.

Then Harris said, 'I'm her father, you see.'

'Really? That's awesome.'

What was awesome about it? Harris wondered. Out loud he said, 'May I come in and wait?'

'Sure thing.' He opened the door and gestured Harris inside. 'I'm Oliver, by the way,' he said amiably. 'Would you like some tea or coffee while you wait for her? Something to eat perhaps?' He began pulling out packets of Batchelors Soup and flat packs of noodles from her cupboards.

'Oh no, nothing for me,' Harris said firmly, raising his hand like a policeman stopping traffic. It struck him that there was something inauthentic about English hospitality: people always seemed more relieved when you refused it. In his world, refusal might cause untold offence. 'I'll just sit here till she comes. You don't need to trouble yourself on my account.'

Oliver mumbled something that Harris didn't catch and then melted away upstairs.

The newly opened hairdressers on Cavell Street was festooned with bunting and Alia had fallen for the cheap offer displayed in the window. The Russian ladies who ran it advertised their hair and beauty services in Cyrillic text, and she was relieved to discover that the language barrier prevented the usual meandering enquiries about holiday destinations, boyfriends and whether she was going out somewhere special that night. She had no plans for that evening, nothing on the cards. The hairdresser, whose auburn hair was like the glossy bright tresses of a doll, scrutinized her in the mirror. Alia returned the gaze, brow furrowed. She wasn't too keen on looking at herself these days. Long brown hair, streaked blonde by the sun, curtained her pensive, oval face. Her olive skin was still tanned and dotted with freckles from her visit to Pakistan, but her eyebrows were too thick for her liking.

'I'd like it shorter,' she said with a vague gesture to the hairdresser, who happily took out her scissors. 'Something different.'

An hour later she emerged renewed, with a short crop and jagged fringe, feeling strangely lighter, as if it was just her hair that had been dragging her down. It wasn't, of course, or not the only thing. Since dropping out of medical school after failing several exams at the end of her first year, she had felt untethered, as if she were rising into the sky in a hot-air balloon, watching the world shrink away beneath her. It was an odd, not entirely unpleasant, sensation. She hadn't told her father yet. Her mother had been volcanic when she'd found out and Alia had ditched the proposed summer holiday with her, not wanting to listen to her ranting for the duration of the trip. Instead, she had gone to Pakistan with her father, much to his delight.

Harris had long wanted her to meet the cousins who lived there. He was keen to show her off. Of course, he'd been back many times by himself, always bringing a good selection of gifts and photos, but this was the first time he'd brought his real live daughter. The village was hardly a village at all but a miniature urban sprawl in the making: a random collection of low-lying, dun-coloured buildings, scattered at the edge of a bigger town, crisscrossed by open sewers and bisected by a rocky road where young men in tight shirts roared up and down on Honda motorbikes. They had reached it in the middle of the night after a meandering journey by train and bus from Lahore. Their arrival was heralded by a straggle of barking dogs that did their level best to see off the foreign intruders before abandoning them to the night.

Harris guided Alia in the darkness, until her eyes grew accustomed to the absence of light. He was tipsy with the sheer excitement of it and nipped off towards a muddle of dwellings faster than she could manage, struggling to keep up as he hopped over rivulets of effluent skirting the low mud houses. Fumes rose up from oily puddles into the night air, but he barely noticed. He was showing her the place he had come from; the place where, if things hadn't worked out the way they had, he'd have ended up. There were no lights to guide him yet he knew the way. The clear blue-black sky was punched with constellations, which he glanced at for guidance, though he didn't need them. Nimble as a cat, he leapt over drains and hopped from doorstep to doorstep, down narrow streets of dilapidated buildings, never stumbling or hesitating once. It was a part of him, mapped into his being, the memory of how to reach the cousin's quarters on the other side of the tracks.

As Alia headed home, the shop windows reflected a disconcerting stranger glaring back at her. She lingered at the Beigal Bunnies van, a permanent fixture parked between the dental school and the pathology building, wondering whether to get something to eat. The thick smell of bacon and eggs sizzling on the griddle made her hurry across the road to escape. She passed through a column of steam spiralling like a phantom from the hospital laundry rooms and crossed a square expanse of balding grass where students gathered in clumps on the steps and benches eating lunch in the autumn sunshine. She bowed her head to avoid any familiar faces with friendly enquiries about how she was doing.

When she returned to the sanctuary of her house, she was taken aback to hear her father's voice.

'Alia, surprise, surprise!' He stood in the hallway, arms outstretched.

'It is a surprise, yes.' She dropped her bag by the door and gave him a quick hug. 'Or should I say, what's the surprise?'

'I've been waiting for over an hour for you. Read the newspaper back to front – the TV guide, weather forecast, even the fashion section.'

'What are you doing here, Dad?' Her stomach clenched. 'Is something wrong?'

'No, no! What could be wrong? Unless it's wrong to visit my daughter suddenly, is it?'

'I just spent the whole of August with you. I wasn't expecting to see you till Christmas at least.'

'So Christmas has come early!' he cried.

'You never said you were coming,' she said, and went into the kitchen.

'There wasn't time. Just got in the car and drove straight here.'

'You might have called.'

'Actually, I did call your mobile and left several messages.'

She glimpsed at her phone and saw that it was true.

'Your new housemate, however, was kind enough to let me in,' he went on.

She started. 'Oliver, you mean?'

'The tall chap, yes, with the rather long hair.'

'Dad.'

'Is he your new housemate, this fellow?'

She took off her jacket and flung it over the back of a chair, pretending she'd not heard the question, unwilling to elaborate on his status.

'So the other girl left, that nice housemate of yours, did she?' Harris probed.

'She did, yes.'

He said nothing, feeling his own plan was in jeopardy, slithering out of his control. She noticed a turmeric stain on the lapel of his tweed jacket and, seeing her expression, he rubbed at it with a handkerchief.

'I had my own lunch en route to keep me going,' he said.

She smiled, and he ventured, 'Any space for me to stay then?'

'Sofa's pretty comfy, if you need a place.'

'Well,' he sniffed. 'I just might. Depends on the schedule. Alia, what've you done to your hair?'

She sat on an armchair that was trailing stuffing and touched her new hairdo protectively. 'It needed cutting. I'm allowed, aren't I?'

'Did you do it yourself?'

'No! A nice Russian hairdresser did it. Is it that bad?'

'Well, it is a bit short.'

'I like it like that. Short and simple.'

He sighed. 'I hope I didn't interrupt anything. Did I? Why aren't you at lectures?'

'Nothing's on today.' Not for her, at least.

'No lectures?'

'Nope.'

'That seems unusual.'

'It's the timetable.'

Harris rose from the sofa and began to pace around restlessly, as if in search of clues.

'What's wrong?' she asked.

'Just stretching the legs after the long drive. I'm getting pins and needles.'

Alia saw him glancing at her desk, strewn with bills, books and CDs – her open laptop exposed to his probing eyes. She flipped it shut.

Oliver padded quietly into the living room, stopping in his tracks at the sight of Alia's haircut.

'Wow, I like it.'

'Thank you.'

'Hello again,' Harris addressed the interloper testily, surreptitiously surveying his features.

'Oh, hi.'

'Did you . . . Have you . . . introduced yourselves?' Alia's question was staccato with tension.

'Yup, we did just now,' Oliver replied, nonplussed.

Alia shot him a look.

'Shall I go shopping for tonight?' he asked.

Harris jumped. 'Tonight? What's on tonight?'

'Oh, nothing much. I just need some milk, that's all.' Alia ushered Oliver towards the door. 'Go now.'

Once they were alone, Harris looked at her expectantly, anxiously licking a hint of a scar on his upper lip. When she was young, there'd been a mole there, punched with tiny dots of hair follicles that made her think of a ladybird crawling into his nose. It was long gone, having been removed by a surgeon in the Royal Air Force. That was another chunk of life over for him, the armed forces. He'd joined up when he was sick of being rejected for every single job he applied for, his hard-won qualifications as a graduate of the Punjab College of Engineering and Technology mysteriously invisible to prospective employers, and to mollify Alia's mother, who panicked that the handsome man she'd run off to marry would never amount to anything. It was a structure, at least, and provided a regular salary. The Christmas parties were good, Alia always said, with Santa arriving by helicopter. But service life, even as an officer, was not quite Harris's cup of tea.

In the beginning, he'd hoped to realize a childhood dream

to pilot a plane – an ambition that was rapidly quashed after he was taken for a test flight with two airmen whose idea of a joke was to loop the loop and watch him turn bilious. So he was grounded on terra firma as a maintenance engineer, checking the components of the aircraft as they ran test operations: a thankless yet vital task. Perfect for the detail-orientated type, the geeky technician who did not mind the invisibility of the work, only in the spotlight if things went awry.

For a decade or so, the family had lived the itinerant life, moving from posting to posting, unloading their personal things that never quite went with the same old utilitarian furniture that filled every new quarters. Yet beyond the jolly camaraderie of service life, Harris had never really become a member of the club. There was nobody else who looked like him in the officers' mess: no brown faces, or precious few, no place to pray without attracting hostile glances. So he had placed his faith in cold storage, promising himself he'd allow it out only when he was free from that life. The strain of conformity, without the daily ritual of prayer, drove him to despair. Eventually he was discharged on medical grounds related to heart problems. It was a blessed relief at first, civilian life, and for a brief period he had felt a tremendous sense of release and possibility. He was free.

But his wife never forgave him for giving up – for succumbing, as she saw it, to physical infirmity. He never quite forgave himself either, regarding it as a punishment from God for abandoning the faith. For a long time, he battled with the sensation that he was a bad Muslim, a view that baffled and irritated his wife. She looked around and saw better men than the one she'd picked when she was an unworldly undergraduate. And so it was, that in the week before Christmas, she had made her announcement of resignation from the family, as they all sat by the pine tree that Harris and Alia had driven home, strapped precariously to the roof of the car. It was not a happy new year, and after endless bitter rows, Harris reluctantly moved out.

Alia had become bogged down with misery. Not because her parents had separated – that was a blessed relief in some ways – but more because of the aimlessness, the domestic entropy, that settled upon her father in his new home. She'd visit him at weekends to find him poring over neatly penned job applications in plastic folders, a terrified frown corrugating his forehead. Middle age was a bad time to be single and jobless; her teen magazine reading had told her that.

She'd secretly hoped he'd find someone new but she knew he needed a job first. Nobody would look at an unemployed, dumped man like him and pounding the pavements for a job, executive or otherwise, was not easy at his stage of life. Colleagues from his RAF days gradually fell away. She noticed that he devoted more time to reading the Koran and writing letters to his more faithful friends back home. He toyed with going into business with his old engineering college friend Omar, but nothing quite materialized and he had signed on to the dole to keep himself afloat. Alia had been bewildered at how rapidly things deteriorated. Yet, given his impecunious circumstances, she'd managed to secure a bursary and mainte-nance grant for university, and temped during the holidays to make ends meet.

'Why don't you just do something – anything – instead

of sitting around like this?' she'd said to her father one day, unable to deal with the torpor any more. She'd regretted it instantly when she'd seen his eyes widen with panic.

'What does it look like!' he'd cried, and flung the folders on to the kitchen table so that all the laboriously scribed applications fluttered out for her to see.

'So, what really brings you down here, Dad?' Alia said, stealing a look at his compact weekend bag – though a small bag was not always a reliable indicator of a short stay.

'Just a quick jaunt. Mixture of business and pleasure.'

'Really?' She darted around the living room, clearing things out of sight.

'To say hello to you and take you out to lunch.'

'What's the occasion?'

'Does there need to be one? Haven't eaten yet, have you?' he probed.

She hadn't. 'Is there somewhere you want to go?'

'You choose. Anything you like.'

'There's a pub round the corner that does really nice food,' she suggested. 'How about that?'

It sounded most agreeable to Harris, who considered pubs a treat.

A babble of voluble medical students and nursing staff spilled on to the pavement outside the Queen's Head.

'Seems popular with the students,' Harris observed approvingly.

They went inside, where they found themselves jammed up at the bar, waiting for Thai chicken curry and beef Stroganov.

Normally, Harris loved pub lunches, but the rancid fug and raucous outbursts of laughter in this place were very off-putting. It was not the ideal venue for the proposal he had in mind. He took a sip of beer and cleared his throat.

'I have something I'd like to say to you,' he declared, more portentously than he had intended.

She braced herself for a sermon.

'There's something I'd like to give you.'

'Give me?'

'Yes. I've decided to give you my fortune—'

Waves of chatter made him difficult to hear. 'Your *portion*?'

'No, no! My fortune!' he said as loudly as he could without shouting. 'To invest. In a new home. For us both.'

A couple of middle managers paused their boozing to eavesdrop.

'What fortune? Invest in what?'

'Please keep your voice down. I thought you could use it to get your own place and we could own it jointly.'

'Own it jointly,' she echoed, uncomprehending.

'You and me. Makes perfect sense, financially speaking. Then, when you have a husband—'

'A *husband*?'

'As you will, at some point. No, let me finish,' he cried, feeling a tidal wave of protest rising on her side. 'When you start your *own* family—'

'I don't want another family. I've had enough of this one.'

'Alia, listen. You're getting wrong end of the stick. What I mean to say is, we can share the burden of the cost of the place we buy. I could come and stay, or even live there—'

'*Live* with me?'

'—and take care of things for you when you're out at work. It would solve so much.'

'What would it solve?'

'Our need for a home!'

'But I have a home,' she said. 'Right here. I don't think this is a good idea.'

'Alia, the final settlement has come through.'

She concentrated on peeling apart a beer mat. 'That's good. You must be pleased.'

'Yes, I am. I'm thrilled. But you don't seem to be.'

She fixed her gaze on a trail of amber bubbles in his beer. 'I am. For you.'

They sat in silence for a moment and then he had another go.

'I'm offering you a large sum of money.'

'I know.'

'So why aren't you pleased?'

'I don't think I can accept it. It's yours.'

'Don't be silly.' His heart raced. 'Why not? Fifty grand, Alia! Not peanuts.'

He stared at her as if she'd dealt him a mortal blow. The barman bellowed their food-order number.

'That's us.' Alia waved at the man, who slid two plates in her direction along the counter.

The sight of the meal triggered his hunger and he stuck his fork into the steaming dish.

'You could buy a place of your own, get your foot on the ladder.' The food scorched his tongue, distorting his words.

She ate in silence.

'I won't bother you. I'll keep myself to myself. We both

need a home, Alia. Where's the logic in saying no to the offer?'

'None, probably,' she said.

A paunchy man in a wrinkled suit turned around and stared at him. The cheeky so-and-so was listening to their private conversation and laughing at him! His tongue bubbled from the burn and he pushed away the plate of food, wiping his mouth with a napkin.

'Don't you like it?' she said, after a moment.

'Had enough.' His forehead gleamed.

He fished his raincoat off the floor and flung it on awkwardly over his jacket.

'I'm sorry,' she said.

As they pushed their way through the press of merry drinkers, the volume rose unbearably in Harris's ears. Losing his footing, he tripped and stumbled into a young woman nursing a glass of shandy. In his confusion he heard himself apologize more than was necessary for the spillage, which had missed her but hit the lower half of his trouser leg, leaving it pungently sticky for the rest of the day.

They reached the corner of Alia's street.

'Aren't you coming in?' she asked as he hovered by his car. 'I thought you said you'd stay tonight.'

He shook his head. There were things he had to do in the city, business he must attend to, and so she didn't press him as he collected his bag from the hallway. It was only after he had left that she allowed the tingling in her nose to give way to tears – hating herself for crying over nothing, for an offer she couldn't accept.

Three

Harris headed down to Greenwich to meet a potential bride for himself, something he had put off until now. Her phone number and address had lodged in his diary for months, and on his last visit to Lahore, Omar and his wife had pressed him to get in touch with her. Now that he was alone in the world, they said, why not? Harris had been fearful of embarking upon something new at first, taking the plunge in unfathomable waters. So as he drove through London, he told himself he was just going to look her up, out of courtesy, and take things from there. According to the map, her postcode was SE10, a somewhat unsavoury area, or so he'd heard. The Friday afternoon traffic towards the Blackwall Tunnel crawled to a standstill and he consulted the *A–Z* to locate the quickest route.

Dr Farrah was a widow with an impressive CV, and Harris was nervous that his own accomplishments might pale in comparison. Apparently she had a PhD in something related to English literature. Shakespearian tragedy, wasn't it? That was all he could recall. Her husband, Idrees, had died a couple of years before, not long after he'd left his job at a medical equipment company where he had enjoyed a moderately successful career.

A weather-beaten flower seller appeared before Harris's windscreen, brandishing sprays of cheap carnations in improbable shades of neon lemon and ultraviolet blue. For a moment he was tempted to buy a bunch, then worried they were tasteless. The worry transmuted into low-level anxiety when he realized he would arrive empty-handed at her house. So he stopped at a newsagents close by and armed himself with a box of After Eight mint chocolates. A classic choice, he felt.

She was a youthful fifty, he guessed, observing her at a distance through the living-room windows of her house. Her hair was divided into two heavy black curtains, though her parting betrayed a band of bright silver. Around her neck she wore spectacles dangling on a gold chain that appeared to bother her; she kept pulling them on and off her nose as she moved about her living room. He tried to pluck up the courage to approach the front door and rap its intimidating brass knocker. Personally, he'd always favoured an electric doorbell, a simple ding-dong that resonated pleasantly through the house. Yet he could now see a door knocker was far superior. He was already beginning to fret about this and the other shortcomings of his house, when she disappeared from view. He lost his nerve and nipped back up the road until he was safely out of sight, then dialled her number on his mobile.

'Hello, yes?' she said.

'Dr Farrah?'

'This is she, yes?'

'Dr Farrah, hello, good morning – sorry, afternoon. *Salaam aleikum.*'

'Who is this please?'

'This is Harris. You remember, Omar's friend – his wife, Kamila, suggested I look you up?'

'Yes, yes, of course! *Wa'aleikum-as-salaam!* I'm so sorry, I couldn't place you. Of course! I'm sorry to be so distracted. I've had some problems with a small flood in the kitchen and I was waiting for the repair man to call and . . . Do please forgive me. Where are you ringing from?'

'I'm in town,' he said, floundering. 'London.'

'I see. May I call you back? What is your number?'

'Oh, I was just in the area and wondering if you might like to meet. But given you are very occupied with your kitchen problem we could make it another time.'

There was a pause for consideration, which Harris felt required to fill. 'Or could I perhaps be of some assistance? I have some rudimentary engineering skills,' he added modestly.

A burst of laughter, not unkind, greeted his offer.

'Not at all, I wouldn't hear of it. It's just – today is difficult.'

'Of course. I wouldn't expect you to be free at this very instant . . .'

'But perhaps the day after tomorrow? Is this a possibility or do you have a fixed programme?'

'I have a programme, but it's flexible. Should I call again in two days' time?'

'Do that, Harris. Yes, that would be nice. I really look forward to meeting you then. I've heard a great deal about you—'

'Not all bad, I trust?'

Her laughter was cut short. 'Oh, do excuse me. The plumber is here!'

'Dr Farrah?' But she was gone. The problem of the flood in her kitchen had overtaken her attention.

Harris hung up, retreating to the safe haven of his car, which was parked beneath the protective canopy of a sycamore tree shedding propeller seeds all over the bonnet. It was a leafy area. Quietly affluent, he noted, contrary to his expectations. Then fatigue overtook him and he reclined his car seat and took forty winks.

When he awoke, he saw her letting the workman out. Apart from a water-damaged photograph of her at Cambridge that Kamila had shown him, and sundry glimpses stolen through the front window, this was his first proper sighting of Dr Farrah in the flesh. She seemed shorter. Her full figure was dwarfed by a mint-coloured cable-knit cardigan that skimmed her ample thighs and distracted attention from the tired, peach-coloured sari she wore beneath it. He regretted calling her. Still, a promise is a promise and now he would have the tiresome problem of hanging around for a few days till she would grant him a meeting. What had he been thinking of?

In a state of indecision, he drove around the M25 and wondered what he should do. He stopped to get some fish and chips, gobbling them in a hurry and then regretting it. It was after eleven when he finally headed back towards Whitechapel, hoping to see Alia and patch things up, and to ask if he might stay the night at her house after all. But she was already in bed and the place was shrouded in a kind of darkness he did not wish to disturb. Tired after the day's exertions, he eventually nodded off in the driver's seat, only to be awoken by the warning beep of a van reversing towards his car. As he surfaced from a troublesome tangle of dreams featuring his ex-wife and Dr Farrah, he leaned on his horn and averted a collision. A light popped on in Alia's bedroom window and Harris instinctively looked up to see not her, but Oliver lifting the curtain.

'Hey, I think that's your dad's car outside,' Oliver said to Alia, who was half-awake.

'What?'

'Isn't it? Look.'

She tweaked the curtain aside and saw Harris staring up at them.

'Aren't you going to let him in?'

Had he seen her? She couldn't tell.

'One second.' She held the curtain tightly shut. 'I'm thinking.'

'You want me to?'

'No, don't!'

'Alia, you have to let him in,' Oliver said. 'You can't just leave him out there.'

'But I can't let him in. Not with you here.'

'What is it?'

'You have to go.' She was wide awake and jumpy.

'Don't be crazy. How am I supposed to do that? Climb out of the window?'

'Just go upstairs, hide somewhere till he's gone. Please, Oliver!'

'How can I hide? He saw me earlier.'

'Not in my bed, though, not here. I'll go and let him in. He must be freezing out there.'

Before Oliver could protest, she had leapt out of bed and run downstairs. She opened the front door, but there was no sign of him. A frigid wind surged into the hallway, wrapping itself around her bare ankles. She peered up and down the dark street, for a brief instant wondering if – or half-hoping that – she'd imagined seeing him.

As Harris sped east towards Docklands, the sweet temptation to drop off at the wheel was thwarted by the dip-dazzle rhythm of his headlights. At the edge of his vision was the broken ribbon of white lines, sucking him into the treacherous land between nod and wakefulness. Perhaps he'd dreamed it. Perhaps it wasn't true. He drove faster, heedless of the speed limit, replaying the scene in his mind, but there was little doubting what he had seen with his own eyes. He felt wretched, ridiculous, and it occurred to him suddenly that Alia's secretive activities were the real reason she had snubbed his generous offer. She was romantically involved, no question about it, caught up in the clutches of an unsuitable boy. Of course, he knew that for the great British public this revelation would not have been remotely horrifying. Yet for him, an outsider, it could not have been worse.

Four

Ever since Khalid Ali's eldest son, Rashid, first came to England, Harris had been like a father to him. He rang and visited regularly, counselled him on domestic and professional matters, and bailed him out of minor debts. When he failed his final exams the first time, Harris was at his side as the boy clutched the torn envelope bearing the disastrous news, armed with advice on cramming for the retakes and endless hints on how he must pull up his socks once he was a graduate. Khalid often asked Harris when his son would return home; his skills as an urban planner were sorely needed in that part of the world and beyond.

'He'll come back and transform this place,' Harris insisted. 'You mark my words.'

So the father kept a graduation photograph of the son propped up on an old fan box in his house and lived in hope.

But as time went by, there was no sign of Rashid reversing the trajectory of his life in England. He moved east, renting a room in a house near East Ham, within earshot of the roar from a flyover close by. A bugger to find, as Harris said, whenever he visited that far-flung stretch of London – which he did on a regular basis, most recently to bring him a winter coat at his mother's request. Nasreen worried about Rashid living in that climate. He was vulnerable to frequent chest infections, she thought, and required protection from the foggy damp that rolled off the Thames straight into his lungs. But he was less delicate than she thought. If the truth were known, it was hard for either of his parents to imagine their boy in England at all; so much about his life was inaccessible to them, beyond their reach. So they tended to stick to what was familiar, in the hope that this would be enough to spin out the thread of connection that stretched between them.

Rashid was a slender, mild-mannered young man who favoured extremely shiny shoes that concealed threadbare socks. His thick glasses corrected poor vision, the legacy of eye infections throughout his childhood that went untreated. They were fixed with Sellotape on one side, much to the irritation of his boss, who thought it made a poor impression on clients. After six months as a junior estate agent at Stone & Stone Properties, Rashid had sold two local authority flats in Bromley-By-Bow and a lock-up garage off Poplar High Street.

He was yet to find his true vocation.

But today he was feeling lucky. Blessed, almost. If he sold this flat in Wapping, the first sale in more than a month, he would make a decent commission. Then he would be in a better position to send his father and mother something, which he'd failed to do for more than a year. There was his rent, his food, his student debts to cover, and at the end of the month, he was out of pocket. The sporadic aerogrammes he received from home, written in his younger sister's hand, hinted heavily at the family's creeping financial woes.

Fiddling with his bent spectacle arm, he strove to maintain a cool demeanour in the presence of a potential buyer. It was not easy. She was pretty, Carolyn, a banker with a glossy slab of flaxen hair, and fragrant with something familiar he remembered from home. Sandalwood, was that it? Or maybe jasmine oil?

She looked about his age, mid-twenties, but she was richer than he would ever be. He was showing her a penthouse flat. Probably loose, he decided, not knowing whether to be thrilled or scandalized. Her micro miniskirt barely skimmed her crotch. Her nipples protruded from beneath a tight T-shirt with a designer logo he was unfamiliar with but which looked expensive. Her face and body were uniformly golden, her cheekbones dusted with bronze powder. The sports car she drove was parked at an acute angle on a double yellow line.

'Is that your car?' Rashid asked.

As she glanced out of the fifth-floor picture windows, a traffic warden placed a ticket under the windscreen wipers.

'Yeah, it is.' She really didn't give a toss; she didn't need to. 'The river looks so great from here. Wicked view. How much did you say the maintenance charge is?'

He consulted a sheaf of property specs. It was a two-bedroom apartment designed to look vaguely nautical, perched on a wind-blown stretch of the Thames with an uninterrupted view of converted tea warehouses on a crumbling wharf.

'It's around a five and a half thousand a year, I think.'

'Right. And what shops are there round here?'

'Let me check. Waitrose is supposed to be opening soon . . .

But like I said before, the asking price is definitely negotiable. The vendor's keen to sell, and you're well placed to—'

'Lemme talk to my boyfriend and I'll give you a call in the morning.'

So she had a boyfriend, then. Every thirteen-plus white girl did. They were all hitched. They were all loose. They all had more than one boyfriend.

'Great.' Rashid smiled. 'Call me first thing. I know we can do this.'

He held open the door and followed her out. Her high-heeled mules clicked on the polished wood floors and he noticed her pale nut-brown feet and perfectly pink unblemished bare heels. He conjured an image of his mother's feet: the ringed toes and the blackened fissures that striated her heels. She rubbed them with a special oil she kept in a tin trunk beside the bed in an attempt to keep them smooth but she was working against the odds.

Would Carolyn call so he could close a deal? He doubted it. The property market was as glassily flat as the Thames, which he now contemplated, idly wondering if he could make a break for it and swim to the other side, or whether the current would overwhelm him. A few years ago he had seen a lifeless man in a dark suit carried swiftly downriver. The rapid velocity of the corpse as it headed feet first towards the open sea was startling, jaunty almost, as though it were pursuing in death a lifelong dream of making it to freedom.

Rashid had watched the river police launch speed over the choppy grey waters, go round the body and haul it on board, zipping it into a nylon bag. For a few moments, he'd felt adrift with sadness for the unknown man who had begun the day in suit and tie and ended it shoeless, bloated and bagged on the floor of a boat in the middle of the Thames. Perhaps nobody would miss him, but Rashid doubted it. Everyone had somebody. It was impossible for him to imagine otherwise, for his was a world in which a network of family, fanned out across time zones, kept tabs on you.

The trouble with selling property was that you had to be willing to fudge, and Rashid was discovering that he wasn't. He hated lying to clients, hated the way they looked at him when he showed them dives he had duped them into believing were the answer to their dreams.

He had survived in this world by becoming adept at living a double life, something he'd learned upon arrival in London as a seventeen-year-old, almost a decade earlier. His first port of call had been to a distant relative's place, in a high-rise flat near Aldgate, where he had been almost too afraid to venture down to street level to explore the tatty markets peppered with white extremists touting cheaply printed newsletters full of spelling errors and dubious facts. Things were different around here these days. The so-called extremists were largely camouflaged in the great mess of London, and Rashid had absorbed something of their method: in order to survive, you had to blend in.

He had taken his A-levels at a crammer, and then Harris had helped him apply to a further education college in Hounslow. He had made a small group of friends there, but they'd dispersed and divided as they found jobs scattered across the metropolis, eager to spend their wages in Soho pubs on Friday nights with girls they had trawled during the week. Almost imperceptibly, Rashid had melted from the picture and was not particularly missed. Before long, he assumed he would be lined up with a girl from the village and he would marry her and follow that effortless path for himself. It was predestined yet it didn't happen. No bride materialized.

Since graduating a few years earlier, his projected career in urban planning was yet to take off. He had pursued a series of temporary administrative jobs for Newham Council in the traffic-planning department, but after a row with an unsympathetic line manager who denied him time off to pick up a relative from Heathrow, he was out on his ear. Desperation propelled him into a job as a minicab driver at Star Cabs on the Mile End Road. The work was truly demoralizing. Unlike most of his peers, he did not own a car and, as the job required that he supply his own vehicle, he had appealed to Uncle Harris for help. Harris had duly come to the rescue with a battered Renault, but Rashid could not shake off the nagging sense that cab driving was not his destiny. Not for this had he spent years enduring long English winters huddled in front of two electric bar heaters, memorizing facts to be regurgitated in dusty examination halls.

Had he known what the future held, he seriously doubted whether he would have put himself through the drudgery of endless exams. The extent of his job satisfaction as a minicab driver consisted of ferrying scantily clad girls back to the Isle of Dogs, or south of the river to the eerily well-tended new estates in Rotherhithe and Bermondsey, all the time hoping that they wouldn't throw up and ruin his already ruined car, and that they had the cash to pay him. He had a university degree and yet nobody wanted to hire him for what he was qualified to do.

Then his fortunes changed. His car was idling after dropping off a pensioner at Asda opposite the London Arena, when he was hailed by a sleekly suited man. The man's Mercedes had been biffed and left in a sorry state and he urgently needed to get to a meeting in Shoreditch. Rashid gave him a free ride. Jerry Stone, the owner of Stone & Stone, whose For Sale boards adorned buildings across the East End, said he would be eternally in his debt. He was late for a meeting to close a lucrative deal on Alie Street.

'You saved my bacon, mate,' he said, running his fingers though a pelt of sleek hair that framed sharp features giving him the appearance of a well-groomed stoat.

'Forget it,' said Rashid, glancing in the rear-view mirror. 'It's on me.'

But what was a nice, well-educated Asian boy doing in this skanky car, with its puke-stained upholstery? Jerry wanted to know. The story of the lower-second-class degree in urban planning fell from Rashid in a rush and Jerry was impressed. As Rashid drove him to his destination, Jerry unfurled his own credentials. He was a local, he said proudly, born and bred in the neighbourhood; now he and his family owned entire Georgian squares. For him it was all one big game of Monopoly, snapping up things that nobody wanted: pigeon-infested houses, burnt-out factories, anything Georgian or Huguenot. It so happened that Jerry needed a boy just like him, someone knowledgeable, not your usual spiv, and so he took him on in the front office of Stone & Stone, on a temporary basis.

At first things went smoothly. Rashid's methodical qualities meant that he was a natural at organizing the filing system. When he moved into the field, however, he found he was less talented at shifting property in the blighted areas he was designated. It simply wasn't his bag.

He was struggling to catch his breath by the time he reached the twelfth floor of a housing block in Poplar overlooking a 1960s concrete bazaar with a bewildering array of cockney and Bangladeshi stalls. Compressed slivers of grey sky could be glimpsed between high-rise flats that were stacked up around it.

'Lift's broken, sorry. Can't believe it – it was working last week . . .' he mumbled over his shoulder to the sighing couple trailing up the steps behind him. 'It's ex-local authority, a real bargain,' he added breathlessly, unlocking the flat and showing them inside.

He flung open the bathroom door. The couple were aghast. All that remained of the fixtures was the blackened porcelain stump of what had once been the toilet. 'The council was going to renovate the place, after the old man living here died,' Rashid explained apologetically. The pensioner, who lived alone, had apparently been dead for over a week before the neighbours called Environmental Health due to the ominous stench.

'But don't worry,' he added. 'It's all been totally cleaned, fumigated, and it's going to get cleared out.' It sickened him that he was trying to make a killing on a flat where someone had just died. But the prospective buyers were attracted by the price reduction, indifferent to its recent history. They sized it up, mentally preparing how they'd strip it to the bones.

'The kitchen's not bad,' Rashid said, trying to draw the silent girl half of the couple into the spirit of bargain property viewing.

Her fiancé answered for her. 'Depends what you mean by bad, doesn't it?'

The lino was a buckled, sticky mess of mottled green hexagons. Rashid regarded it critically. Was he fudging or did he honestly think it wasn't bad? There had been no kitchen to speak of in his parents' home. His mother cooked on an open fire. It was certainly luxurious compared to that.

'Let me show you the bedroom,' Rashid suggested, in the hope of saving the situation.

The fiancé shrugged and another sale slipped through Rashid's fingers.

That evening, as he ate dinner alone in his flat, he sifted through the employment section of the local newspaper, pencil poised, ready to circle anything plausible. There must be something better out there than estate agency, surely? He scanned the small print to no avail and consoled himself with a packet of Rich Tea biscuits. He was about to go to bed, when he saw a face peering in at the kitchen window. It took him a moment to see that it was Harris, tapping at the glass, mouthing to be let in.

Rashid dashed to the door. 'Uncle?' he exclaimed, alarmed. Harris often showed up unannounced, but not usually at this late hour. 'Is something wrong?'

'*Salaam aleikum!* Everything's fine, Rashid. Open the door, quick, quick.'

'Thank God. You had me worried for a moment.'

'Do forgive me. I didn't realize the hour. I was driving back home from Alia's, but I'm so tired, I couldn't keep the damned eyes open. So thought I'd drop in.'

'How was the trip?'

'The trip was excellent. Your parents send their love,' he went on, making himself at home. 'And your father sent you this holy water, blessed by his favourite saint.' He handed over a small brown bottle. 'For your good health and wealth. Your mother worries about you, and so does your father.'

'Are they well, Uncle?'

'Yes, they are——'

'And my little sister, is she better?'

'She is OK. A bit thin, but don't worry. They are fine.'

'Mishele and Mazhar?'

'Your sister and brother are both happy and thriving.'

Rashid relaxed at the news. Then he began the familiar routine whenever the Uncle visited: laying on a cup of tea, heating up tasty leftovers and switching on the gas fire no matter what time of year it happened to be, so the elder man could take off his jacket and relax in the lounge. Why the Uncle took such interest in him was a mystery, but it had its benefits at difficult times like these, when he found himself in need of advice.

'What's going on with you these days?' Harris said.

'My work situation isn't improving,' Rashid moaned. The salary was meagre and commission thin on the ground.

'It all takes time, Rashid, climbing the career ladder and all. Be patient.'

'My father needs me to send him more money,' Rashid went on gloomily. 'I've nothing left at the end of the month, I'm constantly overdrawn.'

Harris did not need reminding of the cousin's indigence, and the chain of dependency that stretched from the village to England. The boy complained about the business of estate agency at length before Harris could interject with the job's positives, which were many.

'You found Alia her place to live,' he reminded Rashid. 'I'm eternally grateful.'

'It was the least I could do, after all you've done for me.'

'And it provides you with a steady income, your job,' the Uncle continued. 'Not to be dismissed, given your father's situation.'

'I barely send them anything. A little here and there.'

'Don't dismiss your contribution. Every little helps.'

Harris reflected for a moment, then said, 'There's the company car. Don't forget that.'

Rashid groaned.

'What's wrong with it? It's a very decent Ford Focus, nice metallic paint. Let's not get carried away with listing just cons, Rashid.'

'Jerry drives a BMW.'

'Jerry's the boss, so what do you expect? Advancement takes time. Anyway, BMWs are very expensive, so forget it and learn to live within your means.'

'It's not the car I want, Uncle,' Rashid said. 'It's the recognition. I feel like a nobody here.'

'Nonsense. You simply need to find a hobby or activity. An interest that goes beyond the grind of daily job. What about squash, or ping-pong? Pakistanis are the best squash players in the world.'

'I'm no good at sport.'

'Are you going to mosque?'

'Sure, but it's my job I'm unhappy with.'

There was a short pause while both men silently struggled

to advance any further pros or cons on his career as a junior estate agent.

'What did you do with my old car, by the way, when you left the taxi job?'

The old Renault was deemed too unsavoury for his role at the estate agents and had ended its days at the scrapyard.

'That was a good car!' Harris exclaimed, though he was biased, having overbid for it at a car auction in Huddersfield.

'Uncle, it was junk. I'm not kidding. A death trap, and it stank. All those kids throwing up in the back seat—'

'It could have been cleaned. You should have told me. I'd have had it back.'

'Uncle, I really need a break.'

Harris sipped his scalding tea, fearing the boy was on the verge of quitting. 'Nobody ever said shifting property's easy, did they? Don't throw in the towel, not yet. Give it a go, Rashid, for your father's and mother's sake.'

Rashid wrestled open the sofa bed. 'I won't quit the job just yet, Uncle.'

Harris made himself at home in the lounge that had become a makeshift bedroom, dotted with soft humps of bedding. 'Good chap. Stick with it.'

'But something is missing for me here, you know?'

Harris sighed. 'I understand, but wait till something better comes along, won't you? It will come, I know it.'

Rashid perked up at the glimmer of a fresh prospect on the horizon. 'Will you help me?'

Harris stooped low behind an armchair, modestly changing into his pyjamas for bedtime. 'Rashid, there's something I'd like you to do for me, as a favour. Will you, my boy?'

'Anything. What is it?'

'I'm worried about Alia,' he said. 'Quite concerned, actually. She's all alone here in London and it bothers me. I need you to keep an eye on her. Call me old-fashioned, but what can I do?'

'Not old-fashioned at all. Just tell me what I should do.'

'Look her up. Go round to this house where she lives, go see her. Find out what she's up to, who she's seeing.'

Rashid was abashed. 'What are you asking of me, Uncle?'

'Nothing illegal. Make up an excuse about the landlord sending you. Doesn't matter what. Treat her like your sister. She almost is, after all.'

It was a serious matter, overseeing Harris's daughter, and Rashid was honoured to be entrusted with such a brotherly role.

'I'll see what I can do, Uncle,' he said solemnly, and left the older man to his beauty sleep.

Five

Alia awoke to the mournful thrum of an autumn downpour. It was September and the muddy slide into winter was already under way, fat raindrops jostling for space on her window-pane. She looked out and saw the street below was a slick of trampled leaves and people slithering to work. *The sky is about to fall on your head,* she thought. A grey canopy of cloud shrouded the view of the tower block from her bedroom window, and she wondered if the residents could see much beyond their noses. *Possibly no bad thing,* she decided, given the vista, which took in the hospital incineration tower, a pale red and white striped cylinder that released slim columns of smoke at night with a conspiratorial wink of its glowing eye. Other people's waste, lives gone up the chimney.

A glance at the clock radio by her bed triggered a pulse of adrenalin, until she remembered she had no reason to rush. Not today. She willed herself out of bed, leaving Oliver beneath the covers to sleep. She had no lectures to attend; no reason to root out her grubby white lab coat that lay crumpled beneath overflowing piles of abandoned clothes on a chair in the corner of the room. The day yawned wide open with possibility, its gleaming novelty tarnished by the circumstances that had precipitated it. For she was not going back to medical school this term. Possibly not ever. Things had unravelled early one morning the previous June. After months of work she'd set her alarm for 4 a.m., overslept and woken in a frantic state four hours later, when the phone rang; it was her mother, calling to ask her to collect the rest of her things from the former family home. She was leaving her current job, she said, and going to work for Médecins Sans Frontières in Africa for two years at the end of the summer.

After Alia had hung up the phone, fragments of the exchange had rattled on in her brain as she gathered up her scattered index cards for cramming. She'd raced through her neatly penned bullet points but it was hopeless. As she dashed off to the examination hall on Settles Street, she wondered why on earth she'd ever wanted to become a doctor in the first place. Was it just some spurious desire to placate her father's thwarted ambitions? An attempt to please her mother? Yet that person had vanished, whoever she was, and now she was adrift, uncertain of who or what she should become.

She made it just in time to the examination hall. But as her fellow students scribbled frantically, fuelled by glances at the racing clock, she found herself frozen. The questions were fairly manageable, and she was more than well prepared, yet her mind reeled and there was little she could do to get her answers down on paper.

The news of her failure was something she could not bring herself to tell Harris. She could barely explain it to herself, let alone her father, who had come to depend so much upon her bright prospects. She knew he harboured hopes that in his declining years, if no second wife could be found, she'd be able to step in with support and medical expertise. He had suffered periodically from angina and cardiac arrhythmia, both controlled with drugs, but sometimes the drugs failed. Yet even though she longed to confide in him about her troubles, she was fearful of making him anxious and exacerbating his condition. It wasn't dishonesty, she told herself, as much as protecting him from the unsettling truth. For the past few months, even during their summer trip to Pakistan, she'd maintained the uneasy fiction that she was doing well at medical school, in the hope that she'd retake her exams before he found out. When he'd crowed about her achievements to his cousins in the village, she'd kept quiet, hoping nobody would notice. Nobody had, yet she'd felt exposed even so, unable to meet their expectations.

News of their arrival had spread fast. Lights popped on down the street and every few minutes there were taps on the cousin's wooden front door as more and more people arrived with bottles of Coke and dishes of a milky sweet dessert called *rasmalai*, eager to get the first glimpse of the visitors from abroad. Nasreen, the cousin's wife, was dressed in her best lilac flowered salwar kameez, the folds of fabric falling elegantly about her long limbs, as she and her daughters handed out glasses to the guests. A small boy with oil-slicked hair silently presented Alia with a slab of Madeira cake, sealed in cling film. She knew by the packaging that it was expensive, special, and she'd been reluctant to open it until Nasreen nudged her to go ahead. She'd felt overwhelmed by their generosity, their curiosity, and even as she longed to escape their attention, she wondered what could she give them in return. 'Don't you worry,' Harris told her, as she fretted about it. 'I'll sort it out.' And sure enough, towards the end of their visit, she saw him doling out envelopes of rupees to Mishele and Mona, and their brother, Mazhar. As for Khalid Ali, he would receive something once Harris returned to England. That was best to save face in front of the family, her father explained.

The cousin and his family were the proud owners of virtually nothing. The living area was almost bare, flanked with rope cots hugging the walls, an embroidered cloth thrown over a table, a spray of plastic flowers in an empty cooking-oil tin. There was a photograph of Rashid on his graduation day in England, propped up on an empty fan box. The children had few toys or possessions between them, though they enjoyed the family of obliging baby rabbits who shared the courtyard. Alia rummaged in her bag and found some pink shell soaps for the girls and their mother, who lingered longingly as she unpacked her things. Nasreen blushed, long-lashed eyes dipping with embarrassment, because she had no fresh soap in the household to give the Uncle's daughter. But there were clean towels and a jug of water, which was more than enough, Alia said, making sure her father explained her words to them.

The next morning she awoke to find Nasreen and the two girls flanked on either side of the rope cot, at the ready with a cup of sweet tea, filmed with tiny yellow dots of fat from the creamy milk. Beside her, gathering flies, was a plate containing a small chapatti and a fried lentil patty. As she wiggled into her clothes in the outdoor bathroom, she felt Nasreen's eyes penetrating the curtain. Mishele ambushed her as she eventually emerged, tugging at her sleeve as if there was something wrong.

'Alia, they want to take you shopping for some decent clothes,' Harris explained, eyeing her ripped jeans and wrecked sandals. 'What do you say? I'll give you some money and off you go. Pick out some outfits. Smarten up a bit, huh?'

She saw that they were all fused with a common purpose: her transformation.

'I'm not sure,' she said. She loved her clothes and didn't want to give them up. 'What's wrong with these?'

After a campaign of attrition over several days, she relented.

It was a muddy walk to the bazaar across a patch of wasteland, crisscrossed with streams of bubbling green water that carried rotting flotsam to a sluggish delta on the outskirts of town. They sat her down on the floor of a small jewellery shop and an eager crowd of spectators began to gather. It started with a stack of bangles. Fragile rings of glass, like spun sugar, the colour of boiled sweets. Beautiful, but not for her, she said. Nobody understood or believed her. They squeezed them on to her wrists, all the way up her forearms till they met a bony knot of resistance at her elbows. She could not take them off, not now. And so she paid for them and everyone seemed pleased.

It did not end there. A total look was what they were after for her. So the tatty flat shoes she'd worn for the past year were replaced with strappy white high heels, and then she was escorted to the tailor's shop, where she was urged to hand over her old clothes in exchange for a tight nylon salwar kameez in a choice of colours: salmon or cerise or emerald green? Which did she want? What would she choose? Did she care? Melting in the heat, she did not. But not caring was beyond rude and so she picked cerise, which produced a positive reaction all round.

It was when she tottered home in the new shoes to find her father supine on a rope cot, drinking tea and chewing betel and giggling with Khalid Ali, that she decided enough was enough: it was time for them to leave. For the truth was, she no longer felt herself at all. She tried to pretend that she missed the comforts of city life, sleeping in an air-conditioned room in the big suburban house in Shadman, Lahore, rather than spending the night under the stars with a thousand mosquitoes and a father who, despite his diminutive stature, emitted snores worthy of a giant. But it was more than a childish hankering for creature comforts that made her want to go. She had grown weary of the unceasing attention she attracted, the crowds that materialized from nowhere to get a glimpse, the many pairs of eyes fixed on her every move, everybody wanting a little piece of her. A little piece that wasn't even her. She had come to feel hopelessly unworthy of her designated status as the visiting princess. For what on earth could she, a nineteen-year-old girl, possibly give them in return? What did they want from her?

It was bedtime before she cornered Harris.

'I think we should go back to the city,' she said.

'Back to the city?' He was blank, wounded. 'Why?'

She softened, tried another tack. 'I want to see Lahore again before we go home. The real Lahore, the Old City, the sights,' she said.

He regarded her suspiciously. 'We can't just take off, Alia. There'll be mass protests.'

She gave him a pleading look and he knew he could not refuse her.

Conveying this to Khalid Ali was not easy. The cousin was devastated that they wanted to leave so soon.

'You've hardly been here, Harris,' he said. 'Why the big rush?'

'It's been over a week, and my daughter, you see . . .'

'We love her as if she were our own.'

'I know, I know. But she's more used to the city and we'd like to do some sightseeing.'

Then Khalid begged Harris to stay a bit longer, knowing that it would be a very long time, years possibly, before they would meet again. Khalid wanted to show that his hospitality could rival that of the big man in Lahore. Not that he ventured to say so, but it hung in the air between them like a gloomy line of dank washing, as the two debated for the umpteenth time the one's departure and the other's sense of bitter affront.

Khalid Ali was only a poor man compared to Harris, but they were like brothers and that transcended everything, surely. Would he not honour them by accepting their hospitality for another week, another day? Harris turned glassy-eyed, the corners of his lips twitching as a tornado of emotion threatened to escape from the back of his throat. Alia had seen it happen before, but on this occasion, to her great relief, the danger passed.

On the morning of their departure, Nasreen had come to find Harris as he shaved in the bathroom while Alia packed. 'I want to ask you a favour,' she said, rescuing a stray strand of black hair that reached almost to her waist, and tucked it behind her ear.

'Yes?' he looked up at her. 'What is it?' He was used to requests from Nasreen to courier short letters, tubs of cold cream, trinkets or bottles of special pickles for Rashid.

'Would you take this and give it to our son?' she said, handing him a bottle of holy water that Khalid had procured, blessed by a saint.

'He has a terrible cough.' She was pricked with guilt that he was all alone in a far off, rain-soaked land. Three tarnished silver bangles slid down her left arm and she pushed them back up in an automatic gesture.

'I'll get it to him, don't worry.'

'Thank you so much. And send our love, will you?'

But Harris was distracted by a nick on his chin that was bleeding onto his collar and, as he sought a tissue to dab it, he forgot about the bottle under the table where the bowl of dirty shaving water stood.

Later, when they were standing outside Khalid's house waiting to leave, the crowd gathered to bid them farewell.

'Too many people, like one of those bloody huge English demos in Hyde Park,' Harris moaned. 'Let us say our good-byes right here.'

So after some hefty persuading, the cousin agreed to filter out the hangers-on, leaving only a select number of around forty to wave them off on the train. In the crush, Mishele made her way to Alia and pressed her address into her hand. She was already mapping out her escape route; her passport was her literacy, and she was in constant demand around the village for her valuable skills.

'Will you write to me?' she said. 'Send me a postcard soon. Of a London bus.'

Sitting on a sticky bench in the brutally hot train, Harris mourned the fact that they hadn't managed to get seats on the

Magic Bus, a jewel-painted luxury coach – double the price but much more comfy and reliable, with soft velour seats and air conditioning into the bargain. Years of living in England had taken its toll on her father's tolerance for the inevitable compromises of travelling second class on the Pakistani railways, and his agitation got the better of him. When the train stopped in a station, he hopped out on to the platform without explanation, leaving her behind. It was only when the locomotive began to shunt forward, lurching off in a steady movement, that she leapt to her feet and began yelling his name out of the window.

There was no sign of him in the heaving throngs outside and she began to wish she'd never come. Then a kind of commotion broke out among the other passengers as the train gathered speed, gained momentum. Mass panic spread like a virus through the crowd and suddenly the concourse was alive, rippling: a heaving, tumultuous sea churning alongside the train. Floating on the surface of a hundred outstretched hands was her father, propelled back towards her, elevated over man, beast and any snack vendor who happened to be in the way.

'I was peckish!' he panted, by way of explanation, fanning himself with his canvas hat. He had nipped off in search of pakoras and sweet tea being peddled up and down the platform to console himself. 'The blood sugar was critically low and there was in fact plenty of time. See? It was a false alarm. We were going nowhere, in fact. The train stopped for us, didn't it?'

'I thought I'd lost you for ever,' she said, wiping her eyes.

'Lost me?' He beamed. 'No chance.'

As the train resumed its journey, Harris unearthed a forgotten twist of pistachio nuts from his jacket and shared them out.

'I was destined to marry my cousin, Nasreen, you know,' he admitted. 'But I let her down.'

She was astonished. 'Nasreen? So what happened?'

'I never came back.'

'Didn't you fancy her?'

'Alia! It's not all about this fancying business, you know. It's about securing your future with somebody compatible.'

'How'd you get out of it, then?'

'I met your mother. That was it.'

'So you mean Nasreen could have been my mother?'

It was an unfathomable notion, the idea that the village life she had just fled could have been hers. That she and Mishele could have been sisters, as though their fate had been switched when no one was looking.

'Yes,' Harris said, 'but then you wouldn't have been born.'

'Or I'd have been born as somebody else.'

He did not pursue the idea, but lapsed into a nap, the dome of his stomach rising and falling as he snored.

She became aware of the bangles, hot and sticky on her wrists, yet when she tried to slide them off, they wouldn't fit over her hands. So she began snapping them against the soft underside of her forearms, each fracture of glass producing a tiny bead of blood on her skin, which she licked off. A family of four, sharing the compartment, sat mutely riveted by this miniature display of destruction. When she was done, she scooped up the pile of brightly coloured shards and threw them away.

She felt a sharp pang now as she contemplated the white crescents on her arms, tiny scars that chided her for the way she'd behaved, resisting the things they'd pressed on her and rushing away from them as soon as she could. She looked at Oliver, surfacing from the seabed of slumber, wiry blond hair matted in clumps, cheeks flushed. He was splayed diagonally across the bed and she noted, not for the first time, that he required a lot of space.

She wondered if she should call Harris and tell him everything, and got as far as unearthing her phone from beneath the bed before changing her mind. She was lacing up her trainers when her mobile lit up with a message from him that gave her a little jump. No need to clear him a sleeping spot on her sofa, he said. He had decided to spend a few nights with Rashid instead.

By the time she went for her run along the Thames path, the fog of rain was lifting and her load felt considerably lighter. She would tell her father everything one day. Just not today.

Six

Jerry Stone was fond of telling Rashid what a soft spot he had for that particular corner of east London, having been born around the corner from the office of Stone & Stone. His birthplace was something he mentioned frequently to clients, as if to impress upon them his authenticity for the job, winking at Rashid as he did so. The junior estate agent would look away, studiously avoiding the subject of his own birthplace, though of course his boss knew where he was from. Jerry had lately begun moaning about his beloved neighbourhood being swamped with illegals, the sacred spots of his youth being ruined, overrun by foreigners and their teeming families. Gone were the days when East Enders were free to leave their back doors open so the neighbours could pop in and out of each other's kitchens for a cup of sugar or a natter. Gone, too, were the days when you could let your kids play safely on the streets. It was all Asian kids these days, gangs of them, running around unsupervised.

'Their youth are *way* out of control,' Jerry murmured darkly. 'You've no idea what they're up to.'

Rashid agreed that there was an undesirable youth element at large in the community, but the idea that it was exclusively Asian he simply found offensive. In any case, what could he, a mere estate agent, do about it?

Jerry owned several properties in the street of pitted red-brick houses. It was in one of these buildings that he had been born and had spent the first six months of his life enjoying the view of three brand-new tower blocks from the top floor. The blocks had long been condemned and it broke his heart a little when they were finally demolished, dismantled gradually, rather than blown to smithereens with the push of a button. The house on Newark Street, where Alia was living, had been bought for a song. Now it was a thorn in his side, a cheap student rental pad, thanks to a rapid if sketchy renovation by a contractor who neither understood nor cared about the finer points of plumbing.

At first, the revamp had gone swimmingly. Then came the ominous pools of amber water seeping up from the toilets that spoke of a deeper, darker malaise in the bowels of the house. The dysfunctional shower, the taps that sheared with metal fatigue. The maps of damp that spread unchecked across the Axminster carpets, lovingly installed by a Bengali carpet dealer who boasted they were 70 per cent nylon and indestructible, and that the diamond pattern was 'most forgiving'. The carpet was emerald and gold, and its musty smell ebbed and flowed with the seasons and the propensity of the students to flood the bathroom off the main hallway. One day, when the kitchen sink blocked and the usual plumber could not be raised, Rashid volunteered with uncharacteristic eagerness to sort it out and save his boss some money.

In the tiny toilet at the back of Stone & Stone, he combed his hair, reapplied his deodorant, then sniffed his armpits curiously. English girls were fussy about that sort of thing – personal hygiene – and he was keen to create a good impression. He had heard from his father that when they had visited Pakistan that summer, Alia had been as fair as a princess, English in her dress, her language and manner. He had also heard how she had not wanted to stay in the village for very long, how the poor conditions of his father's home obviously did not please her. The lack of proper bathroom facilities, the eating and living conditions in the village, mosquitoes in spite of the new fan bought especially for her benefit. Harris and his daughter had rushed back after only a short visit to the comfort of the rich friend's palatial house in Lahore. It pained Rashid to be reminded once again of his failings as the first-born son; that after all these years, he had not provided his family with the means to build a decent home in their own village. He dreamed of the marble bathroom, the well-tended garden, but that was as far as it got: a mental blueprint, no more.

Yet it must surely shame the Uncle, he thought, rallying a little as he turned the corner into Newark Street and glanced up at the graffiti-scrawled red-brick house: your only daughter living all alone in an area like this, unmarried, vulnerable to undesirable elements. Boys with pit bulls patrolled the streets; heroin was readily available. How Harris must worry and fret, which was why he, Rashid, had been tasked with such an important role, acting as a brother and keeping an eye on the girl.

'Hello, Alia,' he said when she opened the door. 'I'm Rashid, do you remember me? Your long-lost relative – your father's cousin's son . . .'

She was blank for a second, then a flicker of recognition animated her face. 'Rashid? Of course I remember you – it's been so long.'

'I'm here to unblock the sink.'

She was confused. 'Really? Did we call you?'

'Someone in the office said you did, yes.'

'You're right. Sorry, it was last week. I'd forgotten. Come in.'

The way she spoke, enunciating her words so beautifully, the curve of her lips, threw him. She was prettier than he remembered, more feminine, and this made him dither, stammer, as he struggled to explain why he was on her doorstep rather than a real plumber.

'This way,' she said, and he followed her into the hallway. 'You know I met your family this summer – did my dad tell you? Khalid and Nasreen. And I met your sisters and your little brother, too.'

'Yes, that's right. He told me all about it,' he said, relieved that she seemed less of a princess than everyone had reported, in spite of the fair skin. 'The kitchen sink, is it?'

'Through there. Coffee or anything?' she offered. 'Only got instant – Nescafé, I think.'

Rashid shook his head. 'No, thanks.'

'Rashid, I feel so bad,' she said suddenly. 'I never really properly thanked you for finding me this place.'

'No problem. Your father's done so much for me.' Rashid smiled. 'It was my pleasure to help you.'

She sat down on the sofa and lit a cigarette, feeling his eyes upon her. He saw that the peculiar way she tucked her legs under her, folding them lithely and with amazing flexibility, was not very English at all. What was very modern and Western, however, was her complete lack of embarrassment, behaving in such a manner in front of him. And then, just as he was processing who she was, this Alia girl, he spied an emerald-green arrow, the tip of a tattoo, just beneath her shoulder blade. Was it something her father should be told? Did her mother allow such things?

He noted how sloppily she was dressed. Very English, like a typical student, he thought, in those baggy tracksuit trousers and a kind of T-shirt, sleeveless, like a vest. Yet she was, he could not deny it, alluring. Her bare arms, the rounded slender shoulders, gleamed a little. Her hair was so short at the back that you could see fine, golden-brown hairs like tiny scratch marks etched on her pale ochre neck. She felt him observing her, or perhaps it was more than that, and she shifted to break his gaze. He noticed she was restless. She was not exactly unfriendly, but she didn't make him feel at home in her world. By all accounts, she had not felt at home in his.

'I really like it here, this house,' she said, breaking the silence.

'Do you? Don't you mind living so far from your family, your parents?'

She laughed. 'Why should I?'

'Not like in Pakistan, family living together, right?'

'Far from it.'

'So how did you like Pakistan, then?'

'I never knew my dad had quite so many relatives, that was kind of a shock.'

'And they didn't leave you alone, right?'

Her long, wide smile lit up her face. 'No – who told you that?'

'I just guessed. I'm sorry.'

She saw his shoulders sag a little. 'Don't be. I loved it.'

'You loved it? Did you honestly, Alia?' He longed to believe her. But it was just an English way of saying things, like *wicked* or *whatever* or . . .

'Honestly,' she said. 'Don't you believe me?'

'But then I heard you didn't stay long in the village, did you?' he pressed.

'No,' she admitted. 'Not that long. Dad wanted to see his friend in Lahore, so we left.'

In spite of himself, Rashid felt hurt. Khalid had written to his son all about it, through Mishele, his writer and reader, who had penned the letter. He'd been forced to take a journey to Lahore, his father had said, to bring the bottle of holy water for Harris to take to Rashid. The Uncle had left it behind in the village in their rush to leave.

Rashid rolled up his sleeves and prepared to plunge his arms into the grey water that filled the sink. She watched him as he did so, noticing how smartly he was dressed and wondering if she should do something to help. Did he want rubber gloves? An apron? He shook his head.

'My dad was supposed to marry your mother, wasn't he?' she ventured, hovering behind his shoulder.

Rashid didn't look up, deliberately refusing to be drawn by her curious smile. It rattled him, the way she was: hard to pin down, hard to draw out. Snapping shut as swiftly as she opened up.

'Uncle Harris?' he spoke into the sink. 'Marry my mother?'

'Yes! Isn't that amazing? Did you know that?'

He turned round and saw her waistline peeping over her tracksuit trousers. The idea that he was to take a girl like Alia under his wing was beginning to intimidate him. He did know. The story had been told to him by his mother before he left for England, but he said nothing, flushing water into the sink. In any case, it was history and why dwell on things that didn't happen? He felt a volt of anger. Yet he had to engage her, make friends, behave like a brother. If only he were that.

She saw she had annoyed him. 'But we had a great time, me and Dad. It was my first visit. My mum never wanted me to go. To be honest, Rashid, I got lost at times, not speaking the language. Couldn't follow what was happening.'

'You don't speak a word of Punjabi or Urdu?'

'No,' she confessed. 'I don't. Isn't that awful? It made me feel so out of it.' She looked at him closely, as if seeing him properly for the first time. 'You must have felt the same, when you came here, though. Did you?'

'I did a bit, yes,' he said. It was how he still felt most of the time in England, but he did not want to offend her by saying so.

She was sitting at the kitchen table. 'My dad sometimes talks about going back, when he's sick of it here,' she went on, hugging her knees to her chest. 'I can't imagine he'd cope there, though. Not now. All those cows wandering around. Or do I mean buffaloes?'

Rashid smiled. 'Water buffaloes, probably. Were there many?'

'Yes, a few. Few hundred.'

'Oh, I'm sorry.'

'Why are you sorry? It's not like it's your fault.'

'It's my country,' he said defensively.

'Do you think you'll ever go back?'

'I don't know,' Rashid said, softening. 'I'd like to, one day. It's home for me, and I miss it.'

'Do you? Still?'

'Of course.'

She felt an unexpected blip of guilt that she didn't miss home at all, having escaped it at the first possible moment. 'What do you miss most?'

It was his turn to feel her eyes scanning him, intent with concern.

'Everything,' he admitted, and heard her emit a sigh in a minor key, a groan of sympathy, perhaps. He reflected for a moment, not wanting to lose her attention. 'I just can't get used to it here, Alia, no matter how long it's been.' Squatting down, he pulled out a plunger from under the sink and thrust it into the water. 'I wonder if something's wrong with me.'

'I wonder that about myself all the time,' she admitted. 'I've made such a mess of things.'

'I don't believe that. How?' He searched her features, aware of his heart thudding faster. 'Uncle's very proud. You're a medical student, aren't you?'

She looked at him and wondered if she should tell him. He'd been so nice to her and it seemed wrong to lie. 'I'm not, actually, Rashid. I failed several exams at the end of last term.'

'What happened?' He was quietly thrilled that she was opening up to him.

'I lost my nerve, or something.'

'So what will you do now?' He waited with baited breath to see if the clam shell was closing again, or if he could winkle out more information.

She grew reflective. 'Well, I'll have to re-sit a couple if I want to go back next year.'

'I'm sure you'll do well, Alia, second time round. I didn't pass first time.' They had something in common then, he thought cheerfully, wondering how to build upon that.

'Thanks. That's nice of you, even if it's not true.'

He glowed inside with pleasure. At last he'd got through to her, prised open that shell. But before he could go any further, she grew serious again.

'The thing is, I may not want to go back,' she went on. 'That's the trouble. That's the mess. Don't say anything to my dad, will you? I've been thinking about doing something else.'

Rashid shook his head. 'I won't.' Her eyes were green, he noticed, when she faced the window, illuminated.

She felt a burst of affection for him. 'Thanks. Both my parents wanted me to go for it, really. Bit of a mistake that was.'

'Why a mistake?'

'Well, I'm learning it's best not to try to please them, right? Bound to fail.'

'I agree with you there,' Rashid said flatly.

'Thing is,' she went on, 'I'm not that sure if I'm good enough for it. I've tried to figure out why I'm there, why I chose it, but I've no idea.'

She appeared almost tearful. It reminded him of watching the English weather change, sunny spells followed by dark clouds.

'Your father at least is very proud of you.'

She seemed to shun the idea and fell silent. Then she said, 'So what was it you studied here, then?'

The rank dishwater swirled and resisted his efforts, as if the problem lay deeper, but he was no expert. He straightened up, turning his back on the sink. 'Urban planning. I have a BSc honours degree.'

'Wow, impressive. So did you enjoy it?'

He shrugged. 'I suppose so. I wanted to get a proper career, and this was the only course that would accept my A-level grades, which weren't as good as yours. Your father helped me with the tuition, of course, and the cost of my accommodation. I'm forever grateful to him, and I'm always in his debt . . . If it wasn't for him . . . I'd never have made it to this country.'

He felt his neck flush.

'I didn't know that.'

'I mean, I'd like to think you could . . . treat me like your brother.' He was stammering now and she caught a whiff of deodorant masking sweat as he struggled to get the words out. 'I'm happy to help you in any way I can.'

'Oh no, don't worry, I'm fine.' Was there no way to drill a keyhole to see into her life? 'I can take care of myself. Honestly.'

The water drained away slowly, in increments, leaving a series of lardy tide marks on the sides of the sink. What on earth to do now?

'I may need to come back, finish off the job.'

She was shepherding him out and didn't seem bothered. He could sense she was waiting to go out and could not hold himself back. 'Are you going somewhere?'

'Yes, I'm trying to find a job. But listen, Rashid, don't say anything about me failing my exams to my dad, will you?'

'No, no, of course not.'

'If you speak to him, I mean.'

Rashid felt himself grow warm with shame, thinking of Harris waiting expectantly for a progress report. For a brief moment, he felt terrible, as he looked at her eager face, the green eyes boring into him.

'You have the phone number here, don't you?' she said.

'Yes, I do, at the office.'

'So just call next time – I might be out.'

She flashed a smile, and was gone.

'Any luck, did you go see her?' Harris badgered, the moment Rashid returned.

Rashid sighed and slung his jacket over the back of a chair. 'I went to her house, Uncle, with the excuse of the plumber. She was home.'

'What happened?'

'I unblocked her sink.'

'Yes, yes, but what did she say?'

'She seemed all right, Uncle. We talked about your trip together.'

'Really?' He perked up at the idea. 'Did she mention me? Seem as if anything was going on?'

Rashid was silent for a moment, clutching Alia's confidences to his chest, like precious gems hoarded out of sight for their own protection. Her mysterious appeal had produced a frisson of loyalty in him and, besides, he had promised her he'd keep quiet about what she'd told him.

'Nothing too much, but I will keep an eye, Uncle, I promise,' he said earnestly, figuring out when he might visit her again, and how.

With that blanket reassurance, the older man seemed pacified, temporarily at least, and was able to ease his anxieties about goings-on in his daughter's life in Whitechapel. He turned his thoughts to another part of London, south of the river, where he had a rendezvous arranged for that evening.

Seven

In the aftermath of her husband's death, Dr Farrah had felt no inclination to up sticks and sell the house in Greenwich, where they'd lived for more than a decade. She had been content to remain there, surrounded by the furniture they had chosen together, arranged and rearranged. Then, at the end of the summer, she had realized she must sell it. A large For Sale board had been planted in the front garden and she had been pleasantly surprised to learn that her house was more desirable than she had imagined. A flurry of potential buyers made offers, several at the asking price, and yet she could not bring herself to go through with it. Even though her bills were mounting and the house was too large for her, she found it hard to let go. Young couples with burgeoning families filed up and down her stairs, mentally projecting how they would redo the place, if only this middle-aged Pakistani lady would sign on the dotted line. But she wouldn't. Or rather couldn't. This was her home, and she wanted to hang on to it, just in case.

She was in the bathroom getting ready to go out, when her sister Naela, who lived in Lahore, rang. The interruption flustered her, for they had already passed many hours on the phone going over the business of houses and whether or not she should stay put, or accept the best offer and move on.

But where would she go to? her sister wondered, not for the first time. Doncaster, Milton Keynes, Leicester, Lyme Regis? She was a lone woman in a hostile land, Naela insisted. Naela herself was a spinster.

'It's not hostile, as you call it. It's actually very nice here in England,' Farrah said. She was tired of the snipes about her adopted country. England had treated her and her family rather well.

'Nice? Not if you read the papers, or see the TV shows,' Naela retorted, pouncing on her sister's words. 'I hear there is a crusade against the Muslims now, and things have got much worse in these so-called *nice* places like England. There's a back-lash over there, don't deny it – arrests and detentions, raids on the mosques.'

'Well, it was bound to happen,' Farrah concurred, 'after the horrendous tube bombings.'

'It wasn't *Pakistanis* who did that, you know.'

Farrah sighed. 'Yes, it was. They were second-generation, apparently.'

'See! Even you are indoctrinated now! You aren't safe.'

Farrah ignored this. 'They caught them on CCTV, from Luton to King's Cross. It's there for all to see. Naela, the evidence was incontrovertible. But as far my personal safety living here is concerned, I don't think MI5 have a case against me.'

'Still, you should move back home.'

'This is my home.' It was something she had never thought she would hear herself utter, yet saying so made it a reality.

'You can share my house.'

Naela suffered corrosive envy of her sister's life in England and was all too keen to reel her back home, so that Farrah might suffer a bit too. Yet the bleak prospect of being Naela's other half, holed up in her crumbling bungalow on the less affluent side of Defence Housing Authority was insupportable.

'Thank you, Naela, it's really kind, but I couldn't.'

'You'd have time to write your book,' her sister tried slyly, 'the one you've been wanting to write for years. On tragedy, huh? I'll tell you all about tragedy.'

Yes, Farrah thought, *in between lecturing me on the importance of coming back to the faith and imparting it to my sons.* How Naela nagged and wheedled on that topic! She was not secure enough to be devout on her own; she required everyone else to follow suit.

'No, really, Farrah, listen to me,' Naela purred. 'You don't understand. Time is running out and you should study the Koran and what it tells us, the beautiful lessons and—'

Dr Farrah's heart sank. 'I know. I have read and studied it many, many times—'

'Not enough. You must go back and reread, and go to mosque, regularly, practise the faith in your daily life, for that will ensure your reward in paradise. No, really. I'm serious. And for your boys.'

'My sons are grown up and flown the nest,' Farrah countered.

Her sister ignored this. 'It's very important those sons of yours don't lose their faith, with all the materialistic values these days, the fancy jobs. Dubai isn't it, where Ifran is working now? Expensive cars and big mansions. It's all this generation cares about now. Decadence and personal pleasure.'

'Oh, Naela, you sound like the mullahs.'

'Are you going to mosque?'

'Occasionally,' she lied.

'I knew it. You've lapsed, sister. I feared as much. Shh, and please pay attention, you have to. Now that you are in the last phase of your life . . .'

Last phase! Farrah thought indignantly. *How dare you? The bloody cheek of it! I'm ten years younger than you. I haven't given up yet.* She glimpsed her reflection in the bathroom mirror, then noticed that the bath she was running was almost full. As her sister chuntered on about end-of-life preparations and other nonsense, Farrah gently placed the phone down on the floor so that only a whiny outpouring could be heard leaking from the mouthpiece, nothing more. She slipped out of the clothes – sensible blouse and trousers – she wore for teaching at Greenwich Community College, and undressed in front of the mirror. Normally, she hung a towel over its reflection, but now she looked at herself, wondering how she would appear to another person's gaze. A woman in the last phase of life, flesh folds escaping from their proper places. It couldn't be denied. She gingerly raised her toe over the side of the bath and sank into the warm, silky water, her body pleasantly buoyed in the foam. Was she wrinkled and past it or actually not too bad?

Whatever she was, she knew one thing was certain. She was a woman who preferred not to be surprised by gentlemen callers; she liked to be prepared. So, after her bath and forty-five minutes before Harris was due to arrive, she sat before her dressing table and applied her make-up. It was a while since she had scrutinized herself so closely, but now she went to work on her mottled complexion, carefully lightening it with fine beige powder. Her grey-brown lips were painted coral. A fresh application of colour to her hair had been made the previous evening, so all that was required to bring out the shine was a vigorous brush.

She fretted about what she should wear, plumping eventually for a pair of smart black trousers from Next, and a Marks & Spencer lilac polo-neck jumper, never worn before. She dithered over a large pashmina and then draped it about her shoulders.

The cloudless night was fine and chilly. Flurries of gnarled plane leaves skittered about Harris's feet as he darted along her road. She sat framed in her living-room window, waiting; curtains undrawn, lamps blazing. He rapped the door knocker and waited nervously. When she opened the front door, he was astounded at the transformation, rendered speechless for a moment, before a flurry of salaams on her side rescued him.

'Harris,' she said, as he hovered on the doorstep. 'Do come in.'

He saw that she had made an effort, an observation that pained him, wishing he'd done more to spruce himself up. Even her rotund figure seemed magically reduced. His own paunch shamed him rather and he discreetly adjusted his trousers to disguise it. But appearances, he thought to himself as he went into her living room, are not everything.

She nudged a silver tray hosting a pile of mixed nuts towards him. 'Please help yourself,' she said. 'What would you like to drink?'

'Oh, whatever you have,' he said, trying to oblige. 'Tea would be fine.'

Her warm chuckle made him realize that she meant something stronger. A cocktail. A pint. A glass of pale ale. He rarely drank much now, unless it was a special occasion. There were precious few social engagements such as these in his current existence and he felt a sharp pang for his former life.

'A glass of lager, perhaps? Or a Bloody Mary?' she suggested with a smile.

'Do you drink, then, Dr Farrah?'

'Please – just Farrah. Yes, of course! Why ever not? It's one of the perks of living here, wouldn't you say?'

Harris laughed.

'So. What would you like, Harris, tell me?'

'A small can of lager, if you have one.'

'I do!' she called back merrily from the kitchen. She was beginning to enjoy herself.

'Is your flood problem sorted out?' he enquired as she poured out his drink.

'Not really, but this is England and plumbing isn't one of its strong points, is it? My husband was always pretty good at keeping things going, and we never really had to call anyone in for repairs and so on. Idrees was a keen gardener, you know, and he decorated this house top to toe, single-handed.'

The mention of plumbing precipitated a short diatribe from Harris on the difficulty of securing reliable manual labour in this country.

'Worse than Pakistan,' he said.

'Oh, much worse!' she agreed.

And then, warming to his theme, he recounted the story of how he had been driven to install central heating in his own house. She was all concern.

'Your house was without heating, in this climate?' she ventured, when he paused to take a sip of lager.

'Yes, until I put in the central heating myself.'

'Goodness. I'm surprised there are still such places to be found.'

'Well, there are in the north of England, where I currently live. It's just a temporary arrangement, to be honest. I'm not intending to stay there for ever. My daughter lives in a nice student house in east London.' Then, as an afterthought, he added, 'Heated, of course.'

'Not far from here, is it? Are you staying with her, then?'

The question threw him and the reply he gave didn't really dovetail with her question. 'Not exactly. I mooted buying her a place, for us together, but she wasn't game for the idea.'

'Ah, the young. They wish for their independence.'

He shook his head. 'Yes, indeed. She's studying medicine, you know.'

'How wonderful! You must be very proud.'

'Thank you. Yes, I am.'

Dr Farrah took a small gulp of a red fizzy drink. Campari and soda, Harris guessed, though he was not 100 per cent sure and felt it unseemly to seek confirmation.

'Ifran, my elder boy, is a management consultant, working in Dubai,' she said, swilling the drink in her hand. 'The younger one, Harune, is just finishing his studies at Aberdeen University. Chemical engineering.'

'Very good,' Harris said. 'They've done very well, both of them.'

'Thank you. Yes, they have,' Farrah said.

They both fell silent for a moment, then Harris said, 'I was wondering if you'd fancy a simple meal at one of the kebab houses along the Commercial Road. Proper Pakistani fare, if my memory serves me correctly. Unless you have an alternative preference or suggestion?'

Farrah was secretly relieved. She hadn't planned on cooking. 'No, that sounds very nice, Harris. I've heard of the place, actually.'

'Really? Good. Well, that's easy, then. It's near my daughter's place, as a matter of fact, in Whitechapel. When were you last in Lahore, by the way?'

'The last holiday my husband and I took was there, three years ago last April.'

'I'm sorry. I didn't mean to—'

'No, it's all right, Harris. It was a good trip. Idrees and I visited many old friends. We saw Omar and Kamila, of course, though we didn't stay with them in Shadman. My sister would have been offended, so we stayed over in Defence with her.'

'Oh, really?' Harris thought of Omar's house, where he and Alia had stayed, its marble floors shrouded in antique Persian rugs, the reproduction French furniture draped in clear plastic covering that made a strange crackly sound when you sat down on it. 'We should toast them, shouldn't we, for bringing us the pleasure of each other's company?'

Dr Farrah looked down for what felt like a very long time. Had he gone too far? He was almost convinced he had ruined his chances when she finally looked up.

'I do miss him still,' she admitted. 'My husband.'

'I'm so sorry,' he said. 'Of course you must. I didn't mean to stir up old memories.'

She smiled. 'No, I know. It's not your fault.' Then she left him alone while she went to fetch her coat.

For the first time since arriving, he took in his surroundings. He found himself moved by the professional quality of the paintwork in the lounge. Clearly Idrees had had hidden talents. Harris always eschewed the finer points of DIY and he rarely finished his jobs off neatly: paint was smudged and applied imprecisely. But Idrees had obviously laboured with great care and attention to every detail. Nothing was left undone. His robust spirit seemed to live on in the decor, which was a neatly uniform shade of magnolia. Wherever Harris looked in the lounge, framed photos of the dead man seemed to spring up: Idrees doing all manner of things from graduating to gardening to posing before internationally famous monuments – the Parthenon, the pyramids, the Arc de Triomphe – with his wife and sons. There was even a gold-framed picture of him shaking hands with an army general. No such photos decorated his own mantelpiece, Harris reflected ruefully. Not that he even had a mantelpiece any longer in his front room since Nawaz had ripped out the old fireplace, vaguely promising to replace it with a modern one.

Dr Farrah reappeared in the lounge, dressed in her overcoat, clutching something.

'Before we go, I wanted to show you this,' she said, handing him a silver-framed photo, the glass scarred with scratches. 'I found it when I was sorting out the attic.'

'Good gracious,' Harris exclaimed. 'That's me, and there's Omar and that other fellow . . . Amanullah.'

It was a sepia print of the three young men, elegantly clad in suits and ties, casually posed in a line, sharing a joke. The picture emanated the optimism of youth, when everything is possible and nothing is fixed. 'I'm sure I had a copy of the same picture myself,' Harris went on, 'but I suppose it's lost.'

Omar, the most handsome of the three, beamed at the camera, while Harris looked away, laughing, his arm in blurred motion.

'See I ruined the shot as usual, didn't I?' he said with a smile. He stared at it for a moment. 'Idrees took the photo, didn't he?'

'That's right,' said Farrah. 'He did.'

It was Omar's camera, a Leica, Harris recalled, that he'd bought during a visit to Germany when they were graduate-management trainees in England. It had taken Harris much longer to save up for his Rollei, which he used to take self-timed snaps of his family every year on holiday.

'Omar was very fond of having his photo taken, I seem to remember,' Harris remarked.

'And Idrees was very good at taking pictures,' Farrah added ruefully. 'Shall we go?'

To the jaded eye, the Commercial Road in east London is little more than a conveyor belt for courier bikes and lorries to the east coast; an ancient thoroughfare for the flow of trade now flanked with glassily optimistic city flats, dusty baby-clothes suppliers, the odd haberdashery warehouse, wholesale fashion outlets and a permanently shut Lloyds Bank with only a sprouting of ragwort at its entrance to commemorate the death of business. But Harris noticed none of it as he sought out a suitable place to take the lady Shakespeare scholar on his arm for dinner. What he saw was a road studded with a string of brightly lit curry and kebab houses, each one almost a replica of the last, yet quietly boasting a subtle difference in sauce or cooking method or regional bias, visible only to the naked eye of a true native. The eateries were all Lahori, though they served what they termed Indian food.

'Harris, these all look nice to me. Let's just choose one, huh? I'm truly not fussy.'

But Harris would have none of it.

'No, no, the best one is near here. Just let me find it . . .'

It had been in one of these Lahore establishments that Harris had tasted the most tender, delicately spiced shish kebab he had ever eaten. The exquisite memory of it had lodged itself in his consciousness, refusing to be ousted by any other rogue dish that claimed the same name. The trouble was he could neither remember which Lahore restaurant he had eaten them in, nor distinguish one from the next. Infuriatingly, they all looked the same. Eventually, they settled on the Real Lahore 2, where he vented his spleen to the manager.

'Have you no imagination? Is originality a bygone virtue? Why call each and every establishment Lahore 1, 2 and 3?'

The manager was unable to provide an explanation, but gave them extra poppadums to compensate. They split a mountainous dish of chicken karahi between them. Dr Farrah declined the kebabs, but sampled the saag lamb stew, another of Harris's favourites. By the end of the evening, there were two melting cones of half-eaten kulfi on a pair of plates. Neither could manage another mouthful.

'I'm not used to so much food any more. I rarely cook for myself these days,' Farrah admitted.

'You should indulge yourself sometimes, you know. It's good for the constitution.'

'I like this place, I really do,' she said. 'Thank you for bringing me. I'll come back with my sons when they next visit London. They'd love it.'

Harris was relieved that the choice of venue was such a success, even if he feared the setting was a little basic for her taste. He watched as the pale blue tables were meticulously wiped down by a silent young man with a helmet of black hair, his stiff demeanour exacerbated by a tight-fitting polyester shirt.

'Just arrived,' Harris whispered to her, as the man scuttled off into the kitchen. 'You can tell that, can't you? Poor fellow, completely overwhelmed by it all.'

Farrah gave a sad smile. She remembered the feeling herself, arriving as a student at Cambridge in the 1970s and feeling incapable of penetrating the social circles that were tantalizingly closed to her. She started to pull out some banknotes from a black leather snap purse buried in her large handbag to pay for the meal.

'Put that away,' he cried, happily noting that she cherished her financial independence. 'Whatever do you ladies keep in those bags of yours?'

'Our lives,' she said.

He smiled. 'We should do this again some time. If you'd like, that is.'

'That would be very nice, Harris – I mean, if you ever come down to London, we should meet up again. You have my telephone number, don't you?'

'Yes, but let me give you mine.' He took out a business card and, for the first time that evening, she put on her glasses to examine it. She saw his name and qualifications were printed on one side and in the corner was Omar's company logo.

'I didn't know you were part of Omar's set-up,' she said abruptly.

'Well, nominally,' he said, trying to sound casual. 'It was some time ago now. After I left the air force and couldn't find another job.' In the dimly lit restaurant, she saw his eyes flicker with the crushing memory of that time. It had been Omar who had provided him with work on one of his many Middle East projects. 'It was just a short-term project management position, but it kept the roof over my head when there was nothing else going.' The job had paid well, and given him fresh purpose and direction for a short time.

'Goodness,' Farrah said, 'that was lucky for you.' Her own husband had not been so lucky with Omar, but she didn't feel ready to divulge the story to Harris just yet.

'Yes, it was. I'll always be grateful to Omar.'

'So why aren't you working for him these days?'

'Well, after the divorce, I moved up north and began running a corner shop.'

'That must be quite a commitment.'

'It is. Exhausting, actually. But my cousins help me.'

Dr Farrah regarded him for a moment. 'Do you think you'll work for Omar again one day?'

'Not unless he makes me an offer I can't refuse.' Harris smiled, as he paid the waiter for their meal. 'I never thought I'd end up as a shopkeeper, I must say.'

Later, when the meal was over, they lingered outside. The restaurant's neon sign splashed electric blue and cherry on the wet pavement and they both waited for the other to say something. For a mad moment, Harris imagined himself in the house with her, not in her bed but in an adjacent bedroom, the spare room. He could picture it already, softly carpeted, a bed under the eaves permanently made up and ready for unexpected guests.

'I'd better be getting home, Harris,' Farrah said, interrupting his train of thought. 'Would you mind driving me back? I have a busy teaching schedule tomorrow.'

'Of course,' he said, pushing his thoughts aside.

He dropped her at her house and kept the engine running as she hurried to the front door. She gave a quick wave from the doorstep before she disappeared inside. He waited as the lights in her house popped out, one by one, and wondered if he would see her again.

He drove up north in a state of elation, barely noticing the miles that stretched ahead. By the time he reached his house, it was almost three in the morning and he fell into bed exhausted, his mind reeling. He was enchanted by her, yet he was uncertain whether his feelings were reciprocated. As he drifted off, he remembered the box of After Eights that he had forgotten to give her; he would have to brush up his skills in the courtship department, that was for sure.

Eight

Harris was on his way to post a cheque at the end of his road when it began. A tightening of the chest and a shortness of breath, symptoms that were familiar to someone who never practised keep fit and saw no merit in staying in shape. Physical exertion often made him breathless or double up with a stitch. But this time the attack left him truly terrified. His heartbeat fluttered out of step with the world, throwing him off balance. The pillar box that was his destination shimmered bright scarlet at the edges of his vision and seemed to melt when he leaned against it for support. A hot, peeling sensation crawled up his body, swiftly followed by icy chills, and he crumpled to the pavement, as though it were an inviting bed swallowing him up. There was no one in the street, unusually, and the world turned without him, indifferent in the face of his mortality. It was a revelation.

Am I in a fainting fit, or is this the heart giving up the ghost? he wondered, coming round. He had to get perpendicular to the ground again, get inside the house, away from a world that was suddenly perilous, hard-edged, unpredictable. When his heart regained its regular beat, he got up tentatively, seized by a queasy giddiness that rendered his legs all but useless. As they threatened to fold beneath him again, he became fixated upon reaching home, where he could take to his bed even though it was barely midday.

It vaguely struck him he must dig out his will, which had not been updated since his divorce, though he was not even sure where he'd put it. Would he have to explore the dark basement cupboard under the stairs and search through musty papers in box files that lay there? The thought filled him with morbid dread. Better to start afresh, draft a new will and alert his nearest and dearest that the end was nigh.

No amount of singing Sufi poetry could calm him. A capsule of Valium sent him into a groggy state of anxiety. Prayers provided a brief respite, but by sunset he was desperate. He made his way to the doctor's evening surgery at the bottom of the hill, where he sat for two hours in the crowded waiting room, hemmed in by feverish children, spluttering elders and fractious toddlers munching crisps. Eventually, it was his turn to be seen.

The doctor was kindly and brisk as she examined him, but could find nothing other than the atrial fibrillation he had suffered for several years. An ECG was not really necessary, she insisted, breezily informing him that it was a common, non-life-threatening arrhythmia of the heart and certainly not a coronary. That was a relief to hear, though he told her that lately the medication was not working and the irregular thumping that filled him with dread was becoming an unpleasant daily feature of his life. When he mentioned this, she fixed him with a beady look.

'Are you depressed, do you think?' she demanded.

The question rattled him, as if she didn't take his illness seriously. After all, who wouldn't be a bit down in the dumps in his situation? Depressed indeed.

Out loud he said, 'No more than usual, doctor.'

The doctor didn't notice or have time to probe his mental state: the statutory seven-minute consultation was almost up. She moved swiftly on to the nuts and bolts of his condition.

'Well, it can make you feel low,' she said, 'the arrhythmia. But to be honest, it's only dangerous if the heart returns to normal and a blood clot has formed in the meantime . . .'

She was young and seemed overly keen to outline all the risks.

'A blood clot you say? And then what could happen?' he asked, not really wanting to hear the answer.

'Most unlikely, but it could result in a stroke.'

'A stroke?'

'Nothing to worry about.'

'Wait a minute. You said a stroke, didn't you?'

'In a very rare number of cases. And clearly, you don't have a clot.' She punched the details of the consultation into the computer and issued him a new prescription. 'It's really not something for you to worry about. I'd like you to try these new drugs. They're supposed to be excellent and should work better than the last lot.'

After his visit to the doctor, Harris stayed in his house for three days, fearful that any exertion might trigger another attack that would prove fatal. A cousin kindly fetched him the new prescription, and Nawaz and Jamal took over running the shop. Released from all practical responsibilities, Harris was gripped with a nameless fear that drove him to his bed. He did not leave the house for a further ten days.

Nawaz and Jamal soon began to grumble that they were being overstretched, with all the extra work of running the shop and none of the dividends. Harris sensed that they put it down to idleness, or that it was psychological. Worst of all, he'd heard gossip up and down the hill that it was because he was a bad Muslim, a sure indicator that Allah was punishing him for his errant ways. When he finally summoned the courage to leave his bed, he saw his future in the swirling pattern of the lounge carpet, and had no clear idea how to put one foot in front of the other. Death was imminent. The sins and misdemeanours he had clocked up over a lifetime made him sure that paradise did not await him on the other side.

One day, when he could bear the isolation no longer, he thumbed through his address book, wishing he were not so furious with Alia. He missed the closeness they'd had on their trip, he realized with a pang. In that part of the world, she was simply his daughter, his pride and joy, but here she was so many other things too. She had thrown up a wall between them, and he was afraid to try and scale it. He toyed with ringing his ex-wife, but then thought better of it. In a trough of gloom, he wondered where it had all gone wrong.

He liked to think it was fate that had led him to marry Gillian. It had been almost love at first glance when he spied her: a vivacious brunette in a mock turtleneck and fake pearls, nursing a cup of minestrone soup in the student union café. She had seen him quivering in the cold and offered him a sip of her steaming beverage. Nights of necking at the Odeon followed and after his three years of waiting for her in Pakistan until she finished university, she flew to Islamabad to be with him. After a twenty-four-hour crash course in Islam, conducted by some genial friends and relatives, they were married. 'We'll just do this to keep everyone happy, huh?' he'd said to his bewildered and sceptical bride. It hadn't worked, he reflected miserably as he sipped a glass of lemon barley, cajoling her into something she would never believe in. He had not spoken to her since she left him for a Scottish doctor she had met at a conference. The betrayal still rankled.

He got out of bed and went to his sock drawer. Lodged among the handkerchiefs and Y-fronts was a pleasant 'thank you' card from Dr Farrah. He had not spoken to her since the heart episode and he somehow found the idea of ringing her beyond him.

Still, the phone sat temptingly on the bedside table. It was his lifeline. He could not go on. He auto-dialled Nawaz's number.

'Nawaz, cousin, brother . . .' His voice croaked to a standstill.

'What is it? What's wrong? What's 'appenin'?'

'I think I'm dying, or about to . . .'

The words broke off into a strangulated silence, punctuated with wheezy breathing that sounded not unlike a man in the middle of a heart attack. The normally immovable Nawaz dropped everything and screeched up the hill in his Mazda minivan, a cloud of exhaust fume in his wake. In a state of agitation, he burst through the cousin's door to find him lying in a shivery state on the couch, his complexion putty-coloured, lips puckered and dry.

'This is the final curtain,' Harris murmured. 'I'm on my last legs.'

Nawaz gave him a bear hug. 'Don't be so daft. You're no such thing.' In spite of their differences, Harris's demise was unimaginable. 'You just think you are, 'cause you're living all alone in this place. This is mad, you being like this. You're comin' straight 'ome with me. No ifs or buts. Stay with our lot till you're over whatever it is you've got, orright?' Nawaz lumbered around upstairs and gathered a small bag of clothes. 'Just till you're better. C'mon.'

'It's a kind offer.'

'Did you tell Alia you've been ill?'

Harris shook his head. 'I don't want to bother her when I'm like this. She has her own life.'

Nawaz tutted. 'We'll look after you, cousin, don't you worry,' he declared.

Harris was overcome. 'You're a good man, Nawaz, that's why I called you.'

In a matter of minutes, or so it appeared to Harris, he was whisked out of his house and transported to Nawaz's home. He and his family lived in a small flat, conveniently situated on top of Royale Cuisine, though this meant there was a perpetual whiff of pizza, chips, kebabs and fried masala chicken percolating through the place.

As Harris entered the lounge, he was greeted by a vision of noisy domestic chaos that was oddly comforting. Against the backdrop of blaring TV, the younger kids saluted him like a returning hero, bouncing from the sofa into his arms. The aroma of basmati rice, just cooked, greeted his senses. Safeena finished feeding the baby in the kitchen and produced a cup of stewed sweet tea and slices of sponge cake for him. He took up his favourite spot on the sofa and readied his lap for a tray of lamb kebabs that materialized from nowhere, followed by a bowl of home-made *rasmalai*, his favourite pudding.

'You orright there, are you? Anything you need, just tell us, right?' said Nawaz.

'Cousin, you're too kind.' Harris's eyes filled when it dawned upon him how much they cared for him.

'Forget it,' Nawaz said gruffly.

'I'll never forget it.'

How unworthy Harris felt suddenly. What had he done to deserve all this? How would he ever repay them? He was racked with guilt for all the years when he was married that he had ignored their presence in the world and determined to make it up to them.

'At the end of the day, family's family, in't it?' said Safeena, as she sat down to reheat the leftovers for herself after the family had had its fill. 'Stay as long as y'like.'

For a short time during Harris's stay in the cousin's place on Perseverance Street, an atmosphere of bonhomie prevailed. His health was on the mend and there had been no more funny turns. The fresh set of medication seemed to keep the atrial fibrillation in check. Most importantly, he was at the nerve centre of the extended family, holding forth from his spot on the sofa, watching telly and dandling the baby on his lap till she required feeding or changing, at which point he would hand her back to Safeena, who laid on a constant stream of delicious meals. There was no need for him to cook any more.

He quickly realized the benefits of this state of affairs. True, he was a guest in their household and there were certain constraints that went with the role. But he felt certain he was gracing them with his presence, sharing the benefits of his extensive knowledge on a range of subjects, from religion to DIY, from the education system to mosque politics. And people listened to him. They liked his confident pronouncements, his trenchant views on how to rearrange the lounge furniture, or what to tell a lazy maths teacher on parents' night at school. Cousins and passing friends were riveted by his ideas and he enjoyed his new-found status in the bosom of Perseverance Street.

He was forbidden by Safeena from doing even the lightest chore. Her boy Nassim was dispatched to rub his feet when necessary, and his brother Ali to tread upon his stiff back to ease muscle pain. Safeena would yell upstairs to her eldest, Jameela, to run to the corner shop for the Uncle's newspaper so that he might keep up to date with world events and domestic politics. If his eyes so much as swivelled kitchen-wards, Safeena would appear from nowhere and rush to intercept him before he could reach the kettle to brew himself a cup. He did not fight it; crossing the lounge was a hazardous run, booby-trapped with the boys' electronic toys and sharp outcrops of Lego sneakily camouflaged against the gold and blue carpet. It was easier to remain on the sofa and allow the domestic labour to roll along without so much as lifting a finger. The children adored him. He showered them with pocket money for treats when their parents weren't looking.

'You're spoiling them,' Nawaz grumbled.

'It's nothing, cousin. Just a little something to keep them happy, that's all. Don't deny me that pleasure.'

'You're right generous, Harris. I mean it. What would we do without you?'

What indeed? Harris glowed inside. It was a delicious feeling. Intoxicating, almost. He began to wonder what else he could do to help the family. He ordered cut-priced children's books from the *Sunday Times* Book Club for Jameela, and bought a proper cricket bat and ball for the boys from the Argos catalogue. He kept up the stream of Twixes, prawn cocktail-flavoured crisps and Mars bars, procured at zero cost from his shop. Everybody seemed happy.

It was all too good to last. Everybody felt it, like a slight change in the weather, a cold front moving in, barely detectable: the honeymoon period was over.

Harris began to fret. 'Sure it's not too much, huh, me staying in your place like this and all, Safeena so busy with kids and takeaway . . . You helping out in my shop . . .'

Nawaz was slumped on the sofa, channel-surfing and waiting for his dinner. 'No, no. You're the Uncle, right? What'd we do without you?' he said evenly, addressing the television screen. 'Shop's no bother.'

'Then tell me how can I ever repay you? Your kindness, Nawaz, I'm indebted to you. And to Safeena.'

Nawaz switched off the television, which gave a white flash of relief after being on all day. 'You're not indebted. You're family.'

That night, Harris writhed about on the lumpy sofa in the lounge, unable to sleep. To remedy his insomnia, he went in search of a glass of milk. As he fumbled in the fridge, he overheard raised voices – Nawaz's deep bearish growl interjected with Safeena's squeaky indignation – in the double bedroom next door. Curious to discover the nature of their altercation, he tiptoed closer to the bedroom door as Safeena's voice grew louder.

'And he's like tellin' me to add more salt to me cooking! He can put his own salt on, can't he? Or can't he even manage that? He's eatin' us out of 'ouse 'n' 'ome, I'm not jokin', right. Telly's on all day. Gas fire's blaring, not to mention central 'eating. Electricity bill's going to be sky high, in't it? I'm not being funny, but don't you think he should make a, like, *contribution?*'

Harris grew hot with shame as he eavesdropped. Stunned by what he gleaned from the conversation, his forehead filmed with sweat. Nawaz responded with a low growl of – what? Agreement? He couldn't quite tell. As he gulped down the milk, he decided he must move back home as soon as possible.

Over breakfast the next day, he announced his intentions and mentioned that he would like to visit his shop. It had been a while since he'd paid a visit. Nawaz expressed surprise but Harris was insistent.

'I'm on the mend,' he said, 'and I'd like to get back on my feet again.'

'No rush, though. We're managing.'

'I'd just like to see how it's going, huh. I miss it, funnily enough. Why not?'

'Checkin' up on us now, are you?' Nawaz ribbed him, as he slurped down his tea.

'No, just curious to see if things are running smoothly.'

The shop was in a shabby 1960s building, and even though it was only a few streets away from Nawaz's place, he always drove there. As they pulled up outside, Nawaz broke the news to Harris that they were considering ditching the groceries and newspaper business in favour of flogging cheap electronics, hi-fis, phones, digital alarm clocks, and designer-style anoraks and T-shirts. Harris was taken aback by the stark change. He'd never thought it was more than a corner shop.

'There's like more of a market for this type o' thing,' Nawaz explained. 'It's where you've been going wrong.'

'Oh, I'm sure you're right,' Harris exclaimed, stung by the criticism. 'But then, the nuts and bolts of actual *shopkeeping* were never my strong point. It's a question of how to position oneself.'

Nawaz smiled. 'Yer right. So come see what I've done. It's just a trial run, mind,' he added, as they went inside.

Harris tentatively stepped on to the beige linoleum floor that bubbled ominously in the middle. It had been roughly slashed at the edges to fit the irregularly shaped room, adding to the general impression of great enthusiasm and haste in the shop's refurbishment. Glue fumes lingered toxically in the air.

'See what you reckon,' Nawaz said. 'Wanted your feedback before I do anything else.'

'Absolutely,' Harris declared, surveying the revamped shop.

Most of the old stock had been cleared out, save a few giant boxes of crisps. The chest freezer still held a few gelid hostages: giant bags of crinkle-cut chips, peas, sausage rolls and a solitary box of crispy cod cakes. Jamal was at the far end of the dimly lit shop, balancing on a rickety stepladder as he attempted to pull out some old shelving. A pile of metal brackets lay around the ladder's feet. Colourful sprigs of wires sprouted from odd places and jagged outlines of cracked plaster resembled crazy world maps on the walls. It was certainly in a state of flux, the shop.

'Is it safe, the exposed wires and all?' Harris called to Jamal. 'Don't want any of our customers getting electrocuted, do we? Or you, for that matter.'

'This'll produce much better turnover, trust me,' Nawaz declared, gesturing to piles of Louis Vuitton rip-off bags, fake Burberry caps, fleeces and mobile phones.

'Are you sure?'

Harris was dubious about the merchandise. Gone were the booze and fags, the tabloid papers; gone were the limp, ageing vegetables languishing in dusty boxes.

'Yeah. There's too many Asian corner shops round here, like. They're everywhere. Market's completely saturated. But all this electronics stuff, and the fashion, right, it's what the English lot round 'ere like, in't it? Design Emporium, that's what we're calling it. What d'you reckon?'

'Hard to tell at this stage.'

'Ey up, someone pass us that screwdriver, will you?' Jamal called down to them.

Nawaz wrapped a chunky arm around Harris's shoulder, his face softening slightly. 'What d'you reckon? Are you OK?'

'Yes, yes, I'm fine,' Harris said, extracting himself from his cousin's grip. 'All thanks to you and Safeena. I'm very grateful to you both.'

'No need to thank us,' Nawaz said. 'It's family, in't it? Anyway, I think it'll do better, the shop, don't you? Gotta keep up with the times.'

They wandered out of the shop into watery sunlight. Harris felt light-headed and wondered if it was a result of all these developments, or simply a side-effect of his new medication that needed adjustment.

Nawaz lingered by the car, jangling his keys. 'We'll miss you, when you've gone, Harris,' he said, then unlocked the door and got in.

Harris sat next to him. 'I don't want to overstay my welcome,' he said.

Nawaz stared straight ahead, squinting against the brightness refracted through the windscreen. 'Thing is, I didn't want to mention it, like, you 'aving been poorly and that.'

'Mention what?'

Nawaz cleared his throat and turned on the ignition. 'Things are right difficult for us at the moment,' he said, his voice gruff. 'Money's tight.'

'Ah.'

'And we were both, like, wonderin', Safeena and me . . . '

'Yes?'

'About that lump sum of yours.'

Harris looked out of the window. 'What about it?'

'Me and Safeena, we're working our socks off keeping it all goin', and we still don't have anything left at the end of the month.'

'Never easy, running your own business.'

'You see how 'ard she works, my wife. Day and night. And the family's suffering for it. There's never enough for the kids. Never mind the mortgage and all the other bills, I'm talkin' school uniforms, Harris, and after-school clubs, basic stuff like that.'

There was a heavy silence as they waited at a set of traffic lights, punctuated by the thick sound of Nawaz's breathing.

Then Harris said, 'I'm sorry. I should have offered you something before.'

'No need to be sorry.'

'I feel terrible, staying with you all this time, adding to your burden.'

'Don't be daft.' The light turned green and Nawaz drove on, his face set. 'We just need something to tide us over.'

It sounded so benign, so very reasonable, when couched in those terms. 'Well, let me see. I'm sure I can do that, Nawaz.'

Nawaz gave him a searching look. 'Can you? Just between us, yeah? Nobody else in the family 'as to know.'

'No, of course not,' Harris said. After all, he didn't want a queue of hopeful relatives with similar tales, begging him for credit.

On his last day at Perseverance Street, Harris wrote a cheque to Nawaz for the sum of £50,000. It was all but everything he had left in cash, a considerable amount by anyone's standards.

'Cousin, are you really sure about this?' Nawaz's hand hovered over the cheque.

'Yes, yes, absolutely. It's the least I can do for you.'

Safeena's bright smile of acceptance complemented her husband's solemnity as Harris presented it to them. 'Thank you, Harris, thank you so much!' she gushed.

'My pleasure,' Harris replied, pulling on his overcoat. 'The money's yours for as long as you need it.'

Nawaz was silent for a moment, overcome. 'Thanks, cousin,' he said. 'Really appreciate it. You're right generous.'

Harris was standing by the door, overnight bag in hand.

'Sure you don't want to stay with us a bit longer?' Nawaz said.

'Yeah, what's the rush?' Safeena added.

'No rush. I just want to be getting home,' Harris replied. 'At at the end of the day, I miss my own four walls. But I'll be back for your delicious lamb kofta now and again, if I may.'

Harris scurried across the busy ring road between breaks in the crawling traffic and then back up the steep hill towards his house. The soft greying hairs on his forearms stood on end in the breezy sunshine. Fresh air rushed into his lungs. He chuckled to himself as he approached home. The weather was unseasonably warm and his polished brogues sparkled in the sunlight. As he strode up the street, grizzled Pakistani men on street corners paused their gossip and paan-chewing to observe him. Whereas they never ventured out of their thin baggy trousers that billowed in the wind, he was a smart, well-presented man who wore suits and who deserved their deferential respect. He was one of them, yet he'd made it. A big man with big ideas. Harris could see they thought that, for they stepped aside to let him pass, not wishing to delay his inexorable progress in the world. He was a player, after all.

He paused outside the Kashmiri greengrocer shop at the bottom of his street when he spotted the fruit seller outside. The man was singing merrily to himself as he highlighted starbursts announcing: *Just Arrived Pakistani Kinnus.* When he saw Harris, he greeted him with a hug and a punch to the shoulder, gently chastising him for not coming round to the shop for so long.

'Been ill, brother,' Harris said. 'Staying with my cousins.'

'Sorry to hear it. Here, try one,' he said, thrusting an orange into Harris's hand. 'It's beautiful. Taste of Pakistan. Really. Vit-min C and all that. Look like you could do with it. Go on, 'ave a bag. It's on me, no charge. Coming to mosque?'

'Absolutely. That's why I'm here.' To his chagrin, he had not been once during his recuperation with Nawaz.

The mournful melodic call to prayer echoed off the rows of stone houses up the street and down into the valley. Harris and his friend put on their prayer caps and went arm in arm across the road to the pale granite Jamia Masjid Noor, a former Methodist church, now with signage in Urdu and Arabic, and steel-enforced bars at the windows. The Islamia Girls' High School shared the premises, barbed wire spiralled along the top of the entrance gate to keep unwanted intruders out. Harris removed his shoes in the entrance hall, made his ablutions and stepped inside for prayer. It was a joyful relief to be back in his old stamping ground. He smoothed his hands over his face and stood squarely, palms turned outwards. His own thoughts shrank into insignificance as he gave himself up to the impersonal ritual of prayer. He made sure to give thanks to Allah for his cousins' kindness and prayed that their financial woes would be alleviated now that he had helped them.

He included Alia in his prayers, as he always did. He must call her again. Her voicemail box was full, spurning any more messages. He had already left three, as well as sending her an email. When he tried her landline, not even a machine picked up. A pang of uncertainty curled into his chest. What had happened to her?

Nine

There was no getting out of it, Alia realized. And why would she want to? It was the pinnacle of civilized, metropolitan grown-up city living: dinner with Colin and Monique, as they had been known to their children since they were young. Oliver's mother had invited them over to their apartment in Spitalfields for dinner that night, had actually insisted, Oliver said, because Alia had been avoiding it up till now.

'Jo should be there, said she'd drop by,' Oliver had said, as though the presence of his older sister, who was also a medic, was some kind of draw for Alia. They had met once before, when she and Oliver were still officially just friends.

'Oh, OK,' she had said, daunted. 'Should I bring a bottle of wine?'

'No need. Up to you.' Very unhelpful.

The 1930s sequin factory where they lived in a converted apartment, glimmered in the dusk between a cluster of tower blocks and the detritus of Petticoat Lane market. Alia approached the building with caution, her reflection funnelling up to meet her in the eerie copper gleam of the entrance phone.

She hesitated for a moment. *Hate arriving empty-handed,* she thought, as she waited to be granted entry. As she whizzed up in the elevator, she flicked her jagged fringe back to sneak a glimpse at herself in the bronze mirrored walls and was fleetingly happy with what greeted her.

Oliver's parents lived on the top floor in a glassy penthouse, complete with the inevitable and much-prized wraparound terrace. When Alia arrived, Monique was outside, showing her son her latest crop of unusual vegetables. It was windier up on the sixth floor, the city a twinkling galaxy of cranes and new skyscrapers. London was being remade. Walking on to the terrace, Alia felt a rush of excitement.

'Hi,' Oliver said. 'You're here at last.'

'Hi. Am I late?'

'No, no, I'm just happy to see you.'

He scooped her in his arms and kissed her, apparently indifferent to the presence of his parents, which she found unnerving.

'Would you like a mojito?' his father interrupted. Like his son, he found it hard to make eye contact and wistfully spoke to her chest. Lots of the older consultants at the London Hospital, where he taught were like that, she'd discovered in her first year. 'I've just learned how to make them,' he said.

'Um, I'm not sure,' she faltered. 'Are you—'

'Yes, she would.' Oliver smiled. He was looking well rested, having napped post-lecture in his old bedroom, which his parents kept available for him.

A sophisticated aroma plumed from a matte-black double oven: Alia detected saffron, aromatic broth, seafood. She sniffed delicately, beginning to relax and succumb to the pleasure of her surroundings, the prospect of dinner, an evening with Oliver.

Monique bustled in. She had been a dancer, years ago, a past life she conjured up fondly and frequently. Now she was heavier, her hair greying, but she was still energetically engaged with her work – photography – and passionate about food.

'Wait, darlings!' She grabbed her camera.

'Monique, no.' Jo protested. 'Must we?'

'Relax. I want Ollie and Alia, darling, not you.'

Before Alia could adjust her expression, the camera flashed.

'Lovely.' Monique sighed with deep contentment. 'Well, I've been longing to have you over, Alia. So has Colin. But Ol's kept you to himself all this time!' She prodded her boy fondly. 'Haven't you?'

Alia felt exposed suddenly; under compulsion to explain, yet tongue-tied. How could she give a brief potted history of her relationship with Oliver and not seem desperately unsophisticated compared to them? They had met in the whirlwind weeks of her first term at a party and to begin with she'd held him at bay. At first he was content to occupy that grey area, the sexually charged friendship, but as university became her home, and friends morphed into family, she realized she wanted more. And now they were together all the time, it seemed.

She gave an apologetic smile. 'I'm sorry,' she said. 'It's my fault, really.'

'Oliver, you never said how charming she is. Now, help yourselves,' Monique said, nodding at four slabs of Basque cheese lying on crumpled sheets of waxed paper on an elongated white oval dining table.

'I really love this Spanish deli in Brushfield Street. It's just *amazing*. Celia and I were there today. Course, there's one in Borough Market too . . .'

'Really, darling?' Colin intoned vaguely.

Alia looked around at the apartment as they spoke, trying to assess its provenance. It was messy and disordered, yet confidently so, unlike her dad's house, where mess and clutter were chaotic. Here, in this oasis, matt white walls were crammed with an eclectic collection of art, culled from their myriad travels around the world. Monique's photographs occupied almost every available horizontal surface. Two Burmese cats strolled around with an air of languid entitlement, repairing to their wicker baskets only when the conversation levels grew too loud for their sensitive pedigree ears.

'This is my bolt-hole,' Oliver said, showing her the bedroom.

A double futon dominated the room. Round the edges were unruly piles of glossy architecture magazines. Digital images of his thesis project blipped on a laptop sitting on the floor.

Jo sidled in. 'Oooh – let me see.' She nibbled at a piece of Manchego cheese. 'Not bad, baby brother.'

'It's brilliant, you cow. You're just jealous.' He turned to Alia. 'Sorry. Block your ears. Ignore us.'

Jo shut her eyes in a display of theatrical boredom. 'So Ol says you're taking a year out or something radical like that?'

'Oh yes, I'm kind of deciding what to do next. If not medicine, I mean.'

'Really? Not going back?'

'Not sure.'

Oliver slid his arm around her waist and under her T-shirt. 'Colin's going to get you a meeting with the college Dean about next year.'

She felt a little unsteady and uncoiled his arm. 'What?'

'He seems to think it shouldn't be a problem. Look, he happens to be a great friend, apparently, so why not go and see him? Nothing to lose, right?'

Alia froze for a moment. 'You should have asked me first. I'm not even sure if I want to go back, Oliver. I'm thinking of doing something different.'

Jo rolled her eyes. 'Monique's doing, I'll bet. She heard Col and Ol chatting about it. Tell them to back off. Just you wait till your final year – it's a nightmare, totally cut-throat. Thing is, Alia, they're saying now there's no fucking jobs for us anyway, our year's going to be royally crapped on. I wouldn't blame you if you pulled out and did something else you actually enjoy.'

How can she tell that I don't enjoy it? Alia wondered. *Must be obvious.*

Monique trilled from the kitchen. 'Come on, it's ready!'

Alia was directed to sit at the middle section of the table, sandwiched by Oliver's parents, and trapped behind an outsized, white platter of . . . what was it exactly?

'It's paella. Hope you like shellfish,' his mother enquired anxiously, her forehead rippling with concern. She prided herself on her hospitality and cooking.

'Oh, yes, absolutely. Actually, I've never had this . . . this particular dish. It's Spanish, right?'

'Uh-huh. Darling, pass the wine. Colin. Wake up, dear.'

'What, what?'

'Oh, forget it.' She uncorked a bottle of Prosecco from the fridge and leaned on the door as she waited for Alia's decision. 'Alia? Glass of fizz? Or red? Or white?'

'Um, neither, thanks.'

'Don't you drink?'

'Very wise!' Colin chuckled, and downed both his and Alia's unfinished mojitos.

'Yes, sometimes.'

Monique nodded with the authority of insider knowledge. She was fascinated, clearly dying to hear more.

'Tell me, when you were growing up, was it very strict? Did you observe Eid and all that . . . fasting, going to the mosque, no pork, no alcohol?'

'Monique,' Jo said sternly, 'don't interrogate her, OK? She's not an alien.'

'All right, all right, Jo, but Oliver said her father's a Muslim. Is that right? Or was he teasing us? He's a great practical joker – you must have noticed by now.'

Alia blushed. 'No, he wasn't joking. That's right.'

'Fascinating, must be, for you to have all that as part of your background. I'm so jealous. It must be amazing,' Monique said dreamily. 'Anyway, we've heard so much about you. Been longing to have you over.'

'Really?' Alia was bewildered by the responses she seemed to be generating in his family.

'Yes, marvellous!' Colin beamed. 'I love the East End, the whole big melting-pot thing. It's wonderful – I mean, look at this girl, just look at her.'

'Colin.' It was his wife.

'She's not *from* the East End, silly. Not Bengali, are you?' Jo enquired.

'No.'

'Oh, I know she's not,' Colin burbled, unperturbed. 'Anyway, what I was saying was . . . Um, today I was on the 25 bus, on the way back from Mile End Hospital – do a few sessions there once a month – there wasn't a white face on the bus, apart from my ugly mug. Thank God, in my opinion. I mean, come on, think of the genetic advantages for the long-term survival of the human race! The giant gene pool, people from all races coming together. Miscegenation.'

'What's your point, Colin?' Oliver squinted at his father.

'Alia, would you like to try some pomegranate juice instead of wine?' Monique broke in, enunciating the name of the fruit very clearly. She had lost the thread of her husband's point. 'Or *guava*? Supposed to be tremendously healthy.'

'Oh yes,' Colin exclaimed. 'Do try it. It's very good for you, very good—'

'*Interracial mating*?" said Jo. 'That's the meaning of *miscegenation*, right?'

'Jesus, can somebody put the fucking cat out?' Oliver rocked back on his chair.

'Don't worry. Not staying for dessert, brother.'

'Jo, please.' Her mother was stern.

Everyone fell silent.

'Sorry,' Jo said unconvincingly.

'It's the *juice* I'm talking about,' Colin went on. 'It's all in the pinkness. I'm conducting some research into that area, positive effect on tumour inhibition. Actually lots of the pink and red fruits and vegetables have these miraculous qualities. . .'

'Really?' said Alia.

'Well, we must have a proper chat,' he went on. She noticed how neatly he'd set out a row of glossy black mussel shells on his plate. 'About your course. Oliver tells me it's been a bind . . . I'd like to help. Don't jack it all in. Bet your father would do his nut, wouldn't he, if he's anything like these

Asian parents I've come across? I mean . . . well, would he?'

Alia smiled and nibbled the rice. 'Yes, he would, you're right.' But she couldn't worry about that, not now. She gave a funny groan, then blushed, as everybody looked at her.

'Don't you like paella?' Jo enquired anxiously.

'Yes. Yes, I do,' she stammered.

'I'm actually allergic to shellfish,' Jo said. 'Only Monique here doesn't really believe me. She thinks I'm being a fusspot. Little does she know. It's a certain very pernicious bacterium that thrives in bivalves.'

'Jo, be quiet, will you? You're talking utter nonsense,' Monique cried as she headed off to fetch more food from the stove. 'You're not *allergic*. You once got food poisoning, from that ghastly place . . . you know, that restaurant in Ladbroke Grove – can't remember the name. Anyway, these mussels are from Borough Market – they're *amazing*. Really. The best. From east Kent, the fishmonger told me.'

'Whatever. Want something else, Alia? An omelette? Some cheese?'

'No, thanks. I'm fine.' She was queasy, though it had little to do with bivalves.

'Damn!' Monique gasped. 'Forgot to get the treacle tart out!'

The acrid sweet smell of combusting treacle and cornflake topping unfurled from the oven, triggering a cacophony of smoke alarms. Oliver's parents jumped to their feet and flapped around with stripy tea towels to dispel the smoke. Alia was gripped with an urge to laugh at her hosts, who appeared to be engaged in an ancestral tribal dance, the steps and rules and taboos known to them alone.

★

'They let you do anything, be anything you want, don't they?' Alia said to him afterwards, when they were back at her place.

Oliver shrugged. 'Dunno. S'ppose so, yes.'

She marvelled at how it was such a given, that he'd never even considered it as something very lucky, or special. He lounged on the futon, sipping the remains of tea she had made.

'Mine want me to be this thing I'm not.'

'How'd you know you're not?'

'I *know*. I kind of faked it at the interview.'

'You can't fake it, Alia.'

'No, I know. But I did. My keenness, my commitment. And now it's like I've been found out.'

'Alia.'

'Does it bother them, your parents, you being with someone like me?'

'Why would it?'

She tucked her knees under her chin. 'I don't know, I just wondered. My father's so different from yours. And my mum's much more uptight that yours.'

'Really?'

'Yours is so cool.'

'Yeah, well, cool can be embarrassing.'

Alia stretched out, laughing, till she caught sight of a ladder in her tights.

'Oh, damn,' she said, 'these were new.' And then she tugged at the thread till it unravelled more and more, lifting her legs high into the air, toes pointing at the ceiling.

Oliver was astonished. 'You're very gymnastic, aren't you?'

'Depends,' she said, feeling giddy, and sat up.

She was mildly fuzzy round the edges after a glass and a half of Colin's potent cocktails. She fell back upon the futon, inhaling Oliver's familiar scent. The ceiling light twirled a little.

'Did they like me?' Her words were muffled. She was in a shoulder stand.

'My parents? Who cares? They adore you, Alia, but what does it matter?'

She flopped down. 'You're right. It doesn't.'

He flipped her back. 'Stop thinking about it,' he said, and pushed her arms to her sides.

The sensation sent a sweet shock through her slack body. She was adrift. It was exquisite.

'Don't,' she said, as he began peeling off her clothes.

'OK, I won't,' he said, not stopping.

It wasn't difficult. In fact, it was frighteningly, intoxicatingly easy. She let him explore her from the smooth soles of her feet to the concave hollow of her pale brown back. Face down, she heard him sigh with surprise and pleasure at his good fortune that she was as breathtakingly desirable. And when she flipped over on to her back, she was laughing with the release of it all, laughing at her own craziness in not seeing all along how very, very, very nice it was to let yourself go, and go down further into something unstoppable – for that's where they were going suddenly, his blond head moving southwards, pausing briefly at her breasts, the tiny dip between them no bigger than his fingertip, then onwards down the ribbed steps that led to a birthmark, shaped like Cyprus, and there, slightly eastwards, her navel, a dark uncharted squiggle he circled but kept going past, not stopping again till he'd arrived at the most southerly tip, his tongue inside her.

The pleasure of it, his landing there, was shocking, exquisite. She twisted and curled and gave in to it. Nobody had ever done that to her before.

Ten

'I said I'd fix the radiators and I'm a man of my word,' Rashid announced with a smile, as he stood on Alia's doorstep, first thing in the morning.

'I thought you said you'd call,' she said, squinting at him as though the light was bothering her, her voice croaky with sleep. She scooped up a pint of milk by his foot.

'Is everything OK?' he ventured, afraid he had annoyed her. He was armed with a special key to bleed the radiators, and rebalance the heating system, he explained, following her inside. 'It was taking for ever, finding someone who'd do the job. Don't worry. I know what I'm doing.'

'Rashid, it's not that urgent. We aren't really using the heating right now.'

'We? Is there a new tenant, then?'

'No, no,' she said. 'I mean me.'

He relaxed. 'Your father would be concerned if he knew you were living in such conditions, no heating and so on.'

'I doubt it. He's not that bothered.'

'He's concerned about you. I know he thinks you aren't eating enough.'

'Really?'

'I promised him I'd take you out for lunch later today. On me.'

Alia's heart sank. How to get rid of him without seeming horribly rude? 'That's OK. You don't need to do that, Rashid. I'm kind of busy today.'

'Come. You must have a favourite place,' Rashid pressed her.

'Not round here, no. I'm sort of not really into eating big lunches anyway.'

'Never mind. We can go for coffee instead – I want to hear more about your trip.'

She didn't move. 'Another time, not today.'

'Why are you always so busy?'

'I don't know, Rashid.'

He had irritated her, evidently, and now she wouldn't listen to him, wouldn't open up. That much was clear from her manufactured smile: so reserved, so English.

Seeing his disappointment, she softened a little. 'I mean, don't you have to get back to work?'

He looked at her properly and noticed she was unkempt. Had she been sleeping at this hour? It pained him, but he wouldn't be stopped. He was put out that she wasn't at least a bit pleased to see him, or thankful he'd fixed things. Was he or was he not a relative? Hadn't they a common bond? Did that mean nothing to her? But all he said was, 'Let me show you what to do with the radiators, just in case there's an airlock when you switch on the heating.'

'It's OK, I know what to do,' she said. 'I can do it.'

He didn't seem to hear her and went into the dimly lit hall.

Tilting his head back to survey the ceiling light, he said, 'Ah. This needs fixing, doesn't it? It's very dark.'

She suppressed the urge to snap at him. 'It's not that bad, Rashid. Really, it doesn't bother me at all.'

'Winter is almost here. You'll be turning on the heating any day now.'

She released a long sigh as he got to work in the living room, thrusting the key into a chipped and rusty radiator. It gave a satisfyingly mean hiss, followed by a clank, as black oily water spurted out, splattering a pile of clean laundry in a basket on the floor.

'See? Done the trick.'

Her impatience swelled. She knew she should be more friendly, that he was only trying to help.

'Don't you have a bucket?'

'Um, no – got a bowl, though. That do?'

He said it would and she went to fetch it.

When she returned, he had another go. 'You like Italian food? You must eat pasta,' he said with a grin. Personally, he couldn't stand spaghetti, the way it slithered out of your mouth in such a rude manner, but it seemed to be what the English liked to eat.

'What? Oh, sure . . . I mean I do, but not now.' She was biting her nails, and he noticed she'd bitten down to the quick. A worrier.

'I'm just doing the bedroom now, OK?' he said.

Before she could stop him, he was leaping upstairs, two steps at a time, nimble, determined.

'You don't need to do every one, Rashid. I'll do them! Rashid, listen to me.'

He called back down to her, but she didn't hear. She chased after him.

'Which is your bedroom?' he said.

'Don't go in there.'

He about-faced.

'But you have a radiator, don't you? Don't tell me that mean landlord doesn't heat the bedrooms!' He was hot with fear, but he had to finish the job because he'd promised the Uncle he'd visit her again, and he couldn't let him down.

'Rashid, there's someone in there. Don't go in.'

He saw now that she was not properly dressed, that beneath the skimpy vest she was naked. Her clavicle protruded, her skin was almost translucent, pale with a network of complex veins beneath the surface. He tried not to look but she was his sister. He couldn't let this go on. He had to protect her from undesirable elements.

She put her body between his and her bedroom door, a defiant, provocative move but she had to do it.

'I can do the radiator myself. You don't need to do it for me.'

The warm smell of her hit him like a wind from a distant, inaccessible place.

'Let me go inside.' He spoke evenly. 'I need to do my job.'

'No, you don't! You're not to go in there!'

Why did he care so much about her stupid radiators? He dodged around her and threw open the door. Oliver sat bolt upright in bed, indignant, shocked. Before he could say a word, Rashid became aware that Alia was laughing, doubled up, as if it was some big joke, when all he'd wanted to do was protect her.

Oliver swung his legs out of bed and began pulling on his trousers. 'What're you doing in here?' he demanded to know.

Rashid ignored him and turned to Alia. 'You live like *this*?' His voice whined with disgust. 'A college dropout, sleeping with boys.'

'What's going on?' Oliver said. 'What's he talking about?'

Alia stopped laughing. 'Nothing.'

'You live like this, doing what you please, while your good father is forced to stay at his cousin's place, because you aren't there to take care of him when he's too ill to take care of himself!'

Rashid's words hit her like stinging darts. 'How do you know that? You know nothing about me or my life!'

But he had already escaped out of the door and was running, running as fast as he could down the stairs, not listening to anything that came out of her mouth. The front door slammed and a thunderous shudder went up through the joists.

Oliver looked at her. 'Was he being serious? You're meant to take care of your dad now, or what was he on about?'

She bit her lip, feeling foolish. 'No, no. He was just saying that to make me feel bad.'

He fished a wrinkled T-shirt from a pile and squeezed his head through. 'And do you?'

'I do, yes. Is that OK?' She followed him downstairs.

'Well, you shouldn't, you know.'

Easy for him to say, with his boho parents shopping in Borough Market. He sighed, lifted his bike off the wall and carried it outside. 'Are you really sleeping with boys?'

'Only you.'

'See you later?' He kissed her. 'Got a lecture this morning.'

She pulled away.

He held her face. 'It's all right, he's gone. You can do what you like, you know. You're an adult.'

Well, she thought, *yes and no.*

It had been ages since she had checked her email, having avoided the onslaught that clogged her inbox, overwhelming her with reminders and questions and decisions that must be made. She crouched over her laptop with creeping trepidation. There were a couple of messages from Harris that were innocuous enough, and she wrote back to him, checking to see if things were all right. She was not prepared for the reply that hurtled back to her moments later.

My collapsing episode in the middle of the street shook me a good deal. But by Allah's grace a small change in medication seems to have put me back on track. Heart bypass doesn't seem to be a good option, but threat of a sudden guillotine in the night seems to have abated, thank Allah. I fear I may be on my last legs, and when I collapsed it certainly did feel that way.

After a not entirely satisfactory spell with Nawaz and Co. when I was ill, I am back home again. Being alone is damaging my recuperation.

I would be very glad of your speedy arrival if your schedule with the college permits. Please come if you can spare the time, if only for a short visit.

Love

D

She began to pack a bag.

Eleven

Rashid repaired to the Special Fried Chicken Restaurant in Sidney Square to regroup. He felt such a fool now as he stared blankly at the whiteboard menu on the wall, pushed and shoved by the noisy madrassa boys queuing up behind him, clamouring for their lunch-break chips with ketchup. As he stood there, at a loss, he was overcome by a surge of despair. He would have to tell Harris everything, break the news to him later, that his daughter had gone disastrously astray, and that he had failed to reach her in time to save her from herself, from the undesirable elements that threatened to assail her. He shuddered at the thought of his turbulent feelings for her, buried just beneath the surface of his good intentions.

'You know what you want yet, mate?' the man at the counter barked.

Rashid shook his head and hung back to let the agitators behind him place their orders. Now who would have her? Who would marry her?

He gazed at the confusing menu, his appetite dwindling. Of course Alia wouldn't look twice at a man like him. Never. How stupid he had been to think he was in with a chance. The cousins back home had said how refined she was, how fair her skin was, how she suffered with the sweltering heat and the harsh conditions of the village. But he could never escape his origins and she belonged to another world, even if she wasn't some delicate innocent flower after all. He'd seen with his own eyes. He sat down by the window on a sticky plastic bench, a cardboard box of steaming chicken pieces before him, and wiped the smeared table with a napkin. The *muezzin*'s call to prayer from a nearby minaret filtered into the square, tinny and distorted by a lousy sound system that made the boys snigger. He wanted to yell at them for being so disrespectful, but lacked the nerve. Instead, he gripped the plastic ketchup bottle and squirted the gelatinous condiment in bloody blotches all over the spicy chicken.

He pulled out a tissue from his trouser pocket to wipe his fingers and felt the pleasing crispness of a letter from Mishele that he had forgotten to read. With fumbling fingers, he peeled it open. He was supposed to be showing a studio flat in one of the streets behind the hospital, he remembered, but he still had a bit of time. A swarm of noisy schoolchildren surged past him and he blocked out the sound so he could hear Mishele's sweet voice as he read her letter. It had been years since he'd seen her. He had never met Mona, the youngest, who was six.

Load-shedding again. Our street is in darkness for the seventh night in a row. Luckily, there is the full moon and I am writing in its light. Abu insisted on me writing another letter to Uncle Haaris, to ask for his help. But don't worry. I am not telling him bad news only!

How are you, my big brother? I think about you often.

Rashid crossed the streets towards the hospital. Mishele's letters kept him in the loop, though he dreaded the waves of misfortune they unleashed upon him. His own letters home were scant and sketchy, occasionally bulked out with a money order, but lately, however, he had sent neither news nor cash.

The dogs are back.

A pack of feral dogs from the plains had been terrorizing the village, and Nasreen believed a rumour that they had escaped from a foreign prison on the other side of the Afghan border.

Abu won't fix the rotten front door. Hinges broke months ago.
Amma won't use the toilet at night in case the dogs get her.
Mona has been sick again with chest infection and high
fevers. She is every week in the hospital. They don't know
what she has.

His heart sank at the thought of their rickety set-up, his little sister's poor health, the medical bills his father could not manage. *But you do nothing,* he thought bitterly, *to help them.* As he picked his way along the Whitechapel Road, dodging the market stalls, he thought of his mother, weaving around the bazaar with his sisters in search of brinjals, onions, bruised tomatoes going cheap. Business was brisk today, brown bags of vegetables flying between stall holders and shoppers; socks and vests, carrots and DVDs changing hands.

*Amma stopped working for the tailor. Remember she was doing
ironing? She couldn't go because she had malaria for a month. She
is better now, but the tailor found a young girl to do it instead.*

In a daze, Rashid pulled out a bunch of keys and unlocked
the front door of the flat, wedged between a 7-Eleven and a
betting shop. When his client showed up, he let the man inside
and waited at the bottom of the stairwell. It smelled of ancient
chip fat, the hallway, of fag smoke and dogs. An English smell,
all too familiar. The man descended the stairs with a smile –
was it pity, disappointment? – that told Rashid in an instant
he wasn't interested in the place.

Are you still going to Sainsbury? Or Tesco?

Rashid had told his mother and the girls about the supermarket near where he lived, how you could get every kind of
food under one roof, how it was clean and bright, and everyone
went there, though there were markets here too, not unlike
the bazaar, that were cheaper. He promised her he would take
her to the great British supermarkets one day.

When can we come?

It was a question she posed often. He could not say. One
day. He'd told her about the towns where their relatives
lived. Leicester, Keighley, Burnley: their gentle bucolic
names evoking the soft green patchwork of England's landscape, not that the actual places resembled anything that
matched the fantasy. Once he had sent the family a calendar

with scenes of famous English beauty spots. The girls had plastered their sleeping areas with vivid images of cottages and woods, lakes and mountains. Nasreen had told them it wouldn't be long, that any day now they'd be moving to a place from the pages of the calendar.

How is your work? You never tell us.

What to tell? It was work, that was it. A job, nothing more. Harris had encouraged him to stick with it, estate agency, and to go to mosque, too. The job he'd stuck with; the regular mosque attendance he hadn't. Harris had said he should keep an eye out for his daughter, but where had that led him? Up a blind alley, face to face with Harris's worst nightmare.

On his way back to the tube station, he hesitated by the mosque, wondering. A cluster of young men was chatting excitedly outside and he found himself oddly envious of their camaraderie.

'What's the topic, d'you know?' he overheard one man ask.

'"Our Faith, Our Future",' someone replied. 'Mohsin Begg's the speaker – he's great, man.'

Rashid's interest was fired, but he couldn't hear what the friend said in response before they went inside. He checked his watch and hurried on, walking against a tide of people heading towards the mosque. Once or twice, he found he had to dodge on to the edge of the road when the pavement proved too narrow. Tight throngs of men were gathering, pausing to chat or stub out cigarettes, before going to hear the imam speak.

Suddenly he was struck by the quiet emptiness of the street, as though he alone had eschewed the gathering within the mosque. All he wanted to do was hear what the renowned cleric from east London had to say. His return to the office would have to wait. Shifting property had never seemed so very trivial.

Mohsin Begg was a wiry man in his mid-thirties, his chin dusted with the sparse hint of a beard. His face was vaguely familiar to Rashid, though he could not place him. He was already halfway through his address by the time Rashid arrived, the room packed with young men, a few teenage boys and a sprinkling of women and elders from the community. There was also a small number of hijab-wearing students, who sat bunched together, listening intently. Rashid squeezed his way inside and found a seat.

'Come in. You're most welcome, bruvver,' Mohsin Begg announced in broad cockney, with a grin. 'There is space for you right here – look, here!'

The imam gestured at a row of bearded elders, who grumbled and shuffled their chairs sideways to make room.

'OK. Where was I? Right, so the Muslim youth here in the West are faced with all these temptations. Their mentality,' he went on, 'their goal in life is: enjoy yourself – life's a big joke, right? It's a game, a laugh, whatever. Seek pleasure. Yeah? Muslims are getting slaughtered in Iraq, Afghanistan, Palestine by our Zionist enemies. Night and day. You saw the photos of the latest atrocities in Gaza just this summer. What do you do? Do you jump in the car and switch on the stereo, turn the volume up as loud as it goes, so you don't worry about what's happenin' round the world? Don't worry about the noise disturbing other people! Your heads and hearts aren't in the struggle, bruvvers and sisters.'

'That's right!' a tight-lipped teacher cried, smoothing the remaining strands of his hair over a shiny pate.

The imam shot a glance at him, but ploughed on with his oration.

'It's all distraction from jihad, from the struggle, my friends, fighting the oppressor. Building the *ummah* is why we are here, right? We're not on earth to waste time, playing the video games for hours, going to movies and seeing the violence, the sex scenes. Missing *salat*, missing the five prayers every day,' he added bitterly. 'Some of our youth is going to college, no question: they work hard in school, parents encourage them, and some do very well indeed. They get to college. Then bang. They start with the clubbing, the drinking, the drugs. The sexual "liberation".'

He air-sketched quotation marks around the word and Rashid began warming to his theme. The man had a certain magnetism and knew how to work the crowd, that was for sure.

'See, bruvvers, sisters, liberation is the problem here. Westerners are so proud of being free, aren't they? It's the excuse they use when they invade our lands, murder our sons and daughters in the name of fighting terrorism. Terrorism! They never tire of lecturing us about how we aren't free, how we oppress our women, don't we? Barbarians, aren't we?'

A ripple of mirth traversed the gathering.

'It's all arranged marriages and halal this and that. We're "fundamentalists", all of us. This is how they see us. Primitive, basically. I tell you, bruvvers and sisters, when this lot was still in their caves, we were deeply into mathematics, writing, geometry, astronomy. Hundreds of years before the West got there. We got there first, though you'd never believe it to listen to them. So what can they teach us? Not a whole lot. They want us to abandon our faith, right, and "fit in". They make laws to crush us. They detain us in their prisons without charge in case we *might* commit a crime. It's an outrage. It's cos we're Muslims. Make no mistake. This is their big goal. They want us to act in a way that is alien to Islam. But why should we? Why should we give up our faith, which is a beautiful guide to living righteously?'

'We'll never give it up!' came a strident voice from one of the housewives in the back row.

Rashid strained around to look at her.

'Thank you, sister.' Begg smiled. 'Another thing I'm wanting to talk about today is that other big con they're peddling here. I'm talking about freedom. Freedom to go clubbing, be a rebel, disobey your parents, be in a gang, sleep around, do drugs, charge interest, marry outside the faith. Some of our sisters are even shooting up and dealing heroin now, right on our doorsteps in east London. No, I swear, I've seen it. Shocking, right? Our sisters, our daughters. It's happening, make no mistake.'

A troubled murmuring rumbled through the audience. Rashid sensed the thrill of united indignation all around him and found it oddly reassuring. He thought of Alia once more, her waywardness, her secretive activities. His own many failings pierced him suddenly, made him long to find the path of righteousness.

'Then you get the parents. I can see some of you here, today, in this room. You think you got the answer to the bad effects of Western culture on your children. You tell them: go get a proper career. Be a lawyer, yeah? A doctor, a banker, work for the government!' He paused, then said with a sneer, 'Property development.'

Rashid felt the imam's currant-black eyes, magnified by square, horn-rimmed glasses, pinion him with his glare. He was right, of course. It was despicable what he did for a living. Wheeling and dealing and tricking people into paying more than they could afford, hiding the truth from them, making a fast buck.

Now the imam was smirking at his audience. 'Get a good job, make loads of money. This is the way to keep on the straight and narrow. Keep your nose clean. Do well. Be a Muslim, if you must. But not too much of one! We've seen them, our so-called Muslim leaders, sucking up to the politicians here, the royalty. The hand-shaking, the photo opportunities, the sound bites.' He paused and scanned the room for signs of dissent. 'Don't be fooled by it. Any of it.'

The audience shifted uncomfortably, waiting to hear about the terrible consequences of fitting in. Mohsin Begg paused to sip some water, his face glowing with the exertion of speech-making. Rashid felt stifled in the airless, crammed room and stood up to open the window. The pockmarked elder sitting next to him looked startled to death by the noise as he forced the catch, splintering the wood. A blast of chilly air flowed into the room and a trio of housewives let out a collective sigh of relief.

'I come across a lot of these types, the professionals, the successful ones,' the imam went on. 'What do they want to achieve in life? What is their link to Islam? This is what I'd like to know.'

Nobody had the answer. The imam continued, triumphant.

'So this lot, these pretenders, they'll attend *Jumuah salah* because it's in the lunch break. But do they pray five *salat* at work? No way. Can't manage it. Too difficult. Boss'll get mad. The pretenders make compromises. It's a slippery slope. You see it everywhere. All of us here, we're all doing it. Cutting corners, making excuses. All of us. Thinking we're good Muslims, when we're not.'

Rashid's mind began to race. What corners had he cut recently? The lecture seemed directed personally at him, as though Allah were speaking to him through this man.

'Don't fall for it, the "fitting in" business. Don't think you've found the answer when all you're doing is being selective in your practice of Islam.'

He felt the breezy sensation of a hundred heads nodding, a deep moan of agreement thrummed all around him.

'Don't make the mistake of practising it when it suits your schedule, slipping it in between picking up your auntie from the airport or going shopping for the latest designer gear.'

Rashid had not even entertained the anti-Islamic implications of his day job, all those times he'd complained to Harris about wages, status and the like. Now he felt he had no choice but to abandon his career entirely.

'You got a rude awakening on your horizon, you better believe it!' Begg cried, like a stand-up comedian, deadly serious, delivering the punchline of a gag. 'What we believe is this: that the caliphate, bruvvers and sisters, will finally provide security and stability to all the people in this troubled land, Muslims and non-Muslims. We want a comprehensive solution that will provide sincere leadership that cares for and protects its citizens!'

The audience clapped and cheered, and Rashid held his breath, inwardly fearful of what lay ahead. Then the imam's face grew stern and magically the audience mirrored his gravity. He surveyed the faces before him, merged as one, rapt and still. The effect was awesome. A young man filled his glass with water from a jug.

'Islam tells us that the purpose of life is worship,' he went on calmly. 'We contemplate our world, and we have this rational proof all around us, and we therefore come to believe that there is a creator who shows us the way we should live our lives. Islam is therefore the thinking man's belief.'

Begg arched his head back for a moment, eyes closed, and everyone waited to see what was coming next. Then he exhaled, opened his eyes and smiled broadly. It was over.

Rashid felt sighs of appreciation on all sides before thunderous applause. Then the audience began to disperse, drifting out into the corridor. The imam pushed his glasses up his nose and shared a joke with his helper as he cleared the lectern and tidied away the water jug. Rashid did not move from his seat. He didn't want to rejoin the outside world, leave this cocoon. People gravitated towards a trestle table set with jugs of orange and lemon squash. Rashid was the only one left in the audience now, apart from a female volunteer who was scooping up stray pieces of rubbish from the floor. The dull metallic clunk of someone stacking chairs did nothing to displace him from his seat. Then Begg caught his eye and Rashid felt himself rise automatically to greet him.

'Is something wrong?' the imam enquired politely. 'Did you have a question?'

'Oh no, no, not at all . . . I, um, was really impressed. Really. It was beautiful.'

'Not my words. They're nothing. Allah and his prophet, peace be upon him, and his creation, these are the beautiful things.'

'Yes, yes, of course,' Rashid stammered. 'That's what I mean.'

Was it? He had never listened to anyone speak like that before and he was entranced.

The volunteer hesitated at a deferential distance from the two men, waiting to clean up, before Begg spied her and gestured with a wave of the hand that she should collect the pieces of paper around Rashid's feet.

As she did so, Rashid noticed it was a sheaf of specifications for a property in Sidney Street that he had dropped. They must have slipped out of his coat pocket. Begg peered quizzically at the estate agent's logo peeking out at the top of the pages.

'Sorry, that's mine,' Rashid muttered to the woman, and took them from her. He felt Begg's eyes trained upon him. 'My line of work,' Rashid explained apologetically, and Begg smiled, commiserating. 'Estate agent. Not what I want to do, really,' Rashid went on. 'Actually I'm looking around for other things. I'm not sure what.'

Begg raised his eyebrows. 'Oh yeah? What sort of thing you looking for?'

'I'm not exactly sure. I feel I've drifted away from what's important.'

Begg nodded intently. 'Yeah, bruvver. That's what happens in this world. Before you know it, you're lost. Listen, I wish you all the best in your search. And if you ever want to talk, need advice or anything, here's my card.' He stretched out and grasped Rashid's arms, and then was gone.

Rashid regarded the card for a moment, which featured a

mobile phone number and a website address. He wanted to ask more, but when he looked up he saw that Begg was surrounded by his acolytes, eager for yet more aphorisms. He would pluck up the courage to call him, but not today. Upon the trestle table, beside a tall cone of plastic cups, was a pile of pamphlets: *The Mirage of Assimilation*. He hesitated, then took one. Inside his pocket, he felt the crumpled property specifications he'd dropped on the floor. Hating them suddenly, hating himself, he scrunched them up into a tight ball and tossed them into the gutter as he went outside.

Twelve

A current of commuters flowed towards Alia as she fought her way up the steps of King's Cross underground station. The rush hour that was all hours, that never ceased. Moments later, she popped out on to a wind-blown stretch of the Euston Road, shivering in the cold. Behind her was the turreted outline of St Pancras Station, its high blank windows keeping watch on everything down below. She made a beeline for King's Cross railway station, dipping and diving between cars whooshing past. Inside the breathy warmth of the concourse, the commingled scents of newsprint, greasy pasties, coffee and diesel fumes triggered a queasy churn of her stomach. It was his declaration that he was 'on his last legs' that had made her drop everything and rush to see her father.

Not as organized as Harris when it came to packing a meal for a long trip, she had left in too much of a hurry to consider bringing something to eat on the way. Now there was no time to grab a snack or a coffee. Time was running out. She was hurrying for the train, her father's words pummelling away inside her head: *last legs, last legs, last legs, last legs*. She imagined herself as a doctor, running to the rescue, racing against time, saving him, saving herself. It was meant to be her calling, her job, her vocation, her training, but actually she was a failure and he didn't even know. *Last legs, last legs, last legs, last legs.*

The refrain fused itself with the unfurling telegraph wires as the train hurtled northwards.

Hours passed.

The solidity of Victorian London fragmented, giving way to the gentle countryside of the Home Counties, dinky dormitory towns and finally, as dusk enveloped the carriage, the jagged hills and stone houses of her father's town.

She was nodding off when the train pulled into the station and she jumped out, leaving her scarf on the seat. It was colder here than in London and she shivered in the bitter wet wind as she looked around for Harris. Maybe he had not got her message. She was about to call him, when she spotted Nawaz lurking behind a pillar, looking sceptical and condescending. That was his manner with her, she had come to realize on her trips up here, because she wasn't like the rest of them. She was not a proper Muslim and she'd no clue about her father's community. Alia mistrusted that word, the way it held Harris in its grip. She felt uneasy as Nawaz came towards her with a lopsided smile and a half-wave. Then they tussled over who would carry her bag, which she insisted on doing until she saw that it was a matter of masculine pride to let him. Harris wasn't inside the car and she looked at Nawaz for an explanation.

'He's fine, don't worry. He sent me to pick you up.'

'He couldn't come?' A volt of anxiety shot through her.

'It's all right. I'm just helping him out, that's all,' Nawaz went on.

'I could have taken a taxi,' she said.

'Why waste good money?' He spoke in a growl, but she saw he was joking. 'Student loan's not that generous, is it?'

Nawaz made room for her in the back seat. 'I had to pick up this new TV set for 'im. He blew his one up. Dunno what he did to it. He's been over with us this last month.'

'Yes,' she said. 'He told me. Is he better?'

'Yeah, he's much better than 'e was.'

Nawaz drove too fast around the ring road, speeding and braking in rapid succession. Eagerly displaying his knowledge of the back streets, he skirted the station and the new shopping centre, then sped up to Thornton Lodge, the neighbourhood where her father lived. A cigarette cupped possessively in his right hand grew a long delicate cylinder of white ash that drifted on to the grubby seat beside him. He didn't offer her one and she didn't ask. She couldn't recall it being this filthy, her father's car – paper cups were scattered about the floor and a faint stench of stale milk rose from the upholstery. It had been well used by Nawaz and the whole community apparently. She noticed how every few streets, his attention would drift from the road as he tooted passing Pakistani locals he recognized, occasionally startling them. Alia saw one bewildered old man shake his fist, then grin toothlessly and wave when he realized it was only Nawaz.

'Did he give you his car?' Alia asked.

Nawaz gave a short laugh. '*Give* it me? Your dad? You must be joking.'

Her heart surged with loathing, suddenly, towards this graceless cousin. Her father had always been generous, she'd seen it with her own eyes.

'No, no, we just, like, borrowed it for a bit. My van's outta commission, see. Down the garage. It's family 'elping out family, in't it, type thing?'

Of course. 'How is he?'

'Your dad? Well, he's been poorly, but stayed with us a while. Ate his meals with us an' all. Safeena and the kids took care of him. Shouldn't be on your own when y're like that.' She felt his narrow-eyed glance shift in her direction. 'He'll be glad to see you.'

'I'll be glad to see him.'

Nawaz braked suddenly at the top of her father's street, narrowly missing a ginger cat. He glanced irritably in the rear-view mirror as the terrified creature did a sort of backflip and scampered away.

It had been almost a year since Alia had been to visit her father. Seeing the house again gave her a jolt, not so much its unfamiliarity but the sight of her father framed within it, standing at the window, waiting. He appeared diminished: a wispy, insubstantial figure, dressed in pyjamas and a grey V-necked sweater punched with fraying holes. *I should come up more often,* she thought, pricked with guilt that she'd been avoiding him.

'Dad!' she cried, and felt him sag a little with relief as she hugged him. 'Are you OK?'

'I'm alive, aren't I?' He mustered up a smile. 'Thank God you came, though. What took you so long?'

Her guilt morphed into mild resentment. 'The train was slow,' she said. 'I'm sorry.'

Nawaz squeezed his way past them, importing the television into the lounge.

'Put it just there, will you?' Harris said to Nawaz, who set it down in the hallway.

'OK if I keep the car?'

'Yes, yes, take it. Have it as long as you need.' Harris called to him as he left.

Alia peered into the kitchen. The place looked as if it had been ransacked by a burglar, caught in mid-trawl. Drawers were half-open, their contents spilling out; a bin was kicked over; stacks of dirty dishes and saucepans crowded the surfaces.

'What happened?'

'Nothing. Why?'

'I mean, it's a bit of a mess.' She touched the yellowing net curtains that had belonged to the previous occupants, who had been heavy smokers.

'You really should get rid of these. They're like, *giving off nicotine*, Dad. You'll damage your lungs just standing next to them. Can't you smell them?'

The walls were sallow with pale spectral oblongs where pictures had once hung. Harris stood a little hunched, apologetic, watching her. He was not at death's door, after all, or on his last legs for that matter; a relief, she thought, if a little annoying for the terrible scare his message had given her. His condition was chronic, that was for sure, and would flare up periodically. Still, even though she couldn't have ignored his begging her to come up, she resented the florid language he'd used to whip up her fear.

'Good of you to take time out of the college, Alia.'

'Rashid came over,' she said, 'to fix the radiator. It was him that told me you'd been ill. I felt so bad I hadn't heard.'

'You want a cup of tea?'

'No, thanks.'

'Biscuit? I have some.'

'You could have called me, you know. You didn't have to send Rashid round. I'd have come up the moment it all happened, if I'd known.'

Harris was indignant. 'You didn't call me back! I left messages all over for you. I was worried, wondering where you'd got to. Your voicemail box was blocked and overflowing, so I couldn't leave any more.'

'You didn't say, though. And I've been busy with stuff.'

'Stuff? Burning the midnight oil, Alia. Not good.'

'You look kind of tired yourself.'

He sniffed. 'Old age. I'm in the twilight zone of my life, that's all.'

'Dad, you are not old.'

'Huh. This heart business is dragging me down. Drugs are taking care of it, my doctor claims, but still. I get these dreadful sensations inside. I'm not mad or turning gaga, am I?'

'Course not. Who says so?'

'They look at me like I'm not all there, the doctors – and the bloody cousins. I'm glad you're here now. You're the doctor in charge, Alia. You're all I need.'

An hour later, as Harris lay on the sofa flicking through the news channels, Alia tackled various sites of destruction around the house, marshalling the wheezy powers of the old family Hoover.

'This thing belongs in a museum,' she shouted over the roar, as its feeble suction failed to have much impact on the carpets.

'It's perfectly OK. Nothing wrong with it.'

He refused to upgrade it. Even after all this time in England, he could not get used to the accepted habit of throwing old appliances away and replacing them with new models. It was not meanness on his part, but rather a tender respect for a defunct item that surely, after a lifetime of service, deserved more than to end its days on a rubbish dump.

'Just having you here makes me feel better, you know. It's quite extraordinary.'

Alia's presence lifted his constitution, he decided, no doubt about that. An unbidden image of the boyfriend spoiled his mood for a moment, until he pushed it away.

'Stop all this vacuuming, Alia,' he insisted. 'Relax. What shall we do about dinner?'

His stomach was rumbling. Normally, when the prospect of Alia's arrival loomed, he would make a quick dash around Marks & Spencer, throwing all manner of groceries into the trolley. Not that he was a gourmet cook; rather, he liked to combine his favourite ingredients in random ways to create dishes he considered to be tasty and filling. Lately, he had barely managed to make it through the doors of the supermarket when a glimpse at the cornucopia of choice triggered a spasm of panic. It was most disturbing.

His illness and its accompanying frailty had made him wary of seeing Dr Farrah again, but she had been quite tenacious at keeping in touch. *Any more plans to visit London?* her last post-card had enquired. He'd detected something almost plaintive in her syntax.

Very soon, he had written back. *I've had a spell of ill health, but a trip is on the cards shortly.*

Now he put all thoughts of Farrah aside because Alia was

here. They were marooned in his living room, wondering how to steer the evening forward. They could get a take-away or go out to a restaurant. She shrugged. He didn't mind. Neither did she. He hummed. She sighed. In the prevailing mood of lassitude, they sat side by side on the sofa and she wondered why on earth she was there at all. Then Safeena rang and invited them over for dinner and a solution to the evening was found.

Alia regarded him critically. 'Don't you think you should get dressed?'

'What's wrong with these?' he said, tugging at his thin pyjamas, then caved in when she shook her head disapprovingly and went upstairs in search of trousers.

They walked down the hill and waited at the bus stop, buffeted by wet blusters of wind for twenty minutes before a crimson hopper bus arrived. When they got to Nawaz's place, she spotted her father's car parked outside Royale Cuisine, as though that was where it belonged now. It was an unsettling sight and she could not help but wonder what else of her father's had been absorbed into his cousin's world. When they went inside the flat, she recognized his slow cooker on the sideboard. And was that not his special hardback copy of the complete works of Daphne du Maurier on their bookshelves? His *Concise British Flora and Fauna* too?

'That's yours, isn't it?' she said to him as he sank into a clapped-out sofa that offered little resistance to his slight form, threatening to engulf him.

'What? Oh yes, they wanted to borrow it. The eldest's a big reader and Safeena said she'd like it.'

'And the slow cooker?'

'I brought it just in case I might be doing my own cooking here. I know you don't like it, but it's convenient for my needs.'

'I never said I didn't like it. But why's it still here?'

'Too heavy to carry back.'

'You walked home?' It was uncharacteristic of him.

'Alia, I'm a free agent, aren't I? I left on foot. It's nothing to get all het up about, is it?'

It was dinner in front of the TV. A programme about a radical mosque in Burnley rumbled on in the background, as Safeena handed round white Pyrex plates ringed with a floral pattern, each with a dollop of buttery mutton curry in the centre, from which a ribbon of aromatic steam curled.

'Hope it's not too hot for you. I've left out the chillies, but he likes it spicy,' she said to Alia apologetically.

'Thanks, I like it spicy too.'

Safeena smiled sceptically. 'Really? Well, OK, try it. Y'dad's favourite, this is.'

'Looks delicious.'

She handed a second plate to Harris, who received it happily, and a third to Nawaz, who was too absorbed by the television to make eye contact with her. She watched for a moment as her husband dived into the food and snorted with satisfaction. The mutton flesh was tender and the sauce oily and sweetly pungent. He carefully spat out a cardamom pod.

'Ooh, sorry, best watch out for them,' Safeena said.

'Now she tells me,' Nawaz grumbled, turning his attention back to the TV. 'Crap, in't it? They always show us looking like a bunch of nutters – I mean, this fellah, the imam bloke, he's not representative whatsoever. It's a right stitch-up, this.'

'Napkin, and some pickle, Safeena,' Harris said, between mouthfuls.

'Dad!'

'What? It's OK. She's family. She knows that's what I like.'

What you like indeed, Alia seethed inside, wondering why she'd been dragged up here after all. Her father's so-called health scare was just a ruse to get her back into their clutches. She felt the same impulse to bolt that she'd felt that night in the village, when they'd given her that makeover and forced her into the tight outfit. Now she longed to run back to London to be with Oliver, who seemed to have drifted off the radar, ignoring her texts. She was out of sight and maybe he'd forgotten her.

The baby made a lunge for Safeena's ankles and she nearly tripped with the tray of drinks she was balancing on one hand, then scooped her chubby daughter on to her hip and disappeared into the kitchen, where her elder daughter was piling up a stack of chapattis she had made. Safeena deposited the baby in her playpen and picked up a stainless-steel platter of saffron rice that she placed before the men. Harris shovelled a sizeable heap on to his plate and a smaller one on to Alia's, showering yellowy grains into the carpet as he did so, indifferent to the mess. The mutton stew was being spooned rhythmically into his mouth, relished as though it were his last meal. Alia saw that Nawaz was doing the same thing, only with less intensity.

'Can I get two slices of bread?' Nawaz said to the TV, and Jameela rose to do his bidding.

Alia bit her tongue this time. What was the point?

When they had nearly finished the meal, Safeena and Jameela sat in the kitchen and finished whatever was left in the saucepans. Alia began stacking plates but Safeena came back into the living room and took them from her.

'Don't you worry about that, I'll see to it.'

'Let me help.'

'No, really. Sit down.'

'Good cook, in't she?' Nawaz said to her, as she slid reluctantly back into an armchair. 'You should get the recipe and do it for your dad, while you're visiting.'

'Maybe.'

'So how long you up here for, then?' Safeena enquired.

'Not sure yet. I do need to get back—'

'She has her studies to think of,' Harris interjected.

'Yes, that and other things . . .' Alia mumbled.

Nawaz burped, cupping his hand to his mouth. He leaned over Harris, interrupting the rhythm of his eating, and pressed the mute button on the remote.

'Alia, do you want anything else?' Harris asked her. 'Safeena makes the best vermicelli pudding for miles around—'

'No, thanks. I'm full. Shouldn't we be going?'

'You've only just got here!' Nawaz declared. 'Sit down.' He rubbed his hands together and turned on the fancy new gas fire in front of the sofa.

'Very smart,' Harris observed, warming his hands before the faux crystalline coals that glowed amber and crimson.

'Works like a dream. The old one bust.'

'It's very smart.'

'I'll get you one, if you like.'

'When? This century, you mean?'

'Yeah, why not? Half trade price from Jamal's cousin in Glasgow.'

Harris sank back in his seat and shut his eyes. He'd heard this story repeated many times before: a fly-by-night cousin in Scotland who was a portal to cheap appliances.

'Come on, Dad. We should be going.' Alia nudged him. She wanted to grab him by the arm and flee the stifling flat.

'Not yet.'

'I'll make some tea,' Safeena said. 'Jameela, I told you to go finish your homework.'

'Jameela could do with some help with her biology, right, Jameela?' Nawaz said. The girl shrugged. 'Maybe you could give her a hand with it, Alia.'

'Oh, sure, of course,' Alia said.

She went and sat down opposite Nawaz's daughter at the kitchen table, as her father and Nawaz finished eating in the living room and began a heated conversation. She was desperate to eavesdrop but Jameela was nagging her.

'You a doctor, then, or what?' the girl said.

She had a wan, guileless face, her wide-set eyes half hidden by a thick fringe. Her father didn't let her go to a proper hair-dresser and her mother never had time to do much more than crop it every so often with the kitchen scissors, blunted from snipping up chicken.

'Not yet. One day.'

'Oh.' She looked crestfallen. 'My granddad says evolution theory's all rubbish, in't it? We weren't, like, descended from the monkeys, were we?'

'Look, it's a theory, Jameela,' Alia said neutrally, as she tried to listen in on Harris and Nawaz's chat. It slipped into Punjabi, so eavesdropping was not an option.

Jameela tipped her chair backwards and chewed on a pencil.

'So what are you working on?' Alia asked the girl.

'Cell structure.' She flicked open her textbook. 'This stuff, 'ere. Right boring, it is.'

Alia struggled to focus on the muddle of homework notes and books spread out before them. 'Where d'you need help? Is there anything you don't get?'

Jameela shrugged. 'Not really.'

'OK. So what do you want to do, then?'

Jameela blushed shyly. 'Don't mind. Just stay and watch telly with us, if y'like. Just have to draw this diagram, that's it, really.'

'Right. Go on, then.'

Jameela curled her left hand around her exercise book in a gesture that was both protective and defensive.

'Is this all right?'

Alia glanced at it and then at her mobile. 'Yes, it's really good.'

At last. A text alert from Oliver sent a frisson of excitement through her. *Ditch the veil and come home*, it said. She was relieved to hear from him at last, though the joke irked her. *Don't do veils round here*, she punched back. A smiley face popped up, grinning inanely. *Not sure*, she added, *when I'm home*.

Meanwhile, the conversation in the living room had increased in volume, but she couldn't discern if the cadences were hostile or simply enthusiastic. Harris caught her eye and projected a smile that was meant to reassure her but had the opposite effect. She switched off her mobile and went over to see what was going on, aware that Nawaz was pointedly ignoring her as she hovered in the vicinity.

'Biscuit?' It was Safeena, at her shoulder, with a tray of ginger snaps and three mugs of tea.

Alia took one. 'Thanks,' she said, and sat down next to Harris on the sofa.

'C'mon, you don't want to listen to all this boring men's talk,' Safeena said, nudging her.

'I'm just fine, right here.'

Safeena looked surprised. 'Don't you want to watch a DVD, then? We've a new telly upstairs. Widescreen HD, it is. S'really good.'

'No, thanks. Honestly, I'm OK.'

'Suit y'self,' she said, and padded upstairs, placing a finger to her lips to shush the voluble discussion that threatened to wake the baby.

Nawaz dunked a ginger snap into his tea, holding it until saturation. He sucked on the soggy half of the biscuit, then dunked again. This time he held it in too long and the remains dissolved and sank to the bottom.

'I can't be doing with this, Harris,' he said. 'It's not what we agreed.'

'But you say the shop is now thriving,' Harris insisted, 'so what are you waiting for?'

'Don't rush me, cousin,' Nawaz growled, and reached for another biscuit. 'For a start, we've not enough cash flow.'

'I don't believe it!' Harris cried angrily. 'That's impossible.'

'Believe what you like. It's the truth.'

'Whatever it is, it seems we don't see eye to eye,' Harris snapped, swaying a little as he rose to leave, dizzied by the argument.

'Too right we don't,' Nawaz said, and folded his arms over his stomach.

Harris looked at Alia. 'We're going,' he announced. 'Right

now.' She'd never seen him quite so agitated. Safeena flew downstairs, disturbed by the raised voices.

'Goodnight to you,' Harris said abruptly to her. 'And thanks for delicious supper, as ever.'

'Yes, thank you,' Alia overlapped his words, struggling to gauge the charged atmosphere; she'd have to winkle out of her father later what this dispute was all about.

'Righto. Well, you're both welcome, whenever y' like. Bring her round, don't hide from us lot, will you?' Safeena said, trying to jolly up the mood before the guests left her to a sink full of washing-up and her volcanic husband.

'*Khuda hafiz*, Harris,' Nawaz said, and propped his feet on the table.

'Could we take the car back?' Harris said.

'Yours, in't it? Take it.'

'I only ask because you said you may need it to drive to the shop tomorrow.'

'Forget it, cousin. Jamal's picking me up.'

Alia drove the short distance home, her eyes darting constantly from the road to the dashboard, as the pale orange petrol icon warned that they were running on empty.

'Typical of the bugger, it really is,' she heard her father mutter beneath his breath. 'Nawaz and his lot use the car and never fill it up.'

'What were you arguing about, exactly?' she asked.

'Wasn't an argument, Alia.'

'*Debating*, then.'

'No need to be sarcastic, my dear.'

'I'm not, it just seemed like a row or something.'

'It was nothing.'

'You were both yelling at each other.'

'Is this a crime all of a sudden, then, to raise the voice?'

She stopped at a set of traffic lights, flabbergasted. 'Can't you just tell me what's going on?' She looked at him and saw that his eyes were black and glassy, mesmerized by the head-lights of passing cars.

'It doesn't matter, Alia,' he said gloomily.

'*Were* you arguing?'

'It was a disagreement, yes, I suppose you could say.'

The lights turned green and Alia accelerated up the hill. She parked right outside the house, which appeared dark and uninviting, and neither of them moved to get out of the car. For a moment, they allowed themselves to be absorbed by the view of the town spread out beyond them. The valley was transfigured at night-time, strung with necklaces of white lights from the ring road and clusters of bright yellow lozenges from the lit windows in the houses below. A train snaked slowly across the viaduct, illuminating it briefly before being swallowed by darkness. They went inside.

'Alia . . . don't be cross.'

Was this why he'd urged her to come up to stay? Not physical infirmity, but something else, some weight he was struggling to bear? The thought scared her.

'Nawaz seemed very angry,' she said. 'I heard how rudely he spoke to you, Dad.'

'Don't say that, Alia.' He regarded her, pained. 'He's my cousin.'

So what? she thought, but said nothing.

Thirteen

The following morning she went downstairs to find the house quiet, except for the crackle of perpetual radio that marked the passage of the day. Tangible signs of Harris's presence were all around. A crumpled prayer cap on the sideboard, a crumby breakfast plate in the sink, yet he was nowhere to be seen. She wiped a spyhole in the condensation-speckled windowpane, and saw that the rain clouds had been swept away, leaving a determined blue sky. A wintry chill had settled upon everything, inside and out, and she shuddered a little as she remembered the bitter exchange between her father and Nawaz the night before. Then she put it to the back of her mind, dressed, ate a bowl of cereal, sorted out the living room. As she did so, she noticed Harris had left his mobile phone behind. There was his diary, lying open on the phone table, and she noticed that he had a doctor's appointment later. It made her wonder if he'd remembered it in his rush to get to the shop. She put an accumulation of milk bottles out on the doorstep and headed for the shop to remind him.

When she arrived, she was surprised to find the Spar sign had been replaced with a new shop front proclaiming it the

Design Emporium. Jamal was standing behind the counter, and greeted her silently with a hopeful grin and a nod before shouting up the stairs to Nawaz. The consensus was that her father had not been there that day, or indeed for quite some time.

'What happened to all the other stuff?' she said, looking around at the newly stocked shelves.

'We went upmarket,' Nawaz said. 'My initiative.'

'I can see that,' she said, surveying the fresh merchandise. 'Is Dad not around, then?'

'I've taken over,' Nawaz explained, 'since your dad couldn't manage it any longer.'

'Oh,' she said, confused. 'He never said. I just assumed he'd be here.'

Nawaz put his head on one side, as if in thought. 'Well, he does sometimes drop in, see what we're up to, but not very often these days.'

'Well, if you do see him . . .' she began, unable to finish. It was as if he were divesting himself of all his worldly goods, one by one: his Citroën, the slow cooker, even his beloved Daphne du Maurier anthology, and now the shop.

'What shall I say, if I see 'im?' Nawaz asked.

'Nothing,' she said. 'I'll find him.'

She didn't mention the doctor's appointment. She was determined to protect whatever belonged to her father from Nawaz, even if it was something intangible like his privacy. The newly fitted shop door resisted as she tried to push it open, then gave a jeering beep and jammed.

'I'll see to it,' Nawaz offered, and let her out.

Unsettled by the encounter, she stood in the street wondering which direction she should take. She turned left and nipped up the alleyway bisecting two rows of terraced houses, past a gang of kids playing a noisy game of hide-and-seek between a couple of defunct fridges and a broken fence. There was no sign of him anywhere. She kept going, peering into people's houses as she went. In a tiny kitchen she caught a glimpse of a woman singing to herself as she scoured a cooking pot. Outside in the front garden, a washing line of neatly pegged socks and kurtas, and an embroidered bedspread, fluttered in the wind.

It was beginning to rain and she decided that perhaps he'd gone to the doctor's surgery after all. She bought a sparkly pink umbrella from a selection at Rukshana Fashions on the corner and made her way back to his house.

Several hours later, flopped upon the bed while her wet socks and jeans steamed on the radiators, she heard a sudden banging at the front door that drew her to the window. She peered down and saw her father waving up at her, a bag of shopping in his hand.

'Got the groceries in,' he cried triumphantly.

She followed him into the kitchen. 'That's great. But did you remember to go to your doctor's appointment at twelve?'

He didn't look at her. 'It doesn't matter. I can go to the doctor's another day.'

'Dad, you've been really ill. You shouldn't miss your appointments.'

She tried to catch his eye, but he avoided her, bending down to gather up some stray onions that had rolled on to the floor. Then he started to peel one, hacking at it with a kitchen knife.

'You said you were on your last legs.'

He stole a sideways glance at her. 'I was. I am.'

'I came up to stay because I thought you were very ill.'

He took out some meat he'd bought from a brown paper bag and tossed it into the saucepan. 'Could happen any day, any day,' he muttered. 'I want my nearest and dearest close to me, and that's you.'

'Don't say that.'

'Why not? It's the truth.'

She sat down at the kitchen table. 'You weren't at the shop, were you? I came to find you.'

He wiped his eyes, streaming from the onion. 'Why?'

'I just wanted to remind you about the appointment, that's all.'

The pungent smell of burning meat and smoking onion pervaded the kitchen and made her cough. She took a deep breath.

'Nawaz has taken it over, hasn't he?'

Harris was silent, absorbed by the job of frying meat.

'Was that what the row was about last night?'

'It's nothing to do with you,' he snapped.

'OK,' she said slowly. 'Maybe not. That was your shop, Dad.'

'It was a nuisance.'

'It was *yours*.'

'I've put him in charge, that's all. The Design Emporium was his idea so I said he could run it.'

Alia went over to the stove. 'That wasn't what he said when I went to find you.'

'Well, what did he say?'

'He said he's taken it over from you.'

'Ah, that's what he says, but we're still partners,' Harris said quickly, adding a tablespoon of salt to the pan.

'Dad! Not so much!'

'Alia, do you mind? I need the iodine. My blood pressure is always low, actually.'

'But you have cardiovascular disease, remember.'

'I don't need you to remind me.'

No, she thought unhappily, *you don't.*

In the quiet muffled retreat of her attic room, she contemplated her exit strategy. Her father clearly didn't need her there or, if he did, it was just to fend off his enduring loneliness. Was she being unfair? She felt a pang of guilt, wondering what excuse she would make for leaving so suddenly; what white lie would she add to the mounting heap? She gathered her things in a bag and tiptoed quietly downstairs so as not to disturb his post-prandial nap. As she approached the living room, she heard him speaking in hushed tones on the phone. Something about the dark whispery quality of his voice propelled her back upstairs into his bedroom, where she picked up the extension to listen, her hand clapped tightly over the mouthpiece. It was a woman's voice, resonant, throaty, with a hint of an accent.

'So I am in limbo on this, Harris, but it doesn't mean we can't meet,' the voice said.

Her heart pounded as she listened, guiltily unable to stop herself.

'No, no, my fault for not getting back to you sooner,' Harris said, in a suave tone she hadn't heard in years. 'I've been under the weather, rather . . .'

Her face burned. Under the weather? Wasn't it at death's door? Did he not invoke his last legs?

'Really?' The voice was all female concern. 'Oh, Harris.'

Alia felt stupid, suddenly, duped in her girlish eagerness to rush to his aid, provide the missing female link, when she was clearly redundant.

'Nothing serious, a touch of angina. A heart condition, to be sure, but nothing that can't be managed with medication.'

'Maybe I should just go back to London,' she said to Harris later, when she came downstairs to find him in the hallway, looking for his prayer cap. 'I've been thinking I really should.'

Harris froze, like an animal caught in headlights. 'Of course. Yes. You mustn't miss your lectures and so forth.'

Alia bit her lip. 'No, Dad. It's not that. There's something I should have said.'

'What?'

She took a quick breath. 'I dropped out of uni at the end of last year.'

It took a moment for the information to percolate, like a draught of unpalatable medicine.

'Alia, you're going to be a doctor! You can't just leave the medical school! What happened?' His voice was staccato with fear, eyes flicking around.

'I did badly in my exams last summer – and I decided I needed to rethink going back.'

He processed her words. 'You mean you never told me, all that time we were in Pakistan . . . All that time we were together! Why didn't you say something?'

Alia looked away, avoiding him. 'I don't know. I didn't want to spoil it for you.'

'Spoil it? *Spoil it?* So you lie and pretend, make a fool of me? Is that so much better, in your book?'

Anger ballooned in her chest. 'I didn't tell you because I knew how you'd react.'

He struggled to absorb her words. 'What do you expect? You worked so hard for your A-levels to get into that college! I remember the revision cards lying all over the place when you stayed with me in the holidays.'

'Yes, well, it didn't work out for me, did it?'

'Alia!'

He stood at the foot of the stairs, gripping the banisters for support.

'The thing is,' she said, hesitating. 'I need to find something I can do, and that I really love, maybe a different degree course entirely. I don't know what that is yet.' She took a breath.

'I don't believe it. Are you mad?'

'Possibly.'

'Alia, you can't abandon the career path, not now. How can you do this to me?'

'I'm not doing it to you.'

'Does your mother know?'

'Yes,' she admitted. 'That's why I didn't go away with her. She went mad, so I pulled out.'

Harris stood stock still. 'So this was why you came with me to Pakistan instead, then?'

'No, no – I wanted to come, I did,' she insisted. 'But you've no idea what's right for me. You want a nice doctor daughter, but that's not me.' She sat down on the bottom stair and looked at him. 'It'll never be me.'

'Alia, Alia, how can you say such a thing? Have I not always loved you?'

'It's not about love.'

'What the bloody hell is it, then?' His features clenched, tears springing from his eyes. 'You're my child, damn it! You worked so damned hard to get into the college.'

'I know, but I can do something else,' she said. 'Can't I?'

'It's that boy you've been seeing, isn't it? He's to blame for all this, isn't he?'

She stared at him in disbelief. 'What are you talking about?'

'Rashid has confirmed everything I feared.'

'*Rashid?*'

She mentally rewound the tape of Rashid and his mysterious eagerness to please: his attempts to ingratiate himself with her; the odd phone calls about nothing very much; the way he'd barged into the house to fix the radiators, tinker with the plumbing.

'He came to your place,' Harris went on, fortified with the facts at his disposal. 'Don't deny it. He saw you both together in the middle of the day, in your room! Broad daylight.'

'So what if we were?' she retorted.

'I was sick with worry, and I admit that I asked him to keep an eye on you,' he confessed.

'How could you do a thing like that? Have someone spy on me!' She rifled through her purse, hands shaking, to check there was just enough money to get herself home.

'I asked Rashid to help.' Harris spoke wearily. 'He's like a son to me.'

'But he's not, Dad.' She pulled her coat from the fake brass hat stand, which toppled over and fell apart as she did so. 'He's not your son. You should never have done that. I'm going back to London to be with my boyfriend.'

'Don't leave!' Harris cried as she bundled herself out of the door. 'Alia! Come back!'

Too late. She was gone. Gone back to her other life, her actual life, not the one she had constructed to please him.

For some time afterwards, Harris sat immobile at the kitchen table, trying to understand. Had he forced her into a course she hated? He'd only wanted to help her, when she'd seemed uncertain. She'd always been so good at the sciences and medicine had seemed a natural choice, a venerable career. Was he a miserable tyrant or just a loving father? He grew anxious as he went upstairs to her room, wondering what to do about it all. She often left things behind and then he would have to call her, tutting and complaining but secretly pleased he had an excuse to drop by when he was next in London. Now, as he looked around, he found himself hoping to find something. But the room was tidy, unusually so, nothing forgotten; only a window left ajar.

Fourteen

That Christmas, Alia did not come back for the holidays. She made excuses about needing to stay and work in London, and Harris did not press her. He didn't bother with a tree, but went over to the cousins in Perseverance Street on Christmas Day, pulling crackers with the kids as Safeena doled out turkey legs and lamb curry to the family assembled on sofas in the lounge. The shop was closed on 25 December for the first time in four years, since he'd lived there. Nawaz said there was no point in keeping it open, what with everyone home stuffing themselves and opening presents. Harris reminded him that when it was a Spar it had provided an invaluable service for English people who found themselves short of a six-pack or a packet of sage and onion stuffing on Christmas morning. But he had buckled under the strain of shopkeeping – the narrow profit margins, the rising debts, the stress of dealing with unsold papers and wizened lemons – and so when Nawaz had made his sly request to take over the business, he'd gratefully accepted the offer.

It was the dead time of the year, the days short and turning dark before tea. Harris ventured into the garden for the first time in ages, shaking out a bag of breadcrumbs for the birds. A fuzz of frost clung to the lawn and shrubs, the ground frozen, unyielding. On the patio, a line of forgotten washing hung stiff and immobile, having given up the struggle to dry. In a rush, he snatched the things inside, feeling the clothes thaw and grow pliant in his hands.

Back in the comfort of the living room, he thumbed through the *Reader's Digest Gardening Year* to see what needed to be done. He discovered he should be ordering seeds from catalogues, protecting plants from frost and wind, checking on bulbs, pruning dead growth. It was a good time to tidy everything up; cut back overhanging plants, repair broken fences. Plenty of those, he thought, as he pulled on an old anorak and gloves, and braved the cold once more, armed with secateurs. Even though he harboured no illusions about his horticultural skills – he lacked Idrees's green fingers, his knack with landscaping – he wanted the garden to flourish, having neglected it for so long. His gnarled old apple tree deserved a proper chance this year, he decided, and pruned back the straggly branches. Emboldened, he set about trimming the dead twigs of a climber he was sure must be jasmine. At the back of his mind was the thought that Dr Farrah would visit at some point, and he wanted the place to live up to her standards.

As he worked, a mutton stew murmured gently on the stove, releasing an aromatic fragrance into the wintry garden through an open window. By lunchtime, he was too ravenous to make proper fluffy rice, so made do with three slices of white bread, sopping them in the brilliant oily yellow sauce that oozed around the meat. He was just enjoying the last shreds of meat on his plate, listening to the radio news, when the post arrived.

He was hoping to get another card from Dr Farrah and eagerly sifted through the pile to see if there was anything, his anticipation swiftly tempered as he saw an airmail letter from Khalid Ali. It was heavily freighted with postage stamps, as if to underscore the sender's urgent intent that it reach its destination.

The letter began with the usual heartfelt greetings. Mishele had successfully learned to ghost her father's style over the years and could produce a fully fledged letter in her neat and fluid handwriting that conveyed his news and any requests he had.

> *Dear Haaris-Sahib,*
> *Assalamo-allaikum!*
> *I trust and pray that you are in the best of health and*
> *happiness.*

The next paragraph shocked him, for he had put all thoughts of the cousins in the village on the back burner.

> *Mona is now very sick. The doctor says she must come to*
> *England for treatment for the blood disorder.* Insha'allah *a cure*
> *will be found before she gets much worse.*

A chirpy radio programme began its galling signature tune and Harris switched it off. He read on.

> *Cousin, what has happened to the generous offer of funds you*
> *promised us last summer?*

The question struck him like a blow. What on earth to do about the cousins' request? If only he'd been less eager to give

Nawaz all his money! How he bitterly regretted it now, fearing that he'd never see it again.

> *My fortune trade is rather slow. People are losing interest in knowing what future is holding for them personally.*
> *Please advise on money question.*
> *We live in hope and anticipation of a speedy response as long as the Almighty permits.*
> *Your loving cousin and brother,*
> *Khalid Ali*

The thought of Khalid and his family in the village suffering such hardship filled him with miserable guilt. How to remedy the injustice? Without liquid funds for himself, it was impossible to help them. Nothing was ever enough. He chewed over a number of improbable solutions, before he circled back to the unavoidable: the loan to Nawaz must be retrieved immediately.

He sat down at the computer and typed up a loan agreement, then printed out two copies and signed them both.

> *Islamic terms of loan: interest free.*
> *Repayment of the sum of £50,000.00 in simple monthly instalments of £1,000.00*
> *To be paid back in full on first of each month.*
> *Signed:* . . . .*H. Anwar*
> *Signed:* . . . .*N. Shah*

He then set off to find Nawaz, who was sitting on a bar stool behind the counter of Royale Cuisine, awkwardly balancing the baby on his knee. It was quiet in the restaurant, fortunately for Harris, so he could pin down his slippery cousin. The only customers were two white lads collecting boxes of special fried chicken in masala sauce from the counter and snaffling them in silence, pausing only to wipe their vivid orange mouths on their sleeves.

'*Salaam aleikum*, Harris,' Nawaz called out cheerily. 'What can I get you to eat?'

'*Aleikum salaam*,' Harris replied, and handed him the loan agreement. 'Sorry I've had to do this after all, but I think it's better to be clear for both of us, don't you?'

Nawaz was thrown. He scanned the document and shook his head in disbelief. 'What you on about? What's all this for, then?'

'Just read and you'll see.'

'I did, and I'm right hurt by it.'

The baby let out a peal of cries.

''Ere you go,' he said, and let her sip some tea from his mug.

Safeena appeared in the doorway, holding up her wet hands beaded with washing-up bubbles.

'Ey up, Nawaz! What you doing, giving her tea, you great nutter? She can't drink that! She'll get poorly again.' She scooped up the wailing baby and disappeared back upstairs to the flat.

'Harris,' he said, 'to be honest, I'm right upset.'

'I'm sorry, but I can't help that. The cousins in the village are in dire need. And I did promise to help them in the summer when I was there.'

'Yeah, well, you'll have to wait. This month'll be difficult.'

'Why difficult? I need it back. Damn it, it's my money,' Harris declared. 'You can't have spent it all on your family.

Must be just sitting in your bank account, gaining interest.'

Nawaz exploded. 'Is that what you think?'

'Well, you tell me. Where's it gone, Nawaz?'

'If you must know, it's all gone into the shop – your old business that I'm struggling to save with me own 'ard graft. I did you a favour, taking it on.'

Harris was stunned. 'I just need some of it back, Nawaz,' he said wretchedly. 'Just a little.'

'I can't. Sorry.'

'You said it was just to tide the family over, didn't you?' Harris's voice rose to a melodic high pitch. 'And you don't seem hard up these days, buying new tellies and fancy fireplaces and God knows what else.'

'You never said it was a loan,' Nawaz demurred. 'You said we could have it for as long as we needed it.'

Harris blinked in disbelief. 'Yes, I did,' he cried. 'But not for ever!'

A woman with a straggle of toddlers was about to order chicken tikka, but had second thoughts.

'Keep it down. You're upsetting the customers,' Nawaz growled. 'I will pay it back, just not now. Not today, not next week. We're not breakin' even yet, cousin.'

'You said it's doing very well.'

'Yeah, but profit's a long way off.'

'When can you pay me?' The forlorn question embarrassed him.

'I don't know. The shop's a liability, a right bloody mess. I'd no idea, Harris, till I took it over. To be honest, yeah, if I'd known, I'm not sure I woulda done it. Just that it was you, and I did it to 'elp you outta tight spot, like.'

'Then get rid of it if it's a liability,' Harris declared, 'and bloody well give me back my money!'

'Can't do that. Jamal's involved, in't he? Or did you forget?'

'Then get him *uninvolved*, for God's sake, man!'

'I'll see what I can do,' Nawaz said flatly. 'But I can't promise anything, orright?'

Harris's first effort at penning a reply to Khalid's letter languished unhappily for three days in the barely functioning electronic typewriter that he had purchased years ago on offer from Argos. It began as a letter of apology for not delivering on his promise, but then moved swiftly into a lecture on the necessity of standing on one's own two feet. Could the cousin not drum up some more clients for the fortune-telling business? There was an insatiable appetite for horoscope-casting in that corner of the world, so surely he could make a go of it?

When he read it through, the letter sounded mean-spirited and petty, which was not his intention. He screwed it up and tossed it in the bin, then rummaged through sideboard drawers cluttered with corks, bits of string, empty crisp packets, until he finally laid his hands upon an old Easter card, featuring a kitten cavorting with a ball of wool. He penned a warm and friendly greeting and slid a fifty-pound-note inside. It would keep the wolf from the door, at least, keep them off his back until he could retrieve the money from Nawaz somehow, or come up with a better solution.

Fifteen

Spring came in fits and starts and the capricious London property market followed suit, promising much but delivering little. One chilly morning, Rashid found himself heading under the arches of the Shadwell Docklands Light Railway station on his way to meet Jerry Stone, who was incubating big plans for development, blissfully unaware that Rashid was rehearsing his words of resignation. It had been a protracted struggle for him to summon the strength to reach this point.

For months he had been feeling dreadful, unable to eat or sleep properly, until finally he had called Mohsin Begg. The man's response had been amazing. He'd listened to Rashid's troubles: his disaffection with his life in England, his overwhelming failure in his duty to help his parents back home. Begg had processed it all, oozed sympathy. He'd counselled him on the difficulties of making your way in the West, while trying to live as a true believer and practitioner of the faith. He'd stressed that being accepted and successful in the world that Rashid had chosen was all but impossible; that he'd forever be an underdog at Stone & Stone, forced to distance himself from his brothers and eventually to reject his faith.

'I mean, do they let you have space to pray there?' Begg asked. They did not, Rashid had admitted.

'Think you'll get anywhere working for a kaffir like Jerry Stone?' Begg demanded.

Rashid winced at the ugliness of the word and hung his head in shame. He quite liked Jerry, and didn't like hearing him spoken of in this way by Begg. The man had given him an opportunity, hadn't he, when he was going nowhere as a cab driver?

'I could do with some help on my website,' Begg said suddenly. 'I'm not like these techie whizz kids, but I'm thinking you might be.'

'Do you really think I could help you?' Rashid perked up at the idea that his skill set could be put to use for a higher purpose. He was not completely redundant after all, just debilitated by his situation.

'Sure. We'll find you something.' Begg smiled.

'I can't tell you how grateful I am,' Rashid said. And so it was thanks to Begg's intervention, that the sometime urban planner, turned taxi driver, turned estate agent would no longer pretend and lead the double life. He no longer needed to.

'Allah will give you strength to make the right choice,' Begg intoned. 'Your job, the *property* business. It's just a con, a mirage.'

Yet the mirage had provided the prospect of income. Thousands of miles away, it still shimmered with hope for Khalid Ali.

'My job isn't working out, Abu,' Rashid told his bewildered father, who had called him from the tailor's phone at his shop, a favour in exchange for a fortune-reading. It was a rare event, getting a call from his father, and usually meant something.

'What do you mean, not working out?'

'Abu, forgive me, but I need some time to explore the faith. I've wandered away from it and it's done me no good.'

Rashid felt the hiss of long distance in his ear. 'But you *can* explore, Rashid,' he heard his father say, quite reasonably. He was a devout man, but had no truck with jihadis or the Taliban overrunning the beautiful valleys of his homeland. The Bearded Ones had despoiled the countryside, made people's lives a misery. Everybody feared their tentacles would stretch further and further into the heart of their beloved Pakistan.

'Follow the true path, my son, but just don't give up your actual job. What will you do for wages?'

'I'll work something out, live more simply,' Rashid told him. 'Maybe go to see Harris.'

'To live with him, you mean?' Khalid sounded hopeful.

'Maybe, yes.' Rashid was silent for a moment. 'Abu, what's been happening with you all? How's my mother, the girls?'

Khalid gave a low moan, invoking Allah's mercy, and then he told Rashid everything. He had begun selling amulets to boost his paltry income. Unhappy lovers, farmers with blighted crops, toothless old biddies with archives of ailments, they'd all come and sought out Khalid for his blessed charms. Yet they made little money and the wretched mullahs were giving him a hard time, saying it was un-Islamic. Khalid had scoffed at the idea, saying such strictures laid down by the Beards had nothing to do with the beauty of Islam.

'I'm so sorry, Abu. I've been a hopeless son,' Rashid said. 'You shouldn't have to do this.'

'It isn't your fault, Rashid,' his father said. 'It is just how things are.'

Rashid swallowed hard as Khalid went on. 'Then your mother reminded me of Harris's promise last summer that he would send us something of his windfall, due from the iron lady, his ex-wife. I hadn't forgotten but I was waiting, hoping, praying. I don't wish to pester.'

'And hasn't Uncle sent anything? Nothing at all?'

'He has sent us fifty pounds, but that is all.' Khalid sighed. 'Inside a card, no letter. Is something wrong, do you think?'

'He has been ill – heart trouble, I heard – and there were problems with Alia.'

'Hah, I see,' Khalid murmured. 'Anyway, it was your mother's idea I go and see Harris's friend, Omar, in Lahore.'

'And did you go?'

'I did, yes.'

Khalid Ali had rung the doorbell several times before a servant let him in, he said. Nobody appeared to be home and he had hovered in the marble hallway, his lambskin hat held deferentially in his hand, waiting for Omar to come.

'At first he thought I must be one of the gardener's helpers, because he walked straight past me. I tried to catch his eye, and then I said, "Omar-sahib, don't you remember me? Harris's cousin?" And then he recognized me from the time I brought the holy water, and was most kind and gracious. So I asked about the money we were expecting from Harris and if he knew what might have happened to it.'

Rashid was amazed by his father's tenacity. 'What did he do, Abu?'

'He led me into a beautiful room – his library, full of books, rosewood carved furniture. I said that I was sorry to bother him but that his good offices were my last hope.'

'What did he say?' Rashid guessed that a man like Omar would be skilled at rebuffing such requests from fellows like his father.

Khalid sounded hopeful. 'He said he had heard nothing from Harris about it yet, but that he would ask him when he was next in London.'

'OK,' Rashid murmured. 'That's good.'

'Then I gave Omar one of my amulets – as a token of gratitude, for long life and a prosperous future. He said he didn't believe, he wasn't a superstitious type, but I insisted, so he took it.'

'Let me speak to Harris. I'm sure he'll send money,' Rashid said.

'Will you?' Khalid cried. 'I'm worried that something bad must have happened to our cousin if he has forgotten. I told him about Mona and he's always been so good to the children.'

Rashid picked his way along the uneven pavement that skirted the back of Cable Street. The decision to quit Stone & Stone had left him feeling profoundly relieved. There was a lightness in his step as he passed a semi-derelict estate patiently awaiting its turn for demolition. Inside, you could still detect signs of life: a faded poster of a pop idol, a drooping sheet acting as a blind. The area was in flux, on the up and up. He knew it spelled opportunity. He knew that he should be excited by the prospects that it presented him, yet he felt nothing. Seismic change rippled in the pavement beneath his feet and when he looked up he saw the skyline morph as old buildings crumbled and new ones flew up. But he had no desire to be a part of it at all. The promise of worldly riches seemed hollow and ephemeral. The myth of Western capitalism, of sexual freedom, romantic love: it was all a huge bad joke, a trick played by governments and the media on people like him. He'd explored Begg's website, strayed on to a portal to another, brighter world, and now he was ready to move on.

He crossed the street, keeping an eye open for Jerry Stone, who had told him they should meet on the corner of Rosen's, a Jewish grocery in the process of being blitzed. All that remained of the original shop, a purveyor of salted anchovies and gefilte fish, was ghostly signage etched on cracked white tiles. The shop had succumbed after a short battle by its proprietor to boost business with cheap offers chalked up on a blackboard outside. The resident Bangladeshis had proved resolutely indifferent to Mr Rosen's efforts and headed next door to the strip-lit Cash and Carry (*Quality is Our Moto*), where they could find spiny jackfruit, great bundles of coriander and murky polythene bags of shock-eyed 'fresh frozen' fish.

Jerry was emerging from the door of the Cash and Carry, skinning a Twix of its wrapper, when Rashid spotted him.

'How they can eat those things beats me.' He was referring to the fish. 'Feeling a bit better, then?'

Rashid had been off work for over a week.

'Uh, yes, much better, thanks.'

'Glad to hear it. We were getting worried.' Jerry chewed his chocolate bar reflectively for a moment, then said, 'End of an era, really, isn't it?' He picked his way through the ruined delicatessen. 'They're off to Finchley, apparently.'

'Don't want to stay round here, do they?' said Rashid.

'Can you blame them?'

'What d'you mean, Jerry?'

'All mosques round here now, isn't it? Synagogues've gone.

Bloom's relocated a few years ago to Golders Green. Remember Silver's Dry Cleaners on Whitechapel Road? Got taken over by the Uddin brothers last spring.'

'What do you want me to say?' Rashid said. 'It's like you blame us all and I'm not even one of them, am I? I'm not from Bangladesh, by the way.'

'Maybe not, but you're all, as it were, under the same banner, religion-wise. Goes beyond national boundaries, isn't that what they're saying now? I've heard them shouting outside the Whitechapel mosque, handing out those leaflets.'

Rashid felt his face grow hot. 'We're not all like that, you know. Islam's not a violent faith. That's not what the Prophet taught us.' *Peace be upon Him*, he thought.

'Pull the other one. Nowhere's safe.'

Rashid sighed and wished he were a million miles from the East End of London.

Jerry flashed a smile. 'I know you're not like the rest of them, my friend. Don't worry. So, I have a favour to ask you. I'm getting nowhere with this tricky Bengali vendor for the Hanbury Street house. He don't trust me cos I'm a Jew. Or he thinks I am. Amounts to the same thing.'

Jerry snorted with laughter as Rashid looked down at his shoes, noting that they required a polish. Was he meant to laugh too?

'You couldn't like . . . smooth things over, could you?'

Rashid gazed steadily at him, wondering. *They think we're all the same*, he mused, *us Pakis. That's why he hired me. Nothing to do with my degree – just a brown face to deal with the nuisance Asian types.*

'What do you reckon? Offer's been in for two months. He's withdrawn the house. Yada, yada. Usual family thing. It was *given* to him in 1972 by the council, right, for two bob. Now he wants six hundred and fifty.'

'Thousand?'

'Yes, thousand! What are you taking? Are you on something, Rashid?'

'No,' he said dully. 'Course I'm not.'

'What is *up* with you, then? You don't seem yourself.'

'I just need some time off.'

'Time *off*?' Jerry snorted. 'You were just away a week, weren't you?'

'Jerry, I need a break from this kind of work. I'm going to stay with my uncle up north.'

'What uncle?'

'I want to spend time up there.'

'You have a degree, Rashid, don't you?'

'So what?'

'Don't waste yourself.'

Rashid said nothing.

'Look, just help me with this landlord schmuck, say the magic Allah word, get him to see sense – if he sells it, it'll mean he can retire in luxury to his dream home in Sylhet. If you do that, you can take off for a month.'

'It could be longer.'

'So go find yourself, if you must. Have a sabbatical. And come back after that, if you get hungry or whatever. If that isn't love, what is?'

The Hanbury Street deal was clinched by Rashid over a chicken tikka roll and a can of Irn Bru at the Karachi Café on Fashion Street.

Then he was free to go north.

Sixteen

'Is 'e staying 'ere for a bit, then?' It was Harris's elderly neighbour, a notorious curtain-twitcher, who lobbed the question when Rashid arrived on his doorstep with a suitcase and a laptop bag.

'As long as I'm welcome,' Rashid replied with a polite but nervous smile.

Harris beamed. 'Mrs Evans, allow me to introduce my cousin's son, Rashid. Just visiting from London.'

'Pleased to meet you.' She sniffed, retreating inside to her usual vantage point behind the china shepherdesses in her front-room window.

Rashid's sudden visit came as a bit of a surprise to Harris but was not unwelcome. Without Alia around, and having reached an impasse with Nawaz, the lack of company was becoming a bind, especially in the evenings. As Rashid changed into a fresh kurta, he tucked a tea towel around his waist and knocked together an improvised spicy meal.

'Smells very good,' Rashid remarked, as he came into the kitchen. 'How are things, Uncle?'

'Hah, yes, everything's fine,' Harris said. 'Hungry?'

'Yes, very,' Rashid said, and padded into the lounge, settling upon a scuffed leather pouffe in front of the gas fire.

Harris stirred his concoction. 'Make yourself at home!' he cried happily.

'Uncle, is it true that you have given up your shop? I heard as much from the cousins.'

'Ah, the bush telegraph. Well, yes and no. My role is more non-executive these days.' He replaced the lid on the pan.

'That's impressive,' Rashid said. 'Sounds like you're doing well, then.'

Harris wagged his head. 'Could be worse.'

'That's good. We were worried about you.'

'We?'

'My father and all.'

'Your good father. And how is he?'

'He's struggling, Uncle.'

'Yes, I've heard.' Harris stirred the pot vigorously.

'I have something very important to ask you. You've always been like a father to me.'

'Come, let's sit down. Ask away,' Harris said, warming up to giving the boy yet more advice. He still enjoyed the esteem in which Khalid's eldest son held him.

'It's my family.'

'Yes, what has happened?'

'You probably heard my father's without a proper job now.'

'He's given up the fortune-casting, then? I thought he was doing well with it – and amulets also, isn't it, now?'

'Yes, but the trouble is, Uncle,' Rashid said, 'there are so many people not paying, taking advantage of his good nature.'

'Ah, well, that was always his biggest vice, his good nature,' Harris reflected. 'Blocked his ambition.'

Rashid ignored this and went on. 'See, Uncle, there's no money to support the family.'

'I know, I know. He's always complained about that.'

'My little sister has been ill again, Uncle, and the doctors are suggesting they bring her to England. The bills are beyond their means.'

Harris swallowed. 'What about you, Rashid? Can't you send them something? Property in London is booming, so they're saying.'

'Uncle, I've left the estate agent to pursue other things.'

Harris threw up his hands in despair. 'Why ever did you do *that*?'

'I want to concentrate on Islamic pursuit.'

'What kind of pursuit requires you to give up your day job?'

'I am intending to find the path again.'

'You don't have to give up your job to do that. I only said you should visit the mosque, get involved with the community.'

'Actually, I've been discussing this very issue with my spiritual mentor and it seems that perhaps I do need to stop working.'

'What spiritual mentor?'

'His name is Mohsin Begg. Perhaps you've heard of him.'

'Is he world-famous?'

Rashid looked down. 'He's highly thought of in some circles. He's an imam, a writer and a teacher.'

'Aha, one of these polymath types, huh?' Harris mused as he sifted through the rice, plucking flecks of grit from the pearly white grains. 'Has he taught you anything, then? Learned anything useful, would you say?'

'Uncle, please—'

'Other than to quit the job and live off the bloody welfare state or the gullible relatives?'

Rashid sulked. 'He's not like that.'

'Are you sure? These fellows are a bunch of windbags, most of them, and some are quite nasty.'

'He has helped me, Uncle,' Rashid said.

'And what about me, all these years? Haven't I helped you also?' Harris scrutinized the boy closely. 'So this little holiday up north visiting me and the cousins isn't actually a bloody holiday at all, is it? It's a cop-out.' Harris flung off the tea towel he had tucked around his waist. 'You've left your job and you've no bloody plans to find another! Isn't that it? You've become a full-time layabout.'

'I'm through with lining the pockets of the enemy.'

'Never mind the enemy, Rashid, what about supporting yourself and your family back home?'

Rashid was quiet for a moment, then said, 'It's over for me, all that. Deluded, I was.'

'For God's sake, don't talk this way, Rashid. Have you joined the ignorant bigots now in your thinking? Why study all these years if you just want to bugger off with the Beards and do their mischief?'

'Uncle!'

'So are you joining a training camp and fighting jihad, is it, or what's the plan? They don't pay well and your reward in paradise is not 100 per cent guaranteed, you know.'

Rashid brooded in silence. Begg had warned him he might run up against this kind of hostile reaction and that he must be prepared and ready to arm himself against it.

'Whatever you think about my career decision, won't you support me?'

Harris tossed a frayed gingham tablecloth into the air, shaking it for crumbs, before carefully spreading it over the dining table.

'Quitting your job is not a career decision, Rashid, it's economic suicide. How will you survive?'

Rashid sat down at the table, gripping the puckered cloth. 'I was hoping you'd support me, Uncle, while I explore the faith.'

'Support you? Am I a charity now or what, a walking cash machine? You're supposed to be supporting your elders, boy, not vice bloody versa. What nonsense are you speaking? I told you in the autumn not to leave your job, whatever happens. You'll never get another, not now you're unemployed.'

Rashid looked down. 'I understand you're angry with me. But can't you help my father at least, send him something?'

Harris began setting the table noisily with a muddle of cutlery. 'God knows the situation is bad for your family. Let me think about what to do.'

'We heard you were going to acquire some money, after the summer,' Rashid continued. 'That's what you told them.'

'Yes, well, stories of my wealth have been greatly exaggerated and in fact I no longer have anything very much. Various things have conspired to stagnate the cash flow.'

Rashid was unconvinced. Like the cousins in the north, and those in the village, he imagined the Uncle must be a wealthy man. After all, he owned a three-bedroom house, a swanky Citroën and a shop as well. As for that sum of money, reputedly very large, it had not vanished into thin air. How could it have?

'Have I not been of help to you, keeping an eye on Alia, finding out the truth about this boy she is living with?' Rashid pressed.

'You have.' Harris sighed. 'And I do appreciate it.'

Rashid looked at him. 'So why have you not acted, then?'

'What do you mean?' Harris gasped, wondering where the lines were drawn in the economy of obligation, favour and debt. Was gratitude insufficient all of a sudden?

'Send my family the money they desperately need, Uncle, please,' Rashid cajoled, steely with insistence. 'Mona's in the hospital so much these days and the medical bills are killing them.'

Such a simple request, so impossible to fulfil. How could he admit to Rashid that he'd given his fortune to Nawaz? How foolish he had been to think that his beneficence could be concentrated in one branch of the family without fallout from the other.

A plume of fragrant steam escaped from the kitchen.

'Rice is done,' Harris declared with relief.

'Should I fetch it?' Rashid asked, but Harris said nothing. 'Uncle?'

'Yes, yes. I'll send them something,' he began vaguely. 'I'll do it now.'

As he voiced the intention, his stomach double-flipped and the silvery hairs on his body stood on end with panic.

'Uncle, thank you. Honestly, you don't know how much this means. What on earth would we do without you?' Rashid said, his eyes brimming.

What indeed? Harris mused.

'Lime pickle?' he offered, as Rashid ate the meal with

his fingers. Neatly, swiftly, contentedly, and without a further word.

Night after night, Rashid sat before the computer, his face illuminated by the pale blue infinity of the Internet. For weeks he had toiled over Mohsin Begg's website, designing the layout of the Live Chat page, until finally it was ready. Begg had asked him to monitor the inaugural session, *Teens and Independence . . . How Far?* and Rashid had been honoured to be entrusted with such an important task.

'How do you deal with teens challenging parents?' was the first question that popped up in the chat room, from a housewife in Slough. 'How do you deal Islamically with the rebellion years? Should I stick to my guns as a Muslim parent?' Not an easy question. The thing was to nip it in the bud. Freedom – sexual freedom in particular – was a seditious thing.

In the meantime, he made himself at home, making use of Alia's room with its wobbly desk, its pleasant view of the street and the mill in the valley below. He visited the mosque near the Islamia Girls' High School and got to know every Pakistani and Bengali shopkeeper nearby, insisting on doing all Harris's grocery shopping locally, rather than supporting the big supermarket chains. He dropped into Royale Cuisine and the shop regularly, chatting amiably to the cousins behind the till – Nawaz in particular. He became mates with the boys who kicked footballs aimlessly around and wrangled dogs on chains up and down the street, and he spent many hours on his mobile to Begg, discussing the website and other pressing matters.

Harris observed all this activity at a distance, slowly realizing that Rashid was becoming more opaque to him than ever before. Eventually, he could stand it no longer and burst into the boy's private domain one night to find him caught up in a thread about creationism.

'I miss our chats, Rashid,' he said, peering over his shoulder with trepidation. 'You used to ask me so many questions about Islam, remember? Got all the answers now, do you?' Harris goaded gently, but Rashid ignored him. 'What's all this, then?'

The fragments of dialogue Harris glimpsed were scrappy and badly spelled, crudely expressed views on the Prophet, the holy book. He had grave misgivings about the masses going online.

'Oh, come on – that's complete and utter rubbish!' he exclaimed, as he read the screen.

Until recently, he had nurtured high hopes for the boy. Not a boy any longer, scratching sums in the dirt outside his parents' house, but a young man.

'You have good brains, Rashid. Just like me when I was your age,' he'd told him when he visited the village all those years ago. It was Harris who had helped the family to send him to England.

Rashid logged off from the site and finally gave Harris his undivided attention.

'Uncle, thank you for letting me stay here, I really appreciate it.'

'Well, you're always welcome, Rashid, never mind what I said before. It's good to have family in the house again. I miss all that.'

'Is something wrong?' Rashid asked. 'Am I in the way? Just tell me.'

Harris smiled. 'Not at all. I'm glad you're here and glad you've become such a part of the community.'

Rashid smiled back, taking off his glasses. 'Me too.'

'In fact, I need you here,' Harris went on, 'so you can help me.'

'Anything you ask,' Rashid said evenly. 'What is it?'

'Reclaim a debt.'

Rashid blinked with surprise at the baldness of the request. 'A debt you are owed?'

'Exactly.'

'Am I qualified for this kind of thing?'

'No qualifications required, just firmness. I handed over a large sum of money to Nawaz, in a moment of weakness,' Harris explained. 'And he refuses to pay me back. I never meant it as anything more than a loan, to tide him over a rough patch.'

'What can I do about it?'

'Well, demand for it to be returned to me, for a start.'

Rashid looked worried. 'OK, I'll do my best.'

'I appreciate it,' Harris replied. 'The thing is, if you want me to bale out your family, I need you to do this one thing.'

'Ah, yes, of course,' Rashid said.

The idea of chasing family for unpaid debts did not appeal to him. It was not spiritually enriching – far from it.

'You get on well with Nawaz, don't you?'

'Yes, but—'

'Then speak to him, please. I've run out of strategies to make the man cough up.'

'All right, Uncle, I'll try,' Rashid said, unwilling to tear himself away from his computer, his blinking phone.

★

Weeks went by and Rashid's trips over to Nawaz produced scant results. Occasionally, Nawaz would offer up a twenty- or even a fifty-pound note that Rashid would deposit upon Harris's kitchen table, but the insultingly paltry sums made little dent in the debt. Once or twice Harris caught the pair chatting over tea and Nice biscuits in Royale Cuisine, apparently enjoying themselves a great deal. How they had so much to talk about was beyond him. Perhaps it was just Rashid's method, he told himself, buttering up the slippery cousin. Whatever it was, it yielded little in the way of financial return.

Rashid began stopping by at Nawaz's place just in time for supper, preceded by a bit of rowdy playtime with the younger children. It made Harris livid, not to mention hurting his feelings, but he kept quiet. Sometimes he'd show up at Perseverance Street himself, only to find Rashid had beaten him to it and was already sitting down to a plate of something delicious. Safeena seemed to like Rashid a great deal. She mended his shirts.

'C'mon, man!' Harris lost patience with Rashid. 'Must I spell out the bloody job description! Beg, plead, cajole, threaten! Do whatever you have to do in my name. And in the name of your father, because I cannot give your family a penny until Nawaz coughs up.'

The Uncle's outburst frightened Rashid; he didn't want to be thrown out – he'd given up his flat in London. In any case, Harris's place was congenial and the pressure to earn money was lifted. He fretted about what to do but nothing came to mind. It so happened that Mohsin Begg was in Manchester on a speaking engagement and was due in town the following week. He had contacted Rashid so that they might meet to

discuss progress on the website and was evidently so pleased
with Rashid's work that he wanted to offer him a promotion.

'Can we discuss it when we meet?' Rashid said hesitantly.
'I have some trouble with my relatives.' He went on to explain
the situation regarding his family back home and the awful
business with the money Nawaz had not repaid to the Uncle.
Begg was more than willing to offer help – he prided himself
on mediating familial disputes.

'*Mashallah*, you are like a father to me,' Rashid had gushed
into his mobile phone. 'I'm eternally grateful, brother.'

Rashid gave his excuses to Harris one afternoon, then made a
rendezvous with Nawaz and Begg in Royale Cuisine. A lurid
pink frothy milkshake with a thick head of foam stood on the
table and Begg could not resist it.

'My favourite flavour,' Rashid said. 'Always order it.'

'It's very good,' the imam agreed, sucking on the straw.

'Refill?' Nawaz offered. 'On the 'ouse.'

Begg nodded. He had a few hours before his next scheduled appearance at an Islamic centre in Manchester, and Nawaz
was all charm as he explained the situation with Harris. The
money from the Uncle was a heartfelt gift, after they had taken
care of him in the bosom of their household, as they had done
many times. Contrary to the Uncle's view that they'd squan-
dered it or were hoarding it and collecting the interest, Nawaz
told Begg, he'd obligingly invested it back into the Uncle's
business, a struggling corner shop.

'To be honest, it was a favour, Mohsin. We've always stood
by him, we 'ave,' Nawaz explained, as Begg nodded sagely.

'See?' Begg said to Rashid. 'I thought this uncle of yours

might have some things he isn't telling you.'

'It's all gone into the business, every penny,' Nawaz went on, sweeping the counter with the palms of his hands. 'Is this the thanks I get for my trouble?'

Rashid's burger congealed, untouched.

'Not hungry?' Nawaz enquired.

He shook his head. 'Bit of a waste, sorry.'

'No problem, I'll finish it,' Begg interjected, and took a hefty bite. 'It's un-Islamic, actually, what this uncle of yours is asking you to do,' he mused as he chewed the burger. '*Riba* is strictly forbidden in the Koran.'

Rashid nodded solemnly. 'Well, I was a bit concerned about that.'

'Course you were. It's not for you to do his business in moneylending and debt collection. It's against all we believe, yeah? We must stand firm.'

Rashid bit his lip. 'If you say so, yes.'

Nawaz sat down opposite them.

'Anything else I can get you both?' he said. 'Want some tea?'

'No, no, brother. We're more than satisfied. This is delicious.'

'Cheers, and come back any time for kebabs – I mean it.'

'Mohsin, how to help my family, though?' Rashid ventured. 'They are in serious need of funds and I'm no longer in a position to help now I've quit my job to pursue this path. Not that I regret it.' He smiled nervously at Begg, who reached across the table and clasped his hand.

'Your family will welcome it, when they know what you are pursuing. Trust me.'

Nawaz snorted. 'Harris isn't a poor man. Look at him, how he lives. Does he seem broke to you? Poverty-stricken?'

Rashid looked uncertain. 'I'm not sure.'

'Nawaz is correct. He's a wealthy man, just hides it,' said Begg.

'When he stayed with us, he was on the phone to his lady friend down south,' Nawaz went on. 'That's expensive, keeping that going.'

Begg shook his head with disapproval. 'Sad to see this behaviour in a fellow Muslim,' he said.

'Yeah, well, don't do his dirty business,' Nawaz admonished, wagging his head.

'Have no fear, brother, Rashid won't be hassling you,' Begg said as Nawaz went to serve another customer. 'I'm glad you came to me, Rashid.'

'But you think Harris really has the means to help them out, my family?' Rashid pressed him.

'If he doesn't, I'll help your family, I promise,' Begg said. 'You'll join me, won't you, in London?'

It was an offer Rashid could not refuse.

As Rashid swiftly prepared to leave, Harris busied himself in the kitchen, bitterly disappointed that the cousin's son was departing like this.

'Want these Honey Nut Cornflakes, Rashid?' he called up the stairs. 'And this Nesquik strawberry powder?' Rashid's dietary quirks had punctuated his kitchen for the last month. Now they, like him, were to be gone and Harris feared the empty house once more.

'It's OK, Uncle. You can use up all the stuff.'

Harris darted upstairs. 'You must take something to eat for the journey, huh? Food is very expensive on the train. The things they flog from those blasted trolleys aren't actually fit for human consumption. Apart from the crisps, maybe.'

Rashid shook his head. 'I'll be fine.'

'I could make you sandwiches.'

'No, thanks.'

Harris hovered in the doorway. 'Do you have a place to stay?'

'No, I gave it up. My old boss Jerry's agreed to let us use an empty place in Whitechapel. Needs work and he can't shift it; that'll be the office. I'll live there for now.'

'I see. And the rent?'

'Very cheap. In exchange for fixing it up a bit.'

'Oh, well, that's good. Still, a shame you gave up your old flat. Never a problem parking outside.'

'Some things you have to sacrifice,' Rashid said.

Harris didn't have the heart to contradict him.

Seventeen

Not long after Rashid's departure, Harris learned that Omar was scheduled to visit London with Kamila and their daughter, Layla. Omar rang Harris to tell him they would be staying in their usual Hampstead flat, and was insistent that Harris come down and help him – the pretext being some business venture that needed attending to – as soon as possible. Harris leapt at the opportunity, eager to lend a hand in whatever way he could. For no matter what anyone said, Omar was a magnanimous and loyal friend, their friendship spanning three decades and two continents, enduring the vicissitudes of life. Or so they both believed, and to a certain extent it was true.

Omar was dressed in pyjamas, reclining on a beige leather sofa the size of a boat when Harris arrived, stroking his tufted toes through rubber Bata sandals with one free hand, while the other worked the phones or fed the fax machine that sat on the floor next to him. His hefty girth bore testimony to a lifetime of easeful consumption, yet he was a handsome man, suavely put together with a silvery mane of hair. He boomed his *salaams* and then got down to the business of complaining.

'Bloody thing. Jamming all the time now.'

'Here, let me try.' Harris was blessed with nimble fingers that did the job.

'Harris, didn't you order me the Panasonic 270, remember, the one we saw on the Tottenham Court Road?' Omar peered over half-moon spectacles, as he punched a series of numbers into a fax machine. Terrified of hackers and viruses, spies and opportunists, he refused to use a computer for business purposes. In any case, there were some documents that could only be faxed.

'It's on order,' said Harris, who had given up trying to convert him. 'Out of stock till June.'

Omar cursed softly under his breath. 'Let's redo this fax, OK? Now, where the hell was I?'

'"Thank you for your fax of 29 Feb,"' Harris read. '"Your proposition sounds interesting. I look forward to your elaborations in April. Earlier, *insh'allah*, if you can." That's as far as we got.'

The fax machine sighed and broke into melodic shudders as news of a contract for offshore cable in Karachi fluttered through the machine. Omar fumbled with the missive.

'Excellent news, Harris!' he burbled. 'Let's take a break, shall we?'

It was late afternoon and cones of light slanted across the sofa, setting the scene for English teatime, something Omar fondly recalled from his spell at Cambridge. Toast with Gentleman's Relish, home-made scones with cream and strawberry jam, plus a pot of Earl Grey tea, served with milk and sugar.

Harris laid down his pen as Omar helped himself to a large slice of cheesecake that Kamila had brought back from Marks & Spencer.

'Mmm,' he purred through a mouthful of crumbs. 'Won't you take a slice?'

Harris shook his head. 'Weight watching.' It was their little joke. 'My heart and all.'

'Aha, yes, mine's in good shape, the doctors tell me,' Omar said. 'Which is thanks to the jogging machine I use daily.'

Harris tried to visualize Omar jogging but could not.

'Now then,' Omar declared. 'Whatever must we do with this cousin of yours, Haaris-sahib? Khalid Ali, is it?'

The mention of Khalid was a shock. 'Yes, Khalid Ali. But what about him?'

'You know he's been over to Shadman, wanting to know where his money has got to. Did you not know this? Took us by surprise, I must say.'

Harris shook his head. 'I had no idea. Forgive me, I'm sorry.'

Omar was nonplussed. 'Makes no odds to me, huh. No need to be sorry. But just tell me if we should forward him anything, so he doesn't need to keep making the long journey to our place. Let us know, will you?'

The news of his relatives pestering Omar's family disturbed Harris deeply. 'Things aren't easy for me right now, Omar-bhai,' he confessed, his voice betraying his woe.

'To be frank, old man, I guessed as much,' Omar said, balancing his fingers together. He smiled sympathetically, as if he understood everything. 'What should I tell him, the next time he comes? Is there some account I should use?'

He was such a good friend, Omar, it was almost unbearable. 'I did send them a little something when I last wrote to them.'

'Is it enough?'

'Ah, well. Probably not.'

'I see, I see.' Omar licked the remaining bits of lemony filling from his fingers with surprising delicacy. He wheezed slightly: a creaky, mournful sound. The turquoise carpets that flowed throughout the flat were dusty and aggravated his asthma; or at least, he blamed them, and the skin-flint landlord, who refused to have the place cleaned properly while Omar and his family were in residence. The problem was that they were incapable of functioning without a retinue of servants to keep the place in order. Careless of what they spilled, or how often the bathroom was flooded, the luxurious Hampstead flat came to resemble a makeshift camp.

'Only the English would have carpet in their bathrooms,' Kamila had remarked when she returned from Selfridges with Layla. 'It's the cold here, I suppose. Marble is much more practical, and beautiful, of course. But, my God, he is so mean, this landlord fellow.'

If the truth were told, the flat particularly disappointed her because it was too far from Harrods. The last place they'd rented was handily located right opposite that shopping Mecca, where she'd bought the crystal chandelier that hung in spangled glory in her dining room at home.

'Uncle Harris!' Layla squealed, and dropped her pile of bags on the floor. It always took the servants back home several days to unpack after they'd been to London.

'Hello, Layla. Come sit next to me.'

'Is Alia not here?'

'Alia's in Whitechapel, actually'

'Will she not come to Pizza Express tonight with us, then?'

Harris was silent for a moment, then said, 'I'm afraid she's too busy this evening. Maybe another time.'

'We aren't going there anyway tonight, Layla,' her father informed his daughter, readjusting his pyjama cord as he watched his wife unpack her shopping conquests.

'But I wanted to try those garlic bread balls!' Layla wailed plaintively.

It was the sort of thing that meant the world to her, Harris observed. So different from his own daughter, whom he missed suddenly, in spite of their standoff.

'We'll go tomorrow, Layla, I promise,' said her mother, who was busily arranging her purchases on the glass coffee table so she could survey them all. She'd bought the latest pressure cooker, a deep-fat fryer and a cordless kettle.

'Not another one!' her husband protested.

'No, a different one. This is the Braun model, that boils very fast,' Kamila explained patiently. 'Actually, I haven't bought so much this time, Omar. It just seems a lot with the packaging. Oh, you know, I couldn't see those saucepans Pinky wanted,' she said, referring to her daughter-in-law. Then she said to Harris, 'People always ask us to bring back so much, and we have to pay such exorbitant excess baggage fees these days. It's criminal. I suppose you have the same dilemma, when you visit the village and everybody wants you to bring things over from England.'

'It's so sad when people in the villages just want these things so badly, isn't it?' Layla suddenly piped up.

'What's so sad, darling?' her mother said, as she bit off the plastic tag from a satin scarf she had bought for herself.

'As though it's the most important thing in life, you know,

having these consumer goods, when it isn't at all, is it?' the girl babbled, swivelling her glance at her father, as her point foundered.

Omar smiled indulgently at his daughter and she took this as a cue to sit next to him on the sofa, sinking into the sausage-like cushioning of his extended arm. Harris was struck by the startling resemblance between father and daughter as they sat beside one another, Omar's curly lashes and liquid camel eyes resonating eloquently in his plump, pretty daughter.

'I do try to bring things that my cousins in the village really want, or need, but I don't always manage it,' Harris reflected. 'Of course there's no point in bringing kettles and electrical appliances and so forth because the electricity is terribly unreliable, all this load-shedding.'

'Yes, well, it is hard. Life is very difficult in the rural areas,' Kamila mused. She delved into a Selfridges bag and pulled out a stack of V-neck sweaters she had bought for her husband. 'Winter evenings can be cold in Lahore, you know, Harris.'

'I know,' he agreed.

'See if you like these,' she said to her husband. 'If not, I have the receipt to return them.'

Omar glanced at them for a split second. 'I like them,' he said. 'But tell me, my darling, how many did you actually buy?'

'You need them all. There are seven in total.'

'Seven!'

'Each day of the week, Omar.'

'Give one to Harris. He's got holes in the elbows of his and no wife to darn them.'

'Not yet, Harris, but let's not jump the gun,' Kamila said. 'So we heard about your date with the lovely Dr Farrah,' she said, her hooded brown eyes flashing with intrigue. 'I'm glad you two got together at last.'

'Aha! So the word got round, did it?'

'Did you think you could keep it a secret?' Kamila gave an arch smile. 'But tell us. How are things with her? Did you find you have a great deal in common?'

'More than I imagined,' Harris said, though he did not elaborate.

'Why don't you call her from here, Harris? Invite her over. We've not seen her in ages.' Kamila handed him the phone. 'You have her telephone number, don't you? Here.'

Dr Farrah's phone rang for an agonizingly long time.

'You'll never believe it, but I'm here with Omar and Kamila!' Harris said, when she answered. 'I'm in London, so I thought I'd look you up.'

'Oh, I see,' she said. She sounded chilly, almost brusque. 'That's nice of you.'

'Are you . . . Is somebody there with you?' Harris enquired.

'Is it OK?' mouthed Kamila. Harris nodded vigorously.

'No, no,' Farrah said quickly. 'I'm alone.'

For a few minutes Harris struggled to redeem the conversation with chit-chat about the weather and random gossip he had heard from Lahore, but her reserve could not be broken down. There was a pause, during which Omar grew impatient and shouted, 'Tell her just to come! Come join us in Leicester Square! We'll send for a taxi to bring her!'

'Did you hear that?' Harris said to Farrah.

'Yes. I'm sorry, but I really can't, Harris.'

'Ah, OK, I see. That's a shame. Could we arrange something for another time?' he asked, turning away from his eager hosts. His heart banged, fearful of what was wrong.

'Yes, let's do that,' Farrah replied in a brittle voice. Another suitor must have put himself forward. Suddenly the thought of losing her made Harris despair.

'How would you feel about a trip to Greenwich Park? I'm right in thinking it's close to your home, am I not?'

'Yes, it's not too far,' she replied, softening.

'We could have lunch there, if you'd like. Would tomorrow suit you?'

The suggestion seemed to thaw her.

'It would, yes,' she replied.

'Good. Then let's meet outside the National Maritime Museum café, shall we?'

'OK, around 11 a.m.?' she suggested, and hung up the phone when he agreed.

'So why not bring her along tonight?' Omar said, puzzled that their extended invitation to her had not been taken up. 'We're going to some ice-cream parlour in Leicester Square – what is it, Layla?'

'Ben and Jerry's. For chocolate-brownie-cheesecake ice cream,' said his daughter, licking her Boots No. 7 cherry lips. 'Have you tried it, Uncle Harris?'

'No, though it sounds very nice,' said Harris tactfully. 'But I think Dr Farrah wants it to be, you know, just the two of us.'

Kamila beamed with satisfaction. 'You see? I knew she was good news. Aren't I always right in these matters?' she crowed, and then disappeared into the bedroom for a much-needed rest.

Layla announced she was going to take a long bath to soothe her aching limbs before going out for dinner.

Omar closed his camel eyes for a moment; it was a strategy, like pulling down the shutters, when he wished to banish the outside world from his ruminations. Harris waited patiently for him to rejoin the world.

'So, how's tricks, old fellow?' Omar said, when he opened them again.

'Not great, to be honest. I'm at a bit of loose end, tell you the truth, work-wise. The shop's a dead end.'

Omar was silent, waiting. Then Harris girded up his courage. 'Omar, I can't help thinking it's time we got some of these big ideas going, before we get too old and decrepit. We're engineers, aren't we? We've got the skills to make a difference in our country.'

Omar remembered Harris's thwarted dream of setting up a megawatt power plant to supply the rural areas around Sahiwal. It was their last adventure in business philanthropy, which had gone badly wrong, and he was loath to repeat it. He delved an index finger into a waxy ear, rotating it rhythmically.

'It's a nice idea, Haaris-sahib, doing good and all, but I'm not sure. It's a crazy, unstable time. Nothing's easy any more, not like it used to be.'

Harris shifted uneasily. 'The thing is, I'm in a bit of a bind. I need a spot of work, to keep me going. I'm game for anything. My debts are like rising waters, Omar-bhai. I'm drowning.'

Omar's untamed eyebrows arched high into his brow. 'Oh, my God,' he exclaimed, 'I had no idea things were so bad. Why didn't you say?'

'I'm saying now, am I not?'

Omar stroked his pudgy knuckles, deep in thought. 'There *is* some work I need doing. I've something in the pipeline and you could help me with that.'

His kindly, conspiratorial tone made Harris want to weep with relief. It was not the first time in his life that Omar had come to the rescue.

'Tell me, Omar, what is it?'

'An exciting opportunity has just arisen in fact,' Omar began, languidly stretching out on the boat-sized sofa. 'We've been looking into acquiring suitable land near Shorkot for a power-generation facility—'

A shriek from the bathroom interrupted him.

'Yes, go on,' Harris urged. 'Something similar to our last project?'

'No, no, this would be on a bigger scale – more lucrative for us, though the rural community would also benefit, in the long run.'

'Papa, we have no hot water!'

It was Layla, who had dipped herself into a tepid bath. Her father shouted to her to be patient, that the hot water would come presently.

'It won't come! I've tried. And I want the bath now, as we're going out soon!' came back the appeal.

Omar sighed and went to switch on the immersion heater. 'See, Harris, my engineering prowess knows no bounds.' He smiled as he settled himself back down. 'We're proposing to form a company to be named Shorkot Power. The share capital of the company is going to be twenty five crores, to be contributed by ten to twenty persons within our circle, and the balance will be raised through public subscription.'

'*Acha*, and what would be my role in all this?'

'Simple. What is required is really very easy from your side,' Omar went on. 'You simply raise share capital, through these twenty or so people we know. Friends, people we trust. Just a fax and computer, that's all you need.'

'Really?'

'You stand to make a tidy sum.'

The words, so casually uttered, hung temptingly in the air.

'You're so good at this type of thing – it'd be of great help to us to have someone on the ground in the UK. Come, Haaris-sahib, tell me what you think?'

Harris's heart thudded against his ribcage. 'Is it definitely going ahead, then?'

Omar's face clouded. 'Would I have asked you if it wasn't?' Like the mercurial English weather, his mien turned from sunny to overcast in an instant.

'I was just checking, Omar-bhai,' Harris said, abashed. 'Keep your hair on.'

'That's good, because you're my closest friend here and I could do with your help.' The storm clouds rolled back to reveal a hint of a smile. 'So will you do it?'

'Of course I'll do it.' Harris exclaimed. 'Why not?'

Kamila emerged from her room and began to make tea in the kitchen.

'Isn't it beautiful?' she said as she arranged a new stainless-steel tea set before the men. 'Should I not get one for your sister – I'm just wondering what to bring her and she did complain hers is really just so *battered* now.'

Omar wasn't tuned in to his wife, so Harris replied on his behalf.

'Oh, you should. She'd love it, I'm sure.'

'By the way, I've made up the bed for you in the guest room, Harris. You'll stay the night, won't you?'

'Thank you, yes, that's very kind.' But Kamila had already disappeared back into the bedroom to prepare her face for an evening on the town.

As he stirred the tea, Omar said to Harris, 'In the meantime, should I send something to this cousin of yours? A regular allowance?'

Harris was overwhelmed. 'Omar, you're a dear friend. How can I ask such a thing of you?'

'Nonsense,' he said, and smoothed out an imaginary wrinkle in his cuff. 'Save the chap these long bus journeys over to Shadman, huh?'

'I don't know what to say.'

'Say nothing, Harris,' He dabbed his forehead. 'I'll take care of it. Just come on board, huh? Join hands with me in this enterprise, will you?'

Eighteen

When Harris spotted her standing uncertainly amid a swarm of tourists beside a rubbish-strewn table, he instantly regretted the choice of rendezvous spot. He had suggested they meet outside the café, before touring the park and grounds around the National Maritime Museum, not guessing it might be quite so teeming and unkempt.

'Harris,' she said, holding her hands out to greet him. 'How nice to see you again.'

'You too,' he replied, glancing around at the half-eaten baguettes and plastic cups that lay scattered upon the tables. 'I'm sorry. This isn't the nicest place for you to be waiting. Please forgive me for being late.'

She gave her tinkling laugh, dismissing the apology. 'It's fine, Harris, honestly.'

He noticed she was dressed optimistically for the weather, in a woefully thin jacket that had seen better days, and open sandals that revealed her crimson-painted toenails. Her hair was pulled into an elegant French pleat, and she touched it now and again, to check that it was secure. He found himself longing to embrace her properly, yet the memory of her brittle voice on the phone resurfaced and he pushed the longing aside.

'Come, Farrah,' he said. 'Let's get some coffee inside, shall we? Or would you prefer tea?'

It was a little too early for lunch, but the smells of roasting meat and the clatter of cooks behind the scenes made Dr Farrah suggest that they return after a walk around the park. The Sunday lunch menu tempted them both.

'Are you sure?' Harris said uncertainly, sneaking a look at her unsuitable footwear.

'Why not? The jonquils are out and we'll get a beautiful view if we make it to the top of the hill.'

'If? Why should we not make it?' Harris smiled. 'Don't tell me we're past it yet, are we?'

She giggled, and he relaxed a little, feeling that he wasn't completely out of the running after all.

'Have you visited your daughter this time?'

'No, but I may well drop in on her.'

'You aren't staying with her, then?' She seemed surprised.

'There isn't really room for me, unless of course I want to bed down in the living room, but that's not ideal.'

'Of course not, I see,' she said, looking at her feet. 'I'd love to meet her.'

'Yes, well, let's see,' he said, wondering how he'd explain Farrah to Alia.

The sun was slowly burning through the clouds, and the air smelled warm and earthy. They walked up an avenue of trees that led to the Royal Observatory at the top of the hill, pausing from time to time while Harris regained his breath. Dr Farrah expressed concern and asked him if he was all right.

'I'm fine. Really. Just admiring the view. Such beautiful buildings,' he said, surveying the serene, elegant lines of the Old Royal Naval college. 'I wonder who is the architect? Do you know?'

'Sir Christopher Wren, I believe. Plus others. Hawksmoor, I seem to remember may have worked upon it, possibly later, though I may be wrong. Let's check.'

When they reached the top, they paused in a paved area outside the Observatory to take in the view of the Millennium Dome. There was the Isle of Dogs, reined in by the bend in the river, a curved strip of silvery ribbon. A pall of mist hung over the glass and steel towers of the City and Docklands. The white light on top of Canary Wharf winked in benign approval of the lesser buildings stacked up around it. Harris turned when he heard her calling his name and saw she was outside the gatehouse to the Observatory. She had removed her spectacles to read a notice about its history.

'Harris, you must see this. This is the home of Greenwich Mean Time, did you know? The Royal Observatory.'

'Yes, of course,' he said, feeling worried that she was about to test him with further comments, questions or enquiries. *I'm not as culturally knowledgeable as she is,* he reflected. *An upstart, a pretender. That's what she'll think.*

'It's the official starting point for each new day, year and millennium. Right here,' she went on, oblivious to his anxiety. 'It says: "Founded in 1675 by Charles II, by international decree, the official starting point for each new day . . ."'

Perhaps her interest in me is purely cerebral, he thought. *An intellectual type of companion, someone to accompany her on cultural trips. Well,* he consoled himself, *there are worse things.*

'"Sir Christopher Wren's original building houses London's only public camera obscura."'

'Really?' he said, feeling at sea.

'Did you know that he designed this building?'

'I thought you said it was this Hawksmoor fellow.'

'Yes, him also. But according to this, Wren designed all the original plans.'

'Is that so?'

'Shall we go see it?'

'Of course! But tell me – see what exactly?'

'The camera obscura! Are you not listening?'

Before he could say another word, she had ushered him over to the compact building where the camera was housed and into a small dark chamber, sealed off from the outside by a curtain. Inside the room, a panning mechanism that travelled over a table in an arc produced a phantom rendition of London. Together they moved slowly round the table, piecing together ethereal outlines of the Thames, the Old Royal Naval College, a copse of trees, a scrap of cloud.

'Should we go – I mean, if you'd like, we could see something else?'

'Whatever you wish. I'm easy,' said Farrah.

So they went outside. Then Harris noticed the Meridian Line.

'I read about this when I was a boy,' he exclaimed, excited.

'Oh yes, what's that?' Farrah enquired.

Harris put one foot on either side of the line. 'I'm so happy we came here. I've always wanted to do this. Farrah, we are at the centre of world time and space!' he cried ecstatically.

'Whatever are you doing?' she said.

'Look! I have one foot in the eastern hemisphere and one in the west – at the same time. This is us, Farrah, isn't it? Eastern Westerners.'

She looked at him intently. 'You're right,' she said. 'We are.'

Three Canadians broke away from the cohesion of their tour group for a moment to observe Harris's demonstration; one even snapped a photo of him before the guide herded them back into the moving blur of plastic macs in his charge.

'Have a go, Farrah. Go on,' he urged.

She gingerly stepped over the line, a foot on either side as he instructed, while he steadied her with his hands.

'Thank you. What a true gentleman you are,' she said, as she found her balance.

She blinked a little and he noticed a tear roll down her left cheek, making a tiny channel in her face powder and revealing the shadow of an age spot. He wondered if it was just the chilly wind, or something more.

'Farrah?'

She wiped her eye and delicately dabbed her nose. 'Yes?'

'Is it . . . are you – all right?'

'I'm fine,' she said.

'Is anything wrong?'

She looked down for a moment. 'There's something I ought to tell you,' she began.

'I could tell something was wrong when I spoke to you yesterday. What is it?' he pressed her. 'Please say. Is it a question of another more suitable companion waiting in the wings?' He immediately regretted the theatrical metaphor. Her laughing made him feel relieved and silly at once. *Why jump the gun? Let her say what she has to say, you idiot,* he chided himself. *Don't pre-empt things always.*

'Not at all,' she said. 'I'm fond of you, Harris.'

This was a thrilling shock. He'd had no idea. He waited for more delicious revelations.

'It's Idrees.'

Relief coursed through him, loosening the knot in his stomach. If his only rival was her dead husband, he was almost home and dry.

'I understand. No, really, I do. But, Allah bless his soul, he is in paradise and we are here on earth, and I am sure he would approve of this, this . . . however you wish to describe it, our friendship. It's barely a liaison, yet, but aren't we . . .'

Farrah looked pained. Had he overstepped the mark?

'It's not that,' she said.

'Then what exactly? Please tell me.'

'It's none of my concern, really. None at all. I keep saying to myself, what you do with Omar is your business.' She paused briefly, then, seeing Harris's stricken face, said, 'I think I'd better go home.'

'Farrah – whatever is it?'

'Forgive me. I'm being so silly, aren't I?'

'Not at all. But at least let me drive you back.'

Two hours, three pots of tea and a round of crumpets later, Dr Farrah and Harris were sitting opposite one another on her twin sofas, with a cardboard box opened on the coffee table that separated them. The box contained an accumulation of Idrees's personal effects collected during his lifetime and devotedly squirrelled away by his wife. There were newspaper cuttings and notices of awards, a cartoon caricature drawn by a colleague, certificates and photos, tissue-thin airmail letters, an old leather wallet, a wristwatch, a packet of Wilkinson razor blades and a small brass letter opener. It did not amount to much, yet to Farrah it was everything. At last, she took out a manila envelope and handed it to Harris. Inside was a document that said: 'Certified Copy of an Entry Pursuant to the Births and Deaths Registration Act 1953'.

'I'm not sure why I'm showing you all this,' she said. 'I suppose it still feels so unreal to me, that's all.'

The baldly stated facts were hard for Harris to grasp, so impersonal and incontrovertible were they. It took him a few minutes to process what was written in the entry under Cause of Death.

'Idrees took an overdose? He killed himself?'

Farrah nodded. 'At first we thought it was an accident – he'd been on medication for various things, as well as antidepressants. But then, when the toxicologist's report came back . . .'

'I had no idea.'

'The boys and I decided we wouldn't tell people. So I've kept quiet about it. It's too humiliating. It tarnishes everything. I want to preserve the best memories of him.'

'Oh, Farrah. How terrible for you.'

'He'd been through so much, losing his last job.'

'How dreadful.'

'He was struggling to hold on to his position there. They were making cuts at the firm, you see, and many employees were being made redundant. It had been a huge adjustment coming here from home but we'd all settled in well, and he didn't want to go back to Pakistan and lose face.'

'Lose face about what, Farrah?' Harris asked, glancing at the precious keepsakes from her late husband's life.

'When we visited Lahore, you remember I told you – the last holiday we ever had together in Pakistan, the two of us? We stayed with Omar and Kamila. It was all very nice, as you can imagine. Omar was treating us to all this hospitality, trips to the best restaurants in town, the club for cocktails by the pool. You know how he is, Harris, don't you?'

'Oh yes, I do.' Harris nodded.

'Omar promised my husband things that he never should have,' she went on. 'but he wanted something in exchange. There was nothing he would not do for Idrees, but always with strings attached. Or at least, this was how Idrees put it to me. He wouldn't go into it. Idrees was old-fashioned, Harris, you see, he was of that generation of men who would lay down their lives to protect their wives from certain things. He wanted to shield me. The company he worked for manufactured precision medical instruments, and they made a specially restricted component that Omar wanted, I don't even know for sure what it was. Anyway, after we got back to London, Idrees struggled with what Omar was asking him to do. He was afraid of losing his job, but Omar kept saying it would all be fine. He wouldn't tell me exactly what it was about. Went to mosque more than usual – he never used to go that often, you know. He wasn't like you, Harris, in that way. Not a devout man, but he was always the kindest, nicest, most . . . I loved him so much, so very much. He was a good man.'

Harris laid his hand gently over hers as she pressed her fingers into the corners of her brimming eyes.

'I'm sorry,' she said, when she had regained her composure.
'Don't be. Please, you mustn't bottle this up. Go on.'

'Where was I? Oh yes. He went for long walks down by
the river, at all times of the day and night. He stopped going
to work, as though he was afraid of something there. The
office was constantly calling him because he was taking more
and more time off. It started with a day here and there, and
then it became weeks. He refused to go to the GP for a sick
note. By this time, his health was in a terrible state. I begged
him to do it, but he wouldn't. There were so many long phone
calls to Lahore and the bills were enormous. After a while, he
hardly dared to open them. Omar would call him in the middle
of the night, hounding him – "Have you done it yet? Can
you do this thing for me? We have this contract and we've
promised these things, and if you don't deliver now, we'll lose
all the money." It was awful. And you know what was unbe-
lievable? In the middle of it all, Kamila would call me and chat
about her daughter's marriage prospects, complain about the
cost of fees for their son at Vassar College in America. She'd
go on about all these things and not a single mention of this
other business, as though nothing was happening. We were all
just friends, and it is friendship above all things, isn't it? This
was the credo.'

Harris's mouth was dry. He took a sip of cold tea. 'And so
what did he do – Idrees, I mean?'

'He did nothing. Omar kept pestering, but he refused to
supply the component. By this time it was too late, though,
because someone in the company was suspicious of him and
he was placed under an internal investigation.'

'For what?'

'They claimed unprofessional conduct, whatever that means. The trouble was, he'd become erratic, less reliable, they said. But Idrees was the most careful, meticulous man I have ever known.'

'They can't just do that – investigate an innocent man.'

'Harris, you have no idea. They can do what they want, actually. Anyway, they couldn't find anything amiss with his professional conduct, but he was made to feel worse than guilty. You see, if you are accused, people think, "Well, he must have been up to something, mustn't he?" He was tarred, ostracized. So they accepted his resignation. He felt it was the only honourable thing he could do. And after that, he was no longer himself. I hardly knew him. He wouldn't go out. We weren't getting any more calls from Omar in the middle of the night – or any other time, for that matter – and all his promises about a contract in Dubai came to nothing. He was utterly furious with Idrees for not doing his bidding. Nobody crosses him or his family, you see. Haven't you noticed?'

She stood up and began to clear the tea tray.

'Let me do that,' Harris intervened.

'We were up to here in debt,' she went on, tapping her neck to convey the extent of their troubles. 'He left without collecting redundancy or pension. Oh, I know, we may not look like paupers but don't be fooled. The last few years have been such a struggle. My teaching has kept me going. Believe me, Harris, I'm not complaining. But as for making ends meet, well . . . I'm not managing very well at all. So now I've put the house on the market and everything you see in it is also up for sale.'

'No, Farrah. This is terrible. Does Omar know about this?'

She shook her head. 'He owed Idrees an awful lot of money from a contract in Kuwait. Omar made a fortune, but after Saddam invaded – the first Gulf War – the operation fell apart and he never stumped up what he owed us. I wrote to him but he's never written back.' She started methodically replacing Idrees's things into the cardboard box, arranging and rearranging each item so that they all fitted perfectly inside. 'I spoke to Kamila last week and she said we must all meet for tea in some fancy hotel she likes in the West End. I've not called her back, but I suppose I will see them at some point.'

'Oh no, this is awful. What will you do now, do you think, if you have to move?'

'I'm not sure. I keep thinking I should go back to my family in Lahore – what's left of it. My sister's unmarried and she's begged me to come live with her.' She thought of Naela's shrill entreaties. 'Oh, you know how it is, Harris. There are the usual aunties and cousins and God knows who around, but somehow it doesn't appeal. It's not my scene, not any more. Never was, really. I like England. I really do.'

Harris felt a glimmer of hope. 'Well, this is your home now.' He scrutinized her to see if she associated him with that notion.

Farrah gave a short laugh that could have been a sob. 'Is it? I wish I were certain. It certainly was home, for a while. We had a good life here, Idrees and me, and the boys. But that time's gone. It'll never come again.'

By now it was dark outside. She switched on the solid brass standard lamp they had shipped all the way from Lahore to London, soon to be sold along with everything else. An old man walking his dog paused to light a cigarette, staring at the two of them as he did so, framed in the lamp lit window. *He assumes we're a couple,* Harris thought, as he caught the man's eye. Dr Farrah went to close the curtains to shut out the prying eyes of the world for a little longer.

'Are you working for Omar, Harris? Is that why you came down to see him? Please tell me,' she pressed him.

'Farrah, I'm in a bind. I've not much income at the moment and there are various demands from other corners of the earth.'

Dr Farrah was dismayed. 'I had no idea you were in such trouble. Why didn't you say?'

Harris hesitated, then admitted, 'I was hoping to sort it out and I didn't want to put you off.'

'I'm not like that,' she said evenly. 'Not at all. But what are you going to do?'

'Think I haven't tried everything, Farrah? Omar's my last hope.'

She looked at him seriously. 'Surely not.'

'If I don't take up Omar's offer, what on earth can I do?'

'I'd like us to have a chance, Harris.'

Neither of them mentioned Idrees, though his spectral presence hovered. But she had made her position clear. If he were to pursue a relationship with her, he must relinquish the opportunity Omar had offered him. *An impossible choice,* he thought, wondering how he might negotiate it.

'We'll find a way,' she implored him. 'Just you see.'

'Oh, Farrah, can we?'

He wondered anxiously how he could extract himself from Omar's proposal now without telling him what he'd learned about Idrees. He did not know which he feared most: losing Farrah or losing his chance to save himself and his family.

'Who cares what people say? Just please say no to Omar. No matter what he has offered you.' She fixed him with an imploring gaze he found hard to resist.

It was getting late and Harris felt that it was time to leave.

'There's a bed in the spare room. I always keep it made up in case the boys come visit,' Farrah said.

'Ah, I see.'

She saw she'd frightened him. 'Oh, you needn't worry. They won't, not tonight. Both of them are miles away.'

'Did you tell them?'

'What is there to tell?' she said, laughing.

They went upstairs, but Harris stopped on the landing. 'Oh dear. I don't have my shaving kit with me. Or my pyjamas,' he said in despair.

'Don't worry. I have some spare things still, if you'd like.'

'Are you sure?'

'Yes,' she said, pulling open a heavy mahogany drawer and releasing a waft of mothballs. She took out a folded paisley dressing gown and an unopened set of flannelette pyjamas and laid them on the bed in her guest room.

'You'll find a fresh shaving kit on the second shelf in the bathroom,' she called to him, then went downstairs to switch out the lamps in the living room.

And so that was how it began, the love affair. Staying in Dr Farrah's guest room that first night in her house and eventually, when the guest bed was sold, sharing hers.

Nineteen

Shortly after Harris's return to the north, he received word from Omar that progress had been made on Shorkot Power and that they were now in the process of acquiring suitable land in the area. For days, he had been worrying about how he might fine-tune his role in the project, with Farrah's injunction in mind. But the precipitous news from abroad sent a frisson of nervous excitement through him and galvanized him to get on with the work immediately. He set up a supply company in his living room, installing his computer and fax machine in the alcove, and a portable shredder beneath his desk. Paperwork was held in a series of wire baskets, then filed in an expandable cardboard file. A number of faxes on the subject of plant procurement were dispatched to companies in Norway and Sweden, Germany and Russia. In due course, a favourable quotation came back from the Norwegians and Harris was spurred on. Soon after that, he received an encouraging response from a high-end British manufacturer, at which point he dashed off a letter to a potential investor in Karachi, a mutual college pal, enquiring if he might be interested in investing in the power-generation game. A warm message came back from the man, who was mildly boastful about his recent achievements in the financial sector, but ultimately non-committal.

Harris's spirits plunged. Was private power generation not merely a viable but also a good cause in their home country? he wrote back indignantly. The friend did not reply. It was worse than shopkeeping, he reflected bitterly one afternoon, as the rain hammered down outside. At least with the shop, you could pull down its metal shutters at the end of the day and enjoy a decent night's sleep.

So let's see, he told himself as he made his way to the mosque for evening prayers, fighting to keep his umbrella braced against the wind. *See what Omar comes up with before I take this damned thing any further.*

In the meantime, he maintained a romantic stream of communication with Dr Farrah, via email and phone, hoping that she wouldn't ask him too many awkward questions about what he was up to. He longed to spend more time with her yet he felt beholden to Omar, and there was the pressure to nail procurement contracts so that he would at last be paid for his work, which was on a commission basis. He pushed harder, working round the clock, freighted with guilt about the cousins in the village. Their visitor visas had arrived, apparently, thanks to his application at the embassy in Islamabad the previous summer. It was still a pipe dream, yet they clung to it, hoping that somehow the Uncle would conjure up the means to establish them in England. He would surely not let them down.

Harris began driving down to Greenwich to see Dr Farrah as often as he could manage. The route to her house became so familiar that it unfolded magically inside him, without his needing to consult the *A–Z*.

It wasn't long before he discovered that one of the most agreeable things about spending time with her was the enjoyable sensation, the blissful relief, of losing himself in her world. Being with her suspended the burden of his own troubles, made him weightless, almost. During his visits he was able to live in the moment, without a crippling fear of the future or dread of the afterlife. In her presence, his demeanour slackened, relaxed, and he felt more at home with her than he had imagined possible. She seemed more attractive each time he visited. Her hair had been styled into a bob and tinted with coppery highlights by a hairdresser in Greenwich. The chain-suspended spectacles were gone. Her wardrobe was unchanged, but in advance of his visits she tried things on in different combinations to make the most of what she had, delving into her dusty jewellery box and scarf drawer. Her rounded cheekbones were dusted with peachy-pink blusher, her soft brown eyes lined with kohl.

Harris noticed her effort and he approved. For his part, he relished the charade of playing her husband, and even though his skills in that department were a tad rusty, he demonstrated an eagerness to brush them up. He was warmed by her attentiveness, her ability to listen to him with intensity, a delicious novelty after years of being alone. What could be nicer than having whisky and ginger ale served to him in polished crystal tumblers, ice cubes chinking in the amber fizz? He couldn't deny that he loved the routine of regular meals and someone to share them with.

Even so, he would never stay for more than a few days, anxious not to miss an important fax or phone call from Pakistan that might require immediate attention. Farrah was quite happy with this arrangement; even when he was gone for more than a week, she enjoyed the opportunity to pen him emails and chat on the phone late at night, like lovelorn teenagers. She understood that he had to keep an eye on his old shop, and he seemed to have an everlasting list of running repairs on his house that took up a great deal of his time.

Yet it was not long before this bifurcated existence began to take its toll upon him. The north–south commute, the contrary tugs of business and romantic love. Opportunities with investors were being missed and faxes from power-plant suppliers were going astray. Harris was always a little behind with follow-up calls to potential investors and Omar soon got wind of it in Lahore. He began to ring him more frequently, his irritation increasing exponentially each time he reached voicemail, because Harris was at the mosque, or the takeaway, or down in London on business. Night after night, he badgered his friend. Why were things not moving forward more quickly? Where were the quotations? Which investors were in the running? Deprived of sleep, Harris's powers of judgement were frayed, so that he began to wonder what on earth was going wrong. He'd sent out letters – the copies were in the file – and he'd made some approaches to a circle of investors in Pakistan. He'd kept things ticking over, hadn't he, when Omar was tied up on the other side of the world? Keeping things ticking over, Omar told him, is not how you get power-generation projects to become more than a bloody fantasy. He was baffled, genuinely stumped. He'd offered his friend a chance to make some real money and Harris was not stepping up.

'Are you on board, Harris old chap, or bloody well not?' Omar wheezed his peevish impatience down the phone line.

'Of course I am. What d'you take me for? Now may I go back to bed, please?'

Then Omar relented and let Harris get back to the comfort of his bed, though he didn't honestly see why this was necessary, for in his world deals were struck across time zones and continents, regardless of day or night.

The next time he visited Dr Farrah, it was pleasantly mild in London and he sat in her conservatory, basking in the tepid sunshine while she filled him in on the news since his last visit. Little did she know that he'd been down to the city one day without alerting her, secretly attending a meeting with a representative of a Swedish power-generation company to discuss possible credit terms on a diesel generator sale. The meeting had gone swimmingly and he had dashed a progress report back to Omar, which seemed to placate him for the time being.

He tried not to think about it now as Farrah chatted away, and found himself surveying her verdant lawn, the pretty rockery that Idrees had landscaped with his own bare hands, lugging each rock into position before filling the crevices with alpine miniatures: saxifrage, purple alyssum, gentian, toadflax. The garden was bursting back to life after the long winter, even though it was still cold at night. Tall, feathery pampas grass grew in the front garden and clumps of scarlet tulips were blooming in the back. At the height of the summer, Idrees's dahlias had been his pride and joy, Farrah said, tight pom-poms of luminescent colour that glowed at dusk. It troubled him that she would soon be leaving her husband's horticultural

legacy behind, but he kept quiet, feeling he was in no position to question her course of action.

He strode into the middle of the lawn and bent down to
pull out a sprig of groundsel that came out of the damp earth
satisfyingly intact, its spray of fine roots flecked with soil.
Lurking in the back of his mind was the knowledge that Omar
had treated loyal Idrees so dreadfully and he wrestled with his
conscience about what he should do. He wanted Farrah: he
could not give her up, even if working for Omar was tanta-
mount to betrayal. Emboldened, he tackled a clump of nettles
that threatened to engulf the rose bushes. He'd come clean on
this visit, he thought to himself, as he admired Idrees's planting.
Farrah ambled over to join him, pointing out the lovely 'Blue
Moon' and 'Peace' varieties.

'Really?' he said, looking up. Surely she'd understand his
position, how squeezed he was, and forgive him? 'I always
wanted a blue rose in my garden.'

'Not blue really at all, but more a pale mauve,' she mused.
'Still, very beautiful.'

'The lawn needs mowing,' he said. 'Would you like me to
do it?'

'Oh, it can wait, can't it? I was wondering, though, if you'd
be up for a shopping trip?'

'Why not?' he answered, relieved at the prospect of
distraction.

A brand-new department store had recently opened in Canary
Wharf and Farrah was keen to see it. Just to browse.

'You could simply let your house, you know, rather than
sell it,' Harris said to her as he negotiated the tight bends in

the underground car park beneath the store. The cement floors were pungent with newness and treacherously slippery.

Farrah was not convinced. 'I'd prefer to sell, then probably just rent a small flat here, and visit Pakistan once or twice a year.' She paused. 'Or maybe not. I'm not a big fan of air travel these days, all those long queues, and this wretched security business – taking your shoes off, undoing your belt. It's madness.'

Harris was perturbed at the idea of her moving. 'You'll have no permanent home if you sell. Doesn't that bother you?'

She reflected for a moment. It did bother her, a little, now that she was falling in love with this man, but she was determined not to show him. She liked the independence the house provided, even if she needed to downsize.

'Oh, I'm not bothered about these categories, Harris.' She shrugged. 'Home, away. East, West. Civilized, barbaric. What do they really mean?'

'I don't know,' he said, sighing.

They had reached the department store and Farrah hesitated by a train of trolleys.

'We don't need one, really, do we? We're just looking,' she said.

'You said you wanted to get some things, though.'

'Just essentials, groceries maybe,' she said. 'I can manage with a basket.'

Suddenly, he was gripped with the urge to buy her something unessential – some lovely outfit, a smart piece of jewellery. A gold bangle far beyond his means had caught his eye in a jeweller's on the high street near her house. The demands on his dwindling funds were already beyond his control, until that blighter Nawaz paid him back, or he won the football pools or the National bloody Lottery. Fat chance. The fearsome thought of his precarious finances put a damper upon everything.

She saw a flicker of worry across his face. 'I honestly don't need much these days,' she said.

'What did you say?'

'I don't need much any more. I mean, we don't have to buy anything. I'm happy just to browse.'

'Nonsense!' Harris declared. He wouldn't let these foolish money fears spoil the mood. 'You choose something, anything you like, a nice suit—'

'A *suit*?'

'I'll pay for it on the plastic card for you.'

She burst out laughing, then stopped when she saw he was hurt. 'Truly, Harris, I don't want anything like that in my wardrobe. My suit-wearing days are over.'

When she saw how crestfallen he was, she added, 'I haven't been as happy as this for ages. I honestly don't need you to spend money on me.'

He glowed with pleasure. Then, arm in arm, they glided into the warm air of the gleaming store, just looking.

Lunchtime was fast approaching at Pret A Manger, and Alia found herself struggling to bisect the Baguette of the Month: crayfish with a light yoghurt dressing. The knife slithered between her plastic-gloved fingers as she sawed diagonally through the resistant crust. *Dissection was always my downfall,* she decided, fleetingly nostalgic for her medical-school life. It had been that first term of cadavers, slicing open a skull, that had made her seriously wonder if she could handle it. It wasn't the smell, which seemed to bother some people, so much as the realization that we're all reduced, in the end, to the sum of our anatomical elements, deconstructed upon the slab.

She had found the job at the sandwich chain when she had returned to London from her father's house and realized that the temp agency was not going to be very forthcoming with work. For days she rose around lunchtime, rarely venturing out of her oldest tracksuit pants, wondering what she should do, until finally she could stand the torpor no longer, got dressed properly and walked west into the City. The streets were teeming with people heading purposefully to work or college: going somewhere, doing something. She was in limbo and that would have to change. Oliver said so, and so did his mother. And his father. They kept telling her she'd have to make up her mind one way or another, and that Colin would help her with the retakes; he knew the Dean, he'd help with the paperwork. They would all help her. They were like a chorus, urging her on. But did she need help, really? It was as if they'd flowed into a vacuum in her life that had opened up now that she wasn't a student. Sometimes it felt as if they wanted to remould her in their own image, set her back on the right track. Yet something made her withhold.

One afternoon when she had found herself sitting on the steps of St Botolph's Church, listening to the bells chime, she was galvanized into finding a new job. It wasn't exactly a Dick Whittington-style epiphany, but it was close. She realized she needed a proper job. Something to sustain herself until she reapplied for college to study something different, something new, possibly at the same place, possibly in another town. She couldn't depend on her father for support, and her mother was on her own trajectory, miles and miles away. The sensation of aloneness was dizzying, yet oddly liberating too.

Something was tickling her nose but she dared not scratch it, because the Quality Trainer was hovering behind her, ready to pounce if he spotted any contravention of Health and Safety regulations. She had spent the last three days prepping the Special of the Week, the caesar club, and today she would graduate to counter service.

At midday, she began serving the great flock of office workers swooping through the doors at lunchtime like voracious gannets, picking over the plastic-windowed packages with intense concentration. They were a stressed crowd, signalling just how harried and important they were by continually glancing at their watches. Their busy-ness annoyed Alia; the smug tightness of their schedules grated on her. But she had been drilled by her Quality Trainer to be perky and upbeat as she took their money in exchange for sandwiches and vegetable crisps, lattes and cups of soup. The blurb about the company had seemed almost appealing, claiming that it was a hip and cosmopolitan place to work, with twice-yearly massive parties. The job more than kept her going – it prevented her from sinking into bed and hiding from the world. It bought her a little time, away from everybody's glare, to think about what it was she really wanted to do with her life.

A City gent deliberated at the counter between a packet of nuts and a brownie. He quizzed her about the differential between a Tall, which was small, and a Very Tall, which was

large, coffee cup. There was barely a moment to exchange
niceties with the man before she felt a warm rustle at her
uniformed shoulder – it was her supervisor, bristling with impatience at the interruption in his production line. The queue
snaked back to the door and twitched with sighing watch-
glancers.

All of a sudden, as her customer slid over a five-pound note,
she spotted Harris hovering outside. Unable to believe her eyes,
she ducked down, and then had a second peek. No doubting
it. They had barely spoken since Christmas. He had rung her
once, claiming she'd forgotten her toothbrush when she'd last
visited, which he'd found in the bathroom. Should he hold on
to it? The question was loaded, of course, and she'd given him
a terse reply, before hanging up. What was he *doing* here? No
time to think about it. In front of her was a long line of hungry
people, so she resumed serving, keeping her head bowed to
her chin as much as was physically possible without people
thinking she had a bizarre disability.

Then she saw that he was with a woman. With her in that
certain way, held within her orbit by something other than
mere blood-relatedness. She was no relative, that was for sure,
nothing so banal as a long-lost cousin or distant half-sister, but
a real live lady friend. Alia could tell, even at a distance, from
the way they moved in tandem, meshed by an invisible pattern,
that this was someone significant. She recalled the suaveness
of her father's voice on the phone that day when she'd eavesdropped, the way he'd reassured the mysterious female at the
end of the line that his condition was nothing to worry about.
It must be her. Was it serious? She didn't know what to feel,
if it was. Was it annoyance at his hypocrisy, or relief that he

was no longer alone, or intrigue at his choice? Or a tossed mixed salad of feelings, a bittersweet medley of them all? He seemed tender and attentive to the woman, from what she could see, but it was hard to tell.

Famished faces loomed before her, thrusting sandwiches impatiently on to the counter. Heads bobbed out of line to cop a look at who or what was holding everything up. There was no time to dodge out of the way, take a break or simply dip down behind the counter – her father was following the woman now, heading to the chilled food section.

She turned to her supervisor, a shaven-headed German who had a soft spot for her. 'Gunther, please, let me go on my break, will you? Just as a favour. Please.'

'Sure, but you'll never get to be Star of the Week.'

She pulled her cap down as far as was reasonable without making her look too silly. Her father seemed unaware that his daughter was on the other side of the counter. She was unrecognizable. *It's all about context,* she told herself; *he's not expecting to see me in here, so maybe he won't see me.* She set down a pair of macchiatos on the counter for two bankers too caught up in gossip to notice the slop she'd made. She saw that Harris had joined the parallel queue to hers, while his lady friend was perched awkwardly on a bar stool by the front window, gazing out.

It would have been fine. He would have paid for their mature cheddar and pickle sandwiches and left without even spotting her if bloody useless Pablo hadn't scalded himself on the milk frother, catalysing a chain reaction of mayhem that culminated in her having to serve at his till. The lady friend joined Harris, having added a slab of fruit cake to their tray.

'Alia?' She heard her name uttered in a tone of disbelief. Her cover was blown.

'Dad! What're you doing here?'

'I was about to ask you the same thing.'

She shot him a look. 'I work here.' What did it look like she was doing?

She saw him give a nervous glance at his companion, who was waiting eagerly for the father to introduce the daughter, eyes darting urgently back and forth as if she were a spectator at a tennis match.

'This is Dr Farrah, Alia. An old friend of a mutual friend from Pakistan.'

'Farrah, please,' Farrah said to Alia.

'Farrah, this is my daughter, Alia.'

'Hello, Alia.' The deep throaty voice was familiar. 'What an unexpected surprise.'

'Hi,' Alia said, and gave up serving.

Gunther took note and she feared her sandwich-toting days were numbered. The shuffling queue of office workers sighed with relief as the service sped up. The awkwardness everyone felt zipped around like an electric current, prickly and unpleasant. Alia longed for them to pay and get going.

'So, am I to understand that this is where you are working now?' Harris asked.

'I suppose this chic cap and maroon outfit is a giveaway.'

Farrah smiled. 'Your father's told me all about you.'

'Has he?' Alia looked at him closely. 'Did you, Dad? I mean, everything?'

'Clearly not,' Farrah said, laughing. 'He certainly never mentioned you were working in the catering business.'

Harris fiddled with the wrapper of his roll. 'Well, she *was* at medical school, weren't you, Alia?'

'Yes, I was, but I dropped out last year, when I failed some of my exams—' Alia said, staring at Harris.

'Oh dear.' Dr Farrah seemed genuinely concerned, in a way that made Alia warm to her. 'Why did you fail, do you think, Alia?'

'I lost my nerve, and messed up,' Alia said. 'Everyone's pretty upset about it. Everyone except me, apparently.' Was he seething? Hard to tell.

'Poor you, how awful,' Dr Farrah said. 'Tell you the truth, I was never very good at exams, either. Were you, Harris?'

'Always top of my class.'

'Yes, and see where that got you?'

'Never mind, Alia,' Farrah said, trying to steer the conversation. 'I'm sure you can retake very easily, can't you?'

'I'm not sure I want to, though,'

'What, what?' Harris looked at Farrah for reinforcement. 'Not retake? Are you mad? Of course you'll have to retake.'

Alia was flustered, afraid that her boss might notice the altercation. 'I need to work out what to do next, Dad. It might not be medicine.'

Harris was on the brink of despair. 'What else can you do?'

'There are other options, Dad. Seriously, I'm working it out.'

She smiled, and he seemed to relax a little. 'So how long have you two been – friends, then?' she said.

Before he could answer, she noticed Gunther staring at her. 'I'd better get back to it,' she said. 'Gunther's getting pissed off.' Maybe she wouldn't be fired, just hauled into the back room for one of his Teutonic warnings.

'Are you eating in or taking out?' she asked her father.

'I think we'll take out,' Farrah said tactfully. 'Have a picnic by the river. It's been lovely to meet you.' She delved into her handbag and pulled out her card. 'And do call me, if you ever want a cup of tea south of the river. I teach at Greenwich Community College.'

Alia was taken aback. 'Oh, thanks,' she said, sliding the card into her back pocket. 'I'll do that one day.'

Farrah wandered away, feigning fascination with a Pret A Manger cookbook that told you how to make the sandwiches you had just eaten.

Alia watched her for a moment. 'I don't mind, you know,' she said to Harris.

'Mind?'

'It doesn't bother me if you have a girlfriend.'

He looked squarely at her, swaying a little in his polished brogues. She noticed how smart he was looking, reminiscent of his old self, dressed in tweed jacket and tie, hair smoothed flatly over the crown of his head.

'Does it bother you if I have a boyfriend, though? That's the question, Dad.'

Her supervisor tapped his watch. Her time was nearly up.

Harris spoke rapidly, as if to wrap things up. 'It's not the same thing, Alia. You're a young girl and you should concentrate on your studies, on things that will secure your future.'

At the edge of her vision, she glimpsed Farrah hovering by the entrance, waiting patiently for her father, clearly eager for his company. 'And what about your future?' she said, adjusting her cap, looking past him towards Farrah.

Harris straightened up, grew a little. 'My future is my concern. Goodbye, Alia.'

Twenty

They drove back to her house in silence, apart from Farrah exclaiming, 'Stop!' when Harris appeared to ignore a red light at a junction, cruising through it in a distracted state. It was not until after they had eaten supper on trays in the lounge and watched the news together that he felt able to bring up the question of his daughter's situation.

'It's only a temporary thing, this sandwich job she's doing, you know.'

Farrah was busily marking a stack of papers, with one eye on the television.

'Sure, yes, I understand,' she replied, and gave a little yawn. She hated marking tests.

'You don't sound like you do.'

She adjusted her spectacles and put down her papers. 'Well, to be honest, I'm a bit confused by your behaviour,' she said. 'Keeping all this business with your daughter to yourself, not mentioning it when you spoke of her. Why, Harris?'

'I didn't honestly know what she was doing,' Harris admitted.

'I thought she'd gone back to lectures, catching up with her studies for retakes and all. This is what I assumed. Foolishly, I see.'

'Yes, but why didn't you tell me before?'

'Well, once you had got hold of this idea about her becoming a doctor, I suppose I couldn't admit she'd messed it up.'

'Honestly, Harris, I don't understand you. I never had you down as one of those typical Asian fathers, anxious to push their children into law or medicine.'

'I don't know. It's just, well, your children are so accomplished, they've achieved so much.'

'Sons are easier than daughters,' Farrah said. 'Not that they are easy, these boys of mine. They have their ups and downs, like all young people. I just close my eyes and occasionally shut my ears, whenever I have to.'

'I wish it were that easy.'

'I know. Trouble is, the moment you have children, you never escape the fear of losing them.'

'Alia's all I have left in this world.'

'Don't say that.'

'But it's true.'

'If you love them too much, it can send you mad. Shakespeare said it all. Look at King Lear.'

Harris nodded, only vaguely remembering the tragedy.

'In the end, they're all we leave behind when we depart, our children,' she said.

'Is that true? Shakespeare left his great works.'

'Yes, he did, but he is an exception.'

Harris sighed. 'I suppose you're right. Are you an atheist, Farrah? Tell me.'

'Atheist isn't a label I'd choose for myself. It's divisive, which I think is unhelpful. Do I believe in God?'

'Well, do you?'

She was silent for a moment. 'Idrees and I went on the Haj to Mecca. It was something he wanted to do after things went wrong for him at work. When I was there, I was sucked into it all, the beauty, the ritual, the prayers. You know, I actually did believe in God, for about five minutes.' Then, noticing his troubled expression, she added, 'But that doesn't mean I'm not a believer. It's just that I believe in people and their abilities. Don't you?'

'But Farrah, surely you don't think that people, with all their flaws and foibles, are the alpha and omega of creation?'

'Goodness, you sound like the mullah. Actually, I do believe that.'

The revelation, so profoundly at odds with his own beliefs, pained him acutely. Early on in their relationship, he had lent her his most beloved book on the subject of religious thought in Islam, written by a brilliant scholar. He'd read it many times, adding his own thoughts in the margins of the text, scrawled spidery annotations in English and Urdu, cross-references to Rumi and other Sufi mystics. Farrah had dipped into it, only to find a dense clot of semi-mystical sentences on the nature of the faith that failed to satisfy her probing, empiricist sensibility. She had been polite about it at the time but now he saw that she would never be a true Muslim. It saddened him, as if they'd reached a fork in the road where they could either cleave together or cleave apart.

He gazed at the dull dregs in the bottom of his glass. 'She's become very secretive, my daughter, Farrah. She keeps things from me.'

'Ah. That's normal. Though didn't she give some hint about it all on the phone? Surely you are in touch regularly.' Farrah spoke every month to both of her sons, one in Dubai, the other in Aberdeen. 'I always try to give them space, though, the boys. They need it, young people – something I only discovered as I got older.'

'We've been having some differences lately, Alia and me,' Harris went on. 'So the phone calls haven't been such a frequent occurrence.'

'Oh dear,' she said. 'What kind of differences?'

'We've not been seeing eye to eye. Over this boyfriend business, and various other things.' He attempted to sound matter of fact.

'Ah, yes, boyfriends. Well, that's understandable.'

Harris seemed relieved. 'I'm glad you agree.'

'No, no. I mean it's understandable that she has a boyfriend, Harris. Surely. She must be wanting to build her own life, having been upset by the divorce and all . . .'

'Upset? She wasn't that upset, actually.'

'Come on. It must have affected her.'

'I've bent over backwards to make her feel at home in my place. Set up the desk in her bedroom for revision and study, let her use my car whenever she needs it.'

She suppressed a laugh. 'Harris, come on.'

'What? It has nothing to do with the divorce, any of this business.'

'Are you really sure?'

'What are you driving at, Farrah? Spit it out.'

'Nothing. But you have to admit, it's a thorny area, fathers and daughters.'

'Don't tell me. Shakespeare again, is it?'

The taunt stung her. 'I'm just trying to give you my perspective. Or is that not permitted?'

'Well, you're not a father, and you don't have a daughter. So your perspective is surely limited, isn't it?'

'Not necessarily.'

'Can't you just listen to what happened, instead of giving me the potted theories always?'

'I'm *sorry*,' she snapped. 'Well, go on.'

Harris took a breath, trying to be patient with her. 'She came up to stay after I wrote to her telling her about my health episode and saying I needed the company when I was recuperating.'

'Needed company, or needed her as your caretaker-cum-housekeeper?'

'Farrah!'

'I'm right, aren't I?'

'Maybe, but so what? She's my daughter.'

'Yes, exactly. But don't forget she needs your care and support, as much as you need hers. Possibly more.'

'She has all that! I offered to buy her a place of her own, but she refused.'

Farrah arched her eyebrows. 'You Pakistani men always think it's always about land and gold.'

'And you Pakistani women don't?'

'Not this one, no.' Farrah dumped her pile of marking on the floor and went into the kitchen in search of a refill, absent-mindedly glugging back a half-glass of tepid white wine that was standing on the counter. When she looked up, she saw that Harris had followed her and was standing there expectantly.

'So what was the problem, then?' she wanted to know.

She ran the sink full of hot soapy suds and plunged her hands into the water, attacking the dishes.

'Tell me.'

Harris began drying up.

'She's been seeing a boy, in secret, Farrah,' he said wretchedly.

'So?'

'So it was a shock.'

'Good God, Harris! Where have you been all these years?'

'I don't know. I caught her at it, came back late and saw them together.'

'I can't believe this.'

'I couldn't either,' Harris went on. 'So then I had my cousin's boy Rashid keep an eye on her – I wasn't wrong. He confirmed my suspicions that it is an ongoing situation. Essentially, she is shacked up with this fellow.'

Farrah was appalled. 'You had someone *spy* on her?'

'Not just anyone – a relative, Farrah. Not spying, just keeping an eye.'

'How utterly awful.'

Harris was stunned. 'Awful? How can you say that? She's my daughter. What do you expect me to do? Stand by and watch her life be ruined?'

'What are you so afraid of? She's a Western girl, for God's sake. She grew up here, born and bred in this country. You'll be making her wear the veil next.'

Harris was indignant. 'I resent that, Farrah, I really do. You've no understanding, none at all.'

'Clearly not.' Her face burned.

'I was worried.'

'About what?'

'About her well-being!' he cried, furious at her utter failure to get it. 'She's led a double life, told lies, been secretive.'

'And what about you? Are you completely honest?' Farrah exclaimed. 'You can hardly blame the girl. I mean, look how you behave towards her. You're so damned secretive yourself, Harris. Your own daughter has no idea about what you're up to! I mean, look how you've kept your relationship with me a secret.'

'I have no choice, Farrah, but to conceal our shameful liaison.'

Farrah spun round, planting her dripping hands on her hips. 'That's the perfect phrase for it, isn't it? Or perhaps we should call it a brief encounter, like that silly old film, if you'd prefer that?'

A dinner plate slithered out of his hand, shattering in jagged white fragments all over the floor. Farrah saw a flicker of despair crease his face as he stared at the pieces.

'Sorry. So clumsy of me,' he stammered.

'Doesn't matter,' she said quickly. 'It was an old plate, cracked anyway.'

He knelt down and began collecting the pieces, as she went to find a dustpan and brush in the cupboard under the stairs. A thin red line bloomed on the ball of his thumb. As he ran it under the tap, he was surprised at the gush of pinkish-red blood from such a fine gash.

Later, when they were up in the bedroom, he found a plaster in the dressing-table drawer and applied it to the cut. As Farah combed her hair before the mirror, he finished his whisky on the rocks, wincing at the sharp chill of the ice cubes against his fissured teeth. He watched her climb into bed and tried not to think about the other thing he was keeping from her. His earlier determination to come clean with her about Omar had deserted him.

'Are you all right?' she said gently, when he did not join her.

'Mmm, fine. Just, you know, my heart and all.'

She got out of bed and went over to where he was standing at the window, staring out at the sycamore trees that lined the street. 'What is it?'

'It's OK,' he said, as she put her arms around him. 'Don't worry.'

'No. Tell me,' she begged. 'Don't keep it from me.'

'Well, you may as well know I've been having this atrial fibrillation trouble.'

Farrah's eyes widened with concern. 'Whatever is that? I thought it was angina, Harris, your heart condition.'

'They're related.'

'Is this more serious?'

'No, no. It's just my anxiety levels make the heart condition even worse – I get these palpitations and then I get scared I'm going to be drowned in my own blood.'

'Oh, God, how dreadful for you! Have you told the doctor?'

'My doctor's assured me it's nothing more than my imagination.'

Farrah's voice quavered. 'I wish you'd said. I feel terrible now.'

'Don't. I didn't want to worry you. Anyway, they've put me on some new medication, so I'm hoping it will resolve. You must have noticed my pill-popping, surely.'

'I thought it must be for the angina, or maybe vitamins.' She looked at him, her face puckered with grief. 'I'm so sorry.'

The concern in her voice sent a tremor of guilt through him.

'You really mustn't bottle things up, OK?' she went on. 'Whatever it is. Whatever it might be, please tell me. I'd like to help.'

She leaned over and kissed him tenderly on the back of his head. He turned and clung to her for a moment, flooded with pain from his chest to his jaw. The urge to lose himself in her almost overwhelmed him.

'There is something.' The words were muffled.

'What is it?'

Harris sat down on the edge of the bed. It was unbearable. He wanted to retreat, fabricate something. He could not say it. He must. The words flew from him.

'I've been working for Omar.'

Her face was still, blank with shock. Time stretched out agonizingly and he all but snatched back the words he had uttered, but it was too late. She stared at him, her features a volatile blend of anger, indignation, disbelief.

'What did you say?' She spoke quietly.

'Please give me a chance to explain.'

'I just don't understand, Harris.' She could barely look at him. 'How could you?'

He scrambled to reassure her. 'I know, I'm so ashamed, but please just listen for a minute. I had my reasons, Farrah. Let me explain.'

She was retreating from him with every moment that passed, withdrawing for ever.

'You lied to me. You kept working for him, all this time, and you didn't tell me,' she said. 'Your little excuses for disappearing home – that was to do his bidding, wasn't it?'

Panic welled up inside him. Was that what he'd done? He was a liar, a betrayer. She would never forgive him.

'Don't say that. I had to do it.'

'Had to? What, so you mean he *forced* you? There was absolutely no choice in the matter, even after what I told you? After I said that we couldn't be together if you did business with that man?'

'I know. I can explain. But please, please try to understand.'

'*Understand?*' She gave a choked sob. 'What is there to understand?'

Harris took a breath. 'My financial situation is very difficult. I had to make a terrible choice.'

'I confided in you the most painful thing of my life. All I asked was that.'

'What should I have done?' he managed to say.

'Respected my wishes,' she said.

After he had gone, she went into the garden and switched on the sprinkler to water the dead lawn. It was the legacy of a hosepipe ban the previous summer, during a long grey drought, when the sun had barely shone, and the water table had shrunk to its lowest level since records began. In the darkness, the grass appeared a brownish green. She shivered, and inhaled the calming scent of wet earth. The water drenched her. Tears streamed freely down her face for the first time since her husband's death. She cried out his name in the chill night air, knowing that he could not hear her, but she didn't care. She drew no comfort from the idea that he was in paradise, because in her scheme of things the afterlife was pure fiction. Death was the end of the story.

Twenty-one

It was impossible to hear yourself think in the cavernous restaurant packed with diners, let alone talk business. Words echoed confoundingly in Harris's ears as he tried to set out his position.

'Honestly, Omar-sahib,' he shouted over the din. 'I agreed to do this, thinking it might be more feasible than it now appears to be.'

'Really?' Omar sniffed. 'I'm surprised, Harris, knowing how you always have something up your sleeve.'

He snapped off a shard of poppadom and tossed it into his mouth. They were sitting beneath the ethereal skyscape of the palm court in Khan's Restaurant in Bayswater, waiting for their meal. Harris had selected the mixed grill with nan for them to share; unsure what might please his friend that evening, he'd gone for something that would cover all the bases. Just as Omar's eyes began to swivel around impatiently, a waiter appeared with a sizzling plate of food and set it before them. A brief lull in the hubbub spurred Harris to continue.

'So the thing is,' he began, as Omar tucked in.

'Mmm, this is first rate,' Omar gasped, distracted by the pungent delicacies before him. He snatched a napkin to dab his drippy nose. 'So what is it, Harris? Tell me.'

'It's not that I don't believe in the project.' Harris squeezed lemon indiscriminately over the surf and turf dish. 'You know how I've longed to do something of vital importance for our rural population. It's been a dream of mine all these years.'

'Always the idealist, Harris,' Omar mused between mouthfuls. 'It's one of your great qualities. But come on now, I need to know how things are going at your end. Put me in the picture. It's been a while.'

Harris suddenly felt hot. He owed him at least a progress report. 'Well, I gave Khadim Siddiqui a feasibility outline, and even though he was initially very keen, he seems to have lost all interest since. Which worries me.'

'You rang the old fellow, did you?'

'Many times. And faxed his office repeatedly.'

'Just be patient. We have the land purchase in hand now and they're starting to plan excavations. It's moving ahead, slowly, slowly.' Omar beheaded a king prawn and dunked it in a puddle of its own crimson juice. 'And did I mention that Amanullah's now on board?'

'*Amanullah?* I thought you didn't trust him. Is he a partner now?'

'I forwarded his letter to you.'

'Perhaps it went astray.'

Omar ignored this. 'Well, he has many contacts and a great deal of knowledge. And he has the money, of course. The family's rolling in it.'

Harris listened intently as Amanullah's virtues as a sleeping partner were extolled. 'Look,' he said, laying down his napkin when Omar had finished. 'You don't seem very happy with my performance so far. And now it seems, with Amanullah and all, my involvement is redundant.'

Omar looked up from his food, lips dripping with prawn juice, lashes fluttering reproachfully. 'Redundant? Did I ever say that? You can't take criticism, can you? Never could.' He stabbed at a piece of kebab that slid around the plate, refusing to be speared with his fork. 'Actually, your role here is essential, Harris. Are you crazy?'

Harris swallowed a mouthful of nan. 'Well, I am perhaps crazy, yes, I admit it.'

Omar sighed and laid down his fork. 'What's wrong?'

'It's Farrah.'

'Farrah? What does she have to do with it?'

'My relationship with her.'

'What about it?'

'My involvement with you is the cause of a painful rift between us.'

Omar gave a little cough. 'I don't believe it.'

'It's come to me making a choice. Not an easy decision, believe me.'

'Let me see if I'm getting this right, Harris, old fellow.'

'OK.'

'You are seeing Dr Farrah in a romantic context now. Am I correct?'

'Correct.'

'Thanks to me, and to Kamila, I might add.'

'Indeed, yes, thanks to you both.'

'And you like each other, are getting fonder?'

'Yes, yes. What of it?' Harris grew hotter and took off his jacket. Damp half-moons of sweat bloomed around the armpits of his shirt.

'And now you've fallen out, is that it? Quarrelling and so forth. What is going on?'

'I'm trying to explain.'

'Explain, then, Harris, how is this my fault? I'd like to know, chapter and verse.'

'Keep your voice down.'

'Am I shouting?'

'You are, yes.'

'Tell me, then, quickly, so I don't have to shout louder.'

'What she told me is in confidence and I can't tell you.'

Omar gazed at the pale blue ceiling, then looked at Harris. 'You know, I gave Idrees a break on a contract I had in the Middle East when his firm was about to make him redundant. Then when I asked for a favour in return, he refused to help.' He pinched a bit of Harris's bread and mopped up shreds of combusted meat from the iron platter. 'He was one of my oldest friends, you know.'

Harris sighed. 'Omar, whatever happened between you is in the past. But I can't go on with Shorkot Power, however important it is.'

Omar gave a puff of exasperation. 'I can't believe you're letting me down like this,' he said. 'This is extremely disappointing. It will delay everything. Actually, it could well ruin things.'

'I doubt that. The ball is rolling.'

'You were my first choice, and now where can I find an

equivalent partner at the eleventh hour, Harris, old chap, tell me that?'

Harris felt his throat tighten. 'I was not your first choice in actual fact. You came to me when all the others said no because they knew it was too risky, too much work for uncertain remuneration.'

'Who told you that?' Omar retorted.

'I'm not a fool, Omar. Some people were very frank.'

Pockets of cold air punctuated the packed eating hall as the revolving doors swept in ever more diners who loitered, eyeballing tables from a short distance.

'So you're throwing in the towel, all for the love of a woman, huh, a feminist to boot.' He sipped a lassi. 'She was never the same after that spell in Cambridge. Harris, you surprise me, you really do. Did all that time in the north of England with those shopkeeping cousins kill your ambition, then?'

A waiter glided past and whisked away their dinner plates.

'That's unfair.'

'Is it?'

'I don't want to be alone in my declining years, ambition or not.'

'Who does? It was me who got you and Farrah together, remember.'

'Yes, you've done so much for me.' Baying conversations hemmed him in on all sides and he found himself at a loss for a moment. 'You were my first friend when I arrived from nowhere at engineering college, and God knows, you've helped me out over the years when nobody would look at me in this wretched country.'

'So tell me. What did the friend do to deserve abandonment, huh?'

'It's my fault, Omar, not yours.' He fanned out his hands on the white damask tablecloth, almost pristine save for a few breadcrumbs on his own side and a splash of sauce on the other. 'I'm truly, truly sorry it's come to this.'

Omar gave a languid wave of the hand to summon the bill. It arrived instantaneously on a battered silver platter.

'Let me pay,' Harris tried, but Omar fended him off.

'Are we not having the kulfi?' Harris heard himself say, though he had no inclination for dessert.

Omar looked up in surprise. 'Not unless you really want it.'

Harris shook his head. 'I thought it was your favourite, that's all.'

'Ah. Well, I try to avoid sweets these days,' Omar said, turning melancholy. 'My trousers don't fit me as well as they did, and Kamila's constantly chiding me.'

He rose heavily to his feet, tipping his chair backwards so that it clattered on to the marble floor. A waiter scooped it up, removing the cloth in one smooth operation. In less than an instant, Harris noticed, their table was surrounded by diners, eager to nab their seats and eat their fill.

The two men were heading in different directions across London, so they didn't linger very long outside Khan's. A light drizzle began to fall and Omar scanned the street for a black cab, brandishing his umbrella as one approached the kerb. Their parting was brisk. Once inside, Omar pushed down the window.

'Let me know how it all goes, Harris. Keep in touch, won't you?'

It was just a figure of speech, a husk of camaraderie thrown
to him as he stood upon the pavement, waving goodbye. Then
the cab made a miraculous U-turn, spewing out diesel fumes
into the dank night air, and sped away in a blur of tail-lights.
In that moment, it struck Harris that Omar never really bothered to say a proper goodbye, neither on the phone nor in
person. Endings were not his thing.

The Bayswater Road was clogged with traffic crawling west,
but Harris needed to go east, where he had left his car parked
near Alia's neighbourhood outside the congestion zone earlier
that evening. He had half wondered about dropping in on her,
but then had lost his nerve. Without thinking clearly, he began
to walk, dodging the crowded pavement, striding along the
double yellow lines that marked the road, splashing through
oily puddles as he went, careless that his socks were drenched,
his smart shoes ruined.

He walked parallel with Hyde Park till he reached the mouth
of Oxford Street. On the corner with the Edgware Road stood
the cinema he'd visited as a young man, though its undulating
sea of plush red seats and the rippling gold lamé curtains had
long been renovated into oblivion, bringing it into line with
the modern multiplexes that had sprung up everywhere. He
wandered on, past brightly lit shop windows, pausing now and
again to take in their spectacular displays.

After a while, he grew tired and decided to catch a bus. The
route map at the bus stop was incomprehensible and, unable
to stop himself, he let out a groan of despair.

An elderly woman looked at him in grim solidarity. 'Hopeless,
aren't they? Where d'you want to go, dear?' she asked.

'East London.'

The woman nodded encouragingly. 'Hackney?'

'No, it's Aldgate, near the London Hospital. Normally I drive everywhere, but I parked it there near my daughter's place to avoid the congestion charge.' He spoke apologetically, and the woman smiled, as though she understood everything.

'You want the 25 – this one,' she said, as the double-decker bus lumbered into view through the rain. Harris felt a pop of optimism at the sight of its trusty headlights, the familiar boxy red outline.

It was a slow, soporific journey to the East End, past familiar landmarks and half-remembered streets, and Harris drifted off to sleep with a carousel of stations spinning in his head – Holborn, St Pancras, Monument, Angel, Bank – only to awaken an hour later with a crick in the neck, having missed his stop on the Aldgate roundabout. The bus was idling outside a pet shop on the Mile End Road, a faded mural of fish and aquatic ferns above the window of the now defunct store, selling dirt-cheap fridges and done-up freezers. It was vaguely familiar, vaguely not.

He walked west towards the crossroads at the Mile End Road and came across Sidney Street. Alia's place wasn't far from here, was it? Now he recognized where he was. The BP garage, the Methodist Mission homeless shelter, the 1970s relic of a post office, the denuded market stalls, the road sweepers with their long brooms puffing stubby fag ends, the band of livid-faced drunks who greeted him like an old comrade. There was the red-brick façade of the East London Mosque. And there was his car, waiting faithfully to take him home.

Twenty-two

Alia was waiting on the platform at the Shadwell Docklands Light Railway station, clutching an aerogramme from Mishele. The train arrived and she slid into a seat at the back, spreading herself out a little to deter others from crowding her with their newspapers and Starbucks cups, their iPods bleeding unwanted music into her space. She watched the towers of Canary Wharf shrink away as the train sped towards Poplar, and then she opened the tightly sealed letter carefully. Ever since last summer, Alia had been sending her postcards of London with snippets of news. Lately, though, she had been receiving more and more letters from Mishele, who sounded increasingly desperate.

Dear Alia

Asalaam aleikum.

Thank you for the red double-decker-bus postcard. I hope this finds you in good health. We miss you and think of you often.

My mother is asking me to write this letter to you. Because she says we are like sisters, and because she says she knows your father loves us like we are his own children.

*Can you help us, Alia? Can you please ask your good
father, what has happened to the money that he promised us?
Every week my father goes to the bank to see if something has
come, but there is nothing.*

Alia was shocked. Had he promised money and then failed
to send it? It was very odd, quite uncharacteristic of him, she
thought. Perhaps someone had stolen it. But then he'd told
her he was sending them money by electronic transfer. He'd
seemed all too eager to play the part of the magnanimous uncle
from England when they were there, so why would he abandon
them now when they needed him most? She glimpsed up to
check which station they had reached as the train screeched
around the curved tracks, tipping as it did so. Jerking forward
as it ground to a halt, she gripped the side of the seat as the
compartment filled up with more people. She squeezed herself
in to make room and read on.

*So much has happened since your visit to us in the summer. My
father says he is arranging my marriage, sooner than my mother wants.
I do not want it. I want to attend Girls' Grammar School instead. It
cannot be, my father says. We children all have to help what we can
for our parents' burden. It is the same for you in England, I am sure.*

But it wasn't the same at all, Alia thought. She'd never had
to work to support herself till now. The news that her parallel
sister in the village was being edged away from school into
marriage was unbearable to hear.

*Me and my family took my little brother to a madrassa. Do you
know what that is? I don't think they have them in England.*

256

It's a school where you live, like a hostel, and you learn the Koran by heart each day. The school is free. They give you food and a place to sleep. My parents say it will help them save money. And when I am married, that will help them also. On the way, it was a long bus journey, my mother gave me a ginger sweet, to stop me being sick. We all went together. Even Mona. She slept on my mother's lap. It was a hundred miles from our home to the place where we left him.

I was not happy when I saw the madrassa. Rooms are very cramped, with small windows. There are bars. We saw boys saying verses from the Koran. It was a very hot afternoon. They were nodding and rocking, and my brother was scared. My father told him it would be all right and we will take him out of that place when things are easier at home.

Remember the pink shell soap you gave me when you visited? I have it still, I'm saving it.

I send you greetings, my sister in London.

May Allah bless you.

Do not forget us.

Mishele

By the time she had finished the letter, the train had reached Tower Bridge. *Do not forget us.* The roundly formed words popped off the page. Not plaintive, but powerful, like a directive from afar; simple, stark, unadorned. She had run away from them once, and tried to forget, but even as the distance was greater now, so was the urgency. For whatever reasons, it was evident that her father couldn't, or wouldn't, help. Perhaps now that there was this new woman in his life, whoever she was, he wished to distance himself from his ties in the village.

Then she thought of Rashid. Why wasn't he doing anything? She felt a surge of anger, remembering how he'd barged in on her and gone behind her back. It was her turn to see what he was up to and why he'd done nothing for his family. She decided to pay him a visit at the estate agent's, only to be told by his old boss that he no longer worked there these days. He was renting a place in Whitechapel, Jerry said, and gave her the address.

The building Rashid inhabited was a dilapidated Georgian house that bulged precariously towards the pavement, its crumbling facade preserved with a thick layer of dull green paint. The paint job was his handiwork, as was the hand-painted sign proclaiming Crescent Islamia Centre, in Arabic and English. The addition of wire mesh over the ground-floor windows was Begg's idea, after a spate of break-ins and vandalism. When the buzzer rang, Rashid had just nodded off at his desk; he'd been working days and nights on the website, and had lost all sense of time. He could hardly believe his ears when he heard Alia's voice crackle through the intercom.

He buzzed open the door and she found herself in a dark-ened hallway piled with bin bags almost up to the ceiling. The centre was his life and work now, and for months he'd been perfecting the website that was dedicated to dissemi-nating the message of Islam, countering Islamophobia and seeking out converts among local youth. Time passed without him registering the hours, one day bleeding into the next as he strove to realize Begg's vision and to hone his own. Often, after working all night, he'd take his meals in the condensation-drenched late-night greasy spoon café in Stepney.

'Sorry about the mess and all,' he said vaguely, raking his fingers through unwashed hair. 'Been working like mad to sort it out from the previous tenants.'

She noticed that his beard had filled out and that he had gained a little weight since she had last seen him. Crushed empty boxes of fried masala chicken littered the floor, leftovers from a meeting with a group of teenagers he'd culled from the neighbourhood in an attempt to persuade them to join the youth discussion group.

'I never thought I'd see you again,' Rashid said, 'after that time I came over.'

She shrugged, irritated he'd mentioned it first. 'Can I sit down?' she said, sweeping a pile of free newspapers from the couch.

He was shamefaced. 'I'm sorry. I only did it because your father was worried.'

'I don't care. You shouldn't have done it.'

'I'm sorry.'

'Forget it, Rashid. It's not why I came.'

He perked up. 'No? What is it, then?'

'This,' she declared, thrusting Mishele's letter at him. 'Things are getting really desperate with your family.'

He tugged at his hair. 'I know they are, I know.'

'So what're you going to do about it?'

Rashid took the aerogramme and scanned his sister's words. 'What can I do for them when I'm stuck here? I have barely enough to manage myself.'

Alia reflected for a moment, then said, 'What I don't understand is why my dad hasn't sent them anything.'

Rashid shook his head. 'Poor Uncle, he can barely manage his shop these days, let alone send anything very much to my family. He's squandering his money on a lady friend, that's what I've heard.'

'Who says?'

'Everyone.'

She suppressed an urge to shake him. 'I suppose what I don't get is why don't you do something yourself. I mean, they're your family, Rashid.'

Rashid stood his ground, his features set. 'I've been a bad son, I know that. I should have sent them more. But I was leading a sinful life, working in the estate agents. I had to leave, Alia, so I might work in the service of Islam.'

She noticed his kurta was blotched with pale brown tea stains, as though he'd given up worrying about such earthly matters. 'How is that going to help them?'

He shook his head. 'You don't get it, do you?'

'No,' she said. 'I don't.' She glanced at a grubby wall, patched with a collage of cuttings, maps, notes about Islam, quotations from the Koran. 'Why do you believe in all this?'

'Because it's the truth. I've found true purpose in my life, understanding it in terms of the faith. Can you say the same thing about your existence?'

The question confounded her. 'Faith doesn't come into it. I'm trying to work out what I'm doing next, Rashid. I've got ideas, I'm doing stuff.'

'I am too,' he declared. 'Helping the troubled neighbourhood youth, Alia.'

'What are you talking about?'

'You've seen them. You know what it's like round here.

These groups of Muslim youths,' he went on. 'On the street corners, milling around, chatting all day long on their phones. They're wasting their lives, chasing after all the superficial rubbish – sex, drugs, clubs, clothes.'

'So what?' She was laughing.

'Alia, listen to me. By doing this work, I can share the beauty of the faith with them. Help them find the righteous way. Bring them to understand the importance of the *ummah*, the thing that unifies all us Muslims, brings us together, wherever we are. We need to work together to make it happen. This work is my life now. Mohsin tells me I have crossed over into something purer and deeper. He says we'll cast our web wider. Reach brothers and sisters in East Ham and Walthamstow, Dagenham and the Isle of Dogs. Why stop there? The struggle will reach all four corners of the globe.'

'All four corners? Really?'

'I believe it, yes.'

She grew impatient with him – there were more pressing matters than listening to him expound upon the faith. 'But what about your own family? What will happen to them?'

'Have you no faith?'

'None,' she said, though a tiny part of her envied him that sureness of purpose she still lacked. His certainty simplified everything.

Rashid opened a packet of custard cream biscuits and made tea for Mohsin Begg, who had emerged from the office where he had been beavering away during Alia's visit.

'You'll be doing my job next,' Mohsin remarked, popping a biscuit into his mouth. 'Thought we'd run out of these.'

'I went to get more from the corner shop.' Rashid always ate large quantities of biscuits when he was stressed.

Begg grinned, baring crumb-caked teeth. 'You're a born talker, Rashid, very eloquent. I heard what you said to your uncle's girl. I'm impressed.'

Rashid brushed this aside. 'Brother, I could never be you, do what you do. I'm happy working on the website, that's it.'

'Yeah? But you talk so well to the boys and girls round here. They really look up to you, respect you . . .'

'Some do, and some laugh in my face,' Rashid said.

'No matter. God is great. Not for you to save the world, is it? We do our work as best we can, brother, in the service of Allah.' He picked up a snow-globe paperweight on the desk and shook it. A tiny replica of the Grand Mosque disappeared in a flurry of polystyrene snow. 'Forgive me, but I couldn't help overhearing your conversation. Your family need help, don't they, to come here?'

Rashid swallowed hard. 'My sister's health is poor . . . and my father can't support them—'

Outside, the downward curve of a passing ambulance siren defeated the end of his sentence.

'I'm sorry to hear that,' Begg said, when it was quiet. 'But maybe I can help in some way, if you need it.'

His words were like manna from heaven. 'Really? How?'

'Well, I could get you the money to pay for them to come here,' Begg said simply. 'No problem. And if they need passports in a hurry, I know someone who can fix it, for a small fee. Only takes five days.'

'Thank you, but I could never accept such an offer,' Rashid murmured, overwhelmed at his generosity.

'Why not? It would be an honour, after all you've done for me here,' he said. 'Please, Rashid.'

A few weeks later, Rashid dropped into Stone & Stone with the rent arrears in cash in the hope of mollifying Jerry Stone. It was a fortnight overdue and not for the first time. As his old boss chatted on the phone with a client, Rashid hung around awkwardly, so he could say hello and apologize. The estate agent's window was ablaze with bright photos of properties to let, and he scanned them vaguely, wondering if he should mention to Jerry that there would be some more people living in the centre, sharing the space. It'd been a favour to Begg, who'd asked him one day when they were leafleting on the Whitechapel Road.

'Three brothers, passing through London, need a place to stay,' he'd said casually. 'Won't be for that long. No need to tell the landlord.'

Jerry hung up, rolling his eyes, and scooted around the desk to greet Rashid. 'Hello, stranger. How's it all going, then?'

'It's fine, thanks, Jerry. How's things with you?'

'Been better. Bit slow this week, but I'm not worried.' He grinned, drumming the desk. 'Not yet.'

Rashid felt a warm flush rise up his neck. 'Sorry it's late,' he said, handing over the envelope. It pained him, withholding from Jerry, especially after he'd been so nice about letting them use the house for a low rent. Still, it had been the least he could do for Begg, putting up the men there. Begg had honoured his promise to help Rashid's mother and sisters come to England, siphoning excess funds to cover the cost of their journey from a store-front Islamic charity in Ilford, where he was a trustee.

'Thanks,' Jerry said, sliding the envelope into his breast pocket, without checking its contents.

'Been a bit of a struggle this month,' Rashid said, lingering at the door.

'Still cab driving, are you?'

Rashid looked away. 'Not much. Not enough.'

Jerry was pensive for a moment. 'I never really understood why you didn't want to work here any more.'

Rashid smiled. 'I know. Bye, Jerry.'

'Bye, my friend.'

Twenty-three

Sunshine glossed the muddle of houses in Whitechapel, making them all match, and blossoming trees in pink and white promised warmth and longer days to come. Young families with small children sprang up everywhere, congregating around the swings, the mobile library, the ice-cream van, lingering to chat on park benches after months of hibernation.

One fine summer morning, Rashid peered out of the kitchen window, drawn by the sounds of jubilant shrieking as a tangle of schoolboys played a version of British bulldog nearby. Here and there, he recognized a few faces from the youth group. As he swilled the forlorn dregs of a cup of Nescafé, he half-wondered about nipping down to talk to them. Talking to young people was very important, he'd learned, but he had other work to get on with that day – proofreading a speech that Mohsin Begg was preparing for a group of students at a college campus in Essex. The deadline loomed. Begg was nagging him for a fresh printout, even though the printer was acting up. Something else he was meant to fix. At least the website was running smoothly.

These days, his work on that front was limited to fixing glitches, tweaking the layout. The number of hits on the site had increased a thousandfold since he'd been working on it. Advertising revenue was up and Begg kept promising to reward his prized employee with a salary.

Yet Rashid insisted on working for nothing; he was spiritually driven, not a wage slave. The relationship between the two men was one of mentor and mentee, and both were loath to sully it in any way. To earn a bit of cash, he'd gone back to driving occasional shifts for a minicab company near Aldgate. They provided a car if you didn't have one, and the pay wasn't bad. In any case, he had no desire to queue up every Monday at the Post Office to collect social security from the smug-faced guys who worked behind the counter. The driving kept him in pocket, while still allowing him to devote most of his time to his real work for Begg.

Lately, with the website up and running, much of Rashid's energy was poured into organizing a Muslim phone-support service for local teenagers. It had been Begg's brainwave, the scheme. He'd witnessed a few of the group sessions under Rashid's tutelage and had divined a need in the community for young people to share their fears and concerns, and to answer questions they had about Islamic issues. The phone service would operate like confession, Begg had explained, a twinkle in his eye. It would provide an anonymous space in which the most vulnerable members of the youth community could find a sympathetic ear and air their grievances; sins would be confessed, lessons learned. From its launch, the phone-in service was a runaway success, endorsing Begg's view that the community's youth was in crisis.

'People are afraid to go to the police, and we know why that is, don't we?' he confided in Rashid. 'The trust is gone, isn't it? We fill that gap for these desperate young people.'

News of the phone service whizzed round the neighbourhood lightning quick. Its big draw in an area studded with CCTV cameras was its anonymity. In this neck of the urban woods, privacy was a precious and scarce commodity. They were bombarded with calls and questions on topics that seriously challenged Rashid's limited worldliness. Girls running from arranged marriages; boys sleeping with white prostitutes; everyone doing heroin. Rashid wasn't like them, he knew that in his bones. He came from the village, a place where he'd grown up feeling safe, sleeping under the stars at night. Now he was bereft, his sense of home and safety lost in transit, eroded over time. He did his best to listen and advise the unending stream of lost souls who spilled their woes down the phone line, opening up in ways that astonished him. Unlike so many of his Muslim brethren, he didn't lecture, didn't judge – he left that to Mohsin Begg – and gradually he discovered he had at last found his vocation in the service of others.

He noticed that the girls in particular sought him out, dropping into the centre for the once-weekly Muslim youth forum that convened on its ground floor. Numbers fluctuated as the group struggled to define its identity. There was talk of table tennis, a camping trip to the Welsh countryside, bungee-jumping at a place near Bluewater. Most of the younger ones had never ventured beyond London or Essex. One girl recalled she had been to Shoeburyness in Year Six, ages ago, and maybe they should go to the seaside. There was talk of steering the group towards more discussion of Islamic topics, of studying

Islamic texts, just to see what all the fuss was about. Everybody felt under attack, under scrutiny. Their faith excited endless comment and hostility from English people on all sides, ugly stories spattered across the tabloids.

After a while, the boys split off and began a discussion group upstairs and it was agreed that the division of the sexes was preferable. Ideas ricocheted around and sometimes the group dissolved into almost nothing for weeks on end. Then Rashid would grow despondent, obsessively checking the website to monitor the number of hits they were getting. Yet Begg wasn't fussed, insisting that the youth group, however sporadic, was an important element in the next phase of what they were trying to do. The first step was gaining the young people's trust.

'Remember, they've been indoctrinated by the system here,' Begg insisted. 'Which is why we're needed now more than ever, specially in the colleges, the universities. The places of higher education are where they retreat from Islam and become assimilated. Then they are lost.'

'So what shall we do?' Rashid asked his mentor. 'How can we keep them coming?'

'Undoing their old ways won't happen overnight, will it, my friend? And you don't wanna get too heavy with them, yeah? Or you'll lose them for ever.'

A rash of red dots lit up the phone as a string of calls came in. Rashid paused, listening to the voicemail to check that there was nothing urgent. He glimpsed himself in the bathroom mirror, unsure about the beard he'd been cultivating in the last few months. It was thicker, spreading bushily over his cheeks. His mother and sisters were coming to England, due to arrive very soon, and he feared Nasreen wouldn't approve.

An aerosol can of Brut shaving foam stood temptingly on the sink. It was one of an array of products that belonged to Begg's visitors, along with their soggy towels that lay in festering humps on the floor, or dropped over the side of the bath. It could be trying at times, sharing a tight, all-male space, Rashid had discovered.

'Tamidul!' he called.

It was past midday, but the twenty-two-year-old former teaching assistant from Luton slept on. Hamid and Saheel, the other two, lay tangled in a swirl of blankets, head to toe. They stirred at the sound of his voice and sat up immediately. Not that they made a habit of sleeping till lunchtime, but the previous night they'd all stayed up very late, talking and smoking. Saheel was slightly older than Tamidul, a graduate in business studies from Leeds Metropolitan. He had not found much work in the north, he told Rashid, and had ended up as a store manager at Comet on an industrial estate near Burnley. Rashid admitted that he'd also had trouble getting the right work with his degree in urban planning.

Hamid, who was from Dunstable, said that this was a familiar pattern. It was because they were Muslims and the world had come to see them as the enemy within. He was the quietest of the group, though Rashid found his observations piercingly truthful. Hamid was bashful about his meagre qualifications, having left school with very few GCSEs, though in fact he'd managed to get into a community college in Huddersfield and was deciding what to do next. It was the first time since Rashid had graduated from university that he'd been able to relax with a group of like-minded souls, chatting about everything from football to cars, gadgets to TV shows. They swapped stories about their wives and girlfriends; they moaned about their jobs, or the lack thereof. For Rashid, spending time with them was a far cry from those unsatisfactory trips to the English pubs, drinking foul-tasting liquor, getting nowhere trawling girls.

One evening, he found himself opening up to his new friends as they sat gathered in the living room around a takeaway from the Real Lahore Kebab House. To his surprise, they listened intently to his recollections of his mother and father in the village, his struggle to make it here so that he could support them back home, and how he had been thwarted. The three men were united in sympathy for Rashid's predicament, for even though they had all been born here, they had heard their own parents' tales of humiliation, working on the buses and in textile factories, striving to make a go of it for the next generation's sake. Yet they all agreed on one thing: that despite their parents' toil and the sacrifices they had made for the sake of their children, assimilation into English ways wasn't what they wanted. Getting ahead, doing better than the uncles and cousins who'd blazed a trail in the northern factories, made this country rich, was no longer really the point. There was a greater struggle in which they were engaged, something that Begg and the others referred to as the final crusade. The typhoon had begun and it was unstoppable.

'Allah's ways are changeless. His bounties and gifts are as plentiful as ever, but only if we grasp them,' Hamid said. 'May Allah grant us enabling courage, strength and knowledge to do his will.'

The other two grunted in agreement, though Rashid kept quiet.

Hamid noticed that Rashid was bothered by the cigarette smoke, but was too polite to mention it, suppressing a cough. 'I'm sorry, brother, it's a bad habit,' Hamid said. 'We'll go outside.'

They had duly clambered up a stepladder that led through a trap door on to a flat roof pooled with pitch-black water. Fearful that he was being inhospitable, or worse, that they might fall over the rooftop edge and kill themselves, Rashid had gone up and found them standing together under the sodium haze of the night sky. He could make out that the timbre of their voices outside was different and that they spoke in truncated sentences.

'The view's really incredible from up there,' Saheel remarked, when he looked up and saw Rashid. 'You can see Canary Wharf and all these other skyscrapers.'

Rashid took in the view. 'No idea you could see so far from here.'

If he had his doubts about the men and what they believed, he did not admit them to a soul. Instead he bottled them up until he was alone at night, turning over in his head what they'd talked about. For the young men had become his friends; they were as kind as they were devout, sharing everything they had with him – their possessions, their time, their company. Nobody English ever did that, or not in his experience; and they made him laugh.

And yet . . . There were moments when he longed to talk to Harris – the old Harris, who used to visit him at his flat on the pretext of curry leftovers and career counselling. One night he sought out an old letter from the Uncle, in which he'd explained the true meaning of jihad.

Its root meaning is to labour, strive and protest. Protestations against injustice and cruelty can be verbal and peaceful, but can of course develop into armed conflict. Armed jihad must be duly authorized by a designated religious leader.

At the time, Rashid had not worried too much about the Uncle's pedantic distinctions. Now he studied his words more carefully.

The Prophet Mohammed, Peace be Upon Him, instructed the believers to remain in constant vigilance and battle against the wayward promptings of the Self and Worldly Hungers.

His use of capitals alarmed Rashid a little, prodded his latent sense of guilt.

Jihad against the self is considered a greater jihad and more rewarding than the one in the battlefield.

As he pondered this last assertion, turning it over and over in his head, he longed to tell Harris that he agreed with this interpretation. But the Uncle was distant these days, and they'd barely been in touch since he had begun working with Begg in Whitechapel. He thought of his visit from Alia, wishing he could talk to her now, as he tossed and turned at night, weighing up the conflicting notions of jihad. For he under-stood the necessity of struggle against the infidel, which was what they were striving to achieve. It was not the same as terrorism, but the media here made no distinction. Did he sanction the murder of innocent civilians? He did not. And so it was that on those sleepless nights Rashid circled back to a state of calm, safe in the belief that he was simply providing bed and board for his fellow Muslims. What was the harm in hospitality?

The men collected weekly social security cheques from a local Post Office near the centre, where the queues were shorter and the postmaster who served at the counter was helpful and friendly, so Hamid said. Rashid was amazed that they had been so organized as to arrange to collect their money there.

'You have to be, though, don't you?' Saheel said, as he ate his fifth bowl of cereal for the day.

Rice Krispies seemed to be his staple diet. And although Rashid wanted to agree, he was uncertain what Saheel was implying. Organized for what? Not job-seeking, that was for sure. They spoke of finding employment, what a nightmare it was, yet none of them seemed to pursue actual jobs. Or not in the way that Rashid had done so, visiting the Whitechapel Jobcentre, poring over the employment section in the newspapers online, drawing up endless CVs, realigning his skills and experience on the page to catch an employer's eye.

So if they weren't really looking for work, what trajectory might they take? There was talk of going to Europe; had Rashid ever been? Had he visited Germany, Holland, France? When he admitted that he hadn't, they seemed disappointed. One of the men had been to a football match in Belgium; another wanted to know if he'd ever taken the Eurostar to Brussels. A further gap in his experience, he admitted.

After a while, Rashid broached the question of how long they intended to stay. It was beginning to seem as though it would be longer than he'd been led to believe by Mohsin Begg. Nobody answered, nobody knew; and nobody seemed terribly bothered, except for Rashid, whose family was due to arrive very soon.

Now, as he stood in the cramped kitchen, he found himself fretting about where he could fit them all in. Nasreen, Mishele and Mona – three girls in a men's flophouse. It would be impossible, housing them here. They really needed to have their own room, somewhere warm and comfy and safe. It distressed him that he was unable to provide half-decent accommodation for his own family.

'Tamidul,' he called again. 'Can I borrow your shaving foam, please?'

The young man padded into the living room, shielding his eyes from the daylight. 'No problem, help yourself.' He was draped in a large blanket that gave him the air of a fakir, or a prisoner of conscience.

As the men got on with clearing up the bedroom, dressing and cooking their morning eggs, Rashid withdrew into the bathroom. If he didn't get in now, he'd have a long wait – Tamidul was a notorious toilet hog. He'd be in there for half an hour, given the chance, reading the tabloids to pass the time, careless of the stench. Rashid squirted a meringue of citrus-tanged foam into his palm and spread it over the outer thickets of his beard. Using a fresh razor, he drew the wet blade across pristine white peaks, like a snow plough. When he was done, he examined his newly sculpted beard in the mirror and was quite pleased with the result. It was neater, more presentable. He didn't want to alarm his mother, for she was wary of the signifiers of extremism. Religious bigots were ruining huge swathes of their country, closing and bombing girls' schools, laying down an ugly version of Islamic law.

By the time he was finished in the bathroom, Rashid emerged to find the men had left for the day. For a moment, he relished the peaceful silence, then felt a twinge of guilt. He'd been a bit of a curmudgeon over the bathroom, and other things too – asking them when they were intending to leave, for instance. Then his sheepishness modulated into mild resentment. Why should he feel bad? He was providing them with free accommodation, wasn't he? But there again, he was just a peon running the website while they had greater things in their sights. He envied them their courage – courage to abandon their wives and mothers, the security of their jobs, their homes, their lives – and even half-longed to be invited to join them. He longed to be immune to the tugs of his mother's needs, his father's dreams and expectations.

Pushing up the windows, he leaned out on to the crumbling sill to see what was going on outside. It was quiet in the square. The boys had vanished, their game abandoned. Fresh air swirled into the room, replacing the beddy stench the men had left behind. The flat was empty, and that was a blessed relief, gave Rashid time to think. Soon they would be back, in dribs and drabs, coming and going as they pleased.

They couldn't stay here, his sisters, his mother. He mustn't let them see any of it, where he lived, what he was doing. He told himself it was because this was an all-male environment, unsuitable for girls.

★

Alia picked her way through the skeletal remains of Petticoat Lane Market, the road clogged with vans, bumper to bumper, loading up their wares at the end of the day. The snack bar where she worked these days was in a narrow lane that joined Spitalfields to the City, and she'd grown to enjoy being in that strip of connective tissue between disparate worlds. Mario's Cafe catered to both. Speciality sandwiches, buttered bagels, hot salt beef, chicken-tikka sarnies, pizza, chips and cappuccinos, all under the banner of an Italian flag painted on the window. It kept her in pocket for now. The one thing that truly bothered her about the job was that her clothes and hair smelled permanently of deep-fat frying. The tips were better than at Pret and the place less regimented. Even so, she worked in a half-daze, smearing margarine on slabs of white sliced bread from an outsize plastic tub stashed beneath the counter. She avoided her two closest friends from the first year and they'd all but given up trying to persuade her to come out to parties with them because she invariably pleaded exhaustion.

The exhaustion wasn't wholly an excuse. It was a side effect of her break-up with Oliver, the hole that was blasted by his absence. For a while, she had leaned upon him, perhaps too much, she'd concluded in retrospect. He had been her mainstay, only too eager to integrate her into his comfortable existence. Yet it had begun to pall, the niceness of it all – the weekly dinners at his parents' apartment and the family's collective desire to channel her back on to the straight and narrow of medical school. Why did they care so much? However well meant it all was, she had found it stifling.

There had been a round of interminable discussions on a family holiday in the South of France that summer, which led to a row between them. She replayed it in her head as she strode past the market traders, indifferent to their appreciative hoots and whistles. She was working and couldn't go to France, she'd told Oliver, and in any case, she couldn't really afford a holiday that year. Oliver insisted that his parents would pay. She'd refused, saying she couldn't possibly accept that. The more he pressed, the more she retreated, and he'd sulked for a week or two until the bright prospect of another girl arose on the horizon — and the chance, he'd admitted, that she might come to France instead.

Alia had been thrown. For a week, she had called in sick to her manager at Pret A Manger, convincing herself she had a throat infection that confined her to bed. Her throat did hurt, though that was probably from yelling at Oliver during a series of phone calls and, when she was alone later, from crying.

She pushed her way through the hubbub, the yells and clanks and clangs of traders dismantling clothes rails, lingering now and again to see if there was a bargain to be had. A short cherry-coloured skirt caught her eye, but she resisted the temptation. She thought of the girls in the village, the fragile glass bangles they had pressed on to her wrists, and how she'd snapped them off the moment she was alone with her father on the train back to Lahore. She thought of the tight pink suit she'd been unwilling to wear because it constricted her, how ungrateful and silly she'd been.

Another letter had arrived from Mishele.

My Sister Alia!

A thousand thanks and greetings from us all here. I am grateful for your beautiful postcard of the Tower Bridge of London.

I have happy news.

My brother Rashid has helped us to come to England.

He says the doctors here are free and he will find me a school. My father will stay here, with my younger brother, who is back from the madrassa, thank Allah. He begged my father to bring him home. Abu wept when he heard what it was like there.

Soon I will see you again. I cannot wait.

Today we went to the market. I have new shoes, and so does Mona.

Write to me soon.

Your sister, Mishele

That had been a month ago and since then the lines of communication had fallen quiet. She still wondered why her father had let them down, afraid of what it meant. Rashid's explanation that it was the new lady friend seemed unconvincing, or only partial, though she conceded it may have derailed him in some way. She felt a pang of curiosity as she moseyed home, wondering what had happened to Farrah and her father, if they were still together.

The coolness of late afternoon set in and she thrust her hands into her jeans pockets, ripped and frayed at the seams. She'd left for work that morning wearing Converse sneakers and no socks, and now a blister bubbled on her heels after a day on her feet serving customers. She fished around in her bag and found a depleted packet of cigarettes. The find lifted her spirits, sagging at the end of her long day; she lit up and walked away from the market traders.

As she rounded the corner, a figure in the crowd loomed towards her. 'Alia,' a man's voice said – a statement of fact, rather than a greeting. The sight of him startled her, his features unfamiliar in the long shadows of the buildings.

'Rashid?' she exclaimed.

She had not seen him since that day she'd shown him Mishele's earlier letter. It seemed as though he'd been hanging around waiting for a while and she wondered if he knew that she worked round there.

'I have a favour to ask you,' he began. She noticed his teeth were chattering, and she wondered why he was so cold, or if it was something else. 'Please.'

She toed her cigarette into a slab of pavement, in case it bothered him. 'What sort of favour?'

'Do you have time now?'

'I suppose so.'

He gestured inside a café, but the owner shook his head as he flipped the Closed sign on the door. Rashid looked about for somewhere else.

'Is there nowhere we can go?'

'I don't think you want to go to a pub, do you?' she ventured.

He seemed uncertain, which put her on edge. 'What is it? Just tell me.' She always felt the heft of things unspoken whenever she encountered him. If only she could unpack him, like a suitcase, examine the contents to see what he was about.

The market had grown quiet and City workers were thronging in phalanxes towards Liverpool Street Station.

'They're arriving soon, Alia, my family.'

'Yes, I heard. Mishele wrote to me.'

He glanced around. 'The trouble is, I have no room in my place. There are some guys staying in the house and it's not suitable for my mother and sisters.'

Alia was quizzical. 'Can't you just get rid of them?'

He shook his head. 'I need your help, Alia.'

'OK. What is it?'

'Is it possible they could stay with you for a short time?'

She was silent for a moment, considering the request, then said, 'I've got room. Why not?' There was something about his demeanour, the urgency of his appeal, that she could not refuse. 'My dad never sent them the money, did he?'

Rashid shook his head. 'But you were right, what you said. It's up to me, isn't it?'

She looked away. 'I didn't mean it like that.'

They had reached the corner of Wentworth Street.

'No, I know,' he said.

'I'd like to help.' She thought about her ungracious dash from the village, and wondered if she might make up for it somehow, reciprocate the cousins' kindness.

Rashid clasped his hand to his chest. 'Thank you, Alia. You don't know what this means.'

She smiled and shrugged, softening a little towards him. And then he was gone, melting into the shifting street life before she could say goodbye.

Twenty-four

Dr Farrah had spent much of her adult life grappling with Shakespearian concepts. She was adept at analysing the texts and making trenchant connections. The work never tired her; in fact, it amplified her understanding of the world, or it had until now, for she suddenly found herself at a loss, unable to disentangle reason from feeling, appearance from reality, in her relationship with Harris. She was quite uncertain what to do, and doing nothing wasn't an option. When he had admitted his deception, it was as if she'd learned of an affair, so sickened and shaken had she been. For a time, it had made her reassess her powers of intuition, her finely honed judgement. Then, after a long silence on both sides, Harris had written to tell her that he had terminated his business dealings with Omar and was back home. He wondered if she might ever forgive him. His words had produced a sharp pang within her, because in spite of everything, she did miss him. Her reply had been swift and to the point. *Forgiveness is all*, she wrote back, and not in quotation marks either.

Yet still she worried that their differences ran too deep to make things work. When they had fought, Harris had chided her for over-theorizing, as if there were something strange about that. It had stung, the criticism had cut her to the quick and shaken her sense of identity, for she was a staunch believer in analysing everything that affected her emotional state. How could he truly love her, if he felt that that was wrong?

'This is who I *am*,' she said aloud, staring out of the conservatory windows into the garden. Did he only care about those silly women who leapt from one emotional raft to the next, careless of where they might drift? She kept returning to his appraisal of their relationship as a shameful liaison. The prim phrase had stunned her at first, then maddened her. How could he entertain such retrograde views on marriage?

But then what on earth did she expect? He was a typical Pakistani man, accustomed to his slippers being placed by the fire, his meals cooked, his proverbial pipe at the ready. Or was she being a bit harsh? He wasn't that unrefined, actually. On the contrary, his love of literature impressed her, as did his erudition upon Islam and other subjects, even if his tastes weren't always hers. Still, his views on Alia were so old school, they appalled her.

And so she had withdrawn a little, tailoring her replies to his emails with brief accounts of what she was up to, the state of the house, the garden, her teaching. It was as if she were occupying a holding pattern like an aircraft in the sky, circling the relationship from a height, wondering where to land. She had told him about the car breaking down on the way to the Cancer Relief charity shop, freighted with crates of books she no longer read, old paperbacks that belonged to her husband, books the boys had long outgrown. The Renault Clio, which was almost a decade old, had overheated in a traffic jam that stretched back from the Blackwall Tunnel and she'd had to ask for help from a fellow motorist, a kindly Englishman, borrowing his mobile phone to ring the AA.

Things were falling apart; her car was on its last legs. Was it sufficiently reliable to spirit her up to the north? She wanted to go and visit him, find out what was going on. Why, she wondered, had he never invited her to his home? What did he have to hide?

In a state of sleeplessness one night, she rashly mooted the issue with Naela. It was daybreak in Lahore and Naela was eager to check if Farrah intended to fast for Ramadan. The tentacles of sisterly concern reached down the phone line and threatened to choke her.

'It's a bad sign, obviously – means he is not an honourable man,' Naela pronounced, without requiring details or context. Honourable was one of those boxes that had to be ticked in her schema of the male species. 'Why do you ask?'

'Oh, I just value your opinion, as my sister, you know that,' Farrah lied, her mind made up.

What she really wanted was to give Harris another chance. Perhaps a part of her wanted to excavate Harris, the Harris who had been calcified with years of dogma. Could she chip into his insecurities, his sense of unbelonging, and unearth the true man she believed lay beneath? What had happened to the honourable Harris, the funny, lovable man she had fallen for? The cultured man with sartorial style; the bibliophile whose generosity was undeniable; the man who loved his Lahore kebabs, even as he loved Lahore?

If Harris was taken aback by her announcement that she intended to visit, he did his best to conceal it. She wanted to come and stay, she said, to see for herself what he'd been hiding all this time. He was apologetic; the place was far from palatial, his life humdrum. Never mind, she told him, she wanted to see him anyway.

The prospect of her visit tantalized and worried him. He had succumbed, giving his house a proper going-over, an approximation to a spring clean, in her honour. He'd attacked the brown stains on the kitchen sink, thrown his dirty socks and vests and towels into the washing machine, assaulted the toilet with an entire bottle of Harpic. The sideboard was swept clear of any remaining religious pamphlets left over from Rashid's stay. By the time she blew in late one night, the place was homely and welcoming, fragrant with the aroma of Pledge. Farrah was elated.

'I hit ninety on the motorway, Harris, can you imagine? Honestly, I never thought that car was capable of such speed. Seems like it loves speed, hates traffic jams!'

Harris swiftly bustled her inside before word zipped round that he was entertaining a lady friend. 'You were clearly in a hurry to get here.'

If she felt the stark contrast between her house in Greenwich, set back on a tree-lined street, and his more modest quarters, with its tatty front yard hosting wheelie bins and a privet bush, she didn't say so. The boundary between Harris and the people just beyond his front door was far less defined than it was in her suburban English neighbourhood, but it mattered little to Farrah. She wasn't one of those *begums* who could only survive in luxurious surroundings, and she was past the point in her life when she could be bothered with dissemblance.

'How is your heart condition these days, Harris? Tell me.'

'It's OK. The drugs keep things flowing nicely,' he said. He was touchy about the subject and always strived to play down any signs of infirmity. 'Everything's under control.'

The following day, she was keen to explore her surroundings. She lifted a corner of the net curtain that shielded the living-room window and peered out.

'Whatever are you looking at? Nothing very picturesque along this street.'

'I don't agree. It's rather fascinating. And also I just need to see what the weather's doing,' she said. 'What a very long street, and such a steep hill!'

'It's here, look, the weather forecast.' Harris punched the remote and found the channel.

'I've heard it can be very rainy up in these parts,' she mused. 'But I've brought a good jacket just in case and proper English wellington boots.'

The idea of it, of encountering nature in the raw, suddenly appealed to her very much. She was beginning to warm to the idea of an excursion.

'It rains an awful lot, even in summer, and it can be cold and windy too. Maybe we should stay home till it brightens up a bit.'

Farrah was crestfallen. 'Are you not feeling up for an outing, Harris? Tell me.'

'No, no, I'm fine,' he said, slapping his chest robustly.

She studied his features and decided he looked a little peaky; they had stayed up very late the previous evening.

'I was hoping to do some touring around the area,' she said. 'But only if you feel up to it.'

'Yes, of course I do,' he said. She seemed completely at ease here and that pleased him enormously, strengthening his resolve to pursue things with her. 'Where shall we head to?'

'The countryside. You know, I've never been in the north of England before. Only as far as Stratford-upon-Avon, which is actually the Midlands, isn't it? This is my first time in the genuine north. The buildings are quite fascinating. Are we near Brontë country, I wonder?'

'Yes, we are, as a matter of fact.'

'Oh, Harris, I'd love to visit the parsonage where the Brontës lived and wrote all those books.'

'I've always wanted to visit, but never had an opportunity till now,' he admitted. 'Did you ever see the old black and white film of *Wuthering Heights*?'

'Mm, yes, I did,' Farrah purred. 'Laurence Olivier was quite wonderful in that picture. But Harris, do show me around your town. I'd love to see your shop, meet your cousins also. Can we?'

'Not that there's so very much to see. It's an old mill town, a little run down in places. The last of the textile mills closed in the 1970s and the area still suffers from that.'

'Well, where are the nice parts, the scenic bits? Where's your shop?'

'Not far from here. But it's not particularly scenic.'

He thought of the ruined playground, the drifts of debris, the women jabbering together as they hauled their washing out to dry in the backyards, bawling at their children.

'Didn't you tell me it's a corner grocery shop?' she asked.

'It used to be,' he said. 'Now it's more bric-a-brac – clothing, electronics, housewares. Designer goods, actually.'

She noticed a photograph of him with Alia in Pakistan on the sideboard. 'Have you spoken to her since we saw her in Canary Wharf?'

'I haven't, no,' he said, and she caught something unfamiliar in his voice.

'Oh, Harris. You miss her, don't you?'

He pretended not to hear.

While she was upstairs, he turned his attention to his *Shell Guide to Britain*. quickly locating the relevant pages of the place she'd expressed interest in visiting. It gave him much pleasure to put the *Guide*, a rash book-club purchase, to some use at long last.

'*Haworth, a small village not far from Bradford in West Yorkshire, is situated above the Worth Valley amid the bleak Pennine moors,*' he read.

'Listen to what it says!'

'*Haworth is internationally famous for its connection with the Brontë sisters, who wrote most of their famous works while living at the Haworth Parsonage, which is now a museum . . .*'

'Why don't we go this afternoon?' she said. 'After lunch?'

In preparation for the expedition, Dr Farrah kitted herself out in a green, waxed Barbour-style jacket, which she had bought for Idrees in the last winter of his life. He had never worn it. 'We were roughly the same size, you know,' she explained, and Harris reflected that Idrees was, like him, a slight man with a small frame. She ferreted around in her suitcase and took out a pair of green rubber wellington boots.

Harris admired them. 'You came prepared,' he said.

She blushed. 'I always try to be.'

In her waxed jacket, rain hat and wellingtons, she resembled a minor royal and secretly fancied the idea of herself striding across the moors, rather as she'd seen photos of the Prince of Wales and his cohorts doing, in the pages of those British celebrity magazines she flicked through whenever she stood waiting in the supermarket checkout queue.

It was already late afternoon by the time they reached the Brontë Parsonage Museum, only to find it was closed. Harris peered in disbelief through the darkened windows.

'It said it's open every day in my *Shell Guide*. What is this country coming to, I ask you?'

'The guidebook may have been out of date, you know,' Farrah said cheerily, slipping her arm into his. She had a point, for the book was over a decade old.

'I really honestly don't mind,'

Then it began to rain, so they got back into the car. The windscreen wipers groaned back and forth, striving to clear the huge droplets that hit the glass with a splat and spread out hypnotically across the glass. It was hard to fathom where they were – a patchwork of heathery moorland hemmed them in on either side – and they drove around for ages. Just as Harris was beginning to fear they'd lost their way completely, he spied a road sign back to the Pennine Way and followed it. At the very least, Farrah could experience something of the local landscape; after all, she was dressed for inclement weather.

'It's the moors I'm really interested in,' she said. The rain had ceased by now. 'Can we go and see them?'

'That's easy. They're all around us – just look.'

Harris was unsure where the best place to pull over might be. In the ebbing light he saw a signpost pointing towards a

360-degree view. A ruined drystone wall speckled with lichen led to a tumbledown stile. It was the perfect vantage point. Even Harris, who had never fully understood the appeal of the English countryside, was awestruck. Clumps of heather cowered in the wind and the last rays of the sun fanned out behind a mountain range of purple clouds. A piercing violet light illuminated everything for a moment, then faded as the clouds regrouped and seized control of the landscape, enveloping it in shadow once more.

Harris clasped Farrah's hand. He noted she had lost her earlier professed desire to roam the countryside and was content to behold nature at a distance. Her face had turned pink in the wind, and Harris tipped back the brim of her hat and kissed her. Even though it was getting late, and he'd promised to have dinner with his cousins, he found himself reluctant to hurry back. For a mad moment, he wished he could elope with Farrah and live somewhere anonymous like this, find an isolated cottage with no confounded community to bother them. Right here, on these moors.

'What is it?' Farrah said.

'Nothing. I just wish we didn't have to go back for dinner with Nawaz and co.'

'We don't,' she said. 'We're fully fledged adults, remember, and this is Great Britain in the twenty-first century. We can do what we like.'

What they could not do, however, was get the car to start. Harris tried repeatedly, but it shuddered uselessly. Pumping the accelerator too hard resulted in flooding the engine and so they were grounded on the moors.

'Oh, God, I was afraid this might happen,' he groaned. 'I'm

so sorry.' His AA car breakdown membership had lapsed, he realized, and an emergency call-out would be very expensive.

'Surely you could give a shout to those cousins of yours,' Farrah suggested. 'Would they not be able to help us out? It is an emergency, after all.'

Harris was horrified at the humiliation of calling Nawaz for help, having him arrive with a smirk on his face to tow Harris and his lady friend home. What to do? He noticed a smallish pub and B&B set back from the road. They would need to find a place to stay for the night, that was key.

To Farrah's pleasure, they signed into the B&B under pseudo-married names. The subterfuge had a literary quality to it that tickled her. They were giddy with the adventure of it all, devoured a meal of scampi and chips in a basket at the bar and pints of warm beer while the rain drilled the moors in the woolly darkness outside.

Harris slept through the radio alarm and awoke in a discombobulated state. The environment of low-beamed ceilings, busy floral curtains and baskets of dusty pot pourri placed on every available surface was distinctly alien to him, and he was stifled with a sense of guilty regret. On the bedside table beside him lay a fat Gideon Bible, stiff and glossy and unread. Farrah was already singing contentedly in the bathroom next door as she got ready to depart. Harris turned over under the slippery bedspread that had kept sliding off him during the night, then suddenly remembered he had missed his medication. Almost as bad, he'd missed dinner with Nawaz and his family, who had a set of visiting relatives in town he'd promised and failed to meet. And now here he was with Farrah, marooned in an

English B&B, pretending to be something they weren't, like
an eloping couple. He loved her, didn't he? So why were they
acting like fugitives? It was absurd; worse, it was sinful, at least
for him. She might have abandoned the faith, but he had not.

Why not marry her? Make the relationship an honest one?
Propose now, on the spot? Stop behaving sinfully? Put this
secretive, shameful behaviour to an end, right now, here on
the Yorkshire moors?

While she made the most of an English cooked breakfast in
the dining room – crisp golden triangles of fried bread, eggs
and bacon – he tackled the car and mentally ran through a
series of proposal lines.

'Let us put things on a proper footing,' he tried, *sotto voce*.

It sounded so wretchedly legalistic, so unromantic. Heaven
forbid. He checked the gasket, and found the rubber appeared
a little worn but not perished. Miraculously, the car started
first time. He looked up and saw Farrah smiling and waving
encouragingly at him.

'Are we in business?' she cried.

The marriage proposal was on the tip of his tongue, but
then stalled.

'We are!' he shouted back.

To compensate for his failure to show up at Nawaz's gathering,
Harris agreed to invite the inquisitive cousin and his wife over
after dinner the following night.

'They will see I'm no monster, I hope,' Farrah said. 'But
then, monstrosity, like beauty, is in the eye of the beholder.'

'Monster or no monster isn't the issue,' Harris declared. 'It's
the living together, Farrah. That is the problem.'

She rolled her eyes. 'We aren't living together, Harris. I have my own house still, remember? In any case, why are they so concerned in this day and age?'

She had risen to the occasion, wearing her best purple slacks and a demure cable-knit cardigan. For good measure, she'd added a long floaty chiffon scarf that she draped loosely around her head and shoulders, a deft nod at the dupatta that she wore only in certain circles back home in Lahore. But her sense was that Harris's cousins were on the conservative side and she wanted to present a positive impression.

As soon as they arrived, Safeena moved swiftly into the kitchen, while her husband settled into the living room with Harris.

'What canna do?' Safeena asked Farrah, eyes darting about.

'No need, it's all done,' Farrah said, emptying a packet of Dutch shortbread biscuits on to a plate with smooth efficiency. The water was already boiling for tea, a tray set in advance of their visit.

'Oh, we're not staying long,' Safeena said. 'And we've just 'ad a big meal.'

'Then you must take tea and biscuits,' Farrah said sweetly. 'Please. Come.'

She followed Farrah into the living room, where Nawaz had colonized the sofa, arms and legs sprawled over the cushions.

'Shall I bring something?' Safeena offered.

'No, no, it's fine,' Farrah insisted. 'Take a seat. Make yourself at home.' Then she disappeared into the kitchen again and returned with the tray she had set with rose-patterned china.

'Pretty design,' Safeena murmured, examining the cup close up to her face. 'Are they new, then?'

'Yes,' Harris replied. 'Purchased in the sale at Debenhams. Like it?'

'I do, yeah,' Safeena said, flushing with envy.

'Tell me, how are your children, Safeena?' Farrah enquired, changing the subject.

Safeena was taken aback by the question. 'They're orright – bit of a handful. I'm in the middle of decorating our bedroom, and the youngest's been a right pain.'

'Oh dear, I can imagine,' Farrah said sympathetically. 'You have four children, Harris tells me?'

'That's right. They're at home today. Plus me sister's visiting from Keighley.'

'Aha.' Farrah smiled. 'Nice for them to have an auntie or two close by.'

'Yeah, 'tis,' Safeena agreed.

During this exchange, Harris had been standing around at a loose end, not knowing where to plant himself. After dithering a bit, he took up a position in front of the gas fire, where he felt more in command of the room. Safeena sat next to her husband, and Farrah noticed her auditing the place for signs of a woman's touch. The kitchen remained Harris's stronghold, that was clear; the slow cooker still ruled the roost, as did the grease-smudged jars of condiments labelled in his copperplate handwriting. When Farrah poured tea and handed out napkins and plates, she felt Safeena's sly glance scanning her face, assessing her vintage, no doubt. There was talk in the family that she was a widow of a friend of Harris's rich business partner in Lahore. But nobody knew for sure if she was wealthy herself or a gold-digger. People said it was her influence that had made Harris drop all business dealings with Omar, the big man in Lahore, that she had refused to allow them to work together. That she had made him stop supporting the cousins in the village.

'Have you heard from Rashid?' Harris asked Nawaz.

Nawaz rubbed his upper arms in a leisurely fashion. 'Uh, yeah, we spoke the other night.'

'And?'

'They're coming, Nasreen and the girls. Rashid's seen to it all.'

Harris's stomach plunged. 'Rashid? How's he managing that?'

'Guess he has his means and ways.'

'And what's that supposed to mean?'

Farrah glanced at Harris, concerned at his crinkled brow, which shone with sweat.

'It was a shock to me too, cousin,' Nawaz said defensively. 'So don't take it to heart. I'd no idea, did I, Safeena?'

His wife bit her lip. 'None of us did,' she said, toying with a bright gold bangle jammed on to her thick forearm. 'Kept us all in the dark, they did, those cousins.'

Farrah offered her a second biscuit but she vehemently declined.

In the aftermath of the cousins' visit, Harris sat listlessly upon the couch.

'I've let everyone down, Farrah, haven't I?'

'What on earth are you talking about?' She sat next to him and took his hand.

'My cousins are shunning me, I can feel it. I've let them down and now they're leaning on Rashid. The boy's turned his back on me, hasn't he?' He looked at Farrah. 'Everyone's given up on me. They used to look up to me and now see how the tables have turned.'

'No, they haven't, Harris. Don't be silly.'

He jumped to his feet. 'I can't live like this, Farrah, skulking around secretively with you in my house.'

'Oh, for God's sake, we aren't skulking!' she exclaimed. 'Haven't we moved beyond that? They must all know about me by now, surely. I'm not a secret any more, am I? I came up to see you and you seemed happy to have me here.'

'I am,' he cried. 'But I want to be able to live according to the faith.'

Farrah groaned. 'You're a devout follower of the faith, Harris, I'd say. I don't see what the problem is. Tell me.'

He had rehearsed the words so many times. 'The problem is, I don't want to live like this any more. I want you to marry me. Will you be my wife?'

There was a long silence, and then Farrah said, 'I need to think about it, Harris.'

It seemed to her that he wanted propriety in the eyes of his cousins more than anything else. More than love of her, more than a desire for happiness.

It was still light outside when she left the house. A straggle of schoolboys lobbed a football up and down the street, shrieking and yelling at each other's blunders. She strolled briskly past, avoiding the ball, lost in thought. When she reached the top of the hill, she sat down on one of the fractured benches at the edge of the playground, uncertain what she should do next. She caught an acrid fume of turmeric wafting in the dank air from somebody's kitchen. Somebody's wife, dutifully preparing the evening meal, in time for her husband's return. She shuddered a little. A skinny girl in a grubby anorak whizzed fearlessly on the roundabout, showering cheese puffs as she did so, drawing a flock of greedy pigeons. Farrah flapped her arms to drive them away, but the birds were undeterred. She looked round and saw Harris walking up the street towards her, his face tilted against the wind.

'I thought you'd run away,' he began. He lifted his hands in despair, then dropped them.

'I don't need to run. I have my car.'

'Think it'll make it?'

'Who knows?'

'Please, come back, won't you?'

She saw that the girl on the roundabout was too absorbed fixing the buckle on her sparkly shoe to notice that the pigeons had finished her precious puffs.

'Why did you move up here, Harris?' Farrah asked as a light drizzle began, softening the vista of the town below.

'Why?'

He wondered what to tell her, what to leave out. He saw her face was pink, whipped by gusts of cold wet wind that flew up the valley.

'I don't understand,' she said simply. 'How you ended up like this.'

He had nothing more to lose and so he told her everything: how his hateful English wife had left him because he had never measured up, how Nawaz had come to the rescue; how things had fallen apart. How he had given away his money and forsaken his cousins. How Omar had thrown him a lifeline, but because of what she'd told him, he had refused it. In the grand scheme of things, the lost opportunity to make money mattered little. The worst thing of all, he said, was losing his daughter.

Farrah listened intently, then spoke. 'Alia isn't lost, Harris. She's in this world, trying to make her way.'

She had secretly hoped that, since they'd last argued about it, he'd come round to the idea that Alia would have her share of boyfriends, however irksome to him, and that he'd forgiven her, accepted the life she lived here.

'Harris, have you thought that you could just go down to London and see her? Go and make it up with her?'

'Make it up?' he exclaimed. 'You make it sound like it's all my fault. It's for her to see the error of her ways and come back to ask me for forgiveness.'

Farrah let out a wail. 'You want her to beg on her knees, is that it? She's a young woman, barely more than a girl. You can't cut yourself off from her like this.'

He shook his head. 'I can't accept her.'

'Then you're worse than a foolish man, Harris,' she declared. 'You've no idea what love is.'

As she spoke, his face seemed to fall in upon itself, as if a curtain had been drawn, shutters closed against the elements. It was only after she had gone that he found her wellington boots drying beneath a radiator, Idrees's waxed jacket flung in the hallway. Before, the presence of her things would have suffused him with happiness, yet now he hid them in the cupboard under the stairs, unable to bear the reminder of what he had lost.

Twenty-five

Nasreen and her daughters landed at Heathrow Airport one fine blowy morning in June and Rashid went to collect them. He hung back from the tightest press of the crowd, aligning himself with a wall of sign-toting taxi drivers as he waited, penned in by acres of relatives scanning the faces from abroad that surged towards them. There was no escaping it, no avoiding the outbursts of joy that hemmed him in, the squeals of recognition as passengers were swished into the hurly-burly of international arrivals. Unions reforged, families reunited. He should have been overjoyed yet happiness or its approximation was beyond him.

'Amma, over here!' he cried when he saw his mother anxiously looking around.

It took her a minute to register that the skinny boy of fifteen who'd left them was now a fully fledged adult in bulky anorak and jeans; her smile split her face in two when she realized it was him. That was a relief, seeing that she still knew him, still recognized him as her son. Yet, almost as soon as the smile faded, he felt a pang at the sight of her features etched with the years of his absence. There at her side were the two girls, one almost as tall as Nasreen, the other a wispy smudge of a thing clinging to her legs. So these were his sisters, Mona and Mishele. His mind reeled as he embraced them, feeling their thin arms clasping his chest, wondering how they would all fit back together. Nothing had prepared him for his changed family.

As he drove them back to Whitechapel, he tried to explain the arrangements.

'Remember Harris's daughter?' he said to his mother.

Nasreen nodded. Of course she did.

'Well, you'll be staying with her for a while. My place isn't suitable.'

'Why not, Rashid?' his mother wanted to know. 'I thought it was a nice place. Harris said so.'

Rashid was flustered. 'Harris hasn't been there,' he said. 'I've moved from that other flat, Amma. My new place isn't big enough for us all.'

He saw that she was baffled, put out.

'Whatever you say,' she murmured. 'But where is Harris? Can we not stay with him?'

'Harris is in the north of England, near the other cousins, in a different town.' Rashid spoke impatiently, in spite of himself. Why must she bombard him with questions? He had gone to great lengths to bring them here, hadn't he?

Alia opened her front door to find the two sisters and their mother huddled in a cluster on the pavement, defiant in their bright flimsy clothes, vivid against the muted grey of east London. Transplanted from the village, the girls seemed to her like fragile plants that might not survive the uprooting and she shepherded them inside quickly, before the hardened wind got the better of them.

They stepped inside the house slowly, tentatively, as if entering uncharted territory, picking their way past unfamiliar clutter that filled the hallway and stairs. Shell-shocked by the journey, the distance they had travelled, they fell into Alia's arms, dumbstruck, then stood back clutching hands, looking away, smiling sheepishly. When she hugged Nasreen, Alia noticed that she carried the tang of the village with her, a hint of the last meal she'd cooked for her husband lodged in the fibres of her clothes, her hair.

Rashid brought up the rear, dragging a large beige suitcase behind him, double-belted to keep the contents safely inside. He was apologetic that he hadn't been more organized, forgetting to tell them to bring winter clothes as well as summer ones, in case they stayed longer or the weather was bad. But it had all happened so quickly, he'd had little time to prepare.

'Don't worry about it,' Alia said. 'We'll sort them out.'

He felt a wave of relief that she was onboard, ready and willing to help him. He'd been distracted, insanely busy with the website, busy with the guys camped in his place who seemed in need of constant attention for one thing or another, and he'd given it freely. Yet he had his mother and sisters to contend with. How would he manage his work, now that they were here, asking questions, needing his presence, his support? He'd had no time to arrange a thing; no idea where they would live beyond this interim arrangement, or how they would survive.

He stole a glimpse at Alia, feeling her expectant eyes upon him. 'Thank you again for having them here,' he said, lugging their suitcase out of the way. 'I couldn't manage it alone.'

'No problem,' she said, waiting for him to say more.

He was silent, awkward. 'I'm going to have to get going.' He was making his way to the front door, lingering for a moment. 'Work and stuff.'

She was put out. 'Already?' His car was double-parked, ready to take off. Clearly, he'd not planned to hang about. 'They've only just arrived.'

He turned his attention to the girls, his mother, who were congregating around him.

'I can't stay, I'm afraid. I've got to get back to work. Amma, I'll be back soon, I promise.'

'What did you say to them?' Alia wanted to know.

'I said I'd be back soon.'

He kissed his sisters lightly on the forehead, then dashed away before questions or protests could surface.

Alia's thoughts chased up and down. What was expected of her now? She tried not to look at Mona too often, afraid the others would see she was trying to assess how ill she was. The last thing she wanted was to alarm them.

'Alia, are we in east or north London?' Mishele asked.

She had grown taller since the summer, the long plaits replaced by a sleek bun.

'This is east London,' Alia said. 'Why?'

'Is Uncle Harris in north of London?'

'North of England,' Alia said. 'A few hours' drive from here.'

Mishele explained the geography of everyone's locations to her mother, who kept up a hopeful smile, her bangles clanking as she flicked back the tails of her dupatta over her shoulders. Rashid had explained that she and the girls would be staying with Alia for a while. Because his place wasn't suitable, he said.

Unsuitable, indeed. 'But you'll see him soon,' Alia said to Mishele, who conveyed this to her relieved-looking mother. 'Every day, probably.'

She ushered them into the living room. 'Let me get you something to eat or drink. Are you hungry?'

Nasreen raised her hands in a gesture to deter Alia from troubling herself.

'At least have something to drink,' Alia tried, wishing Rashid had not abandoned her quite so instantly. 'I've got biscuits, cake . . .'

Mishele relayed the words in translation to her mother, who gave a sudden nod.

Alia was impressed. 'Your English has got really good.'

'I studied hard this year,' Mishele admitted, a pale flush rising up her neck. 'And my cousin has a TV, with many channels in English.'

'Is that what you'd all like, then, cake?' Alia was absurdly relieved, as though the success or failure of their stay depended upon it. 'And tea?'

It seemed to do the trick. The English nervous tic – putting on the kettle – was also a Pakistani one. When in doubt, resort to a cup of tea. She dived into the cupboard and found the Madeira cake she'd bought the previous day, slicing the yellow sponge into thick hunks, observed closely by the girls and their mother, who sat spectating in a row upon the sofa.

After the cake was eaten, Alia took them to see the sleeping arrangements. She'd laid her double futon upon the floor in the empty second bedroom, next to the single bed.

'You can put your things there, if you like,' she said, showing Mishele a small chest of drawers. 'Let me show you where everything is.'

She led them into the draughty bathroom. 'Will this be OK for you?' she asked, and saw they were cold.

Mishele nodded adamantly and Alia realized she was over-whelmed. The toilet, she guessed, was the problem.

'You sit here, look, and flush the chain like this when you're done,' she went on, and did a quick demo, which made the little girl giggle so much that Mishele shushed her as she strug-gled to take it all in.

Then Alia went to find towels. By the time she returned, they were back in the bathroom, experimenting with the shower spray.

Later that evening, when she had finished clearing up down-stairs, she peered inside their silent bedroom to see that all three were fast asleep. She texted Rashid that everything was fine, then went to bed herself, wondering what lay ahead.

She awoke at the deepest point in the night, disturbed by the wind outside, as if she were aboard a ship on a rough sea. In the corner of the room, the luminous numbers of a digital clock floated 3.00 in muffled darkness; too early to rise, impos-sible to sleep. She tunnelled into the bedding, worrying about what next: what she should do, what she should study and how she would manage. The uncertainty of her own future merged with that of her three guests, their sleeping presence amplifying her fears. As she lay in bed, she traced the spindly shadows on the bedroom wall, projections of branches from the plane trees outside, unable to drop back to sleep. She got up and went into the girls' room to check on them. Mona had crawled into the single bed and was asleep in her mother's arms, her breathing snuffly from a streaming cold caught somewhere between departure and arrival. Nasreen's long lashes fluttered in her sleep, her pale face set like a mask with exhaustion. Harris had promised to marry her, but he'd chosen Alia's mother instead, a choice that had catapulted him into an English life, for better or worse, and given rise to her own existence. The unfathomable thought danced about in her head, till a spate of noisy shouting and baying in the street outside interrupted it, followed by the sound of a front door opening, the affray sucked inside. Was it the neighbours, or other people, in another street? Voices were louder at night, carried further, so she couldn't tell. A post office van accelerated over a manhole with an alarming clunk. She listened till the engine noise dwindled away, then peered into the street. The hospital chimney rose up through swirling clouds, puffing smoke into the night, its red light blinking. She had choices to make – choices that could not wait for ever.

By the time Alia came down next morning, Nasreen was already up and about, having taken charge of the tea-making, and was mixing up an old packet of porridge oats she had unearthed from the cupboard. Alia yawned, bleary-eyed, and pushed aside the corrosive worries that had hollowed out her night.

'Will we go and see Uncle today?' Mishele pressed her, as they ate breakfast.

Mona nestled up close beside her sister. Mishele had plaited her sister's hair into severely tight pigtails, gleaming ropes that would never come loose. Her face shone with expectation.

They were all quite puzzled that Harris had still not appeared on the scene.

'I don't think we'll see him today,' Alia said. 'But I'm sure we'll see him soon.'

Though she was far from sure on that front. Tracking her father's movements, his tendency to shuttle randomly between locations, had never been simple. There was nothing she could do.

Or maybe not nothing. As she cycled back from work, two bags of shopping swinging treacherously against the spokes of her wheels, a memory of her father's concoctions in the condensation-drenched basement kitchen sprang into her mind. Wasn't there a mutton stew he made on special occasions? Now that might be something to make the cousins feel more at home, she thought, suddenly inspired. If only she had the recipe, or some notion of what actually went into it, other than mutton; not that he ever used recipes – he simply made it up as he went along. A born improviser, he made a lot of things up, she reflected, as she bumped over the cobbles, and he was infuriating for this and a thousand other reasons.

And yet, she realized as she turned into her street, she missed him more than ever now that the girls were here. His interfering presence was sorely lacking.

She had a day off from Mario's Cafe and took them on a double-decker bus heading west, away from the pressed streets of Whitechapel, so they might see Tower Bridge, Big Ben, Buckingham Palace – a succession of the postcards she'd sent, sprung to life.

She was their guide this time, and she loved it, the feeling that she was showing them London. She knew her way round, the ins and outs of the place, she spoke the language, and they instinctively clung to her, dogged her steps, hung upon her words. They began to unfurl, enjoying themselves, dazzled by the novelty of it all, and so did she, seeing her city afresh through their unjaded eyes. She noticed they needed jackets, as they shivered on the wind-blown walk home from the bus stop along Cavell Street. And so the next outing took shape: a shopping trip round Watney Market, seeking out bargain outfits, sparkly anoraks and gleaming trainers to replace flimsy flip-flops and shawls. They dropped into Iceland supermarket, peeping into chest freezers for things that Mona might like to eat – waffles and chicken nuggets to bolster her appetite. One warm afternoon, she bought them strawberry flavoured Mini Milk lollies from the corner shop and they sucked the wooden sticks till the last vestiges of pink sweetness were gone. She took them on a special trip to Sainsbury's, which seemed to thrill Nasreen more than anything, as she glided down the aisles, eyeing the produce on display, pausing now and again to feel the heft of a tin in her hands or to prod a piece of fruit. Nasreen had heard legendary tales of English supermarkets from Rashid over the years and had longed to see what the fuss was about. Now she understood.

Rashid dropped by in the evenings, often unannounced. That was his pattern, Alia came to discover, coming and going at random, reappearing in the evenings around dinner time, as his mother sizzled onions or poked at a pot of furiously bubbling dhal. He didn't talk much, bolting down his food before rushing back to the centre, or the minicab company, or wherever it was he had to be, which was inevitably elsewhere – anywhere but there with his family. Alia's resentment took root and grew.

'Amma's very happy when Rashid comes,' Mishele explained to Alia as they walked back from the market, her attention caught by the slabs of blue and green glass that formed part of the new library on the Whitechapel Road. 'She wants him to be with us all the time. But it isn't like that here, is it? All the family living together?'

'Not really, no.'

She'd been at a loss to explain to Mishele why she didn't live with her father or mother, or even with other students in a hostel, as she called it. Uncle Harris was in another town, Alia explained once more. Mishele knew that already. She knew his address off by heart from all the envelopes she had written on Khalid Ali's behalf. But why had they heard nothing from Uncle Harris? The perpetual, unanswerable question.

'You said he'd come soon.' Her eyes were round with incomprehension.

'Don't ask me,' Alia replied, tetchiness creeping into her voice. 'I can't keep track of everyone.'

She was out of her depth, playing big sister, cousin, host, cook and parent all rolled into one. Where was Harris when she needed him? She had rung him repeatedly, letting him know that the girls had arrived with Nasreen and that they were waiting to see him, clamouring for his presence, but he had not been in touch. Once, her heart pounding, she had even rung Nawaz to find out what was going on, only to get a vaguely grumpy reply about Harris's whereabouts, not helped by his thick accent and the screech of children in the background. He'd promised to pass on the message to Harris to ring her.

But her father never did ring.

It saddened and annoyed her that he had distanced himself so completely, so effortlessly, when he was most needed. And what was up with Rashid, for that matter? He'd become adept at disappearing from their orbit, holding himself at bay.

A week drifted by, and then another, until finally Alia could stand it no longer. She cornered Rashid when he showed up one evening, far later than promised, her fury at being abandoned having built up a fearsome head of steam. She sensed him shrink away from her as she sat beside him on the sofa, his eyes glazing over as he scrolled down his phone, avoiding her face.

'Rashid.'

'Huh?'

'Could you stop a minute and listen? Hello?'

'What's up?'

'There are things that need to be organized for them, Rashid. Have you thought about it? I mean, at all?'

She'd been more than happy to put them up for a few nights, she said, even a week, or two, or three. But now it seemed as if they were here to stay with her for ever.

'When are the guys in your place moving out?'

'I'm not sure. Is it a problem, my sisters and mother staying with you?' He appeared fraught and she felt a pang of guilt.

'Not exactly, but I can't keep taking days off work,' she said. 'I'll lose my job.'

She saw that this prospect made no impact upon him.

'I've taken too much time off as it is. I can't afford to lose it, Rashid.'

There was a long pause and she heard him take a breath.

'I'm sorry, Alia. I just thought you wouldn't mind having them, now that your father has abandoned us.'

The accusation winded her. 'Listen,' she began angrily.

'No, you listen,' he cut in, drawing his face up close to hers, so that she could see the open pores in his complexion, a mottled rash upon his chin. 'I don't think you understand just what your father did to my family.'

She jumped to her feet, heart thudding. 'What did he do?'

Rashid gave her a quick, strange smile. 'He promised them a sum of money he was expecting, when you visited in the summer.'

'Did he?' she said, her mind reeling, as she recalled her father's munificence in the village, how he had played the wealthy man who was in his element, even though she knew he wasn't rich.

'And then he gave it all to Nawaz.'

She was uncomprehending. 'Nawaz?'

'A small fortune, everybody says.'

As he uttered the words, she felt the chill of his betrayal blow through her like venomous gas. Her hand flew to her throat, as if she might choke.

'I don't believe it. Why would he do that?'

Rashid shrugged. 'Because he can do what he likes, can't he? He always has, ever since he came to England and fell in love with your mother.'

Alia sat immobile, trying to think, make sense of it all. When the components of her family had been flung apart, she remembered how Nawaz had seemed like the answer to her father's displacement, the blissful solution to his atomized life. With a portfolio of benefits, he'd corralled Harris up to the north, welcoming him into the fuggy fold of his community, prodding him into the shopkeeping business before taking over the shop himself. His precision was astonishing. And hadn't he always disliked her, because she saw through him? She observed how he'd seized on her father's weak spots – his insatiable need for company and home cooking, for family and chatter – and honed in on them, with pinpoint accuracy.

'But maybe you are different from your father. Are you?'

'What do you want from me, Rashid?'

He softened. 'Will you take care of them here just a little longer? It won't be for ever.'

His words reverberated in her head long after he had scuttled off, leaving her in the lurch for the umpteenth time. For ever is a long time, she thought, wondering what she might do to drum up her elusive father's presence to sort things out.

It occurred to her that Dr Farrah might know what her father was up to, or perhaps he was even staying secretly with her in London. She fished out the woman's business card, dog-eared and grubby, from the folds of her purse, where she'd put it that fateful day in Pret A Manger when her father had learned the truth about what she'd been up to since dropping out of medical school – assembling baguettes instead of studying for retakes – and she'd found out about his clandestine affair. She'd forgotten all about it – the card and its accompanying invitation to tea – until now.

Silently, she willed Nasreen to speed up and finish setting out the breakfast things, an inviolable late-night ritual that she performed before tiptoeing upstairs to bed. Barricading herself in the kitchen, Alia rang Farrah's home number, handwritten upon the back of the card. It was an old-fashioned ring, grating and insistent, that threatened to last an eternity. She feared that she was calling after an acceptable hour, but cleared her throat to speak as the ringing mercifully ceased and Farrah's voicemail picked up. She hesitated for a moment and then hung up.

Twenty-six

Nasreen was folding laundry in the kitchen the following morning when Rashid stole up behind her, brandishing a spray of pink roses he'd picked up from Kelly's Florist on the corner of Sidney Street. It wasn't really his style, quite out of character, and the expression on his mother's face said as much.

'Beautiful flowers,' she murmured in Punjabi, unwrapping the bouquet and standing it in a carafe of water. She regarded him curiously.

'It's what sons do for their mums, Amma,' he said with a smile, 'here in England. When they want to say I love you, or sorry for something.'

'Say sorry? What for, Rashid?'

'Never mind.' He flung himself upon a chair and folded his arms. 'What's been happening?'

She'd been up early preparing one of his favourite dishes, a karahi gosht stew. The scent of garlic and ginger had percolated through the backstreets of Whitechapel, sought him out, drawn him inexorably towards the house.

'There's a halal butcher just downstairs, Alia showed us,' his mother said.

'You went there by yourself?'

She nodded. 'Why not?'

'No, that's good, Amma. I'm glad you're getting out by yourself.'

'She left me money to go shopping before she went to work.'

'That's nice.'

Her chatter, so cheery and unassuming, triggered a sense of wretchedness that made him wither inside.

'Where are my sisters?' he asked.

'I let them go to the playground in the square. Did Alia tell you she's fixed an appointment with the doctor at the hospital for Mona? Next week.'

'That's good. I'm glad. I'll come with you.'

Her face lit up. 'Will you?'

'Of course, Amma. I'm your son, aren't I?'

'Let me look at you and see.'

Rashid shrank a little from her hand upon his cheek, her eyes upon him like a steady beam, shining into the dark recesses.

'Are you sure you're well?'

'There's nothing wrong with me, really.'

'Your chest doesn't bother you still?'

'Hasn't since the winter, no.'

'Harris gave you the holy water?'

'He did, yes. I told you that, didn't I?'

'Your father thinks he should get on with finding you a girl.'

'Amma, no. It's not the right time for me, not yet.'

'When is the right time? You're twenty-five. Your father has been thinking about arranging it.'

She dipped her fist into a soft mound of wholewheat flour on the counter, added two or three splashes of water and began to knead. Her hands transfixed him, whirling the sticky mass into a pliable ball; making something out of nothing. How he had missed her. She left the dough to rest and pressed a mug of tea into his hand. He looked away.

'Tell me,' she said, 'what has happened. Why are you keeping your distance from us all the time?'

Rashid swallowed. 'Not hiding, just busy with work, Amma.'

'Busy!' Her stinging disbelief was like a clip round the ear. 'And this place where you stay, that is not good enough for us—'

'Stop, Amma. I told you, it's full of young guys sleeping on my floor. There's no room, and it's not suitable for you or the girls.'

'What are you doing there all day?'

He sighed. 'I've been working for someone there, struggling to educate the young people here about the beauty of Islam.'

'And how are you doing this?'

'We have to make people understand the true nature of the faith and we run a website, and there's also a youth group that's very popular,' he enthused.

'But why are you doing this?' She folded her arms, bewildered. 'You had a good job with the property agent, your father always said. Why did you stop working there?'

Her critical questions lacerated him. 'I explained it all to Abu when he called me. It was an empty, worthless life, selling and buying property, and so I gave it up. Amma, Muslims are under attack everywhere,' he went on, disregarding her interjections, 'and we have to make people understand, defend ourselves. Don't you see how important that is?'

'So, then, what have you become instead,' she flashed, 'that is so very worthy, my son?'

'You don't understand, Amma,' he sulked, turning away from her.

She went after him. 'You think I don't see what has taken hold of you? I'm no fool, Rashid.'

He ignored her, emptying a sachet of fine white powder into the flower jug to prolong the blooms. 'Let's go and find my sisters. It's time they came back.'

In Ford Square, they watched as Mona clambered over a play-ground horse that her sister rocked back and forth, grating the rusty runners with a rhythmic squeak. They were wearing their new trainers and Rashid saw with a pang that they already seemed at home in this tatty London playground. Mishele dashed over to her big brother with a volley of questions about the school she had spotted nearby, the one where the girls wore maroon uniforms. Was it a secondary school or a college? Could she go there, and could they visit it one day, and what about Mona, would there be a place for her too? Was he coming to the hospital with them? Would they be staying in London for a long time or going to Uncle Harris? She hopped from one foot to the other, impatient for answers, and then dashed back to the swings when none were forthcoming.

'I should get back to work soon,' he said vaguely to Nasreen, jangling his keys in his pocket.

'But you'll eat together with us first?' his mother asked, stricken.

'I'm not sure I have time.'

'I'll be quick,' she promised, but he wasn't listening. He was staring up through the leafy boughs of a vast plane tree at a flock of starlings, cawing and scrapping over something.

'Five minutes more!' Nasreen called to the girls. 'Then home time.'

'Rashid!' Mishele shrieked, and he turned to see Mona's tiny inverted form, swinging from the monkey bars, terrifying for a second, until he saw she was being held by her sister's hand. Their ability to adapt so fast amazed him; they would survive here, perhaps even flourish, where he had foundered.

Back in the kitchen, his mother immersed herself in the food preparations. The meal would fuse them back together, he could read her line of thought as she hummed, rolling out the chapattis, teasing out their roundness before tossing them deftly over the blue gas flame. *She makes things so beautifully*, he reflected, watching her slice onions into transparent crescents, studding them around plate rims, setting a lemon wedge on each one.

'Ready,' she said.

'This is too much, Amma. Honestly, I normally don't bother – just grab a kebab, that's it, eat while I'm working.'

His mother pooh-poohed the idea.

'Amma, listen to me.'

She looked up, alert to the tone in his voice, dabbing a floury palm to her cheek.

'I owe a man something,' he faltered. 'Something I can never pay back.'

'What is it?' She sounded more suspicious than worried.

He was far out to sea now, drifting further. 'I did it for you, for the girls, to pay for you to come here.'

She absorbed his words. 'I've been wondering how you managed it all, without Harris's help.'

He watched as she briskly filled water glasses at the sink and placed them upon the table.

'I'm sorry,' he said wretchedly. 'I shouldn't have done it.'

She was overcome. 'But you saved us, Rashid, doing what you did. We will always love you, your father and I, no matter what.'

No matter what. The three words buoyed him as he drifted further and further into the dark choppy waves, wondering if he would ever find his way back again. They were all talking at once now, his sisters bouncing up and down on the sofa, his mother engaged in rapid-fire chat, saying things he couldn't follow, and she was dishing up huge dollops of stew on to plates, but he couldn't sit down, and so he stood there, spooning the mutton into his mouth, swallowing the buttery meat, tasting nothing, and she was asking him questions he couldn't answer. Silly things, unimportant things that made him smile, and he was a small boy again, hiding behind her legs, drifting in and out.

'I'd better go,' he said, forcing himself apart from them. 'I'm sorry, Amma.'

He should have been fielding calls at the centre and preparing activities for the youth group later that afternoon, but instead he found himself in Shoebargain, near Aldgate, searching for trainers with Mohsin Begg. The place was hot, packed with platoons of Russian women sifting through baskets of cheap vests, and posses of teenage girls foraging for anything skimpy and designer. It was madness, all this shopping, and Rashid longed to be back at the centre. Yet the purchase was essential, an integral part of Begg's wardrobe for a forthcoming lecture tour, and Rashid's input was sorely required.

'Which ones are better, you reckon?' Begg demanded. 'Timberland boots or the New Balance trainers?'

Rashid couldn't see beyond the towers of shoeboxes that hemmed him in on all sides.

'I don't know, brother. Whatever's more comfortable,' he replied, not that the imam could hear him over the thudding rap soundtrack. He could see why it was used as torture by the Americans in Guantánamo Bay.

'Or these Nikes?'

'Yes. Whichever you prefer.'

Begg mentioned that he wanted to buy some footballs and a set of ping-pong bats for the youth group. Sport was the way into their psyches, he was fond of saying. There had also been discussions about a camping trip for the Year Eleven boys.

'The carpet seller on Ashfield Street generously gave us a ping-pong table, so we just need to get the rest of the stuff. Can we buy it around here?'

Rashid was out of his depth. He was not the sporting type.

'Oh, sure, we can have a look.'

'See about the kit we might need, Rashid. Tents, sleeping bags, stuff like that, right?' He grinned. 'They'll love it – making fires, right, cooking outside.'

A pretty shop assistant rushed back and forth obligingly with pairs of shoes for Begg to try on.

'I'm going to be on my feet, running around, so they must be comfortable,' Begg explained as he bounced up and down. 'You'll be in charge when I'm away, yeah?'

Rashid nodded, in a dream.

'Would you like to take the Nikes?' the shop assistant enquired. She spoke with a clipped accent, which Rashid vaguely guessed was Polish. 'They are very popular.'

Begg caved in to her charm and coughed up the hefty price tag. Then the two men strolled up and down Commercial Street in search of camping gear and table-tennis equipment, only to find endless digital watches and electric components, light bulbs and lava lamps incarcerated on permanent display behind dusty shop windows.

After a spell of fruitless wandering in the sticky late-afternoon heat, Rashid cleared his throat and spoke up. 'Shouldn't I be getting back to the centre?' he said. 'There's nobody there to take phone calls. And there's that computer virus I need to sort out.'

'Possibly, yeah.'

They had reached a broad stretch of pavement close to Christ Church, Spitalfields. Nearby, some flashy developer had been inspired to transform a former public toilet into a subterranean wine bar, its Victorian railings encased in a Perspex box. The metamorphosis had not worked and Rashid noticed it was up for sale with Stone & Stone. They ambled closer towards the church, where a gaunt man with rope-thin arms begged for money on the steps. Rashid fished around in his pocket for some change and gave the man whatever he had. As he did so, Begg pointed out a security camera, steeply angled on a buttress of the church.

'It'll be on video. Asian boy takes pity on the English junkies. It'll be in the *Daily Mail*.'

Rashid shrugged, feigning indifference.

They sat down on a bench encircling an ancient oak tree in the litter-pocked churchyard and opened cans of Coke. Rashid watched a small group of volunteers as they tidied up the flowerbeds, weeding and plugging annuals into the earth. Nearby, a young mother with a baby in a sling upon her hip chatted to a pale-faced vicar, who swayed a little as he listened calmly and intently. Begg wiped his mouth with the back of his hand and cleared his throat.

'What are we doing here, Mohsin?' Rashid asked.

'It's quiet, away from things,' Begg replied, taking a swig. 'This church was designed by a man called Hawksmoor in the eighteenth century.'

'Really?' Rashid said vaguely, his mind elsewhere.

'And the mosque on Fournier Street? Used to be a synagogue.'

'Yes, I know. Jerry told me that.'

'Hard to believe,' Begg went on, disregarding him. 'Before that, it was a Huguenot church. So you see, my friend, it's happening. Which isn't to say we get complacent.'

Rashid didn't feel complacent in the least, but said nothing.

Begg pinioned him with his pebbly eyes. 'You've been a true Muslim, brother, putting up the guys at your place, taking care of them like that. You've no idea how much we appreciate it, really.'

'No, it was nothing, honestly.' Rashid rose to his feet, suddenly anxious to be on his way. 'I don't want to be late for the youth group this evening.'

'Sit down.' Begg traced a knotty whorl of wood on the bench beside him. 'I want you to know how much I've come to trust and depend upon you.' His glasses glittered in the hot sunlight as he tipped back the dregs from the can, careful to avoid it touching his lips. 'At the beginning, Rashid, I wasn't sure. I doubted your true commitment.'

'Really?'

'But now I've seen what you're capable of. Listen.'

Rashid's mouth was dry. 'What is it?'

'Our brothers will be on their way to Europe soon.'

'Really?'

He didn't want to hear or know any more. He looked up and saw the young mother smiling, laughing.

'And you'll follow in their footsteps,' Begg continued.'

The mother was oblivious to Rashid and the conversation that held him, but her baby fixed him with an astonished gaze, defiant from the safety of her sling. The axis of his thoughts swivelled back to his sisters, his mother, wishing he had not left them alone.

'Me follow them?' Rashid heard his voice, muffled, unfamiliar.

'They are working in the name of Allah, the most beautiful, the Almighty,' Begg intoned. 'You will be rewarded in paradise, Rashid.'

Rashid was mute. He shifted his attention to the gardening volunteers, dressed in matching T-shirts, armed with their trays of bedding plants, their shiny tools, their sensible gloves. He'd never heard of the Spitalfields Urban Gardening Trust, but now he found himself gripped with envy for the pure simplicity of their work, pushing plants into the soil, tugging out weeds, watering, hoeing.

Begg clutched Rashid's forearm. 'Have faith, brother, in your strength. Look at yourself. You've developed from nothing into this!'

'Was I nothing?' Rashid croaked.

'Put it this way.' Begg was matter of fact. 'Your life was worthless, basically. It was empty, brother, but not any longer.'

Then Rashid saw everything drop into sharp focus, just as when the optician places heavy lenses, thick and strong, before your eyes to determine the refraction. Everything stood out with terrifying clarity. How he'd been netted. How he was trapped. How there was no exit, no way back.

An oblong of sunlight somehow found its way into the north-facing backyard of the Crescent Islamia Centre. Until now, nobody had thought of using the dead space for anything other than dumping household flotsam and jetsam. Spurred into action by the promise of table tennis, the boys had cleared it to make space for the carpet seller's gift. By the time Rashid returned, there was a noisy group hard at play with Saheel, who seemed remarkably adroit with a bat and ball. He'd never cut a sporty figure in Rashid's estimation. But what did he know about such things?

His mind began to race. If he went to the police, he'd be walking straight into an admittance of guilt by association and his family would certainly be deported; then what fate would await them back home? The idea terrified him. In any case, what could he prove? They would never believe he was innocent, not now. So he did nothing. He drank old tea. He sat down and went through the motions of work at his computer, aimlessly surfing the net, replaying phone messages, scribbling notes.

A scrawny fourteen-year-old bounced over to his desk, hoisting himself up. 'So Tamidul bought us balls and someone got a net.' He drummed his heels rhythmically to a tune on his iPod.

'Get off my desk, please,' Rashid told him, and the boy slid off.

The heavy plod of teenage feet pounding up and down the uncarpeted stairs made the house judder. What had once filled him with a sense of hope and fulfilment – the centre's vibrancy, a hub for disaffected youth – was now unbearable. In a daze, he wandered outside to survey the goings-on.

'We found the table-tennis bats in the basement!' someone yelled at him.

'Nah, Asif got 'em in Asda, man!'

'Whatever.'

Rashid watched Saheel give up a game so that two girls might have a go. Shrieks of laughter filled the yard as the ping-pong ball flew everywhere but the table. The brother's charm was infectious, that was for sure. A teacher, wasn't he? Or was it a teaching assistant? Either way, he clearly knew how to capture young people's hearts and minds, how to win them over. What a skill to have on your CV! Rashid glanced at the time. The after-school session was almost over and soon the boys and girls would divide into discussion groups; lemonade and biscuits would be served, paid for by donations from grateful parents. The scene was a testament to Rashid's success – success that curdled in his gut.

Alia had finished her fifty laps at the pool and was in the changing rooms getting dry when her phone vibrated.

'Hello? Sorry, who is it?' The voice on her mobile was fragmenting and she moved about in search of reception, settling eventually on a hot spot by a bank of metal lockers.

'Hello, is this Alia?' came the voice again. 'Is this she?' The polite formulation, underpinned with a faint upward tilt, made Alia draw a quick breath of chlorine-sharp air. She rubbed her legs dry with one hand and pressed her phone closer to her ear.

'Yes, that's me,' she said, flicking back a section of wet hair and sending beads of water down her back. 'Who's this?'

'This is Farrah speaking. I think you called me yesterday, didn't you?'

She felt an urge to deny it, but that was impossible. Leaning back upon the lockers for support, she gasped at the coldness of the surface.

'Are you all right?' Farrah asked with concern.

'Yes, I'm fine. I've just been swimming – I'm in the changing room.'

'Oh, is this a bad moment?'

'Not at all, no.'

Her towel slumped in a damp coil around her ankles. She picked it up, rewound it about herself and began to pace up and down, bare feet squelching on the soupy tiles.

'I have your number listed here on my call log, that's how I knew it was you.'

'Sorry. I didn't leave a message. I wasn't sure—'

'Don't worry. I understand,' Farrah interjected. 'I often don't leave messages myself. To be honest, I dislike voicemail – so impersonal, isn't it?'

Alia sat down at the end of the bench, swivelling away from the prying glances of two medical students she vaguely recognized from last year.

'Could we meet?' she said, burying her face in her mobile, her dripping hair forming a puddle on the grimy floor. 'I need to talk to you.'

It took Dr Farrah a moment to realize that the girl standing on the other side of her glass office door was Harris's daughter. She removed her spectacles, just to be sure her eyes were not deceiving her, and noticed how much younger Alia appeared than that day she'd first met her, standing defiantly behind the counter in Pret A Manger. A girl of barely twenty, in fact. She'd seen photos of her on the sideboard in Harris's house, examined them discreetly when he wasn't around, taken note of her looks, the cropped hair, the knowing eyes. Not like her father, yet like him; a percolated blend.

'Good gracious,' she said, pushing aside a sheaf of essays upon her desk. 'I wasn't expecting you to come straight away. Is everything all right?'

'I'm not sure,' Alia said.

The office was sun-baked, its windows sealed, and she found herself gripped with an urge to race outside.

'What is it? Have a seat.'

She remained standing, hovering behind a chair. 'Is he staying with you, my dad?'

'Oh, goodness, no,' Farrah declared. 'Is that what you thought?'

Alia shrugged. 'I just thought he might be.'

'Well, he's not,' Farrah said swiftly.

'Is he OK?'

'I think so. Why do you ask?'

'Have you spoken to him recently?'

Farrah saw her agitation and relented. 'I'm sorry. Let me explain. We've not seen each other in a while, your father and me. Actually, we're no longer together.'

'I didn't know that. What happened?'

Farrah shook her head. 'Well, I don't know. I mean, it's hard to say. We kept disagreeing on things – fundamental things, Alia, not just who does the washing-up or what channel we watch on TV. His sexist attitude to me, I suppose, his rigidity regarding the faith. And his attitude to you also.'

'Me?'

'He has this idea about female propriety, what we women should and shouldn't do. It really made me wonder whether we were suited to one another, in the long run. I mean, do I actually want this? I'm not sure I do. I was married once and that was enough.'

Alia saw that Farrah's cheeks had flushed after the outburst. She looked down, embarrassed that she had triggered something.

'Look, I didn't come here to quiz you about your relationship with him,' she said.

Farrah caught a glimpse of a student hovering in the doorway, but gestured her away.

'So what is it, then? Why did you come to see me?'

'I thought you might know what's going on with him.'

'What do you mean?'

'Since the cousins arrived, he's not returned any of my calls, and I've tried calling Nawaz and the others too. Everybody's vague about what's up, where he is. I don't know why he seems to be avoiding me. So then I thought he might be, you know, hiding here with you.'

Farrah was put out. 'Hiding? Trust me, Alia, he's not.'

She saw that she had caused offence. 'OK, forget it. I'd better go.'

She fumbled for the door, but Farrah intervened.

'Wait,' she said, with a sigh. 'I'm sorry. I told him many times he was very foolish to cut you off in the way that he did and I still think he was wrong. But you must understand that he felt terribly hurt when these cousins were brought over without his knowledge, or indeed his help. His pride's been battered, that's the trouble.'

'Can't you just speak to him for me? Make him understand? He'll listen to you, won't he?' Alia pressed.

'I'm flattered you think I have such influence,' Farrah said. 'But I'm not so sure I do. I think you're the one he's missing.'

Alia felt her nose tingle, her eyes brim, and she turned away to hide it.

'Maybe that's it, yes,' she said.

Farrah noticed her shoulders were damp. 'Would you like a dry towel? I have one in the cloakroom.'

'I'm fine.' Alia shook her head and smiled. 'It keeps me cool. Bye, Farrah.'

Farrah watched Alia for a moment as she disappeared down the corridor. *Foolish man,* she thought, *casting that girl adrift.*

Twenty-seven

In the north of England, Harris sheltered in his house, waiting for the weather to turn. A major storm front was forecast, following a hot dry spell, and people had been warned of heavy rains and hazardous driving conditions. He stood at the window watching a shower of hailstones that bounced about his untended front yard, wondering what ill wind prevailed, cursing the weather men and their blasted warnings prophesying doom. Since parting with Farrah, he'd let himself go, gradually abandoning the small rituals and routines of daily life: the wearing of a tie, the filing of a letter, the supermarket run – all the inconsequential elements that solidified existence. He'd lost the will to deal with ordinary tasks, grown adept at avoidance to the point that even Alia's phone messages went unheard, or were simply ignored. He wished there were a way back but found himself believing that he was quite redundant in the lives of others, even those he had once counted his nearest and dearest. They were only interested in him when he had money to spare and now that he no longer did – the thought welled up, painful and hot, like an angry boil – he was redundant.

A thin ray of sunshine threw slivers of light into the living room, thrusting him into a fresh state of indecision. Should he venture into town or not? Perhaps he would go to the Design Emporium – see who was there, or what was new, catch a bit of gossip, proffer advice on retail strategy – or perhaps even venture to the bank. A series of letters from his personal banking adviser (the pompous title of the callow young man filled him with scorn) on the magnitude of his overdraft made him shrink from approaching the place. He had been forced to give up his business account there since handing control of the shop to his cousin. Fortunately, the credit card companies were more generous, allowing him to make use of their cash-dispensing services, though the interest rates were criminally high. Staring up at the bruised purple sky, he decided it was too risky to venture out and so he stayed home, brooding.

When the fruit seller called by to see why he hadn't been to mosque lately, Harris gave a series of tetchy reasons to explain his reluctance to attend. He'd grown suspicious of the imam and of mosque politics, he said. They were all crazy bigots running the place these days, hell-bent upon raising money for jihadis abroad and for the building of yet more mosques back home. What was the point in that? he wanted to know. The fruit seller was shocked at his good friend's words, but kept his peace, for Harris had always been such a kind and thoughtful man. Perhaps he wasn't well. He had deposited a brown paper bag of his best mangoes from Pakistan on the sideboard and left him alone. Harris spent the rest of the afternoon lying on the sofa, dozing in and out of naps, unable to concentrate on anything.

★

Daylight dwindled and darkness filled the house. A howling wind began to blow, forcing its way in through every crack and cranny, doing its best to penetrate the windows, shaking the very foundations. Harris remained in the living room, as if it were a safe berth on a leaky ship. Tiles flew off the roof, shattering on the patio. An army of storm clouds, vast and tumultuous, gathered its forces in the valley below. There had been gale warnings at sea, severe weather all over the north of England, but the news reports of flooded plains, uprooted trees, of cars like Dinky toys bobbing down high streets turned into rushing rivers, had seemed too distant, too surreal, for him to believe. Dogger, Fisher, German Bight, the shipping forecast intoned, lyrical with menace.

'My house is on a hill,' he told himself, repeating the phrase like a mantra. 'On a hill. Far above the danger of flood.'

Suddenly, he heard a loud insistent dripping coming from the upstairs landing. At first he tried to ignore it, turning the television volume up louder, but the noise was unbearable, drilling above his head and agitating him so much that he dashed around to find out what was causing it. He stood on the landing and looked up to see that the skylight had sheared off, giving way to the sky. The outside poured in.

Down he ran, scurrying everywhere in search of buckets, but there was only one to be found, in the kitchen, and that was already occupied, full of rubbish, lodged under the sink. Who to call on a night like this? Not Farrah, not Alia, both of them miles and miles away when he needed them.

'Nawaz!' he barked into the phone. 'Nawaz, come quickly! My roof is falling in!'

And Nawaz came, for he could always be depended upon in a crisis. Undeterred by the weather, he battled the wind and rain to drive across town, spiriting Harris back to the warm safety of Perseverance Street.

In the days that followed the storm, Nawaz returned to the house to assess the damage, and declared that it was nothing that he and his team could not handle: the roof would be fixed by Jamal's cousin, a builder; the carpet replaced by a contractor friend. Everybody would rally round, whatever it took, for Harris' sake.

'This house is too much for me,' Harris confessed. 'Can I not find lodgers to live there and cover my mortgage, till I get myself on my feet again?'

'Don't you worry about that. There's bags of students round 'ere needing a place to live.' Nawaz was stolid in his reassurance. 'The house is in a very good position.'

'Is it?' Harris cried. 'You really think so?'

In his heart of hearts, he had always doubted it.

In less than a week, two bedrooms in the house were let to a couple of German students who needed rooms for the summer. Everything was arranged by Nawaz, who placed an ad on the Internet, collected a month's deposit and settled upon a weekly rent. The relief that Harris felt now that it was off his hands was like a tonic, rejuvenating him and boosting his morale. He was released from his financial responsibilities, mercifully spared from the need to scrabble around for money to cover the bills that arrived with relentless regularity. He no longer had to think about the future, to fret and figure things out. And even

though he was not given a room of his own in Perseverance
Street, he didn't really mind inhabiting the sofa in the lounge,
which converted into a bed at night. The familiarity of the
arrangement was reassuring, even if the place was perpetually
clogged with the traffic of children, Safeena and her noisy
vacuum cleaner, and Nawaz and his cheesy feet parked on the
coffee table – not to mention the sundry friends and relatives
who streamed through at all times of the day and night.

Harris convinced himself it was for the best.

'We'll buy it from you, that house,' Nawaz declared one
day. 'And then you can get a smaller place, cousin, a flat, somewhere more manageable.'

A smaller place was just the thing. The brilliance of the
suggestion lay in its simplicity. No need to advertise the property or bother with slippery estate agents. The arrangement
appeared to solve everything. As it turned out, there just
happened to be an empty flat on top of the shop, belonging
to Jamal's sister-in-law. Perhaps Harris should stay there,
Nawaz said, rather than remain in Perseverance Street. After
all, he'd get the benefit of enjoying his own space, rather than
having to camp in the lounge.

'And you can always drop by the shop, if you fancy a change,'
Nawaz told the elder man, who was doubtful at the prospect
of further upheaval. ''Ave a natter, get a cup of tea.'

That was true, Harris reflected. A room of one's own might
be just the thing. And if trepidation shot through him at the
idea of living alone again, he remembered that the boys in
the shop would be downstairs every day, and that they could
do with his help, from time to time. There, at least, his presence was required, and even perhaps welcome.

And so he went along with it, the move from Perseverance Street to the flat on top of the shop. In the event, he was grateful to Jamal, who helped lug his suitcases up the uneven and cluttered wooden stairs (the doctor had warned against exertion, after his angina problems). He was struck by a sense of déjà vu, as if this moving business had become a terrible pattern that had dogged him in the past and was now unfurling into the future, the shape of things to come in the latter half of his life. Horrified at the prospect, he suddenly became breathless, a tight fist in his chest that stopped him in his tracks. He sat down on the only chair in the room.

Jamal regarded him anxiously. 'Are you all right, Harris? Do you need something?'

'No, no, it's fine,' he gasped, rallying as he took in his new surroundings. 'Should I move my leather armchair in here, do you think?'

The place was devoid of soft furnishings. There was a larder fridge and a two-ring stove in the tiny kitchen; a battered bookcase stood in the living-cum-sleeping area, but there was no bed or couch. Downsizing had a dreadful ring to it.

Later, Jamal brought over a foldaway bed he had going spare, a fearsome zigzag of metal springs and tubes that resembled a kind of cage. A sense of alarm threatened to sabotage Harris's gratitude, until the bed was safely unfolded and secured in the supine position. Both men agreed that it actually fitted quite well into the bed space, and once it was smothered with a duvet and a pillow, the starkness of its form softened a little. It was like camping, Harris told himself. A temporary arrangement.

★

Alia leaned her forehead against the train window and checked her phone messages as they waited in a siding before pulling into the station. Nawaz would be there to meet her, just as he'd promised when she'd rung earlier that morning. To her surprise, he'd been unfazed by the forward nature of her request to talk to him alone.

She listened to his message: *Wait for me under the clock tower outside the front of the station, on't steps, orright? I might be five minutes late, I reckon, with the traffic an' all.*

Yet now as she stood outside in the designated meeting spot, she fretted that whatever she'd imagined saying or doing to the man who had ruined her father was bound to fail if he was surrounded with the usual bevy of kids, wives, cousins. She'd be outnumbered; she'd be sunk.

He picked her up as arranged and insisted they drove back to the flat in Perseverance Street, which to her astonishment was miraculously empty, hushed and tidied, devoid of domestic traffic.

'Where is everyone? Thought I heard them in the background when I called you.'

He gave her a sideways glance. 'We were downstairs in Royale. Safeena's working there, as usual. So what's up, then?'

'I think you know, don't you?'

'No, Alia, I don't.' His voice was even. ''Aven't a clue.'

'The money you owe my father,' she began, steadying her voice. 'I think it's time you returned it.'

It took Nawaz a moment to absorb the audacity of her demand and then a sardonic smile spread across his face.

'So is that it? That's what you've come all this way for?' he said.

As he spoke, she noticed his teeth were surprisingly white; unreal, almost.

'Should have known it wasn't out of the goodness of your heart, seeing your family. I don't owe him a thing. You ask 'im yerself.'

'I will. I'm going to see him now.'

'Give him my best regards while you're at it. I mean, here I am, doing his shop for 'im, running the takeaway with Safeena, takin' care o' him, like he's me own father, under this very roof when his own collapses, while you're down in London enjoying yourself.'

'Is that what you think?'

'You've no idea,' he cried, warming to his theme, 'no idea just 'ow we've taken care of your father while you've been—'

'What?'

He shrugged. 'Outta the picture. We're all 'e's got left in this world. Go see for y'self.'

'I will,' she said, her hands trembling on the door.

'You won't find him at his house, by the way. Didn't he tell you? He's living upstairs from the shop. Keeping his hand in, you might say.'

She careered down the stairs, pausing at the bottom to regain her strangulated breath. She didn't believe it. How could he have moved into the shop, just like that? It made no sense. As she set off down the road as quickly as she could, she heard the determined click of Safeena's spiky heels behind her, smelled her cheap perfume, as she rounded the corner and approached. Alia quickened her pace, wary of what an encounter might catalyse, so that by the time Safeena caught up with her she was panting.

'Alia, don't make trouble, I'm beggin' you,' she said, her eyes flicking fretfully about. 'You'll get your father's money back, I'll see to it. Don't ruin us, will you? We've our reputation an' all.'

'What reputation?'

'Our family business depends on it. If it collapses, we can't go on.'

She looked at Safeena. 'You're just like him, aren't you?'

Safeena bit her lip. 'So will you ruin us, then?'

'You've ruined yourselves.'

'What's tha' supposed to mean, then?' She tossed back her head and tugged at a gold chain around her neck, fiddling with the links. 'He's just become a local councillor, see, and it's right tough round 'ere. You know 'ow it is. And everyone respects him, they really do, Alia. He represents our community, he really does, stands up for people, and he's not a bad man, no matter what you think he's done.'

On and on and on she went, her righteous indignation clicking in her heels, as she pursued Alia down the street.

'You don't understand us, how our families all stick together and look after each other,' she cried.

Then Alia stopped and turned to face Safeena. 'You're right,' she said, her voice shaking. 'I don't. Because if that's true, then why did Nawaz treat my father like that?'

The question stumped Safeena, left her standing gobsmacked in the street, not that Alia hung around waiting for a reply. She nipped on to a waiting bus and did not look back.

The bus dropped her at the foot of the road and she battled against a wall of wind that did its level best to push her back.

The once familiar landscape appeared disordered, wrecked here and there, and elsewhere untouched. A clump of spindly trees had been blasted by the gales, their leafy treetops sheared like a rash and regrettable haircut. The green opposite her father's shop was transformed, pooled with a sheet of rainwater, a magnet for seagulls that swooped on to its mirror-bright surface.

She found Harris in a room at the back of the shop, perched on a sofa, his face dipped away from her, shoulders hunched. He looked up, alert with hope, when he heard her calling out for him, as if he were a missing animal, which was just about how he felt these days. All those years he had complained about the wretched shop, the endless trips to the Cash and Carry, the arduousness of shelf stacking, the meagre profit margins at the end of the day, and now he had been relegated to the back room, relieved of his duties. Was this what he wanted, she wondered, seeing him there, redundant, dishevelled? In the corner was a sink and a kettle; a giant box of PG Tips tea bags stood at the ready. For now he was the tea boy, he said with a smile, who also gave tips on the retail price index.

'I usually drink Darjeeling, but the boys insist on PG Tips,' he said.

'I serve a few gallons of that stuff at work every day.'

'Still working at Pret A Manger?'

'No, I left there. I'm working in a snack bar near the City. Just till the end of the summer, while I work out what to do.'

After a moment he said, 'I thought you'd never come back.'

She sat down next to him, unable to speak. In the dim light, she noticed a curdy rind of milk upon a saucer on the floor, a half-open tin of tuna beside it. A feline tang pervaded the place.

'Did you get a cat?' she asked.

'The cat came shortly after my arrival,' he explained. 'No idea where he's from. He's a good mouser, actually.'

As if on cue, a tortoiseshell emerged from the shadows, pausing briefly at the saucer, disappointed with its paltry offering.

'I feed him once a day,' he said wearily, when the cat stalked off. 'Never gives up, pestering me for more.'

He rose stiffly and rootled around in the cupboard for a box of Go-Cat, rattling the biscuits as he shook them into a bowl.

'Want to see my living quarters?' he said. 'Not very palatial, I'm afraid.'

She followed him upstairs to the flat. Propped up on the window ledge was an old school photograph of her and next to it was a faded Polaroid of a trip to Mecca, distant and unreal.

'Why didn't you say you were moving to this place?' she said. 'What happened?'

She noticed that his chin was dusted with white prickles and wondered if he was growing a beard again, as he'd done once when he'd returned from the Haj.

Harris shrugged. 'It's just temporary lodgings, Alia.'

A trail of clothes spilled indecisively from a suitcase. She glanced around and spotted familiar belongings: the faithful slow cooker, the botanical encyclopaedia, a small Persian rug, the Parker Knoll chair. The room was dominated by a huge television, its slim black screen sucking everything into the abyss of its reflection.

'Nawaz got me that,' Harris admitted, when he saw her assessing its provenance.

'He took all your money, didn't he?'

Harris blinked, bewildered. 'I thought he'd pay me back.'

'But he didn't.'

'The house was too much for me,' he went on, avoiding her eyes. 'You don't understand these things, Alia – the cost of it all, the repairs, the bills.'

'I do,' she said. 'I know about bills.'

'The roof fell in, the landing carpet was soaked, ruined. It was actually Nawaz who came to the rescue.'

'He didn't rescue you, Dad,' Alia said.

'He'll take it off my hands, the house. What do I need such a big place for now? I rattle around by myself.' He stole a glance at her. 'This is enough for me, isn't it?'

Alia sat down on the camp bed, the springs creaking under her.

'What about Nasreen and the girls, Dad? They'll need a place to stay eventually. I can't keep them at my place for ever.'

'Are they sleeping on your lounge floor?' he asked.

'No,' she replied. 'They're in Oliver's old room for now, till someone else moves in next month.'

'And where did he go?'

'His parents bought him a studio in Bethnal Green.'

'Lucky him.'

'After we broke up,' she added.

'Ah.' Harris looked down for a moment. 'I'm sorry. I didn't mean—'

'Don't be. I mean, I'm not.'

They both fell silent for a moment. Then Harris said, 'I may as well tell you that Farrah and I are no longer together either.'

'I know. She told me.'

'You spoke to her?' He was indignant.

'When I thought I'd lost you.'

'Lost me? Like a piece of luggage?'

'It wouldn't be the first time,' she said, remembering the moment on the railway platform, somewhere between the village and city, when he'd vanished in a sea of passengers and she'd panicked, thinking she'd never see him again.

He raked his knuckles under his stubbly chin. 'I really should shave, shouldn't I?'

'You could change that shirt too.'

'One thing at a time. Give me a chance, Alia.'

'I'm giving you a chance. Come to London, stay with me, and help Nasreen and the girls.'

'What use am I?'

'They can't manage without you.'

'Is that true?'

'Yes,' she said firmly, and saw that the prospect made him rally a little. She knew that she must seize the moment before it slipped away. 'Neither can I, really. I thought I could, but I can't.'

'Oh, Alia,' he said, at a loss. He had feared his own redundancy, had convinced himself he was neither missed nor needed.

'It's up to you,' she went on. 'You can be a part of this family or not.'

Her words astonished her and she felt a flicker of fear at the possibility that there was a choice in the matter.

For several hours after Alia had left, Harris stared out of the window, reflecting upon how she had provided for the cousins when he had let them down. Sitting in the flat on top of the shop, watching the hopper buses toil up and down, feeding the cat, brewing the tea, had come to represent the limit of his capabilities. How paltry it seemed, in comparison to his daughter's exertions. As he said his prayers that evening, he felt more mindful than ever of his moment of folly and weakness, diverting his beneficence in the wrong direction. How foolish he'd been, how sinful, putting his faith and trust in Nawaz rather than in Allah.

Twenty-eight

On more than one occasion since Alia's visit, Harris had packed a suitcase, only getting as far as the dual carriageway before fear made him do a U-turn and go back. The fear was ill-defined and yet substantial, ballooning in his chest as he careened down the fast lane into an indigestible glob that refused to disperse.

A visit to a small mosque tucked next door to a fish and chip shop on the other side of town was his final resort. There were no familiar faces in the dingy space and he found his anonymity was a blessed relief. Prayer laid everything bare, drew out the dregs of his fear so that he could avoid it no longer. He feared what he had done and what he had failed to do. He feared seeing Nasreen and facing up to his responsibilities, the ones he had run from decades ago and the ones that had accrued that year.

It was time to reclaim what he had lost. Gripping the steering wheel of his car more tightly than was necessary, he drove back to his neighbourhood. Weeks had passed since he'd been in his old stamping ground yet to his surprise the streets were welcoming, and so were several old faces. He had made an effort to make himself more presentable, thanks to Alia's comments, which had resonated in his head as he dithered between putting on a shirt and tie or just pulling on the old V-neck over his baggy trousers.

The fruit seller was overjoyed to see him and darted out to chat when he saw him pause at the window to examine the lychees that were on sale.

'Coming to mosque on Friday, brother?' he cried, but Harris kept going, as if stopping to talk and discuss the latest burgeoning fracas in that neck of the woods might interrupt his trajectory and derail him for ever.

The car mechanic greeted him effusively with an oily hug outside the garage. Harris had always been a dedicated customer, until recently, and he'd missed the business.

'Where you been 'iding, bro'? We've not seen you round these parts in ages.'

Harris smiled. There was a slight problem with his carburettor, he said, and he'd be needing the car shortly for a journey. Could he pick it up later? 'Just a tune-up essentially, nothing major. Get me from A to B,' he said.

'No problem, my friend.' It was a troublesome car, the Citroën, yet the mechanic was not daunted. 'We'll get it done. Give me an hour or two. 'Ow long you stayin', you reckon?'

'Just passing through,' Harris said, as he began walking up the hill. For once, there was no wind and the exercise invigorated him. He dropped by his house, armed with the valid excuse that he needed to collect the post that had mounted up, unforwarded and forgotten. There were a number of items that he'd left behind, clothes and other things he might need. He wanted it all back – and the house too.

There was no reply, or any obvious signs of life, when he rang the doorbell. He had not visited since he'd fled to Nawaz's place after the storm. It was a strange sensation, standing upon his own doorstep, as if he were a guest visiting his own home. His chest prickled as he unlocked the door, wondering what he would encounter on the other side. The place was peaceful, in spite of the messy lounge, chaotic with the turmoil of other people's things, the clutter of student life. He nipped upstairs and peeked inside his old bedroom, now occupied by Renate, a German language student. Dirty mugs congregated by the bed; files of paper were strewn everywhere. He'd imagined they'd be neat and tidy, orderly like Germans are popularly supposed to be, and Nawaz had assured him that they were. Still, he was not here to protest about their washing-up or study habits. Not a bit of it. He was here to give them notice to vacate his property – he would be putting it in writing shortly, but just to let them know. He sat at the dining table, and ran through the words, friendly but firm, apologetic yet unbending, and was about to leave when he heard the sound of men's voices outside. It was Nawaz, talking to a man in a suit.

'What you doin' 'ere, Harris?' he asked, when he came into the house. 'What's up?'

'I'm allowed, aren't I? I just dropped in to pick up my post, as you never seem to do it these days.'

'Everything orright, then?'

'Not really, no. Nawaz, I've been thinking,' he began. 'About this house. My house.' Harris glanced outside, and saw the man was straining to look up at the roof, scribbling on a clipboard.

'What about it?'

'I think we should get rid of those students,' Harris said.

'At some point, yeah, I agree.'

'A week's notice should be enough, shouldn't it?'

Nawaz glared at him in disbelief but Harris was unshakeable.

'I'm going down to see Alia and the cousins shortly,' he ploughed on, feeling more bold than he had in months. 'There are some things that need sorting out.'

'I gather,' Nawaz said. 'We 'eard. Will you be back before Christmas, then, d'you reckon?'

Harris ignored the jibe. 'I've sold some shares to pay the mortgage and I'm owed something from Omar which should see me to the end of the year.' At least half of that was the truth.

Nawaz stroked his rotund belly, which was struggling to burst out of his shirt. 'I'd been meaning to say, cousin, thing is, like, it's yer foundations. We got the surveyor round—'

'What surveyor? Who told you to do that?'

'Oh, it 'ad to be done. Didn't want to buy it off you without checking the structure was sound.'

Harris was enraged. 'You did what?'

'There's a problem with the foundations, see. I didn't want to say, till I was certain, but there's been subsidence, apparently. It's hollow beneath the ground, right 'ere. Lucky I found out about it, to be honest. Stamp on it, Harris, go on.'

'Don't be ridiculous,' Harris scoffed. 'There's nothing wrong with the foundations.'

'Thing is, we can fix it,' Nawaz went on, tapping the radiators for signs of distress, as he ambled around.

'Stop it. I put those in myself and they're very sound.'

'There's a local firm I've found that fixes foundations, stops the subsidence. Should take 'em about six months or thereabouts, then it'll be right as rain. Bit of a messy job – we'll need scaffolding and what have you – but in the end—'

'I don't care. I want it back, the house, with or without the foundations! Do you understand me? Are you listening?'

The suited man popped his head round the door, smiling brightly.

'Just a sec, Eddie. Be right there.'

The man nodded politely and backed outside.

'Who's that, may I ask?' Harris demanded.

'He's doing a valuation for us.'

'He's doing nothing of the sort.'

Harris strode outside, waving his hand to catch the startled man's attention. 'We've no need of your services, sir. There's been a misunderstanding.' He turned back to Nawaz. 'I'm not selling it to you. Is that understood?'

Nawaz blinked, dumbfounded. 'Whatever you say, cousin. Keep it. It's yours.' He shrugged. 'It's worthless in this state, so don't say I didn't warn you,' he added, and lumbered outside to find the estate agent.

'Worthless indeed,' Harris muttered, when he was alone. He gathered his post, shuffling through it for signs of anything hopeful. He left a handwritten note for the students and was about to go and pick up the car when he remembered the wellington boots sitting in the cupboard under the stairs.

★

Dr Farrah unzipped a large plastic storage bag tightly packed with trousers and cardigans, laying them carefully back on the shelves in her wardrobe. Flopping down on the bed for a moment, she reflected upon what she had done, taking the house off the market, deciding to remain here in south-east London for as long as she could. She had agreed to teach full-time, filling in for a colleague taking extended maternity leave. It was not how she had envisaged her fifties, not at all, but it was her only choice, she realized, if she wanted to remain here. In any case, she enjoyed her students, most of them, and they kept her on her toes. If necessary, she thought, as she got down on her hands and knees to retrieve some old novels stashed under the bed, she could have a lodger or two, if the bills proved unmanageable. Her eldest boy was all for supporting her, now that he was earning a decent salary in Dubai, but she was a modern widow and she had no desire to siphon off his earnings, embracing infirmity and dependency as many of her peers had done. Not for her that coveted spot at the core of an extended household with all its attendant tensions and annoyances. She knelt back on her heels and smoothed away a film of dust from the duck-egg-blue cover of the book she held in her hands.

The title was *A Reconstruction of Islamic Thought*, by an author with an Urdu name she'd never heard of. 'Harris,' she said aloud. He must have left it here. She remembered he'd enthused about the scholarly writer, though she couldn't quite recall why in particular. She opened the cover and saw he had written his name and the date on the front page. It was a well-thumbed tome that had clearly been revisited over the years. As she flicked through the chapters, she found his neat spidery Biro jottings in the margins, underlined passages, cross-references to verses from the Koran and to other Islamic scholars. Her eyes pricked. The book, she recalled, was extremely important to him.

Harris shivered as he walked down the street, sycamores on the smarter side and dusty planes on the other. For the first time he noticed the punched-metal waste bins at intervals along the pavement, so very English, a utilitarian stab at tidiness that most people ignored.

'I've brought back your wellingtons,' was his opening gambit, when she came to the door, sheepish in her exercise gear. She had clearly moved on.

'It's a yoga class I do, on DVD,' she admitted, when he pressed her later, as they sat in the living room. 'Before I pluck up the courage to attend the classes.'

'I could tell you are looking trimmer.'

She didn't take it as a compliment. 'Was I that tubby before, then?'

He shook his head, embarrassed. 'Not at all.'

'You didn't need to go to all that trouble,' she said. 'Bringing these. I don't really use them in London.'

'It was no trouble,' he said. 'I came to see Alia and my cousins, who are staying with her.'

'Ah. Well, I'm glad you've come at last – Alia was terribly concerned.'

'I heard she sought you out.'

'She did, yes.' She paused, wondering whether to say more. Then she said, 'It's nice to see you again.'

'You too. When are you moving? I noticed the For Sale sign has come down.'

She hesitated, then said, 'Actually, I took my house off the market, Harris. I'm staying in London, for now at least.'

He was astonished. 'Really?' Had a windfall turned her fortunes around?

'I'm more attached to the place than I realized, and I'm working full-time these days,' she said, as if reading his mind. 'I was thinking of getting a lodger in, you know.'

'I let my house out to some students, actually. When it became too much for me to manage.'

'Would you recommend it – the lodgers, I mean?'

A lump formed in his throat. 'Oh, absolutely, yes, I would,' he said. 'They cover all the bills, though not the council tax. Such a bugger, that one. You can reduce the mortgage, if you like. And then there's the company, you know, having other people around, should you need it.'

He stopped himself and looked at her. She didn't need company, or not so acutely. She wasn't like him in that respect. She had her college job, her boys, her house, her exercise classes, and no doubt her reading group. Her life was busy, full, and he was not required. A miserable mood descended and he tried to fend it off.

'I'd hoped we might see each other while I'm around. I mean, depending on your schedule, of course.'

'My schedule,' she mused. 'Let's see.'

His request sounded almost appealing, and it was very nice of him to return the wellingtons. She did miss them, in fact, or rather the idea of them. Perhaps in the same way that she missed Harris – the notion of him rather than the actuality. She was cautious of sinking back into old patterns, wary of agreeing to anything. And yet she could not quite shut the door.

'All right,' she said. 'But if we do . . .' She groped for the right phrase, afraid of misleading him. 'If we do see each other.'

'Yes?'

She saw that he was slightly breathless and she was mindful of his heart condition.

'It can't be the same as it was before.'

'What was it before, in your view?'

Farrah was flustered. 'It was unequal.'

'Unequal?' He was baffled 'How so?'

'You wanted me to be a certain way, a certain kind of wife, to be subordinate in some way, as if that was the key to happiness. You said it yourself, many, many times, Harris. It was improper, in your eyes, our relationship, because we lacked the rubber stamp of marriage.'

He was silent for a moment, wondering if what she said was true.

'Well, that was something I did aspire to, I can't deny it, marrying you. When I sought you out last autumn, it was as a potential wife.'

The phrase threw her. 'Potential wife! I was an actual wife, remember, for many years.'

'Hold your horses,' he interjected, before she went off on one of her tangents. 'I know you were, and once is probably enough. Enough for both of us, actually. To be honest, Farrah, I'm not even sure I'm husband material – perhaps I never was.' Admitting his shortcomings, he grew in stature a little. 'My track record isn't very impressive.'

'The thing is this, Harris,' she said, softening. 'I don't want to be your wife, or anybody else's for that matter.'

'Well, that's all right, Farrah,' he said. 'I'm not proposing.'

It was a foot in the door, he thought, as he cruised in the Citroën back through the Blackwall Tunnel to the other side of the river.

Twenty-nine

That evening there had been an unusually early lull at the Crescent Islamia Centre and Rashid found himself alone in the office. The boys had dashed home for their tea, or rushed off to play football in the square, the girls drifting off in small clusters. He lay down on the couch, wishing he could sleep it all away, reverse events and begin his life again. A sharp, piercing sensation split his temples. Was it too late? Were the wheels set in motion? A TV news report rattled out a story of a foiled plot to attack the Court of Human Rights building in Strasbourg, a city he'd never heard of. The men were of Yemeni origin, living in Germany. There were others like them: hundreds, maybe thousands, toiling away beneath the radar, the report said. Fuzzy details ebbed and flowed in his imagination, tuned in and out. Better to shut down, shut it all out.

Saheel popped his head around the corner and asked if he'd like some kebabs. They were going to the Lahore Kebab House for chicken tikka rolls. The name rang a bell, triggered a recollection of Harris taking him there once for a meal. A memory of creamy yellow chana dhal nudged him out of his misery for a moment.

'Is it the Lahore 1 or 2?' Rashid asked, as if it mattered. 'Can't remember which is the better one. I could call my uncle and ask him.'

He reached for his mobile, but a hand fell upon his shoulder.

'No, no. Don't trouble, brother.'

'No trouble,' Rashid said, half hoping for an excuse to call Harris.

'We're not that bothered, are we?'

'Our last supper,' one of them joked, 'in London. Then we'll be off and out of your way.'

'You're not in my way.'

'Have you ever travelled on the Eurostar?' It was Saheel speaking.

Rashid said that he hadn't. He'd told them that before.

'Something to look forward to, then,' Saheel said. 'They say it's like quicker than flying.'

Quicker than flight was beyond his imagination. The very notion made him queasy.

After the trio had left, Rashid cleaned out their room, filling several bags of rubbish and then dumping them surreptitiously in another street. He didn't want to arouse suspicion; some of the residents were fussy about collection days and he worried they might report him to the council. When he had finished, he went back to the centre, unplugged the office phone and shut down the computer and TV. Disconnected from the world, he felt a jittery sensation, a fractious fear that attached itself to everything in his vicinity. He went into the bathroom and caught a glimpse of his reflection in the mirror. His features were the same, betraying nothing of what lay beneath. He saw that the men's things were all gone: the Brut shaving foam he had borrowed, the lotions and potions. He had made use of their belongings and they had used his: the towels he had lent them were washed and folded neatly in a corner. Nothing tangible remained of their presence. It was a relief that they had gone, as if a penumbral presence, some winged black thing, had passed over his house and spared him. He sank into a deep sleep on the living room couch, not stirring at all.

Nasreen sat waiting in the front room with her daughters, glancing at the street now and again, in case she could see Rashid. Outside it was growing dark. As if on cue, someone switched on the television for the sake of ambient noise, to lighten the silent throb of anticipation that filled the room. She was exhausted, her body limply flung against the sofa cushions. All day long, and half the previous night, she'd cooked chicken karahi, and spinach and potato, and Rashid's favourite hot and sour chickpeas, and the usual dhal and rice, and last but not least her speciality, *rasmalai*, which was Harris's weakness, she knew, and also her own.

The pudding sat in a Pyrex dish in the fridge, a sheen of speckled skin stretched over its translucent pale yellow surface, the milky custard beneath. Touching it was not permitted, no matter how inviting it appeared – not the slightest prod, the merest sniff. It was reserved for Harris, whose imminent arrival had caused considerable excitement, followed by a flurry of activity in the kitchen. There'd been talk of his coming for days, since Alia had made the trip up north to winkle him out of his silence, prise him from the shell of that cramped existence, and finally, after several phone calls and a short diversion in Greenwich, he had made it. The reunion with the girls and their mother was a huge relief, after weeks of fearful anticipation. To his surprise, nobody leapt upon him or made impossible demands. That would come in time, he guessed, but for now his presence was enough.

'I'm touched you've done all this,' he murmured, when Alia showed him the bedroom where Nasreen and her daughters were staying.

Their modest collection of possessions – combs and kurtas, chappals and socks – were nestled neatly around the wall and piled upon the dressing table.

'It's good of you, it really is.' He held back for a moment, till the feeling ebbed, became manageable. 'But this is your place, isn't it, and you need the space. For study, or for work. Whatever it is you choose to do.'

'I've got a new housemate moving in next moth, but I'll keep working at the café while I'm applying for courses for next year.'

He glanced admiringly around the place. A printed bedspread he recognized from home was stretched taut over the bed, the futon lined up on the floor beside it.

'You found that cover?'

'In our old house. You wanted to chuck it away, but I kept it without telling you.'

His eyes flickered with approval. He cast his gaze upon a photo of the two girls and their mother near Tower Bridge.

'Did you take them there?' he asked.

'We did a bit of sightseeing. All those postcards I sent them made them want to see the real places.'

'Ah, well, I can understand that. I was the same way, eager to go sightseeing when I first arrived. Madame Tussauds, I remember. Hell of a long queue, though. And it cost me an arm and a leg.'

They both laughed. After a moment, she said, 'I took Nasreen and Mona to see a consultant at the hospital.'

Harris was taken aback. 'Really? And they agreed to see her?'

'It was a friend of Oliver's father. He was really nice about it.'

'And what did he say is wrong?'

'They've ruled out leukaemia—'

'Thank God!'

'But they'll have to do more tests to get to the bottom of all the infections.'

'I see,' he said, and fell silent for a moment. 'I'd no idea you cared so much about the girls. When we were in the village, you seemed so keen to get away.'

She sat on the bed. 'Yes,' she admitted. 'I suppose I was.'

'You couldn't stand it.'

She looked at him. 'Neither could you. You ran away from the life you might have had. It could have been mine too.'

When Harris came down, he found Nasreen standing outside the front door. It was a warm evening and there was no breeze. She'd grown restless, she said, fed up of sitting inside as the food grew cold; she'd come to watch the comings and goings in the street. In the house opposite, where a family was making preparations for a wedding, a poppy-red awning had been erected over the front door. A string of cherry lights had been strung from the windows, stretched out against the grey stucco wall in an elegant V. Two men rolled out a fat column of red carpet over the gum-studded pavement, in preparation for the guests' arrival.

'What's wrong?' Harris asked her in Punjabi.

She held back, staring down the street, as if her gaze alone might reel her boy back home.

'Tell me.'

She sighed. 'I was pushing him about getting married and I upset him. He's been avoiding us, you see. These work troubles. I shouldn't have nagged.'

'Nonsense. You were right to press. Time is passing and he needs a wife.'

They watched as another batch of relatives arrived, spilling on to the street from stretch limos in a cloud of scent and aftershave, chatter and laughter. The clamour of celebration rose high into the sky as children tore up and down in fancy outfits bought specially for the occasion: pint-sized suits and clip-on bow ties for the boys, sugar-pink satin dresses for girls. Had Rashid forgotten he was expected for dinner tonight? Harris was indignant at the idea that he could be so careless.

'He should have been here hours ago,' Nasreen said, her voice trailing away to nothing, as Mishele came dashing down the hallway with Mona behind her.

Nasreen turned away as Harris hugged first the elder and then the younger, cupping Mona's head in his hands.

'So do you like it here? Will you come and stay with me?'

Nasreen shot him a look. Don't make promises, it said, that can't be kept. He swung around, avoiding her eyes.

'What's for dinner, then?' he said. 'I can smell something

promising – several things, actually. I've got a bottle of Cava in the car.'

'*Dad.*'

'Why not?'

Nasreen went inside and began joylessly doling out food on plates set around the table. She hovered for a moment and then left Rashid's empty.

'It can be warmed up in the microwave, no problem,' Harris insisted, as he went to work on the chicken.

The girls, flanked on either side of him, followed suit. Nasreen served Alia and then wiped her own forehead with a napkin.

'Something has happened,' she said, twisting the paper in her fingers. 'He told me he'd come after work. That was yesterday, Harris.'

'What is it?' Alia asked her father.

'She says she's worried that Rashid hasn't come,' he replied. 'Nasreen, nothing has happened. Don't fret.' His voice was cheery, unconvincing.

'He didn't come to the hospital for Mona's blood tests when he was meant to,' Alia pointed out.

'When was that?' Harris said.

'Yesterday.'

Harris sighed. 'Rashid should have gone with you. What's he up to?'

'He hasn't answered his phone since yesterday,' Nasreen said to Harris. 'The girls keep trying.'

Nasreen nibbled her nail, flecked with scarlet polish from another time. Her anguish was palpable.

'Let us wait, Nasreen,' Harris declared, privately wondering what the devil Rashid was playing at, and imagining how he would deal with his recalcitrant behaviour when he caught up with him. 'I called him on my way down to London several times. He knows I'm here.'

They'd barely spoken over the past months, and Harris guessed that he was avoiding the question of what the future held for his family, now that they were on his doorstep, and not an aerogramme or two away.

'He was doing a shift at this new minicab company, wasn't he?'

'See?' Alia piped up, feeling vindicated. 'This is how he is, Dad, just like I told you. Never here when he's meant to be.'

'I can't help that,' he retorted. 'You want me to send out a search party?'

'Up to you,' Alia said flatly. 'I've already been round to the centre twice. He's not there.'

Nasreen was quiet, unaware of what was being discussed.

'Let's not assume the worst, not yet,' Harris said, his brow gleaming with sweat. 'We should wait.'

'Wait for what?' It was Mishele, standing beside Harris, stiff and unyielding.

'Wait till the morning,' he said to her, vaguely reassuring. 'We should all go to bed, and if there's no news by tomorrow, then we will see what to do.'

Daylight pulled Rashid from a cramped position on the couch and he woke with a crick in his neck. A tight parcel of anxiety sat heavily upon his chest, though it took him a moment before he could locate its source. Then he remembered everything.

He tried to get rid of the feeling; he made his ablutions, said his prayers and ate a simple breakfast of cereal and tea. Afterwards, a calm lucidity took hold.

The day promised to be fine. There wasn't much time. He was meant to work a cab shift and he took the car for a valet clean at the Albanian car wash on Varden Street. The owner knew him well and was delighted that he was opting for something more than the usual quick wash: a deluxe clean inside and out. And then he fled London, saying goodbye to nobody.

Propping up a road map on the dashboard, he drove eastwards, with no clear plan in his head. Shoeburyness didn't look too far on the map, crouched at the eastern terminus of the railway line, where the Thames estuary spilled into the cold grey sea. You could do it in a day and be back before dark. Not that it really mattered to him, for he wanted to disappear that summer's day. He wanted to vanish, somehow, keep driving till the road ran out, but beyond that he had no plan. So many obstacles were conspiring to thwart him. Now, as he sat in a traffic jam in the thick of east London, his mobile juddered with texts, shrieked with messages, as if everyone needed to track him down, pinion his coordinates. He'd never been in such demand, so popular, and it made him smile bitterly to himself, the idea he might be missed, needed, his presence required. Then he accelerated, splicing into the bus lane, elated, adrenalin whooshing through him like high-octane fuel, so that he almost hit an old man tottering into the road, rheumy-eyed with booze, a snapshot of his fist shaking defiantly in the rear-view mirror. Nothing could stop him. Not a bank of speed cameras, not some drunkard ambling in his path.

He kept going until he reached a roundabout, uncertain which way to go, swerving first left, then right, before finally choosing. His destination was the very edge of England, the sea. Yet the city wound on and on, and just when he thought it was almost behind him, road signs and flyovers flared up, bridges and tunnels confounded him, like a maddening puzzle that unfolded to infinity. Was there no end to it, the urban sprawl eastwards? A blank-faced stretch of flats gave way to forlorn semis that dotted the margins of Barking, front drives jammed with battered cars that had seen better days. And then at last it was behind him, London.

He was on the open road.

An hour or so later, an exit sign drew him into another England of villages, fields, hedgerows, copses. Here was a pub, there a parade of shops, a village green, a painted station. He remembered the village he had left behind, the house where he was born. An image of Khalid Ali's face, burnished with sadness, seeped into his thoughts as he drove. Why did he always appear in his mind's eye like that, his father? The question plunged him deeper into the past. As he drove along the narrow lanes, he recalled a brilliant sunny day, like this one, only hotter, windless, when he was ten years old. He had gone with his father to sell wire brushes, bumping along by bus to another town. The day had begun full of promise, his father clutching his wares in a greasy leather holdall, convinced that his boy's presence would help draw custom. Hours passed and nothing sold. When the sun shrank behind the plain, gilding the horizon, his father was beyond exhaustion, the bag still heavy with unsold brushes to be lugged back to the village. They had missed the last bus home.

Rashid slowed down as he drove through the village, the landscape softening around him. A brown metal signpost, half-hidden in the hedgerow, led him down a single-track lane towards an ancient church, its flinty spire looming beyond sleepy meadows. Up ahead there was a railway line flanked by fields of wild flowers nodding gently in the breeze. He came to a standstill at the level crossing, its barriers down. Three warning lights blinked upon a board, like a clown's face, two round eyes and a red nose. The tracks sang with the approach of a freight train to the coast and minutes later a caravan of containers thundered by, the Maersk logo a blur of blue stars. The sheer noise of the locomotive thrilled him, humming in his bones, flooding his senses. He waited, closing his eyes, resuming the half-recalled memory.

They'd been walking along the road for a while, Rashid and Khalid Ali, barely speaking, too tired to talk. Dusk sifted around them, plunging Khalid into a deep and impenetrable silence. Several cars roared past but nobody stopped to pick them up. As darkness fell, Rashid began to wonder what they were going to do, and prayed that if Allah showed mercy upon them now, he would forever be his servant. They trudged on through the depth-less night, his father's misery infecting them both. Then suddenly, to the boy's amazement, his prayers were answered. In a cone of dust, illuminated by headlamps, a bejewelled truck screeched to a halt. Tinny pop music poured into the night as the cab door was flung open and the giddy driver beckoned them aboard.

'Slow down, brother,' Khalid begged the man, as they sped recklessly along the highway, overtaking anything that stood in their path. 'Let's get my boy home in one piece! He's my future, the only hope I have left in this world.'

The driver guffawed and Khalid laughed too. Yet when Rashid caught a glimpse of his father's face lit up by the dashboard, he saw fear in the shadows of his features, fear of enduring loss and disappointment, things he did not yet understand.

A row of old bells hung from slack cable over the railway line, a silent relic from another era. Rashid waited for the barrier to lift. The warning light winked its solemn warning. He glimpsed to see if there were other cars behind him, or anything up ahead. Only the church, the fields, the graveyard. He drove on to the tracks, stopped the car in the middle and turned off the engine. His heart flapped wildly against his ribcage, like a trapped bird. The urge to open a window, find release somehow, almost overcame him; yet he didn't, not wanting to let the outside world in, to preserve this moment of solitude, clamping his hands to his thighs. Beyond the silence, he was aware of the distant roar of an aircraft, high in the sky. He stared straight ahead, along the railway line unspooling towards to the horizon, glinting tracks to infinity. The sight of it was stupefying. Yet he could not stop himself, could not tear away his gaze, and then he recalled that other horizon, the sinking sun, his father's sorrow.

He closed his eyes, descending into the still darkness of his head. So was this how it felt, in the moments before oblivion? His stomach churned, the choppy waves of it made him think of the sea and how he had never been to Shoeburyness. The name sounded so appealing, like many English places, until you arrived and found the destination rather different from what you'd imagined. He wanted to run, he wanted to stay.

Do not kill yourselves, for verily Allah has been to you most merciful.

The words tolled in his mind. He thought of his luckless father, the wire brushes, a desperate promise made on a dark road. The allure of death seized hold of him, blossomed in the pit of his stomach. He thought of the men he'd befriended, housed and sheltered, and felt his tongue like a dry and shrivelled thing that did not belong in his mouth. He thought of the rabbits in his father's courtyard, their bright eyes and glistening fur, their brief time on this earth. He thought of Harris and of a visit long ago, when he'd asked Rashid to look after his daughter.

Life is not to be bartered for some greater glory on earth or in paradise – no matter what the others had told him, the yarns that Begg had spun. Sweat dripped down his forehead, pooled in the fold of his neck. He took off his glasses, felt the metal arms slither between his fingertips. He thought of the truck driver's giddiness and of his father's words that his son was his future, his only remaining hope. At last he understood.

The track thrummed, reverberated in his hands that gripped the steering wheel, as he braced himself for impact. The pungency of his body, slithery with anxiety, hit him like a mocking rebuke. Then something unfamiliar, something unexpected reared up inside him, a visceral rebellion on the part of his body. He turned on the ignition, pushed the gear stick into first, revved the accelerator, heard the screech of wheels gaining traction as the barrier began to dip, its skirt of metal batons grazing the roof.

He thought of the passengers upon the train.

Allah is the One who gave you life, then He shall ordain you to die, then He shall give you your life again.

In the blink of an eye, the train sliced through, four minutes later than scheduled. Barely anyone noticed the slippage. Not a soul spotted the car. It hissed gently on the grass verge, ticking over in the silence after its narrow escape.

Rashid wrenched himself out of the driver's seat and on to the other side of the tracks, then staggered over the road towards the churchyard. It was peaceful, blissfully so. Nobody was around, only the tumbledown gravestones, ancient, indifferent. Lying down on the grass, he squinted up at the white sky, incandescent from the sun hidden behind it, and felt something beyond words: being alive.

The ground was soft, damp beneath the thick grass, yielding to his body. He slept for an age, all day and all night, or perhaps it was only a matter of minutes. Time stretched out. In his dreams he scaled mountain ranges, mined scenes from his boyhood, came upon his family gathered around a shiny new motorbike, played ping-pong on a rooftop, saw the world from the pit of a shallow grave.

When he awoke at dawn, shivering with cold, the sun was gone.

Thirty

Broke down in Essex, the text said, and gave the name of the village. *Please come get me. Parked near station. In churchyard.* It occurred to Harris, who had never heard of the place, that it must have been a hefty fare for Rashid, driving all that way from London. The appeal had arrived early in the morning, and Harris had risen from a fitful snooze on the sofa to go to Rashid's rescue, informing Nasreen before he left that her son had most likely run out of petrol on his shift and was stranded twenty miles outside London. It was a family trait, he remarked, running on empty, and not just with cars either. She'd smiled, her body slackening with relief that nothing dreadful had befallen her eldest son – that soon he'd be safely home.

Covering all eventualities, Harris made sure his jump leads were in the boot of the car, along with five litres of petrol, and left Whitechapel in a determined mood. It was the kind of operation at which he excelled and he decided to look upon it as an excuse for them to shelve past rancour and have a much-needed talk. A considerable stretch of time had passed, he realized, since they'd been in touch. There were things that needed to be said and he planned to say them.

It was a pretty village, quaint rather than twee, encircled with ring roads that kept the coast-bound lorries and shoals of white vans at bay. England was like that, Harris mused, a shrinking space that required considerable shuffling of its citizens and endless traffic to keep it running peaceably. He parked close to the edge of the village, by the station, and trudged along the railway line, coming across Rashid's abandoned car at a short distance from the level crossing. The bodywork appeared unscathed, fortunately, though he noticed that it was jammed at an oblique angle against the verge. What an idiot Rashid had been, abandoning the estate agent's beat for the wandering life of a minicab driver. All that advice he'd offered the boy, the tireless support during the college years, the counselling on career prospects. His peregrinations were beyond belief and things would have to change. As he walked up the neatly combed gravel path towards the church, he caught sight of Rashid at some distance, bundled against a mossy headstone in the churchyard, his head buried in the crook of his arms.

'Must have been a pricey fare, was it?' Harris said. 'Driving all the way to Essex?'

Rashid's stillness was unsettling, an augur of death. At first he did not respond, then slowly, painfully, he lifted his face, and Harris saw in an instant that it wasn't a fare that had propelled him here. Violet circles punched his eyes, unfocused and fearful without his glasses.

'Have you come to take me away?' The flat despair of the question hung in the air.

Harris knelt down beside him. 'No,' he said, putting his arms around Rashid's shoulders. 'I'm taking you home.'

'I can't ever go home, not now.'

'You can.' He grasped Rashid's cold, limp hand. 'Tell me what happened. Will you?'

'Not here.' He fumbled for his glasses, which he'd stuffed in his back pocket.

'It's quiet. Nobody around.'

'I don't want to hide any more.'

'You don't need to. Come.'

Rashid stood up awkwardly, thrusting his glasses lopsidedly on to his face.

'Are you all right?' Harris asked, brushing the grass off his clothes. 'That's better.'

Rashid nodded, and they began walking towards the gate, hand in hand, Harris leading the way until they reached the hapless car.

'You have the keys?'

They were still in the ignition, the window wide open, and Harris got in. He switched on the engine, which started first time. The needle on the fuel gauge pointed to a quarter full. He peered through the passenger window at Rashid. 'This should get you home. Plenty of petrol and the battery's not at all flat.'

'Uncle, I can't go home.' His voice was blank.

'Of course you can,' Harris exclaimed. 'Why not? Come back with me.'

'I can't.' Rashid avoided Harris's eyes. 'I did something terrible.'

Neither spoke for a moment, then Rashid said, 'I drove on to the tracks when a train was coming.'

The words hit the elder man without warning and for a terrible instant he wanted to laugh – laugh it away as a dare, a reckless prank.

'I couldn't, Uncle, I couldn't do it.' He was crying now, softly, apologetically. 'I lost my nerve.'

Harris gazed at him. 'Rashid, what has happened to you, my beloved boy? How could you do such a thing? To yourself, your mother and all the people who love you? How could you even think of it?'

'I thought of them all, of you, and my mother, my sisters, my father, the passengers on the train—'

'But why, Rashid, why did you do it?'

'I accepted money from Mohsin Begg.' He looked down as he spoke, running the index finger of one hand over the wavy line of his knuckles. 'To pay for the girls and for Amma to come to England. I didn't know where else to turn and he'd been so kind to me when I left my old job.'

'Was I not kind to you,' Harris said, 'all those years? Did I not take care of you as if you were my own son?' Tears sprang into his eyes and he dashed them away.

'You did, yes, and so much more. I'm sorry, Uncle.'

'And what did the good imam extract from you in exchange for this? It wasn't an act of charity on his behalf, I imagine.'

'He wanted me to join the struggle. When the time came.'

The glibly righteous words filled Harris with loathing. 'And when might that be?'

Rashid gave a diminutive shrug. He'd agreed to let the guys stay in his house, he said, and they'd become friends, Saheel and Tamidul and Hamid, filling his lonely hours.

'I never had friends like that before, Uncle. They weren't

interested in pubs or who was making more money, and they didn't boast about girls.' They'd shared food and jokes, shaving foam and takeaways, confided in one another what they secretly felt about England. 'Mohsin said it was my turn next.'

'Listen, Rashid. Listen carefully,' Harris said, steadying his voice to control his anger. 'It is not for the likes of Mohsin Begg to pick and choose who lives and who dies. Do you hear me? Not for Begg, nor you, nor I. Not one of us can play the Almighty.'

Rashid bit his lip. 'I tried to imagine it,' he said. 'What it's like.'

Harris shook him. 'You did, yes. But in the end, you didn't do it,' he said, 'because you're not like them. I'm proud of you, Rashid.'

In the high street they found an old-fashioned café which sold egg sandwiches, ham and cheese and chutney rolls, custard tarts and slices of Victoria sponge filled with red jam and fresh whipped cream. A grey permed lady in a lace-trimmed apron poured out two cups of tea, malty and thick, from a large stainless-steel pot. She nudged a bowl of sugar lumps in their direction and explained that if it was breakfast they were after, there was egg on toast, any way they liked.

They sat by the window, at a table spread with a crisply ironed flowery cloth, and gazed out at the traffic.

'I should have taken more care of everything,' Harris said, as they waited for their order. 'I've let you all down.'

'Don't say that. You've been like a father to me and my family.'

Harris sighed. 'Like a father, but not enough of one. It's true, I helped you through the exams, I supported you, got you that first car when you landed that awful taxi job – don't remind me, I know it was a wreck. But in the end, I let you down, didn't I? Let down your parents.'

'You came to get me,' Rashid said. 'I don't know what I'd have done otherwise.'

The waitress set a plate of perfectly domed twin eggs before him. Harris saw his face lighten a little with relief as he beheld the food.

'Anything else?' she said pleasantly.

'I'll take the same, if I may,' Harris replied.

For a precious half-hour they ate and drank together, almost forgetting how they had ended up in an English café eating breakfast that summer morning, and not thinking about what lay ahead.

'We'll drive home after the rush hour,' Harris said eventually, when they had finished. 'The girls and your mother are waiting for you. I won't mention what you've told me, for now.'

Rashid wiped his mouth with his napkin. 'Thank you, Uncle,' he said. 'I'm longing to see them. Just to be back with them under the same roof feels like a blessing to me.'

It happened in the dead hours before first light. A team of plain-clothed police descended upon the shuttered green-painted Georgian house. By the time that Rashid made his way to Bethnal Green Police Station to turn himself in, the final stages of the operation were already under way. Someone had got there before him, a relative of one of the ping-pong players tipping them off. Rashid's account of events was greeted with supercilious smiles all round, as he struggled to tell his side of the story. He loved his family, followed the faith, had been deluded by a preacher who hid his true intentions from the world. Was he duped, led astray? Or had he chosen the path of his own volition? The officers listened, took it all in, said little, until Rashid felt the tight aperture of opportunity to present his case snap shut.

In any event, Mohsin Begg was apprehended at Schiphol Airport in Amsterdam, where he'd planned to address a conference on the limits of tolerance in faith communities. The cleric was accustomed to being harassed, stopped at borders and barked at by uniformed men; it was all part of the job. It would not be easy to nip his protean enterprise in the bud, for it wasn't illegal, hadn't been banned. The case against the others, Saheel, Tamidul and Hamid, was even more slippery. They'd left no trail, nothing incriminating in their electronic footprint. They'd departed from Rashid's place quietly, taken the Eurostar and vanished into the homes of friends, cousins, contacts scattered about the suburbs of Paris and beyond. Not a blip on anyone's radar, not a cause for undue concern or above average surveillance. They were just three job seekers whose families all firmly believed they were willing to go wherever the work could be found: London, Paris, Hamburg, or further afield.

When the police told Rashid he would have to be detained, pending deportation, he was stunned but didn't protest. Could he speak to his mother first? Of course, they assured him – this was a civilized country where people's rights were respected and the rule of law prevailed. The trouble was, he was tainted by association, deemed a potential threat to national security, and his presence was undesirable. A part of him had lost all desire to remain in England. He merely wished that his family would not suffer because of him and he pleaded innocence when interrogated about his knowledge of Begg's operations, his friends and contacts at home and abroad. The copper on duty had been business-like, almost kind, and after hours of questioning by the officer's superiors in a different police station in another part of London, he made a statement through a lawyer they provided.

Now he was on a list, lodged upon a computer, forever branded. A naïve young man on the fringes of something – nothing more serious than that – yet the category afforded him scant comfort. The authorities received numerous calls from concerned citizens who had their suspicions about men like him. Was he one of those enraged souls with half-baked plans cooked up in garages and attics and garden sheds up and down the country? Did he fit that profile? The officers listened to Rashid, who seemed earnest, desperate to relieve himself of information. They knew that there were thousands out there who dabbled and explored and fantasized about jihad. Some even accomplished it and ended up in paradise. Or that was what they had been led to believe by their handlers – preachers and clerics like Begg who wheedled and groomed impressionable young men, though never volunteered their own soft bodies for the cause.

By ten o'clock the following morning, a crowd of spectators had gathered from the corner shop, the adjacent streets and tower blocks and the mosque next door to see what was happening in the square. Paunchy cab drivers abandoned double egg and chips and bacon at the café to observe the latest outrage in broad daylight in their manor. A coven of silver-haired old ladies reckoned it was a murder, blaming the out-of-control youths who ran around the estates, but no bodies were taken out from the building. There was no sign of violence, no evidence of struggle, nothing gory. Only gloved men in papery white overalls, carrying sealed polythene bags containing computers and other hardware. Flimsy yellow tape cordoned off a section of pavement in front of the house, obediently skirted by pedestrians. The centre that had saved Rashid for a short time in his young life was closed.

Thirty-one

When a minor earthquake struck Pakistan late that summer, Harris found himself fretting about Omar, his sometime best friend. They had not spoken to each other in many months, and the idea that they might drift apart forever filled him with anguish. The epicentre was in the Hindu Kush range and strong tremors had occurred throughout the northern and central parts of the country, from Peshawar to Gilgit, Murree to Lahore. Farrah's sister's bungalow was undamaged, which she took as a sign. Others were not so lucky. Harris put aside his past disputes and rang the house in Shadman to see if Omar and the family had escaped unscathed. The moment they spoke, their voices overlapping with excitement, time and distance melted away.

Omar described what had happened the night of the quake. He had awoken to the tremors shaking the foundations of his house in the small hours, he said, when he had noticed the amulet that Khalid Ali had given him, months ago, lying on his bedside table. Harris smiled wryly to himself, knowing that Omar had no truck with the spiritual proclivities of his countrymen. Amulets and saints, shrines and blessings were the preserve of village folk. It had lain there forgotten, Omar said, all this time.

'I spurned it, of course, but your cousin Khalid insisted it would bring me long life and prosperity.'

It filled him with shame now, he admitted, recalling how he had brushed the poor man away like a bothersome fly, and how in the end he had never provided for the cousins in the village, as he had promised he would. Yet by the grace of Allah, his life and his family were all spared.

'Was I *blessed*, do you think,' Omar wondered, 'by your cousin's amulet?' He sounded sceptical and yet intrigued by a possible link.

'Maybe you were. But I'd say more likely you were blessed by first-rate builders. Your house has good foundations, clearly.'

Good foundations or not, Omar resolved to make amends. A parcel of land near the village, on the edge of a fertile plain, would be given to the cousin. Far better than cash, it would be an investment for his future. Omar planned to develop the area himself one day, he explained, adding that he hoped they might work together on the project.

'What do you say, Harris? You could be our project manager.'

The telephone line crackled and Harris was quiet for a moment, contemplating the offer, before declining graciously. Then he thanked his friend for his kindness and generosity towards his cousin, which touched him more than he could say. He did not mention what had happened to Rashid, but said that the girls and their mother would stay in England. Then they mulled over the latest news from the Lahore household: the happy news that Layla was engaged to the scion of a wealthy Karachi shipping family; the difficulties of reconstructing the swimming pool, whose sky-blue cement floor was split by a deep zigzag, spewing rubble on to the pristine lawn.

'I'm considering filling the damned thing in and be done with it,' Omar said. 'We have the pool at the club and the upkeep is a bind. What do you think?'

Harris considered the question for a moment, remembering the beautiful house and gardens in Shadman. 'I think you should repair it. Think of the hours of pleasure it brings your family and friends.'

There was a lull, then Omar said, 'Harris, dear chap, I've missed you. You're sure you won't go in with me on this development project?'

Harris felt a familiar tug at his heart but stood fast. 'I'm sure. You've been a good friend all these years.'

'Have I?' Omar's needy tone surprised them both.

'We've had our ups and downs,' Harris conceded. 'But I'm still here. And so are you, thank Allah.'

Omar gave a wheezy chuckle. 'Will you come to Layla's wedding next year?'

'I won't be visiting Pakistan for a while,' Harris said. 'I have my work cut out here in England.'

'Ah yes,' his friend said. 'I completely understand.'

And for once, Harris believed, he actually did.

The vagaries of retail business would always baffle Harris. He was not a born shopkeeper and never would be. So when he returned to the north and discovered that his old shop was doing quite well, he was astonished, for it had never thrived under his management. Perhaps it was purging the shelves of limp and bruised veg that had done it. Or losing the red-top newspapers and dusty cans of beer. Maybe it was the new name that drew in a younger crowd, more disposed to spend their cash on designer-type items. Or possibly it was the weather – the hottest that summer since records had begun. But they always said that in England, as if it were a matter of national pride.

Whatever it was, and nobody could quite agree, Nawaz found himself basking in the warm sunshine of success, turning a respectable profit at long last. He was always quick to insist, whenever the other cousins enquired, that it wasn't a fortune. Why generate envy or provoke unwelcome requests? The summer evenings were long and the shop stayed open late, pulling business from up and down the neighbouring streets.

When Harris brought Nasreen and her daughters to stay in his house, he proposed that she take over serving in the shop, insisting that she deserved a reasonable share of the profits. It was an audacious proposal for Nawaz to accept, but in time, Harris said, she would be capable of running the place herself, making a living. Nawaz had his back to the wall and, not wanting to provoke any further action or familial rupture on the sunk loan, he relented. Everyone said it was the least he could do. He'd feathered his own nest and now it was time he gave something back.

'After all, cousin, you always said you'd pay me back eventually,' Harris reminded him, as he sipped a salty lassi at the counter in Royale Cuisine, 'when the shop was making a profit. And now, thanks to my injection of cash, it is.'

Nawaz did not agree with this version of events and he never would. Yet he had his public face as a local councillor to consider and it was mainly this that prevented him from contradicting the Uncle.

Nasreen learned to count before she learned to read. Figures were her forte. She enjoyed the heavy feel of the English coins in her hands, the neatly stacked notes lying flat in the till. In the evenings, after the girls were asleep in Alia's old room, she began to learn English with the help of tutorial cassette tapes borrowed from the library, attending a once-weekly ESOL class at an adult education centre on the outskirts of town. During the day, Mishele stood at her side in the shop behind the till, helping her with the language and growing accustomed to the regular customers. They watched Jamal's wife, and how she did things, learning from her example. Mishele told Alia she hoped that they would be there until the autumn, when she might go to the secondary school at the bottom of the hill, wear a navy-blue uniform, trousers and matching sweatshirt stamped with a white coat of arms, like everybody else, girls and boys alike. There was a primary school a short bus ride away that Mona would attend, if they stayed. They would need to remain in England for Mona's sake, her frequent infections requiring constant monitoring and weekly injections of white platelets to boost her immunity.

Mishele wrote neatly penned letters describing it all to her father on thin blue aerogrammes, which she posted in the pillar box at the bottom of the hill. She filled him in on the news: what they ate, who they saw; what the shop sold and what the weather was doing. She did not mention school, because it was only a possibility and she thought it best not to talk about it. The summer holidays were not yet over.

Nasreen was watching the television one afternoon with the girls when Khalid rang. He had saved up his nugget of good news for her, bumping over the potholes on his bicycle to the tailor's house to borrow his phone. Harris put his own phone on speaker, so both the girls could hear what he had to say to their mother.

'We are blessed with a plot of land,' Khalid cried, his excitement spilling down the line. He had felt sure that this news alone would bring his wife and daughters back home, so was disappointed by her silence. 'Thanks to the generosity of Harris's good friend in Lahore, we have something of our own,' he went on, struggling to ignite her enthusiasm. 'For us to live together again.'

Then he told her how he planned to plant an orchard on the land and even build a little house there. The more he talked, the more her silence grew.

'How is it with you all?' he asked.

'All is well. And you?'

'Me? Oh, not much. Fortune-casting is quiet these days, but people are buying up the amulets,' he went on. 'Mazhar is helping.'

'I'm glad, that's good. He's a good boy.'

'And how is Rashid?' he ventured. 'Is he—'

'Yes, thank God, he's better.' The persistent cough had resurfaced during his detention in England.

Khalid had found Rashid's shameful behaviour very hard to forgive. His drift away from his career as an estate agent into the clutches of a scurrilous preacher infuriated him still, keeping him awake long into the night. Had they not brought him up to be a good Muslim and to follow the right path?

'I pray for him, my son. Every week I go to the saint's shrine. Tell him, will you?'

'I will, I promise, when I next visit him,' Nasreen said, and felt the blowback of her husband's relief rush down the line. Then she said, 'He's a good son and we'll miss him.'

'Will you send him my love?' he went on. 'My hugs and kisses to the girls. And you too.'

It was all he could do – send love and hope it would be received.

August came and Rashid left England for good. He took one large suitcase and a second smaller one on board the aircraft, accompanied by a pair of immigration officials. Security was long-winded, but he complied with every command, did what he was told, laying bare his belongings, his body. Upon arrival in Lahore, he had little money, but enough for a seat on an air-conditioned bus home, speaking to nobody on the way.

It was nothing like the return he'd once imagined: the welcoming committee stretching out from the bus stop to his parents' house; the throng of relatives and curious bystanders tussling over the portage of his bags. He was a big shot in that version, returning with tales of struggle and triumph, money in his suit pocket, photos of his house, his car, his wife. That was how it was for Harris whenever he returned to the village. The Uncle had given him the opportunity to follow the same path, but he had blundered off, ruined his prospects for ever.

As he approached his father's house at the end of the narrow street, he recalled the place he had left behind as a boy, the open courtyard, the outdoor toilet, the peeling turquoise paint on the rickety gate, the rabbits that came and went, according to their fate. He prepared himself for what he would find when he pushed open the door, his brother grown tall, his father grown old. He prepared for the familiar and for the unknown.

There was no crowd, no welcoming committee, only his father perched on the rope cot, puffing on a hookah, while his brother fixed a puncture on his bicycle. For weeks now, Khalid Ali had been praying daily for his son's safe return. His release without charge, even after his detention, was proof that he was innocent. The fact that his prayers had been answered and his son had been returned to him, healthy and in one piece, was a sign that Allah had not forsaken him. Nervous after a decade apart, Khalid held back for a moment, but then his face broke into a broad grin. He jumped into his son's arms – the boy become man – talking so fast that the words tumbled on top of each other, about how the tailor, Allah bless him, had always said that Rashid would be back to build him a house one day. Nothing fancy, he'd said. Just solid foundations and walls, something to last for the children and grandchildren.

The house on the hill came into its own under the helm of Nasreen and her daughters. Jamal's wife and their children dropped round with tins of paint left over from some recent renovations of their own, and together they transformed the hallway from glossy chocolate to matte lemon. The main bedroom also enjoyed a swift makeover: the furniture was rearranged, fresh wallpaper hung. Harris gave Nasreen his blessing, along with the keys to the house. It amazed him to see the place was transformed by its new inhabitants, as if his solitary presence there had been the problem all along. He could not deny that he'd never really liked the house, and the house had felt the snub, withholding the promise that one day it would be home.

For Nasreen, it was an entirely different proposition. She luxuriated in the amenities. Hot and cold water flowed, the lights worked and wall-to-wall fitted carpets cushioned her feet. She cleaned and swept the kitchen, polished the chrome taps in the bathroom and shook out the rugs. Unlike Harris, she found the back-to-back terraced houses cosy, full of life spilling on to the street and conversations carried on over fences. The girls ventured into the wind-blown garden, exploring it for games, pegging out the washing when the sun shone. Their mother followed, tentatively at first and then, with encouragement from the next-door neighbour, she weeded and dug the earth with a rusty trowel, planting seeds they'd found in the shed.

Harris watched, from the vantage point of the family sofa he would soon leave behind. It moved him to see how well they were taking to their surroundings, acclimatizing even. So different from his own arrival here, decades earlier, in chilly English digs with dire English food and English plumbing. The plumbing and the food had improved over the years. England had opened its doors just a crack and new people and fresh ideas had flowed in. This was a changed country from the one he had encountered back then, but whether or not it was better, he could not say. Outside in the garden Nasreen crouched down over the soil, absorbed in her new world. He had forsaken her as a young woman, but now perhaps, in middle age, she might forgive him.

Before he left the house, Harris gave Mishele a lesson on how to operate the central heating by using the digital thermostat in the hallway.

'I installed it myself, gas-fired,' he explained, feeling a burst of nostalgia for those pioneering early days in the house, when everything needed work. 'Alia wouldn't come till I made the place warm. All the radiators, even the boiler, I put in myself – and this device here, to set the temperature.' At least he had made one useful addition to the unloved house.

Nasreen came inside holding a bunch of dandelions she had plucked from the lawn. They would be grateful of the heating in a month or two, he told her, when the evenings and early mornings turned chilly.

She gasped. 'So we can stay here in this house, then, Harris?' She scanned his face.

'This is your home now,' Harris told her. 'You can stay here as long as you wish.'

When Harris took his leave of the house on the hill, it was without fanfare. The cousins in Perseverance Street, the neighbours, the fruit seller and the friends from the mosque all got to hear about it in the usual way. The news got around, as news does. Standing on each other's front doorsteps or speaking on their mobile phones, they chatted about him, reminisced about his arrival, the nuggets of wisdom he dispensed, his trips to the daughter down in London. They spoke of his kindness to Khalid's wife and daughters; how his own daughter had taken them in when they had first arrived and how he had given them a roof over their heads, providing his house for them to live in. It was like the village up here, he'd always said as much.

Harris's drive south was interrupted just once by the need to have lunch. It was the August Bank Holiday weekend and

typically rainy, the roads jammed with long columns of holi-
daymakers trying to escape. He stopped at a service station
along the M1, and watched families amble in and out of fast-
food chains as he tucked into his tin of curry and a slice of
white bread, courtesy of Nasreen. She was rather a good cook,
he concluded, the woman he hadn't married.

He had borrowed Nawaz's van to transport Alia's old desk
down to London, along with a couple of essentials for himself – the slow cooker and his fax machine – just in case he
might need them. The desk had been her last request from
his old house, for in spite of its wonkiness she'd grown
attached to it, associating it with a lucky run of academic
success when she'd taken her A-levels that year, revising in
the small attic bedroom.

'I never thought of you as the superstitious type, Alia,' he
said, when he arrived at her house.

'I'm not,' she admitted. 'Not really.'

Then she remembered the bottle of holy water blessed with
special healing powers that her father was supposed to bring
back from the village for Rashid, and how sceptical she'd been
at the time. Only he'd left it behind in their rush to return to
Lahore, and Khalid Ali had been forced to travel all the way
to the city to give it to him. She recalled how the cousin had
turned up at the house in Shadman only to be ushered out of
sight into the guest room, not allowed in the sitting room, in
case he might sully a sofa or step on an antique rug. What had
he done to deserve this chilly internment away from the rest
of Omar's household? Alia had wondered. She'd glanced at
Harris, and seen that he was at a loss, his eyes glassy with shame
that his cousin had been so humiliated.

In the end, the bottle had broken somewhere en route back to London, and Harris had given Rashid a bottle of Zam Zam water instead, picked up for a fiver from an Islamic trinket shop in Whitechapel. After Rashid was deported, he'd confessed to Alia what he'd done. She wasn't shocked at the cover-up that flew in the face of her father's professed beliefs because she knew he'd acted with the best intentions. Whether or not the water possessed medicinal or spiritual benefits, she would never know. She did know one thing, however: her father blamed himself for Rashid's fate, and he would carry those feelings to the end of his life.

As it turned out, Alia's desk would not go up the narrow wooden stairs in the house in Whitechapel, no matter how she and Harris angled it. The carpet seller offered his winch, convinced they could hoist it up through the window, but Harris fended off the suggestion. Instead, he drove it to Greenwich, where it found a home in the guest bedroom that Farrah was renovating at long last. She roped him in to help with rewiring the house and, before long, he was a fixture there himself.

Harris noted that her house was no longer cluttered with the accretions of her old life. Gone were all traces of her late husband: the photos and mementoes had been put away, out of sight. Much of the furniture had been taken off her hands by George, the junk shop owner, who lived nearby. The rest of the things that were beyond repair – a Kenwood Chef, a frayed wicker chair – Harris obligingly drove to the dump in Plumstead. He placed an ad on eBay for her old television set, which attracted no bids whatsoever. Everything had evidently gone digital, he explained to Farrah, who was perturbed by the revelation that she was so out of date.

The guest room was very small, Farrah said, but comfortable. She intended to let it out to lodgers, once she had renovated it with Harris's help. It would not take long to refurbish the room, to repair the walls where the plaster had given way, to refit a lightshade or two. The carpet was thick and fluffy; the bed single. There was an empty bookshelf upon the wall and the desk fitted snugly beneath. They would go shopping together, Farrah and Harris, choose paint, buy curtains, tussle over shades and fabrics before deciding what would look best, attract the right sort of person.

Once the room had hosted the suitcases and packing boxes that had carried Idrees's and Farrah's belongings from Pakistan to London. Now those were gone. The sycamore tree outside the window was so close that the dusty leaves cast a shady green canopy like an awning. The room faced east, filling up like a slender vessel of light with sunshine in the early mornings. It would be the perfect spot to wake up in, Harris said, recalling the times he had stayed there alone, rising at dawn to pray.

Acknowledgements

I am very grateful to Khurshid Anwer for years of friendship and correspondence, and to his wife Ulfat for her hospitality in Lahore. A special thanks to Kim Longinotto for her friendship and the inspiring chats we've had over the years, and for taking the trip with me.

Friends who proffered advice, editorial and otherwise, along the way: Kavita Reddi, Omar Rahim, Margot Bridger, Amanda Coe, Gregory Kennedy, Elizabeth Rubin, Lucinda Rosenfeld, Deborah Baker, Clio Barnard, Mark Brozel, Nick Fraser, Joanne Glasbey, Matthew and Janet Kentridge, Tim Oliver, Jessica Strang and Ben Hall. I'm grateful to Elizabeth Wright for driving me from Whitechapel to Ingatestone.

I owe a lot to my agents, Zoe Pagnamenta in New York and Anna Webber in London. Thanks to Fiona Maazel for her editorial notes and comments at a crucial moment, and to Colin Robinson for his support and kindness. I'm deeply grateful to my editors, Sarah McGrath at Riverhead and Jon Riley at Quercus, for their fresh insights and wise comments.

My daughters, Yasmin and Rachel Gapper, provided powerful words of encouragement around our kitchen table in Brooklyn. Thanks to my parents for stepping beyond convention and in particular to my late father, Ghulam Dastgir, for showing me the place where he came from.

Lastly, profound thanks to John Gapper for making me move to New York, and for contributing so much to the book from its inception.